# Heir of Lies

**Black Dawn Series**

BOOK I

Mallory McCartney

HEIR OF LIES

Copyright © Mallory McCartney 2019

All rights reserved.
No part of this publication may be reproduced, stored in a retrieval system, or transmitted, in any form or by any means, electronic, mechanical, photocopying, recording or otherwise, nor translated into a machine language, without the written permission of the publisher.

Condition of sale
This book was sold subject to the condition that it shall not, by way of trade or otherwise, be lent, re-sold, hired out or otherwise circulated in any form of binding or cover other than that in which it was published and without a similar condition including this condition being imposed on the subsequent purchaser.

ISBN: 978-1-9992547-0-4

The moral right of the author had been asserted.
This was a work of fiction. Any resemblance to actual persons, living or dead, events and organizations was purely coincidental.

Cover Art by Cora Graphics
*Shutterstock.com*
Formatted by Rebecca Garcia at Dark Wish Designs
Map art by Lizard Ink Maps

# CONTENTS

| | |
|---|---|
| Prologue | 1 |
| Chapter One | 10 |
| Chapter Two | 23 |
| Chapter Three | 33 |
| Chapter Four | 43 |
| Chapter Five | 61 |
| Chapter Six | 67 |
| Chapter Seven | 73 |
| Chapter Eight | 82 |
| Chapter Nine | 88 |
| Chapter Ten | 104 |
| Chapter Eleven | 123 |
| Chapter Twelve | 140 |
| Chapter Thirteen | 147 |
| Chapter Fourteen | 150 |
| Chapter Fifteen | 159 |
| Chapter Sixteen | 173 |
| Chapter Seventeen | 177 |
| Chapter Eighteen | 194 |
| Chapter Nineteen | 205 |
| Chapter Twenty | 213 |
| Chapter Twenty-One | 228 |
| Chapter Twenty-Two | 234 |
| Chapter Twenty-Three | 238 |
| Chapter Twenty-Four | 243 |

Chapter Twenty-Five ..................................................................... 246
Chapter Twenty-Six ....................................................................... 252
Chapter Twenty-Seven .................................................................. 256
Chapter Twenty-Eight ................................................................... 260
Chapter Twenty-Nine .................................................................... 263
Chapter Thirty ............................................................................... 270
Chapter Thirty-One ...................................................................... 287
Chapter Thirty-Two ...................................................................... 292
Chapter Thirty-Three .................................................................... 342
Chapter Thirty-Four ..................................................................... 352
Chapter Thirty-Five ...................................................................... 355
Chapter Thirty-Six ........................................................................ 360
Chapter Thirty-Seven .................................................................... 377
Chapter Thirty-Eight .................................................................... 380
Chapter Thirty-Nine ..................................................................... 393
Chapter Forty ................................................................................ 407
Chapter Forty-One ....................................................................... 410
Chapter Forty-Two ....................................................................... 417
Chapter Forty-Three ..................................................................... 424
Chapter Forty-Four ...................................................................... 427
Chapter Forty-Five ....................................................................... 430
Chapter Forty-Six ......................................................................... 432
Chapter Forty-Seven ..................................................................... 435
Epilogue ........................................................................................ 439
Acknowledgements ....................................................................... 259
About the Author ......................................................................... 260

ARKEN MOUNTAINS

RISCO DESERT

THE FORGOTTEN BOG

THE ACADEMY

THE CITY OF NEHMAI

THE BL

PENTHA

# KIERO

## THE SHATTERED ISLES

DRAKEN MOUNTAINS

1. HARBOUR OF NEWSOLL
2. TERDES HARBOUR DISTRICT
3. HRISTE
4. OAKLAND WHARF DISTRICT
5. DURDOVER PORT

For the dreamers who see endless possibilities and the magic in everyday life. And for everyone who has dared to fight for love, in all its forms.

# HEIR OF LIES

## BLACK DAWN SERIES

### BOOK I

MALLORY MCCARTNEY

# PROLOGUE

*Fifteen years earlier,*
*Sarthaven (The Ruined City)*

The note shook so hard in her grasp, Nei Fae couldn't focus on the words splayed before her. With a racing pulse and a sharp ringing coursing through her ears, she crumpled the paper beneath her white knuckles.

*Breathe.*

The words branded her like hot iron to her flesh, her entire being coursing with them. Her hope was consumed by them.

She sat at her desk, like any other day. The afternoon light poured in through the window, catching the various objects scattered throughout, from the copious number of books to the overwhelming stack of papers. A hard glint reflected off her longsword and throwing knives that lay scattered throughout the room.

Her office was one of solace, in a time where peace was very hard to find.

Her golden hair spilled forward as she dropped her face into her hands, covering her eyes while her senses were diluted and muffled, if only for a second.

Her father's voice filled Nei's mind as clear as day in her reprieve: '*You will not marry for love, my sweet girl, but you will sacrifice yourself wholeheartedly so that this world may see a day where peace ensues; so that this war will ease itself into the pages of our history.*'

He had been spot on. It had been one year since her arranged marriage where their world had quaked and shook with the defiance of it: a wild woman from the Shattered Isles betrothed to the *prince*.

People's reactions had been worse than expected, to say the least.

When Nei Runnard had been scuffling around with her sisters and sailing the coast, following her heart wherever adventure was, Roque Fae was being groomed in the politics of his court and his country. Nei had almost laughed when her father sat her down and told her he had sealed *her fate*.

One. Year.

She left her family, her life, her hopes and dreams behind to marry a man she loathed. Now, he was tolerable but still undeniably an arse in more ways than not.

It was a strong union, she was told. One that would end her people's suffering. Her marriage to Roque Fae would ensure that the Shattered Isles would thrive again, trading wine and fruit with Kiero. Instead of what the reality was now: her people being captured and enslaved, sailors' ships being attacked by Kiero's fleets, burned and sent to the bottom of the Black Sea.

So here she was, prettily packaged, trying to quell Kiero's hatred toward her country. It had surprised her at first, how angry the people were. So what if she was a rover, a *pirate*. More warrior than princess.

Every day in this court proved just how deep rooted the people's suffering went; every day, accusations of the government not providing the security and protection the people wanted, that they *needed*, came in.

Sighing, Nei Fae stood, stretching, and her joints popped. Beneath her simple garb, bruises flowered her body from her sparring sessions, reminding her with every step who *she* was, where her roots lay. And she had fiercely promised herself that – to not forget.

Nei's only friend in this forsaken court, Bresslin Stratton, took it upon herself to have daily evening walks with her. Instead of dresses and gossip, they filled their time with clashing steel and aching muscles.

# HEIR OF LIES - PROLOGUE

Smiling wolfishly, Nei reminded herself what her sisters had always said: that amongst them all, she was born with the fury of the sea, with the resilience of the rocks the water crashed upon. She would not break beneath the pressures, lies, and riots of being a hated Queen.

Her sisters had been so sure she had what it took to be Queen. Their excitement, their hope of a better life rather than one of fighting for survival, is what kept Nei from running away and disappearing into nothingness.

Besides Bresslin, that's what everyone here thought of her - That she wasn't as cunning or had the potential to rule beside Roque.

A sharp knock sliced through her thoughts, and she stood quickly, tucking the note tightly against her wrist and out of sight.

The door swung open, and Roque leaned lazily against the doorframe, arms crossed and mischief dancing in his green eyes. Their outfits were matching, black loose pants and shirt; a deep plum cloak was fastened at his throat.

Swallowing hard, Nei bowed her head, rasping, "My King."

Three hundred and sixty-five days later, she was still not used to saying those two words. Two words that chained her.

Lifting her dark gaze, she got a lifted brow in response, as Roque stepped into her office. "Are you ready? They won't wait forever you know."

*The council.*

And like every other day, Nei plastered that splintering grin, making her cheeks hurt. "Of course," she said.

His brows furrowed for a moment before he offered his arm to her, the gentleman he was dictated to be. She was grace and poise as she accepted his gesture, and in tow, they left behind her sanctuary.

Sarthaven, the Capital of Kiero, '*the city beneath the stars*', bustled outside the towering walls, the shouts and chaos a never-ending serenade.

Nei wanted to laugh at the acclaimed name. It was far from the truth. The people here came to seek a better quality of life but found more division; while the only thing that bred here were riots and death.

Dread filled her core as they walked in silence down the winding hallway, the sunlight flickering as they passed each small window. Every footfall, every step was a reminder of what lay ahead, waiting in the shape of four council members. Nervously, she shifted her arm, trying to ease her roaring mind. At the end of the cavernous hallway, twenty steps away, an oak door gleamed, two guards stationed by it.

They wore silver shirts and pants, the material shimmering like stardust, and stood so still at first glance they could pass as statues. She caught the flicker of their empty eyes, the rise and fall of their pale skin. As they drew closer, they bowed their shaved heads, revealed two inky black sigils above their brow. Stomach dropping, a cold sweat clung to her skin as she looked at the men from the Shattered Isles - broken and made to serve a country they hated while Nei lived in luxury.

A cold fire burned in their eyes as they met her gaze, unsaid accusations burning behind their looks. Why had she agreed to this union if more men and women from the Shattered Isles were enslaved to serve the Faes? Her people were seen as savages and were treated as such in Kiero.

*Slaves.*

Nei's steps faltered. Three hundred and sixty-five days of sacrificing everything she was, and *this had not stopped*. It was the only reason she had agreed to go through with this madness. Her people lived a content, happy life on the Shattered Isles, one where they hadn't recognized a king in almost several decades, until the Faes and Roque's father deemed his son the one *true* king.

# HEIR OF LIES - PROLOGUE

Now, the world was divided between a tyrant and a son wanting to make his father proud. She was a pawn, a promise to her people that even though their abilities were different, they were nurtures and healers and wouldn't be made to bow, wouldn't be penalized. That as queen, she would break the preconceived notion that they were lesser in anyway.

*And she was failing.*

Nei tore her gaze from the two rovers and forced her features into a neutral expression. Roque grimly smiled down at her before pushing the door open, and they stepped in.

The room was large, a deep oak table placed in its center. The bay window behind the four figures seated encompassed the world behind them. The sun flared in the sky, bathing the bustling city in light.

*Or burning it.*

Nei gritted her teeth when she and Roque stopped and bowed low, their sweeping arms and submissive figures applying all the grandeur this life demanded. They rose together, and Roque gently held her hand as they walked toward the council, the vision of unity.

The council - two men and two women - were scowling. Their papery skin looking translucent in the sun, showing the map of blue veins rippling along their arms and necks. Their severe features let no emotions pass, and Nei's gut twisted with nerves. These ancient souls in front of her dictated every move, political and personal for the royal family.

Roque squeezed her clammy hand gently, as if to say: *Don't worry, this is the best way; or don't worry you are one of us, they can't hurt you.*

Nei sat stiffly in the chair before her, Roque following suit.

Oren, the head of the council, leaned forward, his watery eyes locking on her. "Your Highnesses, I must be blunt. We are curious as to why you called this meeting. We thought our demands were clear."

It took all of her control not to unleash her fury right then and there. Their "demands" were for her and Roque to sit idly by while every day more of their people were slaughtered. While everyday more of *her* people were enslaved.

Nei slipped on that practiced mask of calm and poise, batt her eyes at Roque, smiling sweetly. *Let them play me for the fool.*

Leaning forward, his deep voice rumbled, "Esteemed council members, my Queen and I come to you today with a proposition. One that will only strengthen our world and help end the suffering that is evident within our society. I must be equally blunt, being a new father now has brought to light the flaws within my own father's arrangement. I will do what is best for my daughter's future, and my country's."

Nei watched Oren's expression for any slip of *his* mask. The council had been Roque's father's private advisors, first hailing from the Arken mountains in the north. She had heard the rumors of their dark magic bewitching Camden Fae, allowing Kiero to turn its back on its people and falling into madness…

Oren scoffed. "Please, no insult intended, my King, but…"

Roque's gaze darkened as he snapped, "You will not interrupt me, Oren. I'm your king. It's time this council embraces the future. And I will not stand for one that's bathed in blood."

Roque was arrogant and entitled *but maybe* her pleas had gotten through to him. She had begged him endlessly, their arguments flowing late into the night. He could not turn a blind eye anymore, even though he was afraid of what the world would think and say. But here he sat, powerful and determined, and for the briefest second, admiration flared within her.

"Nei and I are ready to move forward in our lives, and the council and my father will not be privy to our decisions anymore. It's time for you all to step down."

The council members' voices rose in an uproar, accusations being thrown at them both.

Oren's voice, as usual, cut right through the rest, "This is because of *her*. Roque, you have been poisoned by this, this *witch*

# HEIR OF LIES - PROLOGUE

from those cursed Islands." Spittle flew from Oren's mouth, as his pointed finger shook toward Nei's chest.

Slowly and very surely, she focused on Oren, taking in the old man.

*I will end you, even if it means war.*

Nei swallowed down her thoughts, proud her voice was steady when she said, "No, Oren. I am not a witch, only a healer. A woman who wants to see a world that is not trying to tear itself apart. A Queen that has dreams for her King, her daughter, and to ensure we will rule justly and not be ravished in lies and in corruption." She paused. "Too long has this council pushed the idea that their one true King is one of triumphant power, when our people are taking this notion and abusing their abilities on my kinsmen and enslaving them. When they are hunting and killing desolates because they aren't worthy of life."

Oren spat out, "And what do you think they will do when the world finds out your *husband* is a desolate?"

Roque slammed his fist down on the table, the wood shaking from the force. "It is time my people know the truth. I am a king that is barren of ability. But it takes more than might to rule. It is time to rebuild our world, and this will start with our new government."

Laughter danced around them, and Nei clenched her fist, her nails biting into the flesh of her palms. Roque rolled his shoulders, bringing himself up to his full height in his seat. "The time of this monarchy is done. There will be consequences for slave traders and for the slaughter of desolates. It starts today, with the expulsion of this council. You are all relieved of your duties and services."

Oren pushed his chair back, the wood screeching against the cement. Looking feral, he shook with rage. "And what exactly are you going to do?"

The Roque she recognized flickered back through, as he leaned forward, almost touching noses with Oren and said, "Nei and I are building a sanctuary for all who want to learn how to control their abilities and harness it. To be used for good, not for fueling the death tolls and riots. A place for desolates to take refuge. Most importantly, a place to build a government that will preserve our culture and uphold the rights of our people."

"A place that will never exist."

Nei chuckled. "Oren, you are already behind the times. This place will exist, and you are staring at its founders."

Roque leaned away. "I do believe we are done here."

Each of the council members left in an arrangement of curses and rolling anger.

Oren stared at them both, collecting himself before saying, "I hope you both know that we *will not* let this stand." He left, allowing his words to linger in the air before snapping the door closed behind him.

"We have to go, *now*," Roque whispered.

Nei collected herself. The council would move fast, but they were faster. Bresslin and Cesan Stratton were ready for them, with Emory. They would leave this city behind and flee for their future.

Consuming the distance between them, Nei threw her arms around his neck and said on an exhale, "Thank you, truly."

A flicker of surprise crossed Roque's face before a small smirk tugged the corner of his lips. He quipped, "They will try to kill us, you know."

Abashed from showing emotion, Nei pulled away. "Oh, no doubt. It will take years for people to accept this idea. This mad dream of ours."

Despite her hatred, the confinement of her marriage, there was always something so much more important. Putting her differences aside, Nei had chosen fighting for freedom, above all else. Freedom for the Shattered Isles, for Kiero. For their daughter's future.

Running, the note in Nei's sleeve felt like lead, anchoring her to her decisions. She was torn in two: a queen and a daughter loyal to her people.

# HEIR OF LIES - PROLOGUE

Their footfalls pounded around them, echoing in the hallway, and Nei summoned a flicker of energy, calling to her elements. Her skin burned, and the note ignited quickly, dissolving into ash, the remains soaring behind her, lost and unseen.

No one would know. Not Roque, Emory, or Bresslin.

Her father's reply to her letter seared through her: *I will miss you, my sweet daughter. But know we will wait, and when you are ready, we will answer your call for war. May the winds be with you, and your fierceness never falter. The Shattered Isles will answer to you and you alone.*

Nei ran faster, her heart racing. She dared Oren to come after them, to declare a threat to their peace. Because the Shattered Isles were ready, and they answered to only her

# Renegade

HEIR OF LIES – PART ONE

# CHAPTER ONE

## Brokk

*Fifteen years later, The Academy*

The afternoon sun soaked into his neck as Brokk Foster raised the bow, drawing the string back, his arrow nocked. The bowstring grazed his cheek as his arm shook; he tried not to blink against the sweat rolling down his temple. The courtyard faded away in that second, his hawk-eyed teacher, Professor Iasan, standing to the side, his arms crossed, his face impassive. Brokk's fellow classmates stood near, and the looming structure of the Academy was behind them.

A strand of his golden hair tickled his forehead as he exhaled.

*It's not real, just release the arrow. Just release it.*

At the opposite end of the range, a stuffed dummy was raised with an emblazoned red target where a heart would be.

*Not real, not real, not real.*

Muscles screaming, he tried to empty his charged mind, to convince himself that the undiluted fear that clutched his heart was unreasonable.

With still shaking arms, the arrow flew, cutting through the air with a soft hiss. Laughter erupted behind him, making him cringe as he lowered the bow and saw the lodged feathered end in the ground, not even close to the dummy.

"Enough!" Professor Iasan's booming voice cut off his classmates' jeers.

Brokk turned, lifting his gaze to meet the incredulous look of his best friend, Memphis Carter. Memphis raised one eyebrow as his smooth voice filled Brokk's consciousness, only for him to hear, "*Well, what are you going to do this time?*"

Huffing, Brokk wrenched his gaze away. Sometimes his friend could be such an *ass*.

Tactical training class was Brokk's nemesis, and he met, not for the first time, Professor Iasan's cutting accusations. "Foster! What do you call *that?*"

More chuckles rippled out, and the tips of his ears burned. A minute passed, and then another as Brokk studied the fascinating details of his leather boots.

"Well?"

Raising his gaze to meet Professor Iasan's, that familiar flicker of anger ignited in him. He was *so tired* of being trained for no acclaimed threat. The Academy had taken him in years ago, with golden promises of schooling him in the control of his abilities so he could have a shot at a normal life—that they all could.

Over the years, the Academy had become a school woven from lies. The students here were regimented, honed, and molded into weapons. He did not sign up to be a soldier.

Brokk felt his lips tug upward as he threw the bow at his feet. It clattered noisily, as he threw his hands out to his sides. "I'm done, Professor Iasan."

He brushed past Memphis, not meeting his gaze.

Through the catcalls and hollers, Memphis's voice cut through his mind, "*Brokk...*" Memphis's tone only made him walk faster out of the courtyard, not looking back once.

Passing under the stone archway, its chiseled carvings always struck him as unnerving and beautiful at the same time. It told the story of the Academy: how the Faes and the Strattons had built the foundations for their democratic government, how they had pulled Kiero out from under the shadow of war, how the Academy was—and had been for fifteen years—structured to present the world its golden warriors, fighting of any threat of abuse and injustice. The pupils here were some of the most gifted and were the strongest representation of what Kiero had to offer.

*Or most uncontrolled. Most needed to be caged.*

# HEIR OF LIES – PART ONE

It wasn't that he didn't agree with what the Academy stood for. Brokk was just as well learned in Kiero's history as any other student: about the trade wars with the Shattered Isles, about how Roque's father and his council continued for years to enslave Nei's people and slaughter the desolates—people without or with very weak abilities. The scales of the world had been uneven for a very long time, and the Faes had fought for this freedom away from the past, which was bathed in blood.

Of course, Brokk was honored to be a part of such a movement. He was grateful that Nei and Roque had taken him in. He had no recollection of his parents or what had happened for him to end up alone in the forest that surrounded the Academy so many years prior. Without the Faes, he would not have survived or would have been at the mercy of the raiders. Their world wasn't perfect, but it was at ease.

The raiders had proclaimed separate regency and had, somewhat, left their towns and cities alone. The Shattered Isles were under a peace agreement now with the Faes, but no longer accepted Nei as one of their own blood. The desolates were under the sworn oath of protection from the Academy, and the Academy continued to grow and flourish with the Faes' dream.

Brokk sighed, looking up past the archway to the open sky and the endlessness it provided. He *should* be grateful. He *should* take his instruction without question. He *should* be proud to be a student here and graduate to serve his country. He would be a government official, a warrior and protector of the peace.

But he was not.

There had been whisperings for the last couple of years of what exactly the seniors were instructed to do by Cesan Stratton.

Brokk shivered, his eyebrows furrowed as those whispers pulled at the throes of his mind; creating chaos and fear, unleashing the students as weapons. Everything started as whispers in this place, but the knowledge of what Cesan might be doing, what he was *brain washing* into the hearts and minds of students had shattered Brokk's flawless view of the world around him.

He would not be carved into a fearmonger; he would not use his abilities to crack the frail bond of peace that had been accomplished within Kiero. He would not be a monster.

His throat felt thick as he tore his gaze away and continued his walk back to the main building.

Whether the rumors were true was a whole other problem. Cesan was not his favorite man and they rarely saw eye to eye, but was he an enemy?

Brokk sighed, his dark thoughts whisking away any peace of mind he might have had for the day. A tolling bell rang out behind him, marking their lunch break, and breaking him free from his thoughts.

*By fire and flame, finally.*

The Academy was a sprawling map of concrete. The main building consisting of dorms in the center, a tall cylinder watchtower to the east, and encircling it was the constant placement of adjacent classroom buildings. No gates were needed, no security. Anyone mad enough to try to disrupt the students and teachers here wouldn't make it far. Besides, the closest city was the Capital of Kiero, Sarthaven, and that was hours away.

Brokk was following the well-worn path back up toward the building when a clear voice rang out behind him, "Brokk, wait up!"

The blood in his very veins froze, and he stopped walking midstride. Emory Fae grabbed his arm, turning him to face her. A pale blush bloomed across her cheeks, her emerald eyes bright as for a moment he stopped worrying about Iasan and the Academy. But like every other day, he swallowed down his emotions and wolfishly grinned at his other best friend. "And what could you possibly want?"

She wrinkled her nose, playfully punching him in the arm. "Oh come off it. Memphis caught me after class and mentioned you might be skulking around somewhere in this general direction."

"Of course he did," Brokk breathed out, returning his attention back to his walk.

# Heir of Lies – Part One

Naturally, Emory wasn't deterred one bit. "Was it Iasan again?"

Both she and Memphis were privy to his opinion about their training teacher. Iasan was ruthless, a trained killer, and expected them to have no compassion, no mercy. It was dummies now they were practicing on, but when it wasn't? When they killed without a second thought? He never wanted to lose his empathy or his intolerance for taking another life, even if he attained the skills.

Emory's mouth turned down in a grim line as she walked beside him. "I can talk to my dad again," she offered.

"That went so well last time." A strangled chuckle came out of him. "No, I can deal with Iasan, just not today, Em."

Unclenching his fists at his side, he didn't remark on Emory's father, Roque Fae. Everywhere he went, he oozed of authority and structure; of might and discipline. He was severe, a ruler in every right. He was a desolate and one of the most influential people in Kiero. The fact he was a desolate didn't make him any less intimidating. He thought very highly of his instructors and of his government, and Brokk clearly remembered the last time Emory had gone to him about Iasan.

*"He is the best in his field, the best throughout the country. Brokk should be willing to challenge himself instead of limiting himself due to his heart."*

Emory had relayed his message mockingly, but the words had cut through Brokk. *This* was their leader, the person everyone praised. The man everyone looked up to. The man Brokk never went to with his concerns again after that.

Frowning, his doubts clawed at his mind as they climbed in comfortable silence, the melody of the forest creatures floating out to them. Heard, but unseen. It was soothing and melancholy, the soft music dripping with life and isolation. He knew those melodies fell on deaf ears, but he was always listening, his personal orchestra overlapping in beautiful harmonies, igniting him.

In the ancient woods, that was the place he was truly free. The forest lines blurring as he ran, the moon's light mapping his way, feeling the earth under his paws, as Brokk lost himself in his animal instinct. Those heartbreaking laments of the fellow creatures that could be found in the darkness tugged at him.

Calling him to come back, to come home.

To him, being a shapeshifter was a gift. That part of himself, of his ability, was part of his very core. The yearning for wildness, for freedom, for *power*. People had been afraid at first, thinking that he couldn't control himself - that he would hurt someone. The wolf and man were one; each skin he wore was *him*. That part of himself he was always in control of.

It was his other ability that he kept tucked close to his heart, locked in the darkest shards of his soul. The one that scared him, the one he didn't understand. The one that was growing. Waiting for that trigger moment where it would explode from him, emblazoned and uncontrolled. The one he had told no one about.

Swallowing hard, Brokk brought himself back to Emory's crystal laugh, to her smile, to her gentle brushes of their fingers. He was drowning in the stormy seas of his fears, and she was his anchor. Had always been his anchor.

She raised a delicate dark brow at him murmuring, "It would seem we have a visitor."

Snapping his attention forward, he stalled. "Do you want me to take care of this?"

Emory rolled her eyes. "Brokk, I have known him since I was a little kid. He doesn't scare me. You shouldn't let him get under your skin."

Brokk took in Adair Stratton stalking toward them. He was gangly, tall, and thin. His dark gaze held only one person, and Brokk felt himself blush. Adair held such an intensity for Emory it was unsettling. The Faes and the Strattons were best friends, and that extended toward their children.

# HEIR OF LIES – PART ONE

Adair stopped, sneering at Brokk, and didn't even acknowledge him. "Emory, we are to go see our parents. Immediately." His voice was smooth and deep, like still water.

A sly smirk tugged at the corners of Emory's lips. "To discuss very important matters, I'm sure."

Adair nodded, tilting his head as he practically ravished her with his eyes. The hair on the back of Brokk's neck stood on end, and he wanted to snarl, to protect Emory from Adair's dark seducing gaze. Not a single bone in Brokk's body trusted him. Not. One.

Adair offered his arm to Emory, which she took with an apologetic look toward Brokk. "See you later, Brokk. Duty calls."

Feebly waving goodbye, Brokk bore his gaze into Adair's back as they walked away: light and dark, oil and water mixing. Brokk caught a snippet of Adair's voice as they walked - "Emory, honestly, what do you see in *him*?"

This time a snarl did break through his lips, and Brokk shut his eyes, taking in deep breaths. Adair had a special talent to break his patience, preaching to Emory that she was above her friendship with Memphis and himself. That she was above them. Emory, of course, had always done what she wanted, ignoring Adair's poisonous words. Ones Adair thought was lost to them.

Yet, she always let him in, always answered his beck and call. Brokk couldn't help but see past her façade and thought a part of her was spellbound by Adair and would bend to his will wholly.

He *hated it*. Yet, he also tolerated their friendship with him for Emory.

Soon, they were small figures in the distance, and Brokk continued his way up the path alone.

"On my command... Now!"

Professors Lien's voice sliced through the tense excitement of the room. The auditorium was cavernous and filled with natural light, making every detail clear to the students. The obstacle course was grueling and complicated; laid out before him, the challenge was plain to see.

Various tunnels and scaling walls spread in front of them, and at the opposite end of the room, Brokk counted the teachers: Professor Whilms—a burly man, his black goatee framing his smug features as fire danced from his palms. Professor Remre— her silver hair plaited back as the longswords glinted in her grasp. And in front of him, Professor Iasan stood in front of Memphis.

Heart sinking into his stomach, Brokk pieced together that they were practicing hand-to-hand combat before they could reach their partner.

Brokk looked to Memphis stationed across from him at the opposite end of the room. With a causal shrug, Brokk waggled his eyebrows at his friend and then chaos exploded.

Every time he shapeshifted, it was like falling into piercing, icy water. His muscles tensed as he ran, and then, in an explosion of cracking bones, he bore his second skin, his golden fur rippling. His defined muscles propelled him, like a comet streaking across the night sky, full of flaring life, burning and devouring its path.

Around him, the room exploded with a various number of elements: fire, water and wind bending to students will. To his left was Alby, his red hair and pale skin disappearing as he turned invisible. To his right, Jaxson multiplied himself as all the versions of him raced ahead, trying to finish the course first and reach his partner, Wyatt, who waited for him. Pleasure rippled through his body as Brokk scaled the towering wall in one leap, adrenaline pushing him faster, harder, *better*.

Dodging and twisting from abilities being thrown at him, he missed the Professor's assaults with ease. He galloped through a placed tunnel; the light of the auditorium being swallowed up in an instant. Snarling, he charged, flying out of the end to skitter to a stop. Professor Iasan stood between him and Memphis, glittering sword in his right hand, a small ball of flame dancing in his left. A low growl ripped through Brokk, and Professor Iasan tutted.

"Now, Brokk, you must understand this isn't personal. You are so full of talent. Now *use it*."

Fire swirled and consumed his world. All Brokk could see were roaring flames; all he could feel was heat. Smoke filled his nostrils, his lungs, and he was drowning. He was cornered, and he was suffocating. Blindly flinging himself forward, Brokk shifted back just as Professor Iasan parted the fire to his will, glittering steel cutting toward Brokk.

He didn't think; he just reacted. His muscles were pulled taut, and his fist slammed into flesh, Iasan's jaw cracking, his head snapping back. Panting heavily, a strange ringing filled his ears. Iasan rubbed his jaw, his gaze honing back to his student, malice burning in them.

"Enough, Iasan, *enough!*"

Professor Lein's voice rang out, her cry making everyone stop. Memphis was frozen behind Iasan, his usual pale skin ashen. She glared at Brokk.

"Foster, come here now!"

Heaving, he turned and stalked toward his furious teacher, her glowering gaze cutting through him with each step.

"Foster, what are you thinking? You too, Iasan? Class dismissed!" she exclaimed.

Her grey hair was piled high on her head, her stubborn gaze challenging any of the students to defy her. Ripples of whispers came to life as everyone collected their things and then filed out. Memphis shook his head slightly before turning away.

Turning her attention back to them, Professor Lein nodded curtly, and they followed her out of the auditorium.

The hallway was relatively quiet, considering it was just after lunch. Brokk groaned internally, knowing exactly where Lein was taking them. It was the very last person he wanted to see. Iasan shot him a smug look as they finally turned a corner to a pair of old oak doors, and she knocked twice, the rapt sounding twice as urgent from her anger.

The door swung open, and Roque stood there, his dark eyebrows rising as he took the group in, his emerald eyes holding Brokk's gaze last. His hair was disheveled, bruised skin underneath his eyes. His silver shirt and black plants were rumpled, and Brokk couldn't remember the last time their leader looked so unkept. But the resemblance to Emory was stark; she held all her father's physical traits with her mother's wildness and kind heart. For that, Brokk was grateful.

Roque snapped, "Lein! What is the matter of this visit? You've caught me at a bad time."

Lein sighed, shooting them another glare before answering Roque. "Maybe Foster should explain this to you. Iasan, *I* will deal with you."

Iasan paled slightly under Lein's stern gaze and a flicker of gratification shot through Brokk. Smirking, he watched Lein lead Iasan out, his features dark. He wouldn't be let off easy.

The two professors took off in a low heated conversation, leaving Brokk alone under Roque's stare. Roque hurriedly cleared his throat, blinking hard as he said, "Well, you might as well come in."

Resigning himself to the fact this would not be easy, Brokk stepped into the Faes' office. He noticed immediately the office was a chaos of papers, bookshelves, and maps. Nei and Cesan sat at the round polished table in a heated argument, oblivious at first to their arrival.

"Cesan, for the last time, I will not let you..."

Roque slammed the door behind Brokk, making him jump. Nei's words died in her mouth when she took in Brokk and her husband. She shot Cesan a warning look before standing.

"Brokk, what can we help you with? Cesan here was just leaving."

Brokk studied Cesan, his dark ambiance, much like his son's, filling and suffocating the room. Bowing mockingly to Nei, Cesan strutted by them, Roque looked at his friend silently.

# HEIR OF LIES – PART ONE

Warning, hot and sure, flared within Brokk. What had he just interrupted? A dark curiosity bloomed within Brokk, and he cleared his throat, pushing his thoughts aside.

"It's...well, it's about me punching Professor Iasan in the face during ability training."

Nei's lips curved slightly upward, her kind eyes waiting for more of an explanation but Roque stormed in front of Brokk, snapping, "An assault against a teacher can result in expulsion!"

Gnashing his teeth together, Brokk volleyed, "And pushing students to react in violence doesn't need consequences? Sir, I beg you to listen to what I'm saying. Iasan isn't teaching us. He is forcing us to always be on the defense, to always act with vengeance. To be weapons without compassion. To barely be human."

Roque ran a hand through his tousled hair. "Iasan has his methods as we all do. He pushes you because he believes that you can achieve great things. He is brusque, stern, and disciplined, but he knows no other way. The tides of this world have been pushed into change with great effort from all of us. Without challenge, there is no growth. It is the younger generation that will dictate whether the dream and purpose of the Academy lives on. For it to live on, it must encompass your soul, your beliefs, and your dreams. It once did, did it not?"

Brokk stood awkwardly, the weight of Roque's words falling on his shoulders. He did once, as a young boy. Now, being seventeen and on the brink of entering his manhood, he had let go of his dreams of a full life pinned on childish whims. The last twelve years had ensured that. Brokk sought out one thing above all else. The *truth*. The truth of his past, the truth of the Academy. The truth of the hearts of the Faes and Strattons and how they upheld their students.

A flash of sympathy crossed their leader's eyes, and he rested a strong hand on Brokk's shoulder. "You will understand fully one day. With all dreams come sacrifice. With all freedom comes some form of a cage. It is the lesser of two evils that we all must learn to live with."

Brokk cast his eyes toward the floor, unable to find his words.

He saw Nei's sharp gaze flickered between them before Roque murmured, "You are dismissed with a warning. But if I hear of this sort of behavior again, or you are brought to me, then there *will* be consequences."

Heat flushed his cheeks, and Brokk dipped his head. "Thank you."

With that, he flew from the room. Clicking the door shut, fast low voices danced at him from behind it, and that strong sense of warning pulled at his gut again. Ripping himself away, he sauntered down the hallway. He needed to find Memphis. Something wild and dark was churning for them all in the shadows. He could feel it.

Brokk tried to cage his galloping pulse, but every step, every thought brought him closer to his conclusion. The Faes and Strattons were hiding something at the very heart of the Academy, and he had every intention of finding out exactly what it was.

# HEIR OF LIES – PART ONE

# CHAPTER TWO

## Adair

He was transfixed by the way she moved. Locks of her black hair trickled forward. Her slender body was animated as Emory was lost in what she was saying. The words were a distant hum, never truly reaching him, but wrapping his mind with their warmth. It felt *so* good to be talked to without the condescension from his parents or from the withering looks of fellow students.

The afternoon air brushed his cheek, bringing him back to his pressing thoughts. As usual, he was completely and utterly at Emory Fae's mercy. She radiated with life, and Adair clung to it like a lifeline, desperately and all at once. Chewing his inner lip, he tried to slow his hammering heart, his clammy palms. To suffocate the urge to lean over and run his thumb over her lower lip, to cup her face, to lower his lips on hers and just *feel* what it would be like, to know the possibilities they held together.

Like every other day of his life, he pushed his roaring emotions down deep, chaining them in the restraints of his very core. The afternoon had passed with their parents going over maps and possible borders his father would go to next with his brainless group.

Roque and his father constantly butting heads.

Nei and his mother, Bresslin, talking quietly to themselves.

Him and Emory had sat in the back, watching and ever dutiful.

But as always, he was watching her. Glimpses of her full lips quirking to the side in her crooked smile. How she tucked her long ebony hair behind her ear. How her eyes reminded him of the forest at night, deep and full of secrets. How when she was excited or mad, her high cheekbones flushed deeply. Her laugh. Her scowl. Her stubbornness. Her, entirely.

Breathing in the deep scent of summer, he tried to relax as they sat on the ledge of the grey boulder they had scaled. He knew, with every passing day, the ownership of his heart was being whittled away. A slow warmth spread through him at the thought, because when it came to him and Emory, there was no other way he wanted his story to be written. The first time they had met, he had known - they were destined. Her light had always complimented his darkness, and he was, in every sense, entranced by her.

"Adair?"

Snapping out of his thoughts, he stole a glance at her and faltered, looking ahead.

The sun sat lazily in the sky, and time seemed to stop, each stolen brush of fingers and sly smile tucked away for them both. Emory sought out the comfort of her longest friend. He was her confidant. Who else could relate to what it felt like to uphold their family's reputations? The pressure, the constant scrutiny. He cringed internally, echoes of his father's criticisms filling him.

*You are the best and the strongest, Adair. We are elite. Better than these fools who occupy this place. You will understand, my son. There is more to life than a teenage boy's desires. You will see that you deserve to rule. To be mighty. To grow out of this place.*

Adair sighed. He yearned for Emory to see past his facades, see past his ability, see past their friendship, past their families, and recognize that she was the most important person to him. Above his parents and this school.

To realize that Adair had always loved her.

The bustle of the Academy had quieted, classes being resumed, and the forest that surrounded them had slowed in the haze of the afternoon, except for the gentle tousle of the wind. To him, Kiero was endless, the Academy acting as his prison. He yearned for *more*, to see the world, to experience what it had to offer him. To spend his days challenging himself, finding adventure and never stopping, never looking back. Not being a puppet for a life he had never chose for himself.

Adair sighed. "I'm sorry. What did you say?"

Emory gravitated slightly closer, only an inch, but to him, it felt like his skin was doused in flames. He clenched his hands, stopping himself right there.

*Breathe.*

"What did you take away from the meeting?"

Adair blew air through her teeth. "That my dad is a prat." Her eyebrows shot into her hairline as she stifled a choked laugh. Adair muttered, "Oh, come off it, Em. I know you agree."

Her silence was answer enough.

"He won't stop, you know, until he has what he wants. That's what I took from the meeting today, Em. That our families are becoming more divided."

She huffed. "But what's the point now? Why fight about what kind of freedom people have the right to? Our parents have been best friends for over a decade. What would come in-between that?"

*Jealously. Power. Status. Greed. Expectation.*

"Things change, Em. Sometimes, there are things people can't come back from."

A shadow flickered across her face as she sucked in both cheeks. She mused, "Your dad wants to build a new monarchy. My parents want to uphold the gains they have made, not by force, not by titles. We are the peacekeepers, the protectors of the borders. But what exactly will that mean for *us*?"

Adair wanted nothing more than to fold her in his arms and whisper that it would be okay. That *they* would be okay. He didn't move, wrapping his arms around his knees.

*She's not yours. Not yours.*

His emotions were vicious, his gut twisting, and his ears burned. He had never been one for knowing how to navigate being honest about his feelings. Three years ago, he had tried, and like most things, Adair tried to make good of it. Withered and burned, her rejection still stung him. But there wasn't one day that passed that he hadn't wanted more. That he didn't dream of it.

Hooves thudded in the distance, rolling across the forest like disjointed thunder. Both of their heads snapped up, the hazy afternoon spell over them broken.

"What the…" Emory breathed, standing fast.

Adair stilled, everything within him becoming quiet. There was no movement, but the noise grew, rolling toward them like a wave crashing to shore. Standing slowly, his hands flexed by his sides, brushing against his ability churning beneath his skin. Then, there was a flash of deep green, and their visitors made themselves clear. Fifty stallions pushed toward the Academy, galloping under the sigil of broken steel and a churning sea.

Both he and Emory were already running, curses flowing from him. The Shattered Isles. *The Shattered Isles.*

They both reacted in time of each other. Scaling the hillside, Adair's muscles screamed with the sudden movement. Pins and needles made his legs feel numb, but he pushed, sprinting in between the various buildings in a blur. There could only be one reason the Shattered Isles would come here.

Emory was his shadow, her sharp curses thrown in every direction. Adair sucked in humid air, his lungs feeling clotted with the thickness of it. The world remained oblivious to the fact that their nonexistent gates were being charged by people that were bred for war, for the bloodlust and the thrill of the fight. By people who, Adair knew for certain, would not play fair.

He and Emory were about twenty yards from the main building, their curt breaths marking their tempo as they pushed faster. Men and women's voices floated behind them, their catcalls and untamed hollers chasing on their heels.

Ten yards.

Adair's ability floated around him like a cloak, begging for release, to slip into someone else's mind and overtake them. To fight, to get help, to do *something*.

Five yards.

# HEIR OF LIES – PART ONE

Emory flew past him, wanting to reach the door first, her determination plain. He desperately tried to shut out the sound of the hooves booming behind them. If she was afraid, Adair couldn't see it, and he admired her for that. They *should* be afraid.

She collided with the door, scrambling as she shoved it open. Breathlessly, they skidded to a stop, taking in the empty hallway.

She panted. "Come on. We must find them. Now."

His hands shook slightly, and he looked at her, not needing to ask. Exhaling, he let go of the restraints, and with each snapping cord, his ability billowed from him. He always imagined it like smoke, spilling from him and searching for what his heart sought. What his soul sought. His strength wasn't one made from pureness; it wasn't a *gift*. It was one of darkness, of control, of desire. One that he had at his constant disposal. One that Adair couldn't get enough of.

He was lost in his darkness; in the hunt of the person he was searching for. There was no distinction between his ability and man, not in this. A trigger flared in his mind, as his ability brushed against Nei and Roque's energies.

*Consume, consume, consume.*

Pulling at him, his ability drowned Adair in want. Having the power to possess another's will was intoxicating. He could feel it expand, circling around them like a predator stalking their prey - sniffing and weighing its options, right before landing the killing blow. Adair pulled back, slamming into the present moment.

"The Library," he wheezed, his lungs crackling.

Emory took off, her footfalls echoing down the hallway, not looking back once. Pumping his arms, he followed, seething low under his breath.

Low laughter echoed behind them through the doorway. He swore, stumbling as his knees grazed the unrelenting floor. He felt the skin on his kneecap tear, warm blood trickling down his leg. Pushing himself back up, his legs shook from the defiance of gravity, but he didn't stop. He couldn't.

*Do not look back. Do. Not.*

A sharp tugging sensation caught his left wrist, and gravity left him once more as he slammed into the cold stone floor. Black dots tinged his vision, threatening to pull him into unconsciousness as the cutting taste of iron filled his mouth.

"Adair!"

Emory's scream seemed distant, like he was below water being pulled further away from the world above.

Throwing his weight forward, he scrambled, nails breaking as his fingers tried to find something to hold on to. Pain, hot and consuming, surged up his shoulder and down his side. Someone cackled, and he vaguely realized that he was being dragged backward.

Rolling, he looked at the leather whip cutting into his skin, crimson blood trickling down his wrist. Adair looked to where the group of *pirates* waited for him. Their leader held the end of the whip, his smirk holding the promise of malice. His pale green hair was braided back, his deep eyes flashing as Adair stopped before him, gasping and shaking. A boy around seventeen peeked around his father, his emerald hair glistening like a gem, his pale freckled skin making his eyes look too big for his face.

Adair begged with his eyes, for mercy, for the boy to do *something*.

Jutting his chin out, the boy shook his head so fast Adair almost didn't catch the movement.

Pain flared in his chest as Adair felt a heavy boot crunch against his sternum, pinning him flush to the cold hallway floor. Gasping, he tried to get up, to move, and the man only pressed down harder until Adair was sure he was going to break his bones.

"My, my, this place is very interesting, isn't it?" The man's voice was dry and full of authority, and he flashed Adair his gold teeth, searching his face. He leaned closer, "Now what should I do with you?"

# HEIR OF LIES – PART ONE

Adair couldn't breathe. The walls seemed closer, the hallway blurring. Shouts filled the hallway, and Adair looked up to those leering faces. Teeth snapping, laughter clawing at Adair's edges. Their taunts. Their insults. And the boy standing in the middle of the throng, doing nothing but watching him as the distant words became a sharp humming in his senses. The humming becoming a madness.

And he snapped.

Adair's ability shattered through him, and with its inky claws, he sunk them deeply in his victim, relishing in how quickly the boy's mind bent to his will. Adair flashed open his new perspective and looked at his form still pinned on the floor; his eyes rolled into the back of his head. The man paused for the briefest of seconds at Adair's lack of struggle.

The boy's voice was smooth, and Adair started to laugh slowly. The man turned to look at his son, his back stiff. Only to find that his once emerald eyes were now pitch black.

"What the...?"

Adair didn't wait; he didn't care that he was outnumbered. He launched himself toward the man, aiming low and throwing all his weight forward.

The man dodged his attack easily. Chuckling darkly, he said, "Oh, boys, we have a fighter. Shall we entertain his idea?" Mocking laughter rippled around the group, and the leader lazily took in his son's imposter. "You need to leave my son out of this. How about a fair fight in the body that is yours?"

Adair felt the boy's thin lips pull upward. "You won't fight fair, why should I? You wouldn't dare hurt him. Now tell me why you're here. What do you want?"

The man paused, tilting his head as he assessed him. Adair tensed, his muscles pulling as he prepared to fight. The man bared his teeth, making Adair flinch. Before he could say anything, a low hissing filled the hall.

Spears of ice flew past Adair, lodging themselves firmly in the man's cloak, the force throwing him backward and pinning him to the wall.

"Try touching my son again, and I will make sure I don't purposefully miss."

Bresslin Stratton was a force to be reckoned with as she strode forward, the group of rovers trying to block their leader from her wrath. She smirked, her gaze as cutting as a sword, frost spreading down her fingertips and hands.

"Wrong answer." His mother was fluid as water, as ice shattered their trance. Ducking, Adair let go and slammed back into his own body, scrambling to get out of the way.

"Adair!" Emory ran up to him, dropping to her knees and clutching his bloodied hands. "Are you okay? I went... I got..." Stopping, she gasped as she looked at his open wounds from the leather whip, his blood dripping onto the floor.

"Em, I'm okay. It's going to be okay."

Adair cupped her face for the briefest moment, breathing hard, before strong hands wrenched him up. His father's face was contorted in anger when he said, "What did he do to you? Adair, what did he do?"

Spittle flew from Cesan's lips. Emory blanched behind them, unaware that Adair's blood was smeared on her cheek. Cesan shoved him back, his silent rage rolling in waves.

"Dad, no!" Adair's voice cracked and landed on deaf ears as his father stalked to where the intruders were now pinned by his mother's enchanted ice. Bresslin paced back and forth, her cutting gaze making their visitors wary and, for the first time since arriving, silent.

Lurching at his father, Adair found himself grappling at thin air, his vision spinning violently.

*One more step. One. More.*

Everything happened in clips of violence.

Cesan stalked up to the rover, not giving him a chance to explain, before bones cracked and more blood was spilt. Fists against jaws, might against might.

# HEIR OF LIES – PART ONE

Adair tripped, landing hard on his knees. Yells, protests, and the one voice who could stop his father's wrath - "Cesan, stop."

Roque Fae strode past, Nei followed at his heels, her expression dark and unyielding.

Dry laughter filled the hallway as Cesan turned, his dark eyebrows lifted in surprise. "Roque, I thought this is the very thing we are trained to do when someone threatens our *children* and our *home*."

Spittle and blood flew from the man's mouth as he barked out a choked laugh. "Threaten? I didn't know that stepping foot inside your precious Academy was a threat. We were here to talk when your son *threatened us*."

*Lies.*

Adair stood, forcing his shaking legs forward. His dad had to believe that he wouldn't use his ability for anything but self-defense. He had to see reason.

Cesan grabbed the man's jaw, forcing him to look at him. "I'm glad my son threatened *you*. I only wish he had finished the job."

"Cesan!" Roque roared and shoved him back hard with a pointed looked.

The two men stood in a silent battle before Cesan shook his head. "You will condemn us all, Roque. This is my line. You can't possibly expect me to sit back while you reason with these people!"

"That is *exactly* what I expect you to do."

Cesan's skin flushed, his clenched hands shaking. It was a moment suspended in air, the defiance and betrayal plain in his father's features. Adair's heart stuttered as Cesan bared his teeth and turned away, his anger a wild and tangible thing. He didn't look back at his wife, son, or best friends. It was like a cord snapping; the frayed edges that had held on for so long were no longer able to bear the weight.

Dread spread with a fury through Adair, cold and numbing, and he did nothing but watch. Roque sighed and turned his attention on the group who were still pinned to the wall and looking at them with curious interest.

"Bresslin, if you could..."

Adair's mother snapped her frost-bitten fingertips, and the deadly spears turned to water, crashing down on their guests. Sputtering, their leader recovered first, appraising not Roque but Nei.

"Why are you here?" Roque's voice rang with authority, and the man flickered his attention back to him.

Adair felt Emory brush up beside him, tugging his fingers gently, but Adair was entranced, watching as the man gave Roque a bloody smile, chips of broken teeth and bruised skin making his skin look distorted. He bowed mockingly, and rising, his voice rang clear, cutting into Adair's heart. "I am Tadeas Maher of the Shattered Isles. My companions and I have traveled a great distance, Roque Fae, to come deliver news to you all, but specifically to your wife."

Tadeas shrugged past Roque, a menacing glint in his eye. "Your father has been killed, Nei, and usurped. The Shattered Isles no longer recognize the peace agreement that was made with Kiero, nor do we answer to this pitiful fabrication of a government." He paused. "Most importantly, you all have terrible manners. Don't you know you should bow before the new King, which I am pleased to inform you, is *me*."

Nei's skin paled of all color, her mouth hanging ajar. Tadeas's companions drew their weapons, steel hissing with freedom from the scabbards. Flanking their King, Tadeas spat blood and saliva at Nei's feet, musing aloud, "We have a lot to talk about, but I must say we are famished. Perhaps dinner and some wine are in order?"

Adair wanted to melt into nothing, to disappear in the shadows. Emory gripped his hand hard, yanking him back and forcing his body to walk with her, fleeing from the scene.

They couldn't get away fast enough before Nei's shaky voice chased at their heels. "Of course."

# HEIR OF LIES – PART ONE

# CHAPTER THREE

## Memphis

The voices were consuming and suffocating. Roaring and crashing, they took up all that he was and left a trembling boy in its wake. Memphis Carter sat on the edge of his bed, clutching his temples, willing that blissful wall of reprieve back. He had no such luck today.

He had lost control coming back from class, and he was now drowning beneath the beating waves of the collective conscious that was the Academy. Sitting up too fast to pace around his simple room, Memphis's world tilted. His stomach turned, bile threatening to claw its way back up.

Taking a deep breath, Memphis forced his pained features into a smooth compliance as he paced his room. His body knew the drill: breathe, walk, breathe, walk. Around the two bunkers were the desks and the bookcases. He had been lucky enough to land a suite this year, and the simple cavern-like walls provided more space than previous years, and it was pure *bliss*.

Another wave of white noise crashed down on him, and he cringed, picking up his pace. Snippets of conversation wove tightly around his mind, piling up thicker and thicker. It wasn't coherent sentences when it was this intense, but overall feelings: snippets of words, of internal battles.

And he knew one thing without a doubt—the Academy was at a huge unrest.

Memphis groaned aloud and sat back down, shutting his eyes. He hadn't slipped this bad in a long time.

The chaos blanketed him, and his stomach lurched violently again. He really *might* be sick. Spreading his knees wide, he gripped his thighs and lowered his head below his heart. A sharp ringing pierced his ears as he breathed deeply, rooting himself to this moment.

His ability was strong, but he had learned to be stronger. Thanks to the Academy and his private tutor, Professor Ida, Memphis had learned one thing that he could not have learned otherwise—not to give in to his fear.

It had taken years of getting through episodes like this, of grueling private lessons, of learning he was *more*, that he could have a life worth living. That a title like *freak* could be turned into strength. That he could show the outside world who had preconceived fear about people like him, that they weren't so different.

Curling into himself, Memphis did what he knew and turned the crippling pain into fuel, letting his anger guide him. Memories dropped into his mind like stones into a lake, disturbing the thick layer of assault that blanketed him.

His parents, his childhood home—Sarthaven. It was picture perfect, a small cottage by the coast, hours away from the capital. Breathing in, he could practically remember how the salt crusted air tasted on his lips, the roaring waves, the endlessness of the horizon. How the clouds churned and consumed the sky or how they dissipated and nestled far above the stars that winked down at him like gems.

The comfort of the memory vanished, and Memphis saw himself at the age of six, curled in a ball in their living room, knives and dishware levitating around him in a flurry. His parents screaming at him to *stop*, to calm down. He remembered that day like it was yesterday. He remembered the tears, the anger, the names.

*Freak. Monster. Uncontrolled.*

His emotions were unhinged, and he didn't *know*, didn't understand what was happening. His ability had been quietly

# HEIR OF LIES – PART ONE

building inside of him until a fissure was exposed, and it overtook him.

Memphis cringed as he remembered the glint of steel, the cry of pain. The knife lodged in his mother's shoulder and her blood trickling down her blouse; her shocked expression. The blame in her icy eyes. His parents were desolates, which had never bothered Memphis because he was told he was exactly like them. Unchosen and without ability but living a peaceful life without fear.

Until everything changed.

He remembered his apologies, his raking sobs as his father yelled at him to get out, to get help. That he wasn't safe to be around, they didn't want him to stay. How could *they* have a son like him?

That they couldn't help him, *wouldn't* help him.

The weight of his backpack, his meager clothing sticking out from the top, was the indication of what his parents wanted: *him gone.* Memphis remembered, the ushering of strong hands, the snap of the door. His panicked pleas swallowed up against the crashing of waves. His fists beating, bloodied against the door, his raking sobs. Then darkness.

The memory stretched too thin, dissolving like smoke. But Memphis, despite his grief, would never forget that day. He had left his home, alone and scared. Traveling away from the coastline of the Black Sea and further into unknown woods, he had wandered aimlessly for hours, young and helpless, trees bowing in his wake, pebbles floating after him in a trail as he walked.

It was two men ferrying goods by carriage into Sarthaven that had found him, bringing him to the capital. The rest was history. Roque and Nei had eyes everywhere, looking for people who needed refuge, and he was brought to the Academy.

Memphis sat up straight, taking a deep breath. The pain of that memory had always worked to ground him; why he had come here forced the chaos of his mind to a quiet purr. He knew he wasn't defined by his ability, and his dream was to go back to his parents and show them he wasn't dangerous, that he had control.

He stood, brushing away his tears. Right then, his door exploded open, and his best friend stalked in, his anger etched into his features.

"Memph, you look like your day has gone like mine has." Brokk smirked, but it faded fast as he took in Memphis's ashen complexion. Sighing, Brokk ran a hand through his unruly golden hair. "How bad is it, Memph?"

"Bad," Memphis whispered, resuming his grounding walk.

Brokk was basically bouncing at his heels as he gushed, "Well guess who was taken in to see Roque with the lingering threat of expulsion?"

Memphis felt the corners of his mouth pull upward. "Well that would make sense, seeing as you punched a teacher."

He could practically hear the words before Brokk said them, "Memph, come *on*. You're not telling me you agree with them?"

"Brokk, how many times have we already talked about this? The Academy and the teachers here aren't the enemies. The people who abuse their gifts, the people who prey on the desolates, the people who threaten the peace of our country are the *enemies*."

Brokk huffed, cutting off Memphis's speech, forcing him to stop. "I'm telling you, Memph, there is something more going on here. I can feel it. When I was brought in, Cesan was there, and I interrupted something big."

"Did your heightened sense tell you as much?"

Brokk cuffed the back of his head. "Can't you be serious for once? There is tension between the Faes and the Strattons, and that doesn't concern you one bit?"

"No, it doesn't. Friends fight, Brokk. It doesn't mean it's a threat to us."

Brokk poked him in the chest. "Well, I'm going to find out exactly *what* is. I'm tired of being told what I should and shouldn't know."

For the second time, the door exploded open, making them both jump. Memphis turned around, and instantly, everything else was whisked away. Emory stood in the doorway, her face flushed as she supported Adair, who looked half dead, his nails cracked and dried blood smearing his hands. Dread filled Memphis's core as he saw dried blood smeared on her cheek as well.

"Emory," Memphis breathed her name, his heart practically jumping out of his chest.

"Can I get a little help here?" she snapped, focusing on them. Memphis leaped forward, wrapping one arm around Adair's waist, shifting his weight to him.

Adair looked up to him, murmuring, "Thank you, Carter."

"Let's just get you to the bed, Stratton. You look like you've seen better days too."

Adair chuckled darkly as they shuffled to the bunker. Memphis swallowed hard as the edges of his mind pushed and pulled, and he shut down his wall, hard. He would not slip, not when his friends needed him.

Brokk cut past them, his low voice rumbling, "What happened?"

Emory slammed the door shut behind her, her shaking hands lingering on the handle. "My grandfather is dead. The new King of the Shattered Isles is here."

Lowering Adair onto his bed, he immediately covered his face with his hands. Brokk glared, mistrust filling his golden eyes while Memphis stood between them and whispered, "Em, I'm sorry."

She turned to face them. "I never even got to meet him. My parents thought it best. They told me the Shattered Isles are dangerous, the treaty in a precarious position with them. They always talk to me in riddles, yet they expect us to uphold the Academy. To uphold the future." Her voice cracked as she continued, "I'm tired of it. Who else wants to find out why the new *King* of the Shattered Isle is here?"

Brokk lit up, his grin sharp and wicked. Groaning, Memphis murmured, "You can't be serious?"

Emory sauntered up to him, patting his cheek. "I'm *very* serious. Besides, I will need your help, Carter. If you're up to it."

Memphis flushed deeply. "Fine."

Brokk clapped him on the back. "Excellent. Stratton, can you stand?"

Adair uncovered his face. "Oh, don't feign you care. I'm coming whether you like it or not."

Waggling her eyebrows, Emory threw the door open. "Well, there isn't a moment to waste."

Filing out, Adair shuffled out last. The door clicked closed, and the hallways were deserted, luckily. Emory set the pace, and they all moved fast and silent as shadows. Memphis already knew she had a plan; she always did. Memphis threw a sideways glance to Brokk, who was warily watching Adair.

Sighing, Memphis pushed forward. It was a wonder Brokk hadn't tried to rip Adair's throat out, but the two tolerated each other. And so, their mismatched group was formed—the two royals and the two lost boys.

They veered left, and Emory slipped into an unoccupied classroom, waving them in.

The room was filled with long desks and various hanging herbs covering the walls and the ceiling. Round basins filled the back wall, notes and articles of the properties of different natural healing techniques still on the chalkboard. Memphis briefly took it all in before a cool hand wrapped around his own, and he twisted to see Emory smirking at him. "Sorry. Time is of the essence."

After all the years of knowing her, Memphis would never get used to this feeling. It was like being winded, and he froze as he felt his ability drain from him, flowing into Emory. Being a leech, she couldn't break the connection as she absorbed his ability.

With furrowed brows, Emory concentrated at the far corner of the room where screws started to twist and turn, floating down to them. The panel loosened and floated down to them as well. Behind it was a tunnel big enough for them to fit, if they crawled.

# HEIR OF LIES – PART ONE

Loosening a breath, she let go of his hand, and Memphis's power snapped back into him with a startling fierceness.

"Quick. Help me with this," she said.

Brokk quickly grabbed the other end of the desk, and they slid it underneath the opening.

Memphis muttered to Emory under his breath. "Not your first eavesdropping session, is it?"

Hopping up on the table, she raised an eyebrow at him. "When it comes to my parents, I always find a way to figure out what they are hiding from me."

With that, she lunged forward, hands gripping the ledge and pulled herself into the darkness. Brokk shook his head, smiling, and followed, not looking back.

"Memphis." Adair's voice was small as he sidled up beside him. "Can you help me?"

"Of course. Come on. I will give you a leg up."

They moved slowly, Memphis taking in the angry welt on Adair's wrist. Adair's jaw worked silently back and forth, but he pulled himself up on the desk. His movements were slow and deliberate; Memphis could tell he was swallowing his pain. Silently, he crouched down, cupping his hands. Adair stepped into them, and standing, he boosted him up.

Cursing under his breath, Adair slid into the panel, and with ease, Memphis followed, allowing his eyes to adjust to the darkness. On their hands and knees, they could easily maneuver, and they shuffled forward.

"Stratton, watch where you're crawling there, will you?" Brokk said when Adair got too close.

They all moved as fast as they could, following Emory's lead. The air was cool in the vent, the metal slick underneath their palms. The space curved upward, and after several minutes, Emory stopped and whispered, "Memphis, they are down there."

Nodding, he knew what to do. Closing his eyes, he dipped into his consciousness, meeting his iron wall... and stripped it down.

39

Voices barreled into him, but concentrating, he maneuvered, weaving through the web until he found the voice he was looking for.

"Please sit while you inform us on the manner of your declaration, Tadeas."

Roque's voice was weary, and Memphis gritted his teeth, holding on to the connection as he pushed the wave of other voices back. He flinched, but his hold held true. Taking a deep breath, he wrapped his wall protectively around the room below them and was transported.

Tadeas chuckled darkly. "This place isn't a school as you say it is. Anyone can see the power at your disposal here. Besides, while you have been making no progress with your project, rumors have been coming back to me. Sailing, a man can hear many rumors, some false, but some hidden gems that ring of only the truth."

Nei stated sharply, "Be careful of what you are saying."

"Ah, now that is the Nei Runnard I was told about. I know exactly what I am saying. Your Academy has only created more unrest, more resentment, and more fear. How can the people of Kiero have their freedom when you are grooming the most powerful people for them to answer to if they step out of line?"

"The students here are to help protect the borders from threats, not become them," Nei retorted.

Tadeas laughed. "You are blind if you actually think that."

Roque slammed his fist down on the table. "We are not blind. Don't you remember what happened before we had a peace treaty with the Shattered Isles? When my father was King? We were at constant war and enslaved your people, and your warriors pillaged and stripped our towns. I refuse to recess back to that after we have built what fragile peace we have. It's not perfect, but I promise you that this is a safe place, for both the exceedingly gifted as well as desolates. Why throw away the peace you have achieved for your people as well?"

A ripple of unrest flickered through Tadeas's men as he said indignantly, "Peace? What do you know of our peace? The treaty has isolated us, and while you flourished here, we have been left barren." He looked to Nei. "Your father ruled with an iron fist, limited our sailing routes, our raiding routes, and absolutely under no circumstances were we allowed to trade with Kiero. Now I wonder how this came about because it was not always like this. Maybe you can enlighten us?"

There was silence throughout the room as Tadeas continued, "That's what I thought. Now, since you have obviously done something or are doing something that would've made your father leave his eldest daughter severed from his alliance, I am here to help. I am a man of change, and of vision. I do not recognize any treaty of the past that was constructed, and my people will raid and sail wherever their hearts' desire." His eyes narrowed. "My people also recognize me as their King, and they respect my command. I am a reasonable man as well and don't want to start another war. I am here to see if you can gain my respect, and we can find new terms to move forward with."

"You're a reasonable man but have insulted everything we have worked toward... Can we even gain your respect?" Cesan sneered, malice dripping off every word.

"I could move forward with a man of similar vision to the Shattered Isles."

"No." Roque's voice quivered. "I refuse to go back to regency."

Tadeus said, "You would allow your people to burn? For Kiero to fall into ruin? People will learn to fear the King across the Sea, Roque, if you are deemed a weaker man than me."

Nei cut in, "Allow us, Tadeas, to gather our thoughts. At least allow us the honor of hosting you during your stay."

Memphis's balance was tipped as he slammed back into his own mind, breathing hard.

"What did you hear, Memphis? What's happening?" Emory asked.

Swallowing hard, he looked at his friends, shaking his head. "Let's go back to my room. We can talk there."

They looked at him with pale faces, before they shuffled back the way they came, Memphis reeling.

*Kings. War. Unrest. The Faes are hiding something. Something that broke alliances.*

Goosebumps prickled across his skin, and Memphis couldn't shake the knowledge that the Faes are hiding something; Brokk had been right. What secret would be worth sailing across the Black Sea for?

*A powerful one.*

HEIR OF LIES – PART ONE

# CHAPTER FOUR

### Adair

It was late into the night as Adair walked down the hallway. His body ached with every movement, dried blood cracking underneath his shattered nails, but it was nothing compared to how his heart broke with every passing second.

They had talked for hours, going over what Memphis had heard, every possible outcome, every possible way that it would change their lives. Emory's strong reassurances that her parents wouldn't allow anyone to change what they had built, the *safety* within the Academy.

But Adair saw through her façade and the fear that lingered there. Gritting his teeth, he slowly made his way back to his bunker where he was certain either a message from his father was waiting or his father himself.

The low lanterns on the wall lit his way, as the seconds morphed into minutes, and finally, Adair reached that looming, familiar door. Gripping the handle, he swung the door inward.

His room was simplistic, the bed tucked in the corner, his books piling on his bookcase. Other than that, there was nothing to indicate what Adair Stratton held close to his heart. Locking his eyes on the ivory envelope tucked on his pillow, he moved in a trance, and with trembling hands, he read the flawless handwriting before him:

*Tomorrow, noon, in the Library – C.*

His father was never a man of many words.

Adair flopped on his bed in a defeated heap. This was *bad*. Over the years, he couldn't bring himself to acknowledge to anyone, let alone *talk* to anyone about his father's ravings. About how Roque was weak and his father's wild dream about Adair one day becoming King. The Academy was a fool's dream. About the yelling matches, the hidden bruises, and ashamed tears. Adair had believed he would rise to rule with Emory by his side. In believing that, he had embarrassed himself beyond repair with the girl he loved most.

*His father's vision was an arranged marriage—a union that would make the world tremble and finally bow. The Faes and Strattons building the monarchy...*

As he grew, Adair had let that dream idle into embers and had pushed more energy in repairing his and Emory's friendship.

He was feared amongst his peers, an outcast, a monster amongst the gifted.

Taking a shaky breath, Adair rolled over, covering his eyes, begging for sleep to take him. And like every other day, he reminded himself how lucky he was to have the friends he did and the small freedoms he could relish in before he was whisked away into oblivion.

*The trees around him were weeping blood. Adair stood transfixed as he spun around, taking in the inky black bark, stained by the ruby droplets. There were no sounds at all, like the entire world was holding its breath.*

"Hello?"

*He took a tentative step forward, the mossy ground sinking under his weight. There was a strange dampness in the air, thick and cool. The forest was never ending, and Adair was at the heart of it. A high-pitched giggle cut through the air, and Adair jumped, twisting around.*

*A woman with ebony hair stood behind him, her eye sockets stretching wide into deep empty holes. She reached toward his heart, sharp teeth being revealed as her lips were pinned back into a permanent grin.*

"It's so beautiful, isn't it?"

He breathed out, "W-who are you?"

# HEIR OF LIES – PART ONE

*The woman tilted her head slowly to the side, assessing his question. Another giggle erupted from his right side, and she locked her gaze on whoever laughed.*

*After a beat, she whispered silkily, "Your future, if you choose."*

*Adair had slowly trod backward, his back now flush against the wet bark. The woman sauntered up to him, her features contorting between human and something else.*

*"Don't you want to be powerful, Adair Stratton? Accepted? Loved? The son who is never enough, the student that is feared. Well, I see you, and I do not fear you."*

*His heart raged against his ribcage, trying to break free as Adair whispered, "You're wrong."*

*Giggles erupted all around him in the shadows, devouring his words. The woman was now face-to-face with him, a pale hand against his cheek, forcing him to look at her.*

*Her breath was hot against his skin. "You would be enough, if you accepted the darkness within you instead of burying it."*

*Looking down, the ground started to shift and churn, dissolving into a thick smoke, and the world exploded into whispered promises that sunk their sharp claws within his heart.*

*The woman tilted her head, whispering, "Find us, Adair. Find us."*

*She stepped back, spreading her arms wide, and closing her eyes, she fell into the smoke. It hissed and sparked, embers flying up toward the sky.*

*Shaking, Adair lurched forward, but not before he realized he was soaked with blood. Crying, he shook his head, whispering, "Not real, this is not real."*

*Blood smeared over his pale skin as he tried to wipe it away, but it piled on thicker and thicker. It ran down his face, and as he looked up through the iron and salt, he realized that the world around him was consumed in flames, devoured and lost to the smoke and ash. As he stood there transfixed, Adair realized that he was in the heart of the fire.*

*And he was laughing.*

Lurching out of the nightmare, Adair shivered in a cold sweat, his mouth opening and closing as he shifted back into reality.

*Just a dream, it was just a dream.*

Running a hand through his black hair, gulping down air, and trying to steady his nerves, he closed his eyes, and beneath his lids, the woman waited for him, her sharp, angular features and beckoning calls.

He muttered to himself, "It was not real. Not. Real."

Shaking his head, he jumped to his feet and began pacing his small room, he tried to stop the ice that was flowing through his veins and the odd exhilaration that awakened his senses. It was just a nightmare. *That felt exceedingly real.* He was probably under too much stress, and this was him reacting to it.

He wasn't a monster.

He didn't want more.

Clutching his face, Adair breathed into his palms, each breath wiping away the darkened forest. Slowly, he lowered his hands, taking in his room. It was the same as before, nothing changed.

"It was just a bad dream," he stated to the air.

The quiet of the night pressed back to him, and he resigned to the fact that he was not getting any more sleep tonight.

Numbly, he walked over to his dresser, pulling out his normal outfit of black pants, a shirt, and a jacket, and swiftly peeled his soaked clothes off him. Refreshed, he slipped out of his room, clicking the door softly shut.

Through the bay windows, tinges of dawn peaked over the horizon, and Adair set off down the hallway, knowing exactly where he wanted to be.

He passed the classrooms and suites, basically jogging now, the walls feeling too close, too small. Too much like a cage. He passed the surveillance room, the different cameras capturing almost every ounce of the school.

Dawn was his favorite time of day, the edges of the night being chased away, the world still and silent while everyone was still lost in their dreams.

# HEIR OF LIES – PART ONE

Exploding through the front doors, he breathlessly jogged to the edge of the hill, where a small escarpment overlooked the surrounding landscapes. Scaling it easily, he hung his feet over the edge and settled in as the sun greeted another day. The Draken Mountains to the east were bathed in golden hues with tinges of pink bleeding into the sky. Dew still clung to the blades of grass, as Adair watched the world reawaken. Bit by bit, the light overtook everything.

"Couldn't sleep either, then?"

Cursing, he jumped, nearly falling off the ledge. To his right, the teenage rover sat on the same ledge, his emerald green hair looking more vibrant in the light. He jutted out his chin, looking forward, as he stated, "I'm sorry about my Dad."

Adair appraised him, seeing if he was being sarcastic or not. Lifting a dark eyebrow, he said, "He's not great at making the best first impressions."

The boy's face spilt into a lopsided smile, and his eyes lit up. "So, you're not afraid of us then? The whole sail here, my father prepared me for you bunch of sticklers." His face twisted as he mimicked his father's voice, *"They aren't like us, Marquis. Be prepared for the worst, Marquis."*

Barking out a laugh, Adair quipped, "Afraid? Most people are afraid of *me*. Try being the only one at your school with the ability to possess people. But no, I'm not afraid of you."

The boy faltered, looking forward. "Only the change my father is bringing to Kiero?"

Adair rolled his shoulders, turning his attention back to the sunrise. "Change isn't a bad thing, if it's met with good intentions."

"Ah yes, good intentions." The boy chuckled. "I was brought into this life taught to take what I wanted without a second glance, to always be moving. To dance with the edge of danger, and above all, do what's best for me. I don't think anyone from the Shattered Isles knows what that even means." He shook his head, standing. "Anyways, I will leave you now to your brooding thoughts."

Pressing his lips together Adair ate his retort taking in the other boy, his interest blooming.

He lifted the corners of his mouth with a wicked glint in his eyes. "I'm Marquis, by the way. I'm sure I will be seeing you soon." Gracefully, he bent in a mock bow, and then with that, he was striding back up to the Academy, hands buried in his pockets. He didn't look back at Adair once.

Shaking his head, Adair pushed the strange boy out of his mind. He had more important things to focus on. Soaking in his final moments of peace, Adair hungrily watched as the soft hues turned into a beautiful array of fiery brilliance. The sun peaked higher in the sky, and closing his eyes, sunlight bathed his skin, flushing his cheeks and his vision. Lingering, he could pretend the world was on fire.

"*Find us, Adair.*"

His eyes flew open. Breathing hard, he twisted off the ledge, his heart caught in his throat. The whisper felt like someone breathing down his back, his skin prickling at the thought.

Swallowing hard, he walked back up to the Academy, thinking about the day of classes ahead, trying to ignore the voices in his head.

'*Don't you want more?*'

Stalling, he curled his fingers into his palms, his broken nails sending lacing pain up his arm. Looking behind him, he knew there was no one there. But why did he feel like he was being watched? Adrenaline surged through him, and Adair murmured under his breath, "Don't be ridiculous, Stratton. Keep moving."

One foot in front of the other. The cool morning air brushed past him, and it took all of Adair's control not to run up the sloping hill. He ran a hand through his unruly inky hair, trying not to focus on his trembling fingers.

'*Accept the darkness inside of you.*'

Adair came to a full stop, his limbs taut. The world was still, yet Adair couldn't shake the oppressing feeling of hopelessness colliding within him. Like he was running right into the pit of fire himself, and his course couldn't be changed. Which he knew was ridiculous. It had just been a nightmare, bleeding into his reality. He was hurt, tired, and overwhelmed. This was just his imagination dealing with his stress.

And he would not let *it* control *him.*

Exhaling through his teeth, he continued the climb back up to the school, icy whispers slithering in his mind and soaking into his heart the entire way.

"I am sure you are all aware of our visitors by this point, but I'm afraid the world must go on." The class's whispers only increased, and Professor Jett clapped his hands together, his booming voice encasing them all, "*Enough.*"

Sparks danced from their professor's palms, and his class were instantly quiet, looking at their teacher with wide eyes. Adair felt the corner of his mouth pull up in a lazy smile.

Lowering his hands, Professor Jett continued, "Now, who wants to tell me the magical properties of these two obsidian gems?"

Adair wanted to roll his eyes; going to class was a waste of his time.

"No one?" Professor Jett raised a silver eyebrow at them all.

Sighing, Adair murmured, "Combined, they make the perfect gas to knock out your enemy, and in large doses, an army."

"I didn't see a hand, Stratton."

Locking eyes with the older man, Adair slowly raised his pale hand. "The chemical reaction between the gabnite and the slinte, once weathered, will create the perfect destructive gas."

Professor Jett nodded brusquely. "Yes, thank you, Adair," Flicking his gaze away and, not missing a beat, Professor Jet pushed on about the different kinds of gems, rocks, and minerals that could be mined to find other lethal combinations.

Professor Jett was one of the only teachers who had the nerve to look Adair in the eye, but only barely.

Clenching his jaw, he told himself for the millionth time in his life that it wasn't his fault he was born into the family he was. That he was different.

Sighing, he shifted his gaze to the opposite wall, where a smooth slate of frosted glass hung. Deep within the ice, smoke sprawled and swirled, shifting and ticking, smoky tendrils marking how long was left of the class. And when Adair would meet his father.

His skin crawled, dread pooling in the pit of his stomach. He had nothing to fear; it was his *dad*.

*What happened the last time he demanded a meeting?*

Adair's spine stiffened as he gazed forward, not focusing on anything but being pulled down into his memory.

Cesan had left a note, crisp and identical to the one he received last night. When Adair had met with him, he had two seconds to process what had happened. The door clicked shut. He had looked up to his dad, hopeful and curious. Then his world exploded into white, lacing pain and his father's anger.

'*You are above this, Adair, above them.*'

Adair vaguely remembered the note floating down to the floor, drifting as light as a feather. He had clutched his cheek, desperately trying to stop the wobble in his lips as his father had whispered in a deadly quiet, "You do not need friends. You don't need anyone, Adair, except your family. The more you open your heart, the more people will find a reason to shatter it and bind you to that pain. You are not weak, you are a Stratton, and you will not bow."

He had run out of the room, tears spilling fluidly. That had been only a month ago, and Adair hadn't talked to his father alone since. It was as if the closer he was to turning eighteen, the more his father craved using physical violence to ingrain his morals into Adair, no matter how hard he resisted.

No one else knew what their private talks entailed. No one except the school healer, who had covered up Adair's split, bruised, and bloodied skin without question on various accounts.

A deep tolling vibrated throughout the room, and Adair jumped back into the present moment. His chair squeaked underneath him. The smoke in the ice showed that it was twelve, and class was over. His classmates were oblivious to his unease, and their relief and chatter overtook everything as they relished in their new freedom.

Chairs squealed, books and pages ruffling as everyone else started to file out, Professor Jett yelling over them, "Now remember to read chapters twelve through fourteen! I will know if you don't!"

Adair was frozen. How had the morning passed so quickly? He had felt in a daze throughout breakfast, and then like a ghost, he had sat through his classes. Advanced Ability Training. Advanced History. Advanced Weaponry.

*Breathe, Stratton.*

With shaking hands, Adair swept his useless books into his bag. These classes were just a time filler for him. With parents like Cesan and Bresslin, Adair had already read the textbooks several times.

*Only the best.*

Sighing, Adair forced his body to move, feeling Professor Jett appraising him the entire time. Adair didn't look back as he left and was met with the pure chaos of the hallway. Pieces of paper with inked secret messages soared through the air, laughter and gossip spilling from the entourage of students. Ducking his head, Adair set for the library, desperately trying to ignore flashing shows of abilities, the catcalls, and squeals.

In a place like the Academy, it bred more emotion and hope than Adair liked to admit. A government built on dreams, to nourish the most gifted. But to him, there was no control, and it suffocated him.

Grinding his teeth, he allowed his feet to carry him, having walked the path a thousand times. He tried not to think about what waited for him in that room, tried not to think about last night. Everything was a blur, the people and the school washing out to a dull white noise, as those doors appeared.

Five steps.

Taking a deep breath, trying to stand a little straighter, he smoothed his hair to no avail.

Three.

Adair bit the inside of his cheek, his teeth breaking skin as iron filled his mouth.

Two.

He would not bow. He would not break. He was better than this.

Reaching the doors, Adair gripped the handle and pulled. For a place like the Academy, the library was simplistic. Just a room with a desk, filled with bookshelves and dull material no one with an imagination would find exhilarating.

Cesan leaned against the desk, impeccably groomed, causally inspecting his nails. The door clicked quietly shut behind them, cutting off the roaring commotion from outside. Adair tried not to flinch as his father raised his gaze to him. Indifference etched into his features, the burning promise and hunger for violence simmering behind his hooded eyes.

Adair waited, his lips pressed into a thin line as he desperately tried not to throw up or to dip into his ability.

*It would be so easy.*

He couldn't do it, not against his Dad.

*Protect yourself.*

"Adair, do you believe in fate?"

The question registered slowly, and Adair paused, digesting that his father was talking to him. There was no anger, no violence, no accusations. Just a simple question that Adair was *not* prepared to answer.

Cesan didn't wait for him to. "Fate. It is something that for a long time after I met your mother, I believed in. We were living in a dangerous world, but we knew what we wanted. To see the injustices paid for, to end the war Roque's father had started. For years, I followed the Faes' dream. I followed my best friend and didn't doubt a thing. I had a life and a family, strung along with the promise of more."

A chill snaked down Adair's spine, when Cesan stepped forward, whispering, "Who wouldn't want more? To be powerful, to rule? Roque promised me that our day would come, Adair, to have equal right to the Academy. That it would always be fair, that there would be no secrets. That he would *always* weigh our family's opinion with an equal mentality."

His face contorted, and Adair stepped back.

"It was all lies. Things have changed, Adair, and I'm not going to follow Roque into this trap. I refuse to stay in his shadow."

"Dad?" Adair's voice trembled, his heart trying to catch up with what his mind had already concluded.

"These people from the Shattered Isles shouldn't be entertained or tolerated. And instead of making them our *guests*, I'm going to end them."

"Dad, no."

Cesan had backed Adair flush against the door, sneering down at him. "Are you with me?"

"What, and leave the Academy?"

"If you're not with me, you're with them."

"Dad, you don't have to do this! The Faes aren't the enemy, even these people..." He should have seen the hand coming; Adair's head snapped back as his father hit him. Tears welled in his eyes.

Cesan growled, "You are as weak as the rest of them. These people are a threat, Adair, and I am going to stop them." Cesan's face was flushed, and his eyes sparked with rage as he spat, "You are no son of mine."

With that, he shoved past Adair, slamming the library door with such force Adair was sure the door would splinter.

*'You are no son of mine'*, played in his mind.

He couldn't breathe as he blindly grappled with the doorknob. The door swung toward him, the explosion of noise surreal to him as he looked down the hallway, seeing his father getting further away with every step.

He had to stop him.

Lurching forward, his breath caught in his lungs, burning against his ribcage.

*Move.*

He was numb; he was nothing but the stinging remainder of how his father saw him.

*Weak.*

The word turned to ash in Adair's mouth, and the hallway spun sickly on its axis. He was anything but *weak*.

Someone caught his arm, their cool fingers brushing against his burning flesh, bringing him slamming back into reality.

"Stratton?"

Rounding on Memphis, his friend visibly flinched at his withering look.

Pulling hard out of his hold, he said, "Let me go," through gritted teeth.

He had already wasted too much time. What was his father going to do? What had he already *done?*

Sprinting, he wove through the hallway, through the classmates that hated him, through the school that confined him.

"Adair!"

He hadn't realized that Memphis had been on his heels, and with a flash of blond hair, he was in front of him, arms crossed.

"What happened?" Memphis asked. His voice was quiet, his ice blue eyes piercing into Adair.

Adair's chest was heaving, fists clenched tightly at his sides. He licked his dry lips, trying to begin to explain why he had to go *now*, that he couldn't even begin to explain what his dad had been doing, what he was about to do. He could feel the stares burning into his back, the judgements, the whispers of the students around him. His world was tipping, and he was drowning in it.

Snapping his gaze past Memphis, Adair felt that small protected part of himself crack, falling into oblivion. Falling into darkness.

"Get out of my way now, or I will *make* you."

Memphis's eyes widened slightly, the only sign of hurt flickering across his face.

Adair's anger was liquid fire in his veins, consuming him, incinerating him. It was effortless to abandon himself, diving into his ability that was always waiting just beneath the surface. Waiting for him to come home.

Memphis's mind was an iron seal, but Adair overtook him within seconds. Not wasting any time, he dove deeper into Memphis's muscle memory. Pouring his breaking heart into his actions, Memphis clawed against him, ripping and tearing at Adair, trying to stop him. But he barely noticed.

Adair felt his power overflowing, tipping the scales, knowing he was about to land the finishing blow.

"*Adair, no.*"

Memphis voice was distant and weak, and Adair suffocated him, pushing him further down until darkness snapped liked a whip and consumed them both.

Adair took a gulping breath as he was snapped back into his body, looking at a crumpled Memphis in front of him.

"What did you do?"

Adair raised his gaze to a pale faced boy with flaming red hair. Adair shrugged. "He is just knocked out, Alby."

Rushing to Memphis, Alby yelled something at him, but Adair was already running, his adrenaline fueling him, pushing him harder, faster.

*What had he done?*

The concrete world around him was a blur, and panic sunk its steady claws into his mind. He had crossed a line. He pushed the thought down. Memphis wouldn't have let him go otherwise.

How could Adair possibly start to explain what had happened? Who would understand? Who would listen to the shadows of his heart when they kept him at a distance? Who would see that he was desperately trying to be a man and not a weapon?

A choked cry escaped from him, and Adair threw the doors to the Academy open, the afternoon sunlight pouring over him. Cesan was in the courtyard, his gruff voice snapping commands at several senior students.

"Dad!"

Cesan turned slowly, taking him in. Adair took one step, his mind reeling when thundering footsteps sounded from the hallway.

"CESAN!"

Roque's voice made Adair flinch, and the door exploded open behind him. Roque, Nei, and his mother appeared first. Tadeas and his entourage quickly following behind them.

Adair was swept to the side, but Bresslin stopped to crouched down and cup his cheek, "Adair, did he do this to you?"

Ice crusted over his skin at his silence, and Bresslin stood, her eyes slits as she took in her husband. Cesan, in a fluid motion, gripped a hilt beneath his jacket and, with a hiss, brandished a black steel blade.

His grin was twisted, contorting his handsome features as he yelled to Roque alone, "No more, Roque! I *will* not bow to you! A desolate, weak man! How *dare* you string me along on your empty promises for years! How *dare* you go back on everything you promised my family! Promised me! I *will* be King, and I promise you, you will wish you hadn't crossed me."

A ripple of anger spread through them at his words, and Roque walked down the steps, appraising his best friend.

"Cesan, listen to me. Don't do this. What are my choices? The world constantly changes, and it demands that people either accept it, or they will fall stagnant in this life. I will not make my father's mistakes." He shook his head. "For the first time in years, we have the chance to make our alliances stronger instead of continuing to break them. Stay with me. Please."

Mad, crackling laughter erupted from his father and dread filled Adair as Cesan raised a dark eyebrow and breathed, "No."

Adair saw it in slow motion at first, Cesan running full tilt toward Roque, that mad dark gleam shining in his eyes, and

# HEIR OF LIES – PART ONE

Adair knew in his heart exactly what he was about to do, before anyone else could react. He was born from ice and darkness, and he was his father's son through and through. He was the only one who could stand up to Cesan.

"Dad, NO!"

Adair exploded past the group, shoving arms and bodies out of his way, and flung his physical body off the step, but his ability was already soaring, pouring out of him like smoke. And it wrapped itself around Cesan. It was like hitting a brick wall, battering repeatedly, all his energy pouring into this single action only to get pinned.

He was slammed back into his physical body, the air knocked out of his lungs from the force of his father's ability. He landed hard on the ground, his head cracking from the impact. Wheezing, Adair rolled, white spots dancing in his vision. Cesan's blade slammed into the ground right where Adair had been a second before.

"Do you think you are strong enough to *stop me?*"

Scrambling back from his father, from his words, from his violence, his voice cracked as Adair begged, "Dad, please. Stop. Listen to them. Listen to *me*. I'm asking you not to do this. Don't leave."

Cesan ran, forcing Adair back onto his feet, to duck and dive from his onslaught.

Steel hissed through the air, harsh and relentless. Tripping, Adair fell on to the steps and saw Cesan about to plunge the tip of the blade down. He shut his eyes, flinching as he readied himself to feel the slice of the blade.

"NO!"

The world exploded into ice, rippling down the stairs, courtyard, the blade in Cesan's hands. Bresslin charged toward them, as the sword shattered, forcing Cesan to turn his attention to her. Flickering anguish crossed his face as he took in his wife, spears of ice forming in her palms.

"Cesan, leave. Now."

His dad paused, sweat dripping off him, and whispered, "Bresslin. Come with me. You don't have to do this. Don't make me choose."

Face darkening, Bresslin stalked up to him, not pausing as she slapped his face, ice slicing his skin. Glistening ruby droplets streaked his face. "How do you like it? How long have you been doing this? He is our *son*, Cesan." Her lips twisted into a snarl. "Get. Out. Now."

Each word, she threw at him like a punch, direct and fierce.

"Bresslin, wait."

She snapped her hands down, and a wall of ice exploded from her, forcing Cesan to stagger back. The ice was thick, a thousand colors shimmering in it as the sun sliced through it. For a second, they just stared at each other, unsaid things passing, both of their chests heaving. Bresslin growled as she watched Cesan turn his back on them, snapping orders to his group.

Adair watched as if in a trance as two seniors freed the horses Tadeas's group had brought, and they mounted them.

Cesan hauled himself up on a stallion's back, twisting to stare at them all. His gaze landed on Adair last as he roared, "You will all regret this!"

Then with thundering hooves, they slowly disappeared, leaving them with his ringing threat and their broken hearts.

Cursing, Bresslin snapped her fingers, the ice cracking into a thousand tiny shards, suspended in the air like crystals. She stared at her work before turning her back. The ice melted and dissipated into droplets of water, sloshing onto the ground behind her.

"Adair, are you okay?" she asked.

Her hushed murmur broke him even further. One word burned in his mind, etching itself there permanently.

*Why?*

"Adair, you have to stand for me."

Looking up to his mother's face, her kind eyes, her soft features... she was strong, and he never once doubted that she wasn't *good*. But what was he? Was there any trace of her in *him*?

# HEIR OF LIES – PART ONE

Adair stood, shaking, his already bruised body making each movement drawn out and painful.

Roque still stood on the steps, staring at where Cesan had been, as if willing his best friend back. At their movement, Roque snapped his attention to them, and narrowed his eyes. "Bresslin, you need to follow him now. Take a group with you but do not let him accomplish what he wants to do."

"And exactly what is that?" Adair was surprised at how steady his voice was, and Roque sneered, taking the steps two at a time.

"Your father, *Stratton*, is planning on starting another war. By preying on desolates and people from the Shattered Isles until I step down from accepting my terms as King of Kiero."

*No.*

Roque didn't stop until he was face-to-face with Adair, his breath hot against his skin, "He is doing what he knows will hurt most. It's what my father would have done."

Bresslin stepped in between them. "Roque, enough. It's not Adair's fault."

"You're right." Roque stared at him a moment before wrenching his gaze away. "Bresslin, you have an hour to get ready. Nei, you will go as well. Can we prepare the school in time?"

They all snapped into action at his commands. His mom glanced at him one last time before she whisked herself away, jogging toward Nei. Tadeas gave Roque a sad nod, and anger rose its ugly head within Adair as he took in the scene.

They were preparing for war; in a single moment, his dad had ripped anything Adair thought he knew away.

*What just happened?*

Grinding his teeth, he forced himself to move, following the group back into the Academy. Everything was displaced: the brilliant warmth of the sun, the peacefulness of the forest sprawling behind the Academy. A dark foreboding unraveled within Adair, the pit in his stomach consuming him.

*"Don't you want more?"*

59

Whispers cut through the pain, wrapping around him, and Adair shook his head, pushing himself back into the Academy and to a healer. No one stopped to double check that the shadow of a boy was okay. No one stopped to make sure he was holding himself together.

And like thin ice, a crack split through Adair, reluctant and then all-consuming until there was nothing whole left.

# HEIR OF LIES – PART ONE

# CHAPTER FIVE

## Brokk

Hope was a dangerous thing. It could consume every dream and make them take flight, becoming wild daydreams in one's heart and mind. Or hope could incinerate everything you thought you knew, burning you down to your core, leaving you raw and exposed for the world.

As Brokk walked down the hallway, looking for Memphis, his world was ripped apart in a split second. The hallways were quiet, which should have been his first sign that something was off. Class had just ended for the afternoon, and like every other day, Brokk's blood was boiling after seeing Iasan. His *teacher* had become predatory toward him, trying to push him to his edge but always in ways only noticed to Brokk, putting on the persona for the other teachers.

*Iasan was only trying to ensure a bright future*, they said.

By grooming him into a lethal weapon that would kill on command.

Swearing under his breath, Brokk was hoping for the blissful distraction that the hallways of the Academy always provided. His fellow classmates had a flair for the dramatics; it was guaranteed he would be swept away in their display, along with his thoughts.

Instead, his footsteps echoed as he continued on, dread pooling in his stomach and making it churn. Turning the corner, he was about to stop and go back when he saw him. Crumpled in the middle of the hallway, his blond hair splayed out around him and his skin drained of any color, he looked dead. Alby's appearance flickered as he turned invisible in a panic.

"What happened?!" Brokk's voice cracked, as he sprinted, dropping to his best friend's side in an instant. Alby's eyes were wide, as he grappled with his words, his mouth opening and closing.

Brokk urged, "Alby, what *happened?*"

The doors at the end of the hallway were thrown open, and Brokk stood, slowly taking in the group rushing toward them. Roque stormed down the hall, Nei and Bresslin at his heels, Tadeas and his entourage flanking them. Roque looked at them, narrowing his eyes to slits.

"Foster! What are you doing here? I told the teachers to issue a temporary room curfew effective immediately."

Roque's words were just white noise, as Brokk saw Adair filing slowly in at the end of the hallway, looking like he had just been through a war.

"Foster, I suggest you answer the question," Roque spoke quietly and slowly, and Brokk flicked his gaze up to the man for a second, truly taking him in. And what Brokk saw, for the first time in years, scared him. Rage contorted their leader's features into one unrecognizable. One that consumed the man and left a person that had nothing left to lose.

He took a step back. "I was just looking for Memphis."

Alby cut in, "*He* did it. Adair used his ability against Memphis."

Brokk barely took in the next couple of seconds. Roque stiffened, turning slowly to look at Adair limping behind them all, his hooded eyes swept down to the floor, not realizing that everyone had focused in on him.

*He hurt Memphis.*

His nails dug into his skin, his body quivering. Brokk's body responded before his mind could. He felt his weight shift, anger flaring through his veins, electrifying every move as he sprang forward. He pushed past Roque, yells coming from behind him.

But it was like he was being funneled down, swept away, with only one objective.

# HEIR OF LIES – PART ONE

To make Adair pay.

His blood coursed through his veins, wildly alive, and Brokk lost himself to his adrenaline. His bones cracked, and the world splintered as he flew, landing heavily as a wolf, his lean body and golden fur rippling, his growl tearing through him.

The King of the Shattered Isles slammed himself flush to the wall, looking with wide eyes when Brokk came charging past. The rest of his company followed suit, and Brokk snapped his massive maws at them.

*They should be afraid.*

Adair's head snapped up, shadows and malice dancing across his face. Brokk didn't care about what the Faes were saying. Or the Strattons. Or the strange new King. All that had ever mattered to him was his family.

When it came to him, it didn't have to do with blood. Memphis was his best friend, and their bond was as strong as any kinship. They looked after each other and always had. Always would.

The coldness of the hallway sent shivers up his limbs as his body was tugged sideways, slamming into the concrete, bones cracking. Ice slicked the hallways, as Bresslin sauntered up behind him.

"Mom, no!" Adair lurched forward, his skin draining of any color.

Brokk recovered himself, his nails as sharp as any blade, and they dug into the pale ice. A deep thrumming overtook his senses. He was two lunges away from Adair, and his hackles rose on his back. Bresslin would never reach him in time, and she wouldn't attack him, not with the Faes there.

Adair was a liar, always waiting for the opportune moment to tear their group apart.

It ended *now*.

Adair stopped, slowly raising his chin, fists clenching at his sides. Snapping his massive jaws, spittle flying, Brokk welcomed his rage, his defiance. It wouldn't be a fair fight any other way.

His muscles tensed, and he lowered his body, preparing to cut through the air.

"Brokk, NO!" Emory screamed, throwing herself in front of him as she grabbed his paw, her green eyes alit. His world came crashing down around him. His back slammed into the floor, winding him, as every ounce of strength, every ounce of *himself*, was gone.

Emory stood above him, gritting her teeth, and Brokk knew she was barely holding on to the new surge of ability soaking into her bones. *His* ability.

"What are you doing?" Emory asked. Each word was forced, and she looked down to him, shielding Adair behind her.

Her grip tightened around his wrist, and Brokk licked his dry lips, searching desperately for his power, both the wolf and the *other*. The secret he had held close to his heart for years. The secret he had made sure to keep from his best friends, knowing if he ever got himself into this situation, that she would know in a split second.

Her eyebrows furrowed and sweat slicked her forehead. Brokk wanted to scream at her, to stop, to try to not figure it out. He didn't understand it himself. They had transcended time, and Brokk wanted to form any coherent sentences, to explain. Instead, panic flooded through him, about what he had almost done and about what Emory now knew.

Pulse fluttering underneath her pinning ability, she leaned in closer, whispering only to him. "This isn't over. Don't kill him, okay?"

Letting him go, Brokk shuddered, his ability slamming back into his marrow; relief washed over him. It was like returning home after being caught in a storm. Warm and familiar, he clutched his head, losing himself in the feeling. He never wanted to let go.

"Roque, this can't be tolerated!" Bresslin exclaimed.

Sitting up, Brokk watched Bresslin chasing after Roque, the rest of the group hanging back. Roque stormed right up to him, and Brokk froze. Their leader lowered himself, so he was eye-to-eye with Brokk, his breathing heavy.

# HEIR OF LIES – PART ONE

For a moment, they stayed like this, sizing up the other. Roque ran a hand through his hair, exhaling hard.

"This should result in expulsion, Foster. Attacking a teacher? Now a student? Adair's actions are his own consequences and will be dealt with. Memphis is fine. You're executing penalties leading with your heart and not your logic. That's a dangerous dance to take part in."

Brokk snapped his gaze to behind him, focusing more, and he spotted Memphis wide-eyed but standing meekly, looking more embarrassed than anything.

Roque stared at him, darkness filling his gaze. Sighing, he stood before raising his voice, "Brokk Foster, you are hereby expelled for the act of already assaulting a teacher and now trying as well with a student."

"No, "Adair protested, pushing past Emory, limping, a bruise flowering on his jaw. He flicked his gaze to Brokk before refocusing on Roque. "This is a misunderstanding. Brokk shouldn't be punished. He is just being a loyal friend. Isn't this what the Academy teaches, to protect others above all?"

"Yes, but not to reprimand with violence."

"The world is being ripped apart from its core by violence! Right now, Roque, there are dark forces working against you, to destroy any sense of good that the Academy has built," Adair said and flushed, but his words struck true.

Roque looked to his best friend's son; his features stony. "But to respond with such a reckoning will ensure we tear apart the moral we have built."

Adair seethed. "And to do nothing except ensure there *is* a reckoning will form a security never seen before. In this case, we have to fight."

"He's right." Tadeas stepped forward, making all of them instinctively step back. "Roque follow through with what we have decided. Together, we will stop Cesan and make sure Kiero will not fall into another war. These are your people, your land. Take your claim to protecting it."

Roque growled under his breath and said to Adair and Brokk, "I will deal with both of you later. To your rooms. Now."

Turning to Tadeas, Roque snapped, "Do not tell me exactly what I should do or how I should feel. If this alliance is to work, you must earn my trust. I am not quick to forget the way you came here, Tadeas." His eyes narrowed. "To tell my wife her father had been killed? That our peace treaty is no longer recognized? That our fabrication of a government is pitiful? Don't overstep your boundaries." Roque turned, leaving Tadeas to follow him.

Brokk stood shakily, turning to Emory and Adair. Adair glowered at him, not saying a word then limped down the hallway.

Emory rested a hand on his arm as Brokk started to go after Adair. "You've done enough. Let me go talk to him first. We've all been through a lot."

Emory shot him one more look, disappointment shining in her eyes before catching up with Adair. Linking arms, they left.

Memphis gave him a pitying look then joined Emory and Adair.

Leaving him alone in the hallway, his heart was in his throat, his fear consuming him. Swallowing down his disappointment, Brokk made his way back to his room.

# HEIR OF LIES – PART ONE

# CHAPTER SIX
## Memphis

They walked in silence, unsure of what to say to one another. Adair's shoulders were slumped, curved inward, like he was protecting his heart. Emory was pure energy, each bounce of her step deepening her frown or the pinch between her eyebrows.

He looked to the bland hallways that contained his life, his hope, and his future. This school was so much more; it had been a symbol of change, a promise of a way of life that could get him back home. Back to his parents. To be a part of his family once more. That would mend the displacement Roque's father had created.

He had thrived off this, thrown himself into his studies, private tutors, and endless sleepless nights just thinking of that wish.

And now?

It seemed to be all spiraling, slipping through Memphis's fingers faster than he could manage. Shooting a glance at Adair, he wanted to say something. Clenching his jaw, his drained body chose for him. His black shirt seemed to constrict as Memphis stuffed his hands into the pockets of his well-worn black pants.

Adair had slipped. His fellow classmates, even some *teachers*, had let their skepticism of Adair be known, that he truly was dangerous, that his family shouldn't be trusted. But the Strattons were powerful and were so close to the Faes, that it was a risk to mention it.

Memphis had always scoffed at his peers' judgments; they were harsh and had little reason to think Adair was any different than them. Everyone at this school was a risk, to themselves and to the people around them. Why should they single out Adair?

Finding his gaze drifting once more to his friend, doubt clawed at his mind. Emory caught his gaze, and Memphis flushed, quickly looking away. The hallway curved; they were coming to their crossroads.

*Say something.*

Adrenaline made everything look sharper than it appeared, like fragmented shards awkwardly pieced together. The lighting along the walls seemed too bright, a strange hissing noise coming from them. The classrooms they passed were too distorted, too empty. He felt the air grow thicker, more humid. Gulping, he quickened his pace, knowing he didn't have long before succumbing to another episode of his ability.

"Memphis, wait!"

Emory and Adair's voices overlapped, creating a strange harmony throughout his mind, and he stopped, his body shaking. Sweat slicked every ounce of his skin, but Adair pushed in front of Emory.

"Memphis, I'm sorry. I didn't mean... Well, actually, I did mean to, but let me try to explain!"

Taking a deep breath, Memphis paused, holding on to his control as Adair said in a rush, "I made a mistake. You have to believe me! All I could think about in that moment was how to get to my dad, and I never meant to hurt you!"

Raising his gaze to Adair, Memphis said coolly, "To get to your dad by whatever means possible right?" He looked away. "Just forget it, Adair. It's already done."

"Memphis!" Emory exclaimed.

A cold strong pressure on his wrist made him falter, and he turned. Emory stood, her loose green shirt making her eyes striking. Her pants were padded along her thighs, and Memphis could make out different knives' handles poking out from their sheaths. She was wringing her hands and looking more nervous than he had ever seen her. To him, she was fearless.

"Memphis, I'm sorry for what happened. Are you okay?"

# Heir of Lies – Part One

A pressure had built so fiercely in his mind, trying to break through and overtake him. Blinking hard, he shook his head. "Em, don't worry about it. It's Adair, right? He wouldn't do anything to hurt me, or any of us. It's just been a long day. You know, a lot happening at once."

She chuckled darkly, running a hand through her ebony hair. "I guess it is, isn't it? You know my dad is announcing our family's regency? That as of tomorrow, I will be Emory Fae, Princess of Kiero? That as of tomorrow, everything my parents built will shift back into the mold it once was in."

He took her in, weighing the truth in her words. He was afraid of what exactly this weight would cost. Grimacing, he said, "All we can do is make sure we have each other's backs. And that the decisions being made are ones that will only better our lives."

"And how exactly do we dictate that at fifteen and seventeen?" she asked, her voice demure.

Memphis arched his eyebrow. "We make sure to find the truths in this world and follow them. No matter the cost." He took a step back, and the walls dipped. He breathed deeply. "Emory, I'm sorry, but I have to go."

Turning, his footsteps echoed around him, pushing faster and faster toward his room.

*Hold on.*

He couldn't remember the last time he had two episodes within the same week. It had been years.

Familiar panic set in as each hanging light on the wall flickered as he passed, the whining energy pushing against the frame that held the magic in. It begged for release and knew he could do it.

Everything in the Academy was constructed by the Faes, the Strattons, and the teachers and their abilities. From the steel framing, to the concrete, to the lights, to the desks and the very beds they slept in. Every particle, every structure had traces of strength and magic in it. The idea of technologies met with abilities was something never seen before, and it was catching fire across Kiero.

The Academy was, before all else, a tool, a resource to mend the mistakes of the past. Roque was building an empire with the belief desolates and people of abilities could live in harmony. Roque was living proof by manning an entire school of some of the most powerful kids in Kiero.

As Memphis ran harder, the full weight of what Roque had taken on hit home. The Faes had already achieved an impossible feat. A desolate prince and a fierce woman from the Shattered Isles being forced into an arranged marriage, only to fall in love and reshape their world into freedom.

What was one more impossible feat to Roque Fae?

Memphis reached his room and threw the door open violently. His world dipped, and slamming the door shut, his back slid against the wood. His breath was short and ragged. He was going to be sick, as a wave hit his consciousness, pain lacing through him.

He couldn't hang on.

The white noise sharpened as Memphis let his walls down, tired of fighting, tired of constantly trying to be something he wasn't. Just for this second, he abandoned his control. Letting go, his ability consumed him, and a like a star exploding, Memphis was lost in the sea of a thousand voices, sharpened and clear. The room disappeared, he disappeared, and the voices became clear.

Or one voice.

It shouldn't be a surprise that Roque's voice cut through the rest, powerful and full of secrets. But Memphis tensed before succumbing once more.

*"She is our daughter, Nei, always. Before titles, before us, before this school. Our. Daughter. Her quality of life is priority. I will not put her in danger unless it is the only option. What choices do we have here?"*

*"I could try mending with the Isles, my sisters. Word should have never left our confinement. About what happened. About what we did. About what we have."*

*"In our place of power, it is also our place to protect this secret. Until it is safe. Until we know for certain that after dealing with Cesan, there are no more threats. There has been word of strange things happening*

past Sarthaven. That a darkness is starting to lift its head, tinging the borders. Creatures of the night, strange disappearances, accidents. The people of Kiero are scared and are looking to us to secure their peace of mind." He paused, then continued, "I promise you, as my best friend, that after we deal with this, we will destroy it. We will find a way, find someone who can help. But until then, we make sure it doesn't fall into the wrong hands."

Being slammed back into the present, Memphis fell on his hands and knees, heaving for air. The room spun, and he threw his meager energy into throwing his mental walls back up. A blissful emptiness greeted him, as he staggered to his bed. What had he just heard? What were they talking about? Why were they in danger?

Sitting hard on the edge of his bed, gasping, he tried to sort through his emotions. Brokk had been right. Within twenty-four hours, everything had changed. And his hopes were crashing around him.

Numbly, he looked to the door, his gut telling him to run, to find Brokk. There was nothing they couldn't figure out. But for the first time in eleven years, he couldn't move a muscle. It was too much to digest, to take in. How could he move forward when he couldn't even sort out what he was feeling?

*Anger. Grief. Fear.*

They were being propelled by the fates, out of his worldly realm of control. He was just another body in the sea of reactions, his course still to be determined. The thought was draining on his already tired and hurt body, and so he leaned back, thumping against his mattress.

His gaze drifted to the ceiling, and Memphis embraced that for the first time, he wasn't going to do anything but wait and try to sort out the information he knew. His muscles started to relax, and sleep tugged at the edges of his skittering mind, desperately trying to connect the dots.

As his surroundings bled away and his consciousness floated into the realms of dreams, he couldn't shake the feeling of unease and that they were all running out of time.

HEIR OF LIES – PART ONE

# CHAPTER SEVEN

## Adair

"Please proceed to the Dining Hall... Please proceed..."

Adair awoke with a jerk, completely and utterly disoriented. The Academy's intercom blared through the hallway, the whining pre-recorded message sounding flat.

How long had he been asleep? The walk back to his room had been caught in snippets in his mind, his body going through the actions. Blearily looking at the small clock on his bed stand, he realized it was just on the brink of twilight.

Sitting up, Adair rubbed his eyes, listening to the intercom's drone, his gut tightening with every word. His father hadn't come back.

Scrambling up, he was across the room and flying through his dresser, sifting through clothes in every direction. He grabbed his usual go-to, the black shirt and pants, with his button-down jacket. Throwing a hopeless look in the mirror, he stopped.

Bruises flowered along his jaw and underneath his eye, his skin paler than usual, his ebony hair standing up in every direction. His eyes were hollow. His empty gaze of indifference reflected at him, but locked down underneath the surface, he was screaming.

Ripping his gaze away, he was out of the room before he could register what was happening. His classmates were already flooding the concrete hallways, the curiosity rippling around them in a contagious energy. Classes had been canceled for the rest of the afternoon, and now this?

Turning the corner, looking to the bay windows, the sun dipped below the horizon, the last rays bleeding into the sky, creating a marvelous display. Beautiful and terrible, he thought, as his gaze drifted back to the throng in front of him, that the world displayed most magnificently before the darkness swept in.

Adair pushed faster, his plan forming swiftly.

He hadn't seen his mother since everything that had happened and assumed she had already left with Nei. She hated goodbyes, and so did he. That meant no one was looking for the deserter's son, which left Adair at an advantage.

His feet carried him, twisting and turning, the walls blurring. All the classrooms Adair passed were sealed and forgotten about, as if everyone could taste the change before them. Frowning, he slowed his steps, slipping inside the washroom too fast for anyone to notice. Not that anyone was paying attention to him.

*A ghost amongst the living.*

"Shut up." He stopped as his voice rang out. The washroom was empty, the dimly lit room making it seem like it was already late into the night. Adair growled, whispering to the voices curling into his mind, "Shut *up*."

He was already moving as the taunts and accusations of their cruel voices ebbed. But they were never fully gone. Making his way to the end stall, he quickly closed himself inside, securing the lock. Panting, he lowered the lid of the toilet, and standing on top, his hands roamed, searching for the lever.

The Academy was an amazing place to grow up in, to see it be built from practically nothing. The one advantage to be a Stratton and living here his whole life was that he knew the secrets hidden amongst them.

The lever was small and flush in the stone, but Adair pressed down hard, and the concrete started to shudder to life. Bricks dissolved, crumbling into dust as Adair waited. Soon enough, a small tunnel was revealed, the damp air swirling around him. Adair grinned wolfishly, not looking back as he climbed into the cramped space. As soon as he passed the threshold, the air shimmered behind him, the movement of the wall becoming whole once more.

# Heir of Lies – Part One

The Academy was filled with secret passages designed for his parents and the Faes to have meetings away from prying eyes when they had first formed the school. The school wasn't always praised; it took years for people to be brave enough to utilize what the Faes were offering.

Adair had found out this, as he did with most things when it came to his parents, he had to use his wit and patience: they had documents hidden away, maps of the school, Adair conveniently found when he was pursuing different books of the cultures of Kiero, which his mother took an interest in.

Crawling faster, he leaned into the curves and twists of the tunnel, the dust making his nose burn. It had been years since he had used one of the secret passages, trying to keep his habits of disregarding the rules in check. The concrete was freezing underneath his palms, each movement sending shots of pain from his cracked and bruised fingernails.

He should have really seen a healer, but in a way, he liked the reminder of what he had gone through and survived. Each hot flash of pain, each strained movement reminded him that he was stronger. That at the start of each day he would carry on, bearing his scars like a shield and not a poison that would cripple him.

He would *not* become his father.

The light in the tunnel was becoming a dull grey wash as the concrete suddenly sloped down, and Adair knew he was getting close. He shifted his weight, so his legs were extended, his black boots shining in the limited light. Taking a deep breath, he pushed with his hands, gravity taking over. He dropped, sliding down the makeshift chute, the still air now roaring around him; he gritted his teeth until his jaws ached dully. He had always hated this part.

But just as soon as it had started, he slammed to a stop, his ribs bruising with the impact. Dots danced in front of his vision, threatening to bring him into unconsciousness.

Groaning, he rolled over, cursing, questioning not for the first time if it was worth using this passage. Coughing, Adair dragged his body, scraping across the cold rock, his arms shaking.

A voice boomed underneath him, and he smirked, blood pooling in his mouth. He listened, stilling his body as Roque continued. "Thank you all for coming on such short notice."

Shimmying faster, Adair was met with a small overhang, looking down to the now full dining hall below. Chest heaving, he settled in, having a complete view of his classmates and teachers, their chatter dying down instantly at the sound of their leader's voice.

Adair devoured the scene hungrily, his gaze landing on the four figures standing at the front of the hall.

Roque was dressed in a deep blue jacket, the rest of his wear black, enhancing his proud features. Emory stood beside him, her black hair glistening, swept back and pinned so it tumbled down her back. She wore a simple dress, a matching royal blue, the fabric sweeping down from her waist, creating the illusion of churning water. He was frozen as he took in her turned mouth, her gaze plastered to the floor in front of her. Beside them, Tadeas stood, his broad chest puffed out, his traveling attire now changed into a simple brown suit, his pale emerald hair tied back, enhancing his sharp features.

Adair's hands curled tightly into fists, his breath coming in fast gulps. Before, the Isles were treated with wary and caution, and now? Now an allegiance was forming before his eyes. Marquis stood by his father's side, having not changed since Adair saw him last, his deep emerald hair unruly, his indifference evident. A flash of admiration flared in his chest for the strange boy.

He wasn't the only one who didn't want his family name to dictate his future.

Adair became entranced as Roque said, "First, I must apologize for the abrupt change in your schedules. I wanted everyone here to be the first to know before I send my message to Sarthaven. The tides in our world are starting to change, and I must accept my duty in building this government and school, by accepting

# HEIR OF LIES – PART ONE

my fate. The Academy was my vision, along with my wife's, to have a safe place to teach our children not to fear their gifts. That abilities didn't create monsters. That just because we were different, didn't mean it was *wrong*. My father was a proud and vicious man who brainwashed our world into thriving in our differences, to believe that the weak should be punished, to become our slaves, our lessers.

In my arranged marriage, I was wed to a fearless woman, who at first loathed me, being connected to the son of a man who had shackled her people, the people from the Shattered Isles, to a husband who was too scared to allow my wife to bear the weight of my greatest secret." His eyes swept the crowd. "We witnessed war, bloodshed, the world tearing itself apart with a wild magic that was uncontained, and no one cared. But against all odds, we started to trust one another. We shared a vision, of a world at peace. And I dared to trust her with my secret, that I, a Fae, was a desolate."

Roque took a shuddering breath, peeking down at Emory, a sad smile tugging at his lips. "We stood up to my father's council as you all know. We broke away and changed our future and the history of Kiero. You all also know the story of how Nei was my strength through the dark days ahead of us, as we arranged a Peace Treaty with the Isles and broke away from the capital, forming the first democratic government." He paused and the crowd shifted in the silence.

"It is a sad day today, as I must be honest with you. I have failed, in my dream, in my vision of fairness and equality. Peace has been a fleeting thing, something that we have been able to grasp here, but beyond our borders? There are still so many people who believe in the old ways of my father's reign. The people of Kiero have been suffering, and I have too long ignored that state of our world." Another pause.

"May I introduce to you all Tadeas Maher, and his son, Marquis Maher, King and Prince from the Shattered Isles. They have come with the sad news my wife's father has passed, and they are here, with their company, as our guests while we negotiate our terms." Roque's voice hung, allowing the weight to settle.

Emory shot a sharp glare at Marquis, who raised his eyebrows in response, making Emory glower.

Clearing his throat, Roque's voice dragged them all back into their reality. "Today marks the end of our democratic society, and I ask you, my students, my friends, my family, to accept me as your rightful King. Together, we can rebuild our world, escape this hovering darkness of war, and enter a true era of peace."

He lowered himself to one knee before the crowd, causing ripples of unease to grow amongst them. Laying a hand across his chest, his voice turned gravelly, "I promise you all that I will not fall into my father's mistakes. I will never forget our safety or to turn deaf ears to you. I will never betray you or lead you astray. A threat has become clear to me, and as King, I will stop it with help from Tadeas. Kiero will flourish and prosper. No dream will be too big, no alliance too obscure. It is time to set our differences aside and unite Kiero as one."

He stood, eyes blazing. "My wife and her team are already chasing after a man I trusted with my *life*. A man that promised he would never betray me, but his greed, his close-mindedness has made him blind. He has threatened acts of terrorism until I step down from being your leader. I will not falter under his violence. I will not throw away everything I believe in. That we have worked toward. The Academy, above being a school, is a promise that we will not sit idly by."

Emory's eyes widened at her father's words as he roared, his voice bouncing off the walls, "Will you have me?"

Adair watched from above as the spark of Roque's words caught, turning into an inferno. Tadeas clapped Roque on the back, grinning broadly as teachers and students started to yell, to chant, to praise: "Long live the King! Long live the Faes!"

Adair covered his mouth, his screams clawing against his throat, begging for release. The pounding booms of feet stomping, of yells clambered up the walls toward where Adair, shattering into a thousand pieces, lay hidden. His father had made a mistake, had been lied to and jaded by Roque. He promised him greatness and handed him the shadows. Was it wrong for his father to want more?

*Yes.*

Groaning, Adair covered his eyes, wishing to disappear. He knew firsthand how vicious his father could be, how twisted, how dark. He had been trying to break him for years and had left his family, tried to kill his best friend. For what? A title? Responsibility of ruling a country?

His muscles cramped and complained against his movements when he took a gulping breath and moved his hands underneath him. Getting ready to leave, Adair paused as Roque's voice roared far below him.

"We are gathering senior students as well as teachers who are willing to become part of Tadeas's group to assist in going to Sarthaven, to bring Cesan and his followers back."

Roque was immediately lost in the chants, in the yells of approvals.

Adair gritted his teeth and left, maneuvering through the tunnel. He didn't want to hear any more, to see his friends sign up to bring his father back. He didn't want to watch Emory stand by her father's side, knowing that there would always be a division between them now.

He was a traitor's son, a scorned boy, harboring a dark ability. He was a weapon. He was barely a name, more like a shadow, one everyone was skittering away from.

Hot tears ran down his cheeks, and Adair didn't stop them. A sharp buzzing filled his hearing as he shuffled to the left, starting the long climb back to the washrooms. The filtered grey light had dulled considerably, making the walls seem endless, like he could freefall into nothingness. Silently, he pushed ahead, trying to forget, trying not to fall into numbness. But for him, what was the point of trying? Everyone that resided in this cursed school had made up their judgements about him and his family.

But as he continued to climb, his thoughts went to his friends. What about Emory and Memphis? His heart dropped into his stomach at the thought of his small group of friends. What did they think of him now? Would they have forgiveness in their hearts for him, to know that he wasn't following in his father's footsteps?

His pulse picked up, making his skin slick and clammy at the thought.

*"Don't you want more?"*

Adair froze, the hissing voices encircling his consciousnesses. He stuttered, "W-who's there?"

His voice bounced off the tunnel's walls. Peering into the darkness, Adair waited a beat. One, high pitched giggle bounced back from the other end of the tunnel. Scrambling back, Adair slipped, slamming his head against concrete, dots flickering in front of his eyes. It was like being doused in freezing water, every sense on overdrive, his nerves sparking with adrenaline. Fear coiled underneath his skin, soaking into his core.

It was the same voice, the same giggle from his nightmare. *Impossible. You are just tired and stressed. Move.* His thoughts egged him on, but he couldn't. He curled his limbs into themselves, his breath quick as he made himself flush to the wall. Seconds passed, and all Adair could do was stare farther into the tunnel, where the voice had come from.

The light was fading, and to his left, Adair saw them first. The slim figures, crawling toward him, their tilting heads. Their permanent grins. He was mesmerized as they started crooning to him, "Adairrr. Adair, we have found you. Don't you want to be noticed? Come with us, and we will show you the way. Come."

It was impossible, yet Adair saw them crawl steadily to him, pale arms and black holes where their eyes should be. The air rippled, and Adair flinched, as he felt the ancient magic shudder through his bones. He somehow had bled the rules of reality and dream together.

They were in front of him now, caressing his arms, reaching for his face, tugging at his hair.

# HEIR OF LIES – PART ONE

"Come with us. *Follow your destiny.*"

Their teeth glinted in the dark, sharp as knives, and Adair buried his head beneath his hands, shutting his eyes tight.

"This is not real. Not real. *Not real.*"

The giggles erupted around him, orchestrating his terror, and he felt a tongue lick up his cheek. Tasting him.

He was screaming now, flinching away from their touch, from their promises, from their hungry expressions. Clutching his knees to his chest, Adair fell into the fetal position, pressing his eyes shut.

The minutes turned into hours, the darkness swallowing him and the creatures whole. Adair was frozen, talking to himself, yelling at them to go away. His blood had slowed. His circulation cut off from being curled into a ball for so long. It wasn't until the traces of dawn flickered into the tunnels that Adair lifted his head—his eyes swollen from crying and his voice hoarse—to see that he was utterly and completely alone, no trace of anyone ever being with him.

He uncurled his limbs, leaning over to empty his stomach, the bile burning his throat and nose. The acid made his eyes water, and coughing, he looked up the tunnel. He stayed like that, sweaty and shaking, unable to move. Unable to do anything but feel the hot tears slide down his cheeks.

# CHAPTER EIGHT

## Brokk

The energy in the Faes' office practically overtook all of the students, and Brokk wished breakfast had lasted longer.

Memphis stood stiffly beside him, and Brokk leaned closer to his friend. "Can we talk?"

"You really think this is the time, Brokk?" Memphis arched a pale eyebrow. "We are about to go into a warzone."

"Which is exactly why it's the only time. Just hear me out. I'm sorry about yesterday. About how I reacted. I talked to Roque last night after the meeting, and he said if I helped the cause, I wouldn't be expelled from school. You didn't have to follow."

Memphis smirked, whispering, "Yes I did. Do you really think I would allow you to get all the action? Besides, who is going to keep you in check with Iasan?"

Brokk grinned. "I would suspect you."

Memphis looked ahead, lost in his own thoughts, not answering him. Brokk hated this. He hated being pulled into a movement fueled by politics and alliances. But what choice did he have? He had been a member of the Academy almost all his life, and now was the time they were all put to the test. It was either do this or leave.

They were protectors. Guardians of the peace. Or so they had claimed.

Rolling his shoulders, Brokk stood straighter when Roque opened the door, seeming tired. Tadeas followed closely at his heels. The door closed with a snap, and Roque eyed the thirty students and smiled slyly.

# HEIR OF LIES – PART ONE

Reaching the front, he folded his hands neatly in front of him. "Thank you all for coming so promptly. I have been reassured that you are all the top of your class or have volunteered on your own accord."

Vigorous nods met his words.

His gaze lingered on Brokk when he continued, "You are all representing the future of Kiero. Tadeas and I have reached the decision that if anyone doesn't follow his orders while you are away from the Academy, those individuals will be brought back and tried for treason. Your mission is to tell anyone who is seeking refuge to come here until we have the situation under control and bring Cesan back. I hope you all know I wish I could come with you, but I am needed here. I expect you all to show Tadeas the same respect you would show me. He is here to help us."

Brokk's blood ran cold, his mind running into a thousand different possibilities. Here he was, trading his freedom to a man who had waltzed in proclaiming he was a King from across the Black Sea? To lead them to the capital to find a madman?

Looking over to Memphis's furrowed expression, he knew his friend was thinking the same thing. Swallowing his doubt, thinking about what exactly they had gotten into, he took in the rest of the young men and women potentially ready to lay down their lives for this.

*To do Roque's dirty work.*

Of course Roque was staying, to get word to the capital, to sway all Kiero to his regency. Or, he was staying to ensure no one found what he was hiding here... The thought had him practically bouncing on his heels. If Brokk knew one thing for certain, it was to never trust the Strattons, and things had gone from bad to worse in a matter of days. Somehow, when they got back from this, he and Memphis would get the truth and the full story.

*If we get back.*

He knew they were all underprepared for what Cesan was planning.

At the end of Roque's speech, Tadeas started talking about the fierceness of him and his people and how they shouldn't be worried. They were on the same side, a *team*. By flame, Brokk couldn't care less, and his gaze flitted to each person, looking for an ebony head of hair.

*Where was Adair?*

He didn't remember seeing him last night at the meeting or this morning in the dining hall. He didn't realize Memphis had been watching him, and his voice was low and urgent as it shook through Brokk's consciousness, "*Adair isn't here.*"

He had to admit, it surprised him. If anyone would have volunteered, Brokk thought Adair would have been the first. Icy shivers ran down Brokk's back, but it was too late.

The room exploded in a flurry of movement as they gathered weapons, Tadeas beaming down at them all as his men distributed an assortment of weapons. Brokk pushed through the crowd, Memphis at his heels, as he stormed up to a rover, ripping the sleek bow from his hands. "This is mine."

The man raised his eyebrows at him, but Brokk slung the bow securely over his shoulder and with the quiver of arrows strapped onto his back he realized that any humanity within him was quickly being destroyed with every passing second.

Turning, he filed out of the room with the stream of students. The Academy was quiet, and Brokk liked it this way. No fellow classmates were there looking wide-eyed at their entourage, no one seeing what he was seeing—the darkness that was bleeding into all their hearts with what Cesan had done. He had forced the Faes' hands, forced them to fight fire with fire or else be afraid that Kiero would see them as weak.

Brokk furrowed his brow, the steady pace of his boots against the floor was like a pulsing heartbeat, but in his mind, it was a war drum. His body moved lethally, his muscles taught, his adrenaline spiked. On the outside, he was the epitome of a warrior.

# HEIR OF LIES – PART ONE

Could no one else see the sadness when they caught his gaze? When they talked to him? Did no one else care that the Academy was ripping their morals from their very cores, leaving behind empty shells? Leaving behind nothing but the echoes of dreams?

"Brokk, Memphis, wait!"

Stalling, they turned in unison to see Emory running down the hallway, full tilt, her garb from the previous night gone, replaced by a black shirt, pants, and boots. Her royal blue jacket was too bright for what was happening around her. But to him, it made perfect sense. She had always been a flaring spark when things went dark. It had never mattered what was going on in her life, she was always there for them. His heart gave a painful tug as he wished for the courage to be able to leave Emory behind.

Colliding with him, her arms wrapped tightly around his neck, and she buried her face in the crook beneath his ear. She was trembling, her heart beating out of her chest.

"Please, don't go. I'm sorry about earlier. I'm begging you not to do this. We will figure everything out, we always do. I can't follow you down this road," she said.

Releasing Brokk from her chokehold and stepping back, her gaze landed on Memphis. Memphis cleared his throat, shooting him an apologetic look before grasping Emory's face in between his hands, fiercely. "We have to go, Em. But I promise you we will come back. I will come back to you."

Heat flushed Brokk's face as he watched Memphis swoop down and kiss her. Not caring there was an army of students and teachers filtering by them. Not caring *he* was right there. That she was a Princess now, the face of their country.

The turmoil and emotional charge of their situation had taken hold, and Brokk could practically hear Memphis's mind, shouting out to her, begging her to understand. That he loved her, had always loved her, would always love her.

Averting his eyes, Brokk looked anywhere but at his friends, suspended in their embrace. They broke away breathlessly, and

Brokk looked up. Tears were streaming down Emory's face as she whispered to Memphis, "Don't go."

Brokk could see Memphis's resolve cracking before he turned away brusquely, and with one last look at Emory, her face drained of all color, Brokk followed him. Words were lodged in his throat, drowning him with their weight. They walked in silence, feeling Emory's stare burning into their backs the entire way.

Swallowing down his jealousy, he tried not to linger on what had just happened between Emory and Memphis. Instead memories of laughter and hope swirled all around Brokk, as they left the Academy behind. He could feel the balance of their world shifting, back into their bloodied past, back into the unrelenting darkness. The doors swung open, and sunlight beat down on them, making him blink fiercely. The students and teachers were leading horses, making sure everyone had a mount from the Shattered Isles, from what was left.

It took him less than ten seconds to find Tadeas, to find the king smiling wolfishly at him already. *Deep breathes.* He couldn't afford to lose himself when the king from across the sea had already seen him lose control. Rolling his shoulders, he took the steps two at a time. There was no turning back now.

His gaze drifted to the forest, to the canopy of trees, reminding him of the wildness in his heart. He could run away from all of this. The chatter of birds and echoes of ancient magic stirred his heart, shivering down his spine.

Averting his gaze, he followed as Memphis broke away from the throng toward two dappled mounts. The horses pawed the ground nervously as they approached, and he internally cringed. Animals had an acute sense when it came to *seeing* people for who they truly were, and Brokk made them nervous. The powerful creature before him knew he was more beast than man.

With a pounding heart, he gripped Memphis's arm. "We look after each other. If things go south, we escape."

Memphis nodded, his smooth voice echoing in his mind, "*Agreed.*"

# HEIR OF LIES — PART ONE

Gripping the pommel of the saddle, he lifted himself up with ease, sliding his boots into the stirrups. Easing the reins into his grip, he gave the mount a reassuring brush of his hand, begging the horse not to throw him off.

He glanced over his shoulder. The Academy, and the courtyard nestled amongst the rolling hills and the ancient forest behind them. He said a mental goodbye to his friends who lingered behind its walls and snapped forward when Tadeas's voice roared over them: "Let's visit this city under the stars, shall we?"

Cheers and catcalls sounded, and lurching forward, the horse's hooves pounded against the ground, the group moving forward in a gallop. Brokk leaned forward, gripping with his legs, causing his stallion to shoot forward, his powerful hooves pushing them faster.

Brokk's heart was in his throat as he settled into the speed, leaving everything behind. Memphis's stallion pulled close to him, the two galloping together, spirits unleashed.

"Did you see who else is here?" Memphis's voice was clipped as it bounced around his consciousness. Brokk shot him a glance, and Memphis nodded to his left where Professor Iasan was galloping, his black stallion frothing at his bit.

The Professor looked sideways at them, his lips turning upward in a sickly-sweet smile. As if to say that out here, in the wild, they weren't protected. Out here, they would be at his mercy. Baring his teeth in answer, Brokk dared Iasan to try. If it came down to it, he wouldn't falter - not again.

# CHAPTER NINE

## Adair

The excited voices around him felt dull and far away. *Everyone* was talking about the group of students that went to assist in bringing Cesan back. *Everyone* was talking about what his father had done. Whispers chased at his heels, one word standing out from all the others.

*King. King. King.*

He rubbed his eyes, the heaviness of them making everything seem too bright, too fast. The world was charging forward, and he wanted to curl into himself and make it stop. Classes had been suspended until further notice, which meant until Roque dealt with his father.

His traitorous, lying father.

Leaning against the cool wall, Adair closed his eyes.

*"Follow us, follow your destiny."*

Those voices curled around his mind, and in response, he slammed his iron walls up. What happened last night wasn't real. He had stayed in the tunnel until he had willed his body to move toward the new light, and images of those creatures lurked behind his every waking moment, chasing him further and further into himself.

Feeling reckless, he needed some form of normality—which had led him to this moment, waiting outside the Faes' office.

"Adair, what are you doing here?"

Eyes flying open, he took in Emory, her face gaunt as she wrung her hands together. She wore her usual loose black pants and leather boots, but today, she was adorned by a velvet royal blue button-down jacket.

Pushing himself off the wall, he said, "I assumed, even though classes were canceled, we would still get our training. Especially now that you are royalty. Despite...what has happened."

She loosened a breath, a slight tremor through her body. Stepping closer, her voice was soft, as if she was trying to coax a feral animal. "Adair, please try to understand. My dad met with me this morning after the group was dispatched. Things are moving fast. We are trying to reach Sarthaven's communications to let them know what Cesan is trying to do. Things are in a precarious situation. My dad has decided to not recognize your family as part of his court after yesterday."

She bit her lip, her eyes wide, waiting for him to respond. Roaring had filled his senses, as his heart tried to catch up with his mind. He took a step back, feeling unhinged.

"He is pushing us out then? Just like that? Like the years we have all put into this means nothing? That my family means nothing to him? To you?"

Emory reached toward him, whispering, "Adair, no..."

An ugly aggression raised its head within him, wanting to lash out. To destroy, to bleed darkness within all their hearts. This was madness. Complete and utter madness.

Backing away, he shook his head. "And you agree with him? That you, alone, will rule Kiero? That you, alone, are the rightful heir to the throne? No allies, no court? No one you trust by your side?"

"Adair, I will have a court."

"Just not one with me in it."

Her eyes begged forgiveness, but all he saw was the blade as she landed the killing blow. "Yes."

Running his hand through his hair, Adair looked at Emory. They had been best friends since birth; he trusted Emory with his *life*.

Ice licked at his heart, churning through his veins, as his pulse roared in his ears. Stepping closer, and with shaking hands, he gently tipped her chin up toward him. Her skin was silken, her breath coming faster as Adair watched her emerald eyes fill with tears.

"I wish I could go back in time, Em, and be brave enough to tell you how much you mean to me. Maybe it would have changed things between us. But I will be damned if I don't try."

Swooping down, Adair gripped her face tightly as his lips collided with hers. Heat tore through his core, chasing away any icy shock. His lips moved against hers, wanting more. Pressing Emory against the wall, she gasped. Mussing her hair, his hand swept down her side, grabbing onto her hips. Adair felt the pressure of her hands against his chest. Slowly, breaking away, Adair registered her answer in her features, pale and drawn.

"Adair, I'm so sorry... I just don't feel the same way. You're my best friend, and I will always love you—as my *friend*."

The world had tipped, and he was freefalling. All the pieces he had been trying to hold together for his future, for *her* scattered into that void. There was only one thing that remained beneath all of that. His ability, which was born from fury and darkness.

Brushing by her, his feet carried him, his entire body numb. Her pleas were lost in the hallway, his classmates looking between them. At her tension and his indifference.

*"Don't you want more?"*

The words sunk their claws into his heart, and for a fraction, he opened himself to those voices: those chilling, soothing voices that beckoned to him. Emory's rejection smothered his logic as his anger wildly encompassed him. He refused to bow anymore.

The shift around him was subtle, the world carrying on like it always did. But to him, as he charged down the hallway, his world was quaking. His best friend, severing him for the power that was now handed to her. Until his parents returned, Adair had every inclination to reveal Roque's skeletons to Emory.

Over the years, he had caught snippets, that Roque, generous kind Roque, had very interesting rumors kept sealed tight.

Rumors only his parents had heard. Adair, once a couple years ago, had accidently slipped into their consciousness, and he hadn't told anyone what he had found lurking there.

Swinging by his room, quickly, Adair let his emotions ravage through him before succumbing to his numbness. Throwing open the door, he grabbed his high collared jacket and a bag which he stuffed a short blade into, several history books, and a hidden supply of jerky. Zipping it closed, he swung the bag over his shoulder, looking at the empty room. Steeling his nerves, he walked out.

The door shut behind with a snap, and an arrogant voice sounded from behind him, "Going somewhere?"

Twisting to find mischievous eyes, Marquis Maher leaned against the wall, arms crossed and a lazy smile splayed on his face.

"Go away," Adair said before turning and walking steadily down the hallway; Marquis jogged behind him.

"Had enough of this stuffy pace then?"

Groaning under his breath, Adair looked at the spots where the hidden cameras lay. His ability unfurled, its talons clicking themselves along the wiring, spreading like a disease until it reached its target. The new surveillance team before the main doors collapsed at their desks, unconscious. Stalking by the room, a stony silence filled him as he looked at the bodies. They would wake up in a few hours, and who would piece together that he was gone? It would be too late at that point.

He shifted the bag on his shoulder, turning to face an amused Marquis. He snapped, "Look, I'm not joking. Leave me alone."

Throwing the doors to the Academy open, the empty courtyard splayed before him. Rushing down the steps, he was desperately trying to escape the ghosts of what had happened here.

"Well, that's not very welcoming. We did travel a long way, you know."

Adair turned, stalking up to the heir of the Shattered Isles. "I do not care. Now leave me alone, or I will make you."

Marquis waggled his eyebrows. "I dare you to try."

His ability roared in response, exploding from him, rushing toward the rover. Marquis grinned wickedly. Adair's talons rushed forward, about to sink themselves into his flesh, his muscles, his nervous system.

All he met was an iron wall.

The wind howled around them, and Adair found himself encircled in a mini cyclone, his ability scattered to the winds.

Sauntering up to him, the prince snapped his fingers as the cyclone dropped immediately. "Now, where are we going?"

Adair was breathless, his words lodged in his throat. "How did you do that?"

Marquis sported a lazy smile. "Because, like yourself, I am gifted. *Different*. The sea bows to me, and I control the water. But I can also block abilities, if the occasion calls. Seeing as you were just about to try to either kill me or force me back, that is a perfect example of when I use it." He faked boredom. "Now, since we are over that, what exactly are you planning?"

Running a hand over his mouth in exasperation, Adair shook his head. It would draw too much attention to try to send him back.

Adair shrugged. "If you slow me down or try to stop me, it won't end well. I'm going to find answers."

The prince lit up. "That's exactly what I was hoping you would say. Back in there, they have their futures paved out, you know? Their judgements made, and their accusations ready. But... you, Adair Stratton, are worth more than their judgements. Crave the adventure that it will bring. I find it quite refreshing."

Adair huffed, continuing to walk toward the woods. "Isn't that a bad thing though? My father will likely be killed, my family holding no title or status. My future here has come to a standstill."

Marquis slapped him on the back. "Then it is up to *you* to change the course. Seek what you want, not what others want for you."

He whispered, "I want the truth."

Marquis nodded. "Don't we all?"

# HEIR OF LIES – PART ONE

Adair let his words sink in. "Why are you being so nice to me?"

Pulling at his jacket, the prince replied, "Because the world is changing. Because I know what it is like to be forced into a life you don't want. Take this situation as a gift, Adair. A gift not to be locked down in the politics of kings."

Adair picked up his pace, the wind gently tousling his hair. The afternoon was clear and crisp, the threat of autumn on the air. This had been his life, being groomed for court with Emory, with the Faes.

He looked to the forest line, pausing for a moment. His answers, his *truth*, lay in the depths of those woods. At the heart, where an ancient magic lay dormant. He had always had a fascination for the history and mythology of Kiero. His father had battered against him for years, saying that it was a waste of time to always have a nose in a book.

Those years of research hadn't been wasted, when a year ago, Adair found a map and instructions to a lair of ancient magic that had been long forgotten. After the Great War had happened and the lost city of Nehmai had fallen, dark magic and creatures were forced to the shadows, never to be awoken again. But Adair had found them.

Pausing, Adair turned to Marquis. "This won't be easy. Or safe."

The Prince of the Shattered Isles smiled slyly. "The best things never are."

Adair stepped through the forest, the coolness of the shade washing over him as he murmured, "Agreed."

He had always loved how as soon as he passed underneath the trees, it had seemed like he had stepped into another world. One consisting of weathered bark, mossy ground, and above all, mystery.

"Come find us, come find us, come find us."

The whispers on the wind pulled at his heart, at his betrayal, his pain. Those chilling voices from his nightmare pulled into the heart of the woods.

Sweat rolled down his neck, and he rolled his eyes as the prince didn't stop *talking*. Marquis quipped at his back the entire time while they navigated the denser part of the woods.

The Shattered Isles had been painted vividly, each word stroking Marquis's home into life before Adair's eyes. Of a community that was wild and unkempt, strong and unyielding. One that was united, despite its conflict. Marquis told him about cave exploration and how he could swim for hours, the ocean bending to his demands. Of the merpeople that dwelled in the darker parts of the Black Sea, and the sea dragons, called caines, which took entire fleets down.

Exhaling, the prince caught him off guard as he lifted his eyebrow and asked, "What I don't understand is how the Faes have achieved such loyalty. What did they do?"

Adair chewed his bottom lip as he hopped over a fallen tree trunk then looked to Marquis. "They were the dreamers in a time when culture, creativity, and equality were being butchered. The Academy was the foundation of that dream, for the desolates, for the people with weaker abilities. For everyone. The people of Kiero followed Roque because they can't fear him, they can only admire him. How brave he was for standing up to his father, for breaking free of his reign, to start his own."

"It sounds like you have a different opinion of him."

He threw up his hands. "I was born at the Academy. Raised in the Academy. Who am I to doubt the intentions of the Faes? They are practically family."

Shrugging, Marquis cooed, "Sometimes it is the ones closest to us that betray us first."

A shiver ran down Adair's spine, as he looked at the shadows collecting around them. The trees towered far above them, their branches looking like veins, a lifeline.

"Adair."

# HEIR OF LIES – PART ONE

The whisper tugged at his core. His whole body shook with the recognition, with the knowing that they were getting close. He stopped, slipping his bag free from his shoulders. Choosing not to answer, he grabbed a thin leather book, flipping the weathered pages open quickly.

The wind picked up unnaturally, and the Prince of the Shattered Isles stepped closer, "What is that?"

"My offering."

He found the page he was looking for, the illustration of the trees bending, forming a doorway to where the mirror lay beyond, and the man bent before it. Before Marquis could react, Adair stood in one fluid motion, unsheathing the blade. Striking it across his forearm, the skin ripped, forming a deep gash. His blood welled and bubbled, looking a deep crimson in the fading daylight.

Taking a steadying breath, he softly said, "I am here."

The world before them exploded into movement and a brilliant array of colors. He felt the ground shudder. The forest fell silent. Light fractured, spilling and washing them, as everything spun into chaos. Glancing over, Marquis stood in awe.

Blood trickled down Adair's arm dripping thickly onto the ground below them, which was smooth and golden now. An archway rose, intricate carvings of the forest bowing together, and at the top, two gleaming red jewels stared down at them. A thick oak door was all that stood between them and the truth.

The forest was long gone, and with his shaking bloodied hand, Adair reached to grab the smooth doorknob. The handle twisted and then released, the hinges creaking loudly as the door slowly swung inward.

Adair whispered to Marquis, "Follow me, and *please* let me do the talking."

For once, the prince just nodded, at a loss for words.

Their footsteps cracked like thunder as they passed under the archway, into a cavernous room. The floor glowed brilliantly, parts of it turning into liquid silver and forming four walls around them. It was quiet and empty, this place lying between reality and dreams; it was like walking into a jewel being melded and molded into shape.

Adair pulled his jacket closer around him, slinging his pack over his shoulder. He popped his collar out of habit, his hair standing on end. Marquis had frozen by the archway, in horror or fear, he couldn't tell. His blood trailed behind him, flowing hot down his arm as he stared ahead, walking surely.

A throaty laugh bounced off the walls, distorted, as smoke started to spill from the middle of the room, crawling toward them like grappling hands. It stopped right before his boots, rising like a fog.

"Adair Stratton, you dare come see me again?"

The voice tolled with ancient magic, malice, agony, and despair. An iron tang filled his mouth as he rasped, "I have come with my offering. Will you answer my questions?"

That chuckled reverberated throughout the fog, as one by one, the golden hues started to fade, the inky blackness rippling throughout the room.

"Are you offering yourself or the prince?"

He sneered. "The prince has nothing to do with this."

That throaty voice chuckled again, whispering, "Oh, I highly doubt that."

The room was dipped into full-fledged night, like a flame being blown out. Adair's breath hitched in his throat, and he twisted, trying to spot Marquis. He felt the slight shift of the floor, and before he could react, he was falling. Through the fog, through time and space.

The world roared around him, and he squeezed his eyes shut. His heart dropped into his stomach as he tried not to scream. The wind ripped at his jacket, his hair, and skin. The temperature dropped, ice crystals forming on his skin and exposed blood. He clamped his jaw so hard, he thought his teeth would shatter.

His body flipped violently, his limbs flaying. He dared to look, opening one eye and then the other. The sun hung low in the sky, bleeding into a sunset. At the same time, the full moon hung beside it, the remnants of night bleeding into the light. He fell through clouds, the ground below him, speeding up to him. Too fast. He could see the snowy tops of mountains below him, rushing up with their granite might.

His scream ripped through him, and his limbs flailed, trying to stop, trying to claw back up. The fog ripped the peaceful scene away, and Adair fell faster, briefly seeing the tunnel he was being swallowed by before slamming into the damp earth.

Everything went dark in a sweeping instant. It was like diving into the ocean, being pulled down by the waves, the sense of self stripped away. Hot blood filled his mouth as he bit through his tongue. Trying to find his bearings, shadows churned before him, those icy whispers cutting through the fog.

*"Adair, you have come. You have come!"*

Trying to slow his breathing, Adair watched as a pulsing light exploded below him. Its pale essence was like a lone star in the sky, entrancing him and pulling him in. His body slammed into something solid, cracking hard against it. The night clung to the room around him, besides that sole light.

With shaking limbs, Adair pushed himself up, standing slowly.

Adair was in another room, Marquis nowhere in sight. If the one they had entered was the heart of light, then this was the sealing promise of obscurity, the promise of danger heavy on the air. The coolness of the room sent shivers raking through him. Orbs of dew clung to the roots, hanging from the roof, and the smell of the forest after a rain filling his senses. It was both calming and unnerving.

Running his hand through his hair, he took in the creature he sought. Spindly arms hugged his legs toward his chest, his papery skin looking translucent. Adair could see each pronounced rib sticking out of his sides, each vertebra in his spine. His brown hair hung loosely, framing his sharp features.

But it was his silver eyes that made Adair freeze. Those eyes, holding every promise, every secret. Those mysteries that pulled him forward, whispering, "Gortach, I hope the years have treated you well."

The starving man smiled, revealing rotting teeth as he rumbled, "You, Adair Stratton, haven't changed much since your last visit."

Lowering himself onto his knees, he shrugged. "I have and haven't. But you would know that already."

Gortach's grin spread wider. The ancient shapeshifter dwelled in the depths of Kiero. Adair had learned that sacrificing blood to the creature caused it to see into the future, answering one question brought forth to it.

With a slight tremor, Adair held out his forearm, the dried blood caking his skin. Those silver eyes flicked down to the wound, ravenous. Slithering fear uncoiled throughout Adair, but he could barely process it as Gortach lowered his cracked lips to Adair's skin. The wound reopened, and the world tilted as his blood flowed.

Gortach rippled, the appearance of his decaying body fading, replaced by a haunted youth. Adair balked as he saw the familiar appearance. Gortach had a dark sense of humor and took on the form of whoever came to pay its price.

That ancient voice shook through him, his mind, his core. "Now what is it you seek? Your heart, Adair, is consumed by your desires."

Swallowing hard, he whispered, "What is Roque Fae hiding in the Academy?"

The creature paused, tilting his head. When he replied, it was as sharp as a sword's edge, "Are you sure that is the secret you wish to hear? You know the rules."

"Yes, my blood will grant me *one* answer. I am certain. What are they hiding?"

Gortach crawled toward him, his nails scraping against the dirt. "The time for Kiero's reign in prosperity is over. Darkness tinges the future, submerging it in death and destruction. Be prepared, Adair Stratton. We will all be unmade. Roque Fae has in his possession an ancient, binding magic. One that was never his to keep. The secrets of ultimate power in the form of the Book of Old."

Something clicked within Adair.

Gortach was face-to-face with him, his breath putrid as he whispered, "Find this, and you will be free."

Sweat started to collect at the base of Adair's neck. "Free from the unmaking of our world? What do you mean? What is the Book of Old?"

He paused, and when Gortach spoke again, his voice was gravelly, "Are you requesting another answer?"

Adair froze, practically trying to hold his breath, then exhaled, "No."

The image of youth drained from Gortach, showing his true form. Baring his teeth, he spat, "That's not what it sounded like to me." Lunging forward unnaturally fast, his now sharpened nails slashed at Adair.

Stumbling back, Adair cursed, running back to the wall of the room. Gortach stood to his full height, chuckling darkly. The crevices caught shadows across his features and body, making him look distorted.

Then, the only light source in the room went out.

Pushing his back flush to the cool, earthy wall, Adair's heartbeat thundered within him. Images flashed through his mind, and panic flooded him. Giggles sounded in the darkness as the shadows moved. Their sickly movements, those pitiless eyes. The pinned back grins, their sharpened teeth.

And the world, ripped to its core, bleeding.

Adair didn't know if he was hallucinating, but as the Gortach stalked him in the darkness, his image flicked back and forth.

Gortach.

Those pale faces.

Gortach.

Their sharpened grins.

Gortach.

Their empty sockets pinned him, as a dim green light pulsed again in the darkness. The room was empty, Gortach gone.

Four of them circled him, reaching for him. Long black stringy hair, skin as white as snow, their bones practically poking out from underneath their flesh. Their hands stroked his skin and his wound as they cooed to him, "Adair, don't let our watcher scare you. Don't allow us to scare you. You must go. Find the Book of Old. Help us."

The creature to his right tugged his hair, exposing his throat as she whispered in his ear, "We will watch as the world burns. Together."

Their giggles encircled him, the darkness washing over him once more. Hot tears spilled down Adair's face, and as he blinked, Gortach roared back into his deadly reality. Mounds of dirt exploded around Adair, and he threw his body weight forward, rolling.

Gortach said, "I will have all of you, Adair. Your dark desires, your soul. It's *mine*."

Adair heard the scuffling as Gortach loped behind him. He was blindly running full tilt, his blood, his tears, his sweat, burning his skin. Stumbling, dirt filled his mouth, his muscles screaming.

*Move, move, move!*

He wasn't about to die in the throes of dark magic. He rolled onto his back just as he saw the skeletal body fly forward, pinning him to the ground. Gortach used his forearm to press down hard on his esophagus, cutting off his oxygen. Adair used all his remaining energy, kicking hard, clawing at his back.

Gortach grinned down at him. "You are just a man. I am made of magic. You cannot win."

The smell of rotting flesh filled Adair's senses, and frantically, he spiraled in those silver eyes that churned with knowing, with victory.

Spots filled his visions, and he couldn't let go. He wouldn't stop...trying...

"You best get off my mate there." Marquis's voice sounded behind them just as the light flared, chasing away the darkness.

# HEIR OF LIES – PART ONE

Gortach snapped his attention to the young prince, roaring.

Marquis's lips pulled upward as he looked annoyingly calm. Emerald eyes flashing, he snapped his fingers together. The earth underneath them churned, droplets of water oozing from the dirt, floating up, spinning around Gortach. The droplets suspended and grew until a hissing ball of water consumed the shapeshifter. With widened eyes, he clawed and snapped, his anger lost in the water as the sphere ripped him away from Adair.

Choking, Adair rolled onto his side, gulping for air, blissfully taking it in.

"Adair, you have to get up. Come on."

He complied, wheezing, as Marquis supported most of his weight. More lights flared as they ran, the underground room expanding much larger than Adair had thought. The world shuddered, and Marquis pulled him down, *hard*.

Gravity pulled their weight, and they slipped through a small crack. There was a compressing darkness, and then the wind howled fiercely as they freefell into a different world. Snowy mountains enraptured by a starry sky was all Adair saw when they plummeted toward the ground.

Their screams were lost in the wind, snow, and ice. Adair blinked, as they were sucked in faster, the scene changing with the heavy scent of iron. The sun beamed now, a rolling sea of green below them with flowing plains. The scene changed again, and they were falling through dense clouds, moisture clinging onto their skin.

Squeezing Marquis's hand tighter, they continued to fall.

Adair snapped his eyes shut as the tang of magic rattled in his bones. He opened them, just in time to see the golden floor rushing up to meet him. Slamming into it, the coppery tang of blood filled his mouth and lacing pain shot through his body. Marquis lay still beside him, his deep emerald hair rumpled.

The floor shuddered just as Adair took in the oozing, black fog coming up to meet them.

*No.*

Through the pain, his blood and tears, Adair lunged forward, grabbing Marquis's hand. Screaming in frustration, he threw his body weight back, dragging the prince with him. Darkness filled his senses, as he watched the poisonous fog rush at them, wanting to tear through them, to bring them back to Gortach's lair. His blood pounded a vicious beat, and he snarled at the unconscious prince.

"Adaiiiir."

Somehow they had defied logic, having fallen through time and space, ending up in the original room they had started in. Cursing, he moved faster, the golden floor turning an opaque black at the sound of Gortach's voice.

The once silver walls started to crack, debris falling and shattering all around them. It felt like fire splintering through the marrow of his bones.

Yelling, he dipped into that well of ability, begging internally for some hidden strength. He could feel the magic of Gortach looming behind them, wanting to pull them back down into his depths. Slipping in his own blood, he didn't stop. The archway was maybe ten more steps. Their freedom was just beyond that door.

Guttural growls escaped from him, and he lunged, black spots threatening to overtake him.

*Don't stop.*

The floor trembled, and Adair heard the shrieking crack, like nails scraping against stone.

*Don't look back.*

The floor tipped, gravity clawing at them, to pull them down. Adair screamed, throwing his weight forward, scrambling at the doorknob.

A deep throaty laughter echoed behind him, panic choking him. The floor gave way entirely just as Adair leapt through the threshold, dragging Marquis behind him. They plummeted back into the woods, and Adair slammed the archway door shut just as he saw the translucent claws break through the swirling smoke.

# HEIR OF LIES – PART ONE

Sweat dripped off his nose, and he let go of Marquis. In one motion, he had his backpack in front of him, and he shakily ripped it open. The books and jerky spilled out, as well as his sheathed knife. The archway remained, the oak door shuddering from the force behind it.

*Move.*

Throwing the book open, his eyes flicked over the passage about *closing* the gateway to the ancient realm. His gaze flicked up to the two blood rubies. He didn't delay.

Shooting quickly toward the passage, his body screamed at him to *stop*.

Jumping, he swiped the two jewels from their perch, just as the oak door was thrown open. Gortach stood there, his withered, rotting body shaking with rage as the gateway was shielded. He couldn't pass through.

Adair bared his bloodied grin as the arch melted like fired metal, cutting off their world. They were finally safe.

Once the arch was nothing but dust on the wind, he quickly lurched to the side, emptying the contents of his stomach. Inhaling hard through the bitter taste that coated his mouth, Adair looked down to where the blood rubies had been clutched in his hand. In their place, blackened liquid ran through his fingers, dripping onto the forest floor beneath him. The same putrid smell that had come off Gortach filled his senses.

He watched as the substance ran down his forearm, mixing with his own blood, his breath coming in fast gulps. His skin turned cold and clammy, his stomach churning. He looked at Marquis, his still body starting to look uncharacteristically like Gortach's. Marquis's body churned into a nightmare until the world spun, and the forest floor rushed up to meet him, as he collapsed.

# CHAPTER TEN

## Memphis

Memphis *hated* traveling by horseback. His legs were numb, his pants having chaffed burns onto his inner thighs. His shaking hands gripped the reins as his steed followed the breakneck pace, the hooves around him rolling like thunder.

Brokk rode beside him, looking worse than he felt.

The hours had quickly bled in to having no meaning. The scenery was a churning organism of blurred colors, rolling hills, dense forest, and more rolling plains. It was wild and unbound, the cool wind pricking his skin into numbness.

His breaths came out in misty puffs as the sun quickly sank into the horizon. The chill in the air sank into the marrow of his bones, and Memphis could practically taste the change in the air. Arching his shoulders inwards and gritting his teeth against the wind, every tactical training class and lesson kicked into high gear within him.

Because as much as Brokk liked to turn a blind eye to the facts, being able to protect innocents meant being prepared to handle situations like this one. Being able to beat men like Cesan meant being a talented soldier.

Mud flecked his mount's side, and they ploughed through soft earth, chunks flying around them. Brokk raised his eyebrows as he steered his mount closer to his left side, their gallops falling into unison. Memphis felt the presence on his right before he looked. Tadeas must have looped around the side to the back of the group, then cut through the middle.

# HEIR OF LIES – PART ONE

The King of the Shattered Isles grinned wolfishly at them. His pale green hair flew behind him, his eyes shining with mischief. He dipped his head in acknowledgement before pushing his white mare faster, ripping forward with a speed and grace Memphis had rarely seen. Dread clawed through him, swift and unrelenting.

Why had Roque decided to trust him? The King bled with dark authority, arrogance, and cunning. Voices slammed against Memphis's iron walls locked around his mind, begging to be let in. It would be easy to let those guards down and find out the truths he wanted.

Growling under his breath, he squeezed his legs against the horses' heaving sides. Shooting forward, *faster*. Memphis wasn't going to be the monster half of the world saw them as - that his parents had seen *him* as.

He hadn't been back to the capital since all those years ago as a young boy. Lost, wandering the bustling streets filled with art merchants, traders, and remnants of Camden's, Roque's father's, loyal men. Memphis remembered the rumors that had floated around his mind, secrets at his disposal. Secrets that he hadn't understood then but had kept locked away, the memories tugging at him now.

That day, before he was taken to the Academy, the world was buzzing about the death of Camden, how he had mysteriously dropped at his dinner table. No health problems. No sign of tampering. Nothing. His court had frantically scattered, disappearing on the wind, leaving conflict between governments.

Leaving Roque to play the savior, to brandish the Academy with welcoming arms after years of fighting against his father. Memphis hadn't forgotten that one emotion roaring through Camden's guards that day.

One of betrayal.

Sluggish memories came into his mind's eye, fear slithering through him. That day, almost eleven years ago, Memphis had overheard Camden's men stirring, anger burning deep toward

Roque Fae and the murmurings about how the prince had finally chosen his path. His love over his blood ties. It was like unblocking a dam, the emotions, the clipped conversation slamming into him. He had looked around, wondering if the panic was evident behind his eyes, if anyone had seen his revelation. That Roque had somehow managed to kill his own father.

Had Memphis just as blindly played into the Faes' motives? Like so many others, he had been cut off from his family, scared and dangerous. That Academy had never been just a school for him but a lifeline. A place where he could learn control. He had buried those memories down into an iron vault, not thinking of Sarthaven until now.

Because if Roque Fae was willing to have spun lies and killed his father for the Academy, how far was he willing to go to protect it? How much loss would he justify for the greater good?

Memphis knew, without a doubt, that Camden had deserved his end. He had cast the world into a madness that wouldn't soon be forgotten.

Chewing his bottom lip, he wondered how much Roque was willing to sacrifice to rise to be King.

The thought clung to him, loud and ugly. Its claws sank deeply, erupting chaos as scenarios ran through his mind. He could feel every mile behind him, the distance between Emory and him searing into him.

*Just find the truth.*

Dusk clung to their surroundings, washing the world in a dreamy haze. Deep violets and blues chased away the golden hues of the day as the forest thinned before them. A sharp whistle cut through the air, and their horses slowed from a gallop to a canter, and finally slowing to a walk.

Hissing through his teeth at the momentum change, his muscles ached deeply.

Tadeas's voice boomed over them, "We will camp here tonight. We are about an hour from Sarthaven."

# HEIR OF LIES – PART ONE

They snapped into action, his group dismounting first. The teachers from the Academy flanked together, talking quietly. Professor Iasan, tactical training. Professor Whilms, ability assessment. Professor Remre, weapons specialist.

Memphis froze as he looked at the most ruthless teachers of the Academy. It made sense; they had no idea what would be waiting for them in the capital. They needed them here with a potential battle looming. Yet, the back of his neck tingled with foreboding.

"Well, you look like you have seen about ten ghosts in the last minute."

Brokk limped up to him, his horse much more relaxed around his presence than a couple of hours ago. Memphis loosened his feet from the stirrups, lowering himself onto solid ground. Hot pain laced through him as he practically fell off, his mount whinnying nervously.

"Next time, I am shifting to travel." Brokk clapped his shoulder.

"Must be nice," Memphis muttered under his breath, which made Brokk chortle. The happiness was quickly lost as Brokk fell in stride with him. "I don't trust this lot. What are we going to do?"

"We are going to play the faithful students of the Academy. But I agree. It's time to find out what is really going on here. I'm not sure…I think you might be right about Roque."

Brokk raised an eyebrow at him. "Why the change of heart?"

Two men from Tadeas's group gathered their mounts, whispering to the horses in soothing tones as they led them to the babbling stream at the forest's edge.

Memphis rubbed his frozen hands together. "I remembered something I had…attained with my ability before I was brought to the Academy. When I was a kid. I just think there is more to Roque than our best interest."

Brokk nodded but didn't push for more. Tents were being pitched around them and fires being lit, as the chatter of the camp broke out. No one noticed them as they slung their packs over their shoulders and navigated to the far corner of the camp.

Absentmindedly Brokk grabbed a tent and poles, murmuring, "Do we deal with Roque when we get back?"

Sighing, he shrugged. "We have to be careful about how we go about this. Emory is our *best* friend."

"I know." Brokk said.

Memphis felt heat flush his cheeks. The memory of Emory's lips against his ignited him, hope bubbling in his chest. When they made it back, he daydreamed of what he would say to her. He didn't care if she was a princess; titles were nothing compared to belonging to another human. Emory had enraptured him in every sense of the word.

"Memphis! Brokk!"

Turning, Memphis saw flaming red hair cut through the crowd. Alby, a bit out of breath, ran up to them grinning. "Am I ever glad to see you both here. Come on, let's catch up."

The three of them turned, Alby chattering away, as Memphis shot Brokk a glare, his ability wrapping around him as he stated in his mind, "*We will talk more later.*"

Brokk waggled his eyebrows at his tone, making Memphis shoot him a vulgar gesture that made him bark out a laugh.

Falling into step with Alby, the three of them set out to make camp.

Embers floated up, twisting and churning through the bleak night, as they sat around the fire. Propping himself up against a decayed log they had found, Memphis eyed the other side of the camp warily. Tadeas's men were roaring with laughter, having broken out some ale. On their left, the teachers and seniors from the Academy watched their animated chatter with darkened gazes.

It would seem they weren't the only ones who didn't trust the King from across the Black Sea.

# HEIR OF LIES – PART ONE

Brokk passed him the dried-out meat and water jug they had acquired from Tadeas. An hour before, Tadeas had hungrily taken in his best friend like a prized possession, ignoring him and Alby. Memphis exhaled through his nose as he took a deep swig.

Running a hand through his flaming hair, Alby whispered, "How far do you think Cesan will go?"

Brokk snapped his attention to Alby. "Who knows, Alb? Cesan has made his decision, and we have to go through with ours."

The unsaid words hung in between them all.

Staring into the flames, Memphis tried to find his answers in the flickering oranges and pulsing embers. The tides of Kiero were churning. Now, a battle loomed, caused by two friends over spite and power.

How many would die before the Faes were sated?

Turning his gaze upward, he took in the starless night. Deep, never-ending clouds had whisked away any trace of them. It felt like the entire world was holding its breath. Maybe it was. In the end, it wouldn't matter.

Memphis knew he should tell Brokk about that day in Sarthaven. About the whispers of Roque and Camden. Rolling his shoulders, he said, "I'm going to try to get some sleep."

Brokk raised an eyebrow, sensing his turmoil. Alby nodded, saying goodnight, and Memphis grabbed his pack and weapons, stiffly making his way to the tent.

Groaning, he threw the flap back and lowered himself onto the floor, pulling his jacket tighter around him, using his pack as a pillow. Breathing deeply, his eyelids fluttered closed, and his body slowly uncoiled, muscle by muscle. The voices of the camp became a distant hum, as Memphis fell deeper into his exhaustion, but his ability was waiting for him at the other end.

It was like sharp talons shredding his barricade, his dark desires throwing all he had into the action. Memphis flinched, his eyes flying open, and a cold sweat broke out over his skin. He felt each wall dissipate, breaking to his will. His world tilted sickly, and he was pulled under.

He was a hunter prowling, swiftly and surely. It took him *seconds* before his ability curled around Tadeas's mind.

*No. no. NO!*

He was scrambling, trying to throw those walls back up. His ability shattered through Tadeas's mind with ease and precision. The King was talking adamantly to his companions and had no idea that Memphis was swept into the depths of his consciousness, searching and reaping.

He was obliterated in the current of memories and thoughts, pushed under them. His power shifted through the unnecessary details like a bloodhound on a scent. He now had one intention, and he would not fail. Emotions and images flew by him until a name started echoing through him. *Roque. Roque. Roque.*

Memphis was slammed into the memory, and everything he knew bled away.

*Roque slammed his hand on the oak table, breathing hard, looking completely unhinged. Tadeas raised his eyebrows, crossing his arms. "How are we going to trust one another, Roque, when you won't break away from the mistakes of the past?"*

*He laughed darkly, shaking as he sized him up. "What happened with my father has nothing to do with the situation at hand. You waltz in here, expecting not only me, but my family and my school, to bow to your every demand?"*

*Tadeas became very still. "We have bowed to Kiero's demands for years. I have watched my people, people that I love, be shackled, enslaved, and destroyed. I'm not asking for your bleeding government. I'm asking for your trust. Allow us to build together, Roque. You and I both know how precarious your situation has now become. Do not allow one man to destroy it."*

*Roque frowned, staring at the polished oak as if he would find his answers. "He is my best friend."*

*"Who has now put your world at stake."*

# HEIR OF LIES – PART ONE

*Roque raised his gaze. "There are innocents in Sarthaven. They will get caught in the crossfire if I go through with this. Cesan is too cunning and knows me too well. He will expect me to uphold my word in giving justice with a fair trial."*

*Tadeas smiled sadly. "No one said achieving the greater good was going to be easy. People will die, but it won't be for nothing. We need each other as allies. Cesan will expect a trial, but what he won't foresee is our allegiance. Let me end him."*

*Roque snarled. "And what do you expect in return?"*

*Tadeas smoothed the front of his jacket, clucking his tongue. "As I said, I want our trading routes reinstated. I am here to compromise, not to threaten you. We can both keep our secrets and uphold our life, Roque."*

*"And what is that supposed to mean?"*

*He smirked. "Sailors gather a lot of information on their travels. Let's just say you are a hot topic amongst the Shattered Isles."*

*Roque paled, chewing his lower lip. "I don't want to enter another war."*

*Tadeas nodded. "Leave it to me. We will bait Cesan, and then it will be done."*

Memphis collided back into the present so hard he rolled over and emptied the contents of his stomach. Gasping for breath, he threw up his iron walls, sealing them tight, and the well of voices quieted until it was just him.

But then he noticed how silent it was outside the tent.

The hairs on his arm rose, and Memphis silently stood, slinging his pack over his shoulder and unsheathing his weathered sword. Everything made sense. How hard Tadeas pushed them to reach the capital, how loud they were being. It was practically ensuring Cesan would come sniffing. To fall into the King's trap. Only for Tadeas to kill him with no chance of justice.

Rage ripped through Memphis at how fast Roque had risked them all, had bent to the claim of being King.

*What did Cesan know?*

*What was Roque afraid of being found?*

Cursing, he pushed the thoughts down for now. The firelight danced outside, and he could see Brokk and Alby's silhouettes, their voices a low murmur.

Settling into what felt like a restless sleep, Memphis sighed. Closing his eyes, a sound cut through the night so suddenly, the hair on his arms stood on end. Eyes flashing open the howling was distant at first, a low humming in the night. Lurching out of the tent, Memphis's heart leapt into his throat. His breath was misty puffs in front of him.

Brokk and Alby were standing as well, swords out, faces drawn. Squinting into the bleak night, he tried to make out what was making the sound. On the horizon, nothing stirred. Bringing his sword in front of him, he exhaled slowly, gripping the handle with white knuckles.

The sound of hundreds of thundering footsteps filled the night as his heart dropped into his stomach.

It was the same effect as losing all sense of clarity. The lurching panic and then helplessness, as you grappled to hold on to *anything*. The screaming started first, at the north end of the camp, as Memphis took in what was causing the chaos.

Their bodies were like sleek armored plates, gleaming and muscular. Their elongated torsos were like serpents, twisting and flexing as they propelled forward with long black legs. Their bald bodies shimmered like water against the fading firelight, reflecting their drooling maws and inky teeth. Their orange eyes gleamed with madness as they cut through tents and bodies.

Memphis had heard of creatures of dark ancient magic before; ones that were told to children as myths to scare them. But as he saw the first monster rip the throat out of one of Tadeas's men, this was the furthest thing from bedtime stories of old.

Terror gripped Memphis as Brokk threw himself forward, shifting in one motion, and his colossal paws rumbled, shaking the earth. Alby in one motion, became invisible; roars rose from the creatures as he assaulted them, unseen.

# HEIR OF LIES – PART ONE

Everything moved in slow motion. Memphis felt himself take in the numbers of monsters as they poured into the camp, their rage and might crashed into their own.

It was a battle of tyrants.

Yelling, Memphis bounded forward, his ability already two steps ahead of him, reacting to his fear. Wielding it like a sword, Memphis slashed his ability into the minds of the monsters, his talons sinking into their wills. Simultaneously, Memphis held their bodies, ten at a time, as Brokk made his killing blows.

Blood trickled from Memphis's nose when, screaming, he let go, moving with his blade. Slashing, his steel cut into the side of the creatures closest to him, blackened blood spurting over his face. Ducking, Memphis parried another onslaught of attack, raising his blade as talons swiped toward his chest. Panting, his ability reacted, unbinding the creatures mind as it fell, twitching in front of him.

He was a darkened duet of body and ability, the two forces creating a lethal harmony.

Their inky talons and severed bodies filled his senses as he heard the King of the Shattered Isles roar.

Memphis's consciousness slid into Brokk's, *"Brokk. The Isles."*

They were one unit, had always been one. The giant wolf before him flung himself onto one of the creature's backs, his talons digging into the black flesh. The anguish of the monster's cry split through Memphis, adding to his adrenaline. This was too convenient. Too easy. These creatures born from the night had known where they would be.

Memphis ran. Blood curdling screams surrounded him, and to his left, a man was crying. To his right, a student was screaming as a monster slowly tore into his arm socket, his blood spurting over them both. The smell of smoke clung to his lungs as bile seared his throat, spilling through his lips. But through his panic, Memphis didn't stop.

His mind whirled, trying to connect the dots as he fought his way over to Tadeas's men. Too many had already fallen: fellow students, teachers. Iasan was the only one in Memphis's peripheral left standing, his body fluid and blurred as he cut through them. He was pure malice, yelling, as he found his way to Tadeas as well.

Sprinting, not looking back, Memphis's mind brushed up against Alby's and Brokk's consciousness. They were following behind, weaving through the carnage. His fear sliced through him, consuming him, as one-by-one, the fires were extinguished.

From the shadows, to his left, a monster exploded from the night, its teeth flashing as he barely reacted fast enough to save his life. The monster dropped when the tendrils of his ability fanned out, making a protective shield around Alby and Brokk as well.

*They were outnumbered.*

It wasn't a fight—it was a slaughter.

Running faster and trying not to falter, Memphis blindly maneuvered through the madness of this attack. There was a flash of steel to his right, as the man dropped his sword, the monster impaling his chest. The orchestra of screams rose as bile climbed up his throat again.

Five more men rushed in front of him, disappearing too quickly in the night.

*Remember your training.*

A cold fury coiled in his chest, and Memphis allowed more of his ability to course through him, and for the first time in his life, he allowed himself to become the monster his parents had claimed him to be.

*Move. Move. Move.*

The power was intoxicating as he snuffed out each creature's mental stability, his ability like a poison. Memphis relished in it. Their executed blows became sloppy, giving them the upper hand. Tadeas clapped his hands, as he revealed his ability. Wind roared over the land, circling the monsters in a cyclone. Thousands of droplets of water rose from the bloodied earth, as Tadeas roared, the water collecting into one in the cyclone—drowning the creatures.

# HEIR OF LIES – PART ONE

"Memphis!" Alby's yell cut through him as his friend flickered in view beside him.

There was a crack that was deafening, and hot pain laced through his back. His body was dragged down and then back. Dirt and blood filled his mouth, as his scream ripped from his throat. A thick muscled tail wrapped around his torso. The snarling creature dragged him closer.

The creature's voice was silken as it rattled throughout the folds of his mind, "*You are not like the others. You have pieced together that we are here under our new ruler's orders.*"

Memphis flung his weight back, kicking, trying to twist out of its tight hold. The creature chuckled. Its eyes seemed to grow brighter the harder he resisted.

"*The true King has come. We grow hungry and tired in the darkness, always skittering to the shadows. The era of your kind is coming to an end.*"

He dove through the creature's walls. His consciousness was sleek and dark, no kindness, no humanity to be found. Only a hunger for death.

Memphis snapped down their mental connection. "*What are you?*" He was now pinned under the monster, its saliva coating his face.

"*We are the dabarne, centuries ago we roamed Kiero freely, but with the Great War dark magic fell—as did we. The fey warriors of Nehmai bound us in the shadows, but what they never foresaw was that darkness would rise again, and us with it. Our King not only freed us but promised freedom to roam once again, if we started with your camp.*"

All Memphis felt was the creature's dark joy as Memphis honed in on its features. Its long serpentine body flexed, supported by its muscular legs. It surpassed the size of a horse. Its wolf-like snout inhaled his scent, pointed ears flush against its skull. Thrashing back and forth was a whip like tail, pounding against the bloodied earth.

One word came to mind *demon*. This dabarne unlike anything Memphis had ever seen before. The dabarne pushed its giant paws into his chest, lowering his teeth, snapping and vicious...

There was a flash of golden fur and immense relief as the monster was ripped free from Memphis's chest, leaving him wheezing and his lungs crackling. Brokk flipped it on its back, the *dabarne* screeching, withering under his friend's pin.

And then silence.

Brokk bared his teeth at the lifeless form before loping back to him. His giant muzzle nudged Memphis's shoulder, and he could practically hear what he was saying.

He had to move.

Warmth spread as blood trickled down his back, energy draining with his movement. The chaos of the fight reigned around them, swords meeting flesh, bodies being lost in the darkness of the night. Memphis heard men crying, their curses, their pleas for mercy.

He endured their inner most thoughts as they died, grief gripping his chest.

Taking deep breaths and with shaking hands, he gripped Brokk's heaving side, hauling himself onto his friends back. Brokk didn't delay. Charging through the carnage, Memphis gripped his fur, taking in snippets of what was happening around them, as if his mind couldn't process it fast enough.

His panic was in full bloom, choking him, making his world spin, his ability roaring around him as he soaked up the destroyed camp. Absorbing the monsters' rage, he swooped in and destroyed their sanities. Each dip down into their consciousness as it resonated within him, and he realized that the dabarne were all thinking in unison, as if their minds were linked. Memphis broke through another iron wall.

*We work for the acclaimed King.*

And another - *We turned to the darkness and were shown that you were coming.*

And another - *We know you are coming to kill him.*

And another - *So, we will kill you first.*

# HEIR OF LIES – PART ONE

His mind was reeling. Brokk twisted, almost throwing him off as they avoided a roaring dabarne. Cesan had used these dark creatures to flush them out. It wasn't a rouse for Cesan at all but a trap for them.

Memphis searched in the night, for *anyone* they recognized. The air rippled with slithering bodies and glowing eyes. Tadeas. Iasan. They were nowhere to be seen.

"Memphis! Brokk!"

Alby ran full tilt towards them, covered in blackened blood that wasn't his. The tents around him crashed to the ground as the dabarne that was hunting him roared, charging forward.

Their friend flickered in between visible and invisible, undulating in fear as he sprinted through the destruction, and Memphis noticed that his weapon had been discarded. Brokk growled, but they were across the camp—they wouldn't make it in time. Brokk ran, but Memphis knew he couldn't carry him and run at his full potential.

*Do something. Anything.*

The world tilted, and Memphis prepared to shift his weight, throwing himself onto the ground so Brokk could make it there. He felt the ripple through the air, like a charged electric shock.

There was the pounding of hooves, then a blinding white light as Nei Fae appeared from the night. She galloped into the heart of the fight. The light beamed from her palm, radiating. Her pale hair was tied back, and she sported several fresh cuts and bruises, but she pushed her horse right in front of the *dabarne* fearlessly.

"You cannot have them!" she screamed and met Alby's outreached hand, hauling him onto the saddle. Tears slid down his bloodied cheeks, and Nei pushed her horse out of the way just as the monster slashed forward, teeth and claws snapping at the empty space.

Brokk skittered to a halt as Nei shouted, "Sarthaven is already lost! We must go! NOW!"

*Sarthaven had fallen. The capital of Kiero was gone.*

Memphis's blood pounded in his ears as his pulse echoed his shock. He snapped his ability in, gnashing his teeth at the force. Brokk tensed underneath him, and then they were flying. The hammering of Brokk's paws filled Memphis's senses, and he gripped his friend's golden fur with blood-soaked hands.

The dabarnes roars filled the night behind them, chasing at their heels.

The ground quaked and shuddered from the sheer force of their chase. Reigning in his ability was like trying to dominate a feral animal by sheer force and then reeling from the impact of it. Memphis gripped Brokk's fur tighter, and a trickle of blood streamed from his nostrils. It was *too* much; he was losing himself to that sick serenade of destruction, of ripping the *dabarnes* minds apart.

Shred by shred by *shred*.

Leaning lower, he breathed himself back into his body, to the present and the looming forest ahead.

*Don't look back. Don't look back.*

Nei's mare broke the forest line first, and Brokk charged. Gravity left them as they cut through the air, landing hard in the sanctuary of the woods. Nei had reined her mount to a stop, sweat dripping off her brow. Raising her palm, she concentrated on the tree line, white light pulsing from her palm once more.

Brokk flattened his ears, whining as they all took in the bloodthirsty army galloping toward them. No movement stirred from the camp, and pulsing embers died in the night. The world swayed, as Memphis prepared to meet his end.

Everything seemed to still, and blinking, he looked down to his blood-soaked clothes, to his best friend, to their queen. Despite the bloodshed, despite their losses, he choked on his anguish as thoughts of Emory filled every orifice of his being. He wouldn't see her again; this was their end. He grappled for any way out, any way they could beat this.

Instead, he numbly watched the army of darkness sweep down upon them, their blood coated teeth, their deafening roars. Suddenly, the ground rolled and churned underneath them, like they were in a boat on the ocean. Brokk jumped back, growling, just as the trees shuddered to life all around them, as if they had just been in a deep slumber, waiting for their siren call.

Branches, thick and unyielding, snapped down before them, the trees bowing to the movement. Quickly, they layered, branch by branch, thick bark crunching from the impact. The forest, within seconds, was creating a shield. Bowing to the whim of their commander, which as he turned and looked at Nei, it fell into place.

She bared her teeth as she wielded her mighty orchestra, the trees bowing and responding at a rapid rate. She was buying them time, commanding and controlling the elements, the earth beneath them and the trees surrounding them.

A guttural groan escaped her lips as she looked at them and croaked, "*Run.*"

Brokk shot forward, not looking back as he carried Memphis. Screams echoed in the distance, and then he heard the pounding of hooves behind them, as Nei and Alby followed. Each tree they passed sprang to life once they were all clear, building and creating a deadly labyrinth for the dabarnes, their sharpened branches landing blows to the monsters. Branch met flesh, ripping and tearing as their screams splintered through the night. He cringed at the sounds of the woods dragging the creatures within their depths.

Intricately, they wove through the twists and turns, the night turning darker with every passing second. Spotting movement from their side, he barely had time to react, as a dabarne suddenly cut into their path. Jumping, Brokk swerved severely to the right. Right where his companion waited.

Teeth met teeth as Brokk bit against the dabarne's sleek throat. Memphis's world twisted as he was thrown off, his head cracking against a flat rock on the forest floor. Dots blared in his vision, threatening to pull him under, just as the monster slammed his weight into his best friend; bone crunched from the force. Brokk's cry tore through his heart with a shattering force.

Shooting up, he dove into his power, as it laced forward, every nerve, every fiber, being latch onto by him. Those orange eyes turned to him as the dabarne sensed him.

Letting go, every ounce of his energy exploded, and his ability crushed and broke everything that the dabarne was until nothing remained. The body hit the ground, and Memphis ran to Brokk. Relief coursed through him when his friend stood, his hackles raising, turning his golden gaze to him.

Collapsing, Memphis mentally whispered, *"Are you okay?"*

Snapping his maws, Brokk curtly nodded his giant head once, conveying he was. Quickly, he didn't waste another moment as Memphis climbed onto his back, and they were off. Brokk's legs wobbled as they flew over the woven trees, Nei galloping ahead of them.

They had fallen behind.

Crashing through Nei's magic, the trees responded fiercely. It was like fighting against an hourglass. If the sand ran out before they covered ground, they would be at the mercy of the darkness and the monsters that called for their blood.

Branches snagged their hair, shredded their skin, as Brokk clambered over and under, weaving powerfully, snapping at trees when they mistook them for the enemy.

"Nei! Alby!" His voice was hoarse and was instantly lost in the sounds of the fight that surrounded them.

Brokk pushed faster, the forest blurring, sounds blurring, and all Memphis could digest was the fierce pounding of his heart, pleading for survival.

Howls erupted behind them, and more trees bonded together in response. A makeshift wall was weaving before them, another shield. Brokk's sides heaved as he cut to the left, and Memphis spotted his intention.

A small opening *just* big enough for them to fit through was left as the trees solidified, the ripple quickly spreading through, closing any gaps. Brokk's footfalls reverberated through him, and he watched in horror. The trees became thicker, sharper, preparing for them, to destroy them.

# HEIR OF LIES – PART ONE

Gravity left as they launched forward, aiming for the shrinking gateway between their life and death. Memphis closed his eyes, waiting for the impact. Screams echoed around him, or maybe it was him: he couldn't tell anymore.

Cool air howled, licking at his exposed face, sinking deeper and deeper into his bones. There was the sensation of his clothes ripping, talons digging into his calf—sharp and unrelenting, ripping through his flesh effortlessly. Pain, hot and lacing, shot up through his body, consuming his every thought, every movement and internal battle.

Until it was nothing but the fire in his bones.

Memphis cracked his eyes open, his vision spinning and blurring, but he saw enough to take in the ground rushing up to meet them. They collided with such force; he was thrown viciously from Brokk. He was suspended in time for a moment before his back cracked against something hard. The taste of dirt and blood filled his mouth, and he wheezed for air. Brokk's growls ripped through the night as he stood from the mounds of dirt they had churned up, shaking. In one motion, he shifted back to his human form.

Bruises peppered Brokk's skin: dark purple, blue, and green overlapping in a colorful display. His clothes were in tatters, revealing bleeding, open wounds. Memphis watched in wonder as sinew and skin healed, Brokk's ability working in overdrive.

In one motion, Brokk was kneeling beside him. "Memphis, breathe. We are okay. Just breathe."

The howls from the other side of the thick wall of interwoven trees slammed their reality in Memphis, and he lurched forward, gasping. "We have to get out of here. Back to the Academy."

"Brokk, Memphis!"

Nei galloped through the forest, reigning her mare to a hard stop. Panting, she dropped from the saddle, leaving a stunned Alby in her wake. Her voice was thick as she ran toward them. "We lost sight, and I couldn't get back. I couldn't stop what I unleashed." With wide eyes, she studied them. Cursing, she snapped, "Brokk, can you still carry him? We have to warn the others."

Brokk's voice was barely above a whisper when he asked, "What is else coming for us, Nei?"

She grabbed his shoulder, her features solemn. "A reckoning."

Ice licked at Memphis's veins, through his pain, through his nausea. He wanted to claw out the remains of the demons' whispered voices, of their acclaimed king, of *Cesan*. Of the promises of their unmaking.

He was distantly aware as Brokk shifted back, making himself flush to the ground.

Nei's whispered words were an anchor in the chaos. "Memphis, you have to try and get up."

Shifting his weight, clambering for his friend, the pain almost made him succumb to oblivion. Was that him crying? Had he completely unhinged? His weight shifted, and Memphis breathed deeply, Brokk's fur tickling his nose.

Nei said, "No matter what you see, don't stop until we reach the Academy."

Brokk heaved a shuddering breath, dipping his head once. And then they were running. Leaving the bloodthirsty howls rushing through the air behind them, as they dove deeper into the heart of the woods.

And they didn't stop.

HEIR OF LIES – PART ONE

# CHAPTER ELEVEN
## Adair

They came to him in his dreams. Their beckoning voices were soft and comforting, and Adair groggily smiled, looking around him. Nothing was clear in his dreamscape; the colors and shapes all blurred into a giant grey mass. Stuffing his hands into his pockets, he shrugged his shoulders.

Stepping forward, the ground rippled, like he had dropped a stone into the water. Green hues shimmered below his feet, crisp and sharp against the grey backdrop. Taking another step, the world shifted, exploding before him. The smell of damp grass overcame him, and looking around, he was in another forest, one he didn't recognize. The trees here were oversized, the leaves a deep purple, creating the illusion that he was in the heart of a gem.

"Adair."

The hair on the back of his neck stood on end, as the soft voice changed into something he recognized. Turning slowly, the creature was behind him, her head tilted, like a predator watching its prey before it pounced.

She stalked up to him, slowly, the leaves turning to scorched earth with each footfall. He couldn't move. He just watched, his heart lodged in his throat as she came face-to-face with him, her pale hand resting gently over his heart.

Those pitiless eyes pulled him in until he wasn't sure he was breathing at all.

Leaning in, her sharpened teeth clicked lazily as she whispered, "You are so close. You can't falter now."

"Close to what?" His voice was a whisper on his exhale.

She pressed her hand harder on his chest. "To freedom."

Adair stared in horror as black flames erupted from her fingertips. They twisted up and down her arm until they erupted, consuming him. It was like having his head shoved underwater. He flailed and writhed trying to escape her grasp, but he couldn't break free.

He watched as the inky flames, twisting all around him, kissed and caressed his skin. Starting to sink *into* his pores, turning his veins black. Choking him, deafening him. He felt liquid burst from his tear ducts, black tears streaming down his face.

His screams echoed through the forest as the she giggled, lowering her sharpened teeth to his throat, making *him* submit to her will, her dark desires. He clawed at her, but the fire just raged, crawling into his mouth, his eyes, his nose. Suffocating him as he was turned to ash beneath her hold.

His screams tore from him, jarring him back to reality. Sweat clung to his skin, making his clothes sticky beneath his jacket. The tinges of dawn bled into the sky, making the forest around them seem innocent as the shadows were chased away.

Scrambling back, he clutched his heart, ripping at his clothes, tearing them so he could see, could *check*, that it had been just a dream. The cool air made his skin prickle when his chest was exposed. His skin was starkly pale with no trace of inky lines. Sighing, he held his head in his hands, trying to shake the nightmare.

"I thought you might have died."

Adair snapped his attention to the figure looming over him. Marquis was pale in the morning light, dark shadows lining his piercing eyes. Slowly, he lowered himself, so he was eye-to-eye with him. Marquis's voice was raw as he said, "A little warning might be welcome next time we go visit a creature of death."

Adair raised an eyebrow at the young prince. His voice was scratchy when he said, "I thought you would relish in the life-threatening experience. Also, I *did* warn you."

Marquis grinned wolfishly, extending his hand down to him. Adair grasped it, welcoming the help as his body protested from the movement. Bruises flowered his arms, the dried blood cracking from the old wound.

Sighing, he looked at Marquis skeptically. "How did you find me anyways? Gortach's lair is almost impossible to pass through."

Dusting off his jacket, the Prince of the Shattered Isles murmured, "It's hard to say. A horrible wrenching gut feeling? That the golden room we started in started to turn into itself? It was like I was looking through a mirror once I found the crack, and I stepped into it. Turns out, it was a portal straight to you."

Adair dusted himself off slowly. "And a good thing at that. Bleeding dark magic."

Marquis lightly coughed under his breath, arching an eyebrow at him in anticipation.

"Yes, thank you for saving my life, oh noble Prince."

Chortling, Marquis clapped his back. "That's more like it. Anyways, did you find what you were looking for down there?"

Adair popped his collar up, shivering against the misty morning. He looked around at the empty forest, absentmindedly rubbing his chest. He could still *feel* the echoes of those black flames burning through him, through his core, and running through his veins.

"In a way."

He started walking, his boots thudding wetly against the ground. Marquis was right beside him, chomping at the bit.

"I just saved your life, and you decide now is the time to be cryptic?"

Adair tiredly rubbed his eyes. "What? So you can report back to your father what I'm up to?"

Marquis squared his shoulders. "No. Because we just visited a hidden realm where creatures of ancient myths *do* exist, and I'm curious how exactly you found them and what is worth that kind of desperation."

Walking in silence, Adair chewed his cheek. He glanced at the prince, who had buried his hands in his pockets, waiting patiently for him to answer. Would it be so bad to confide in someone? To *have* someone to confide in? Someone who would listen with no judgements, no pre-conceived notions of who he really was. Or who he had to be.

"I like to read. History is my passion." Adair shrugged. "Look. All my life I have been groomed to become part of the Academy's successors. Which means not having regular classes and having access to materials the Faes have brought in for their own personal use. I found this book, and well, I devoured every word."

He frowned and Marquis motioned him to continue. "Is it so wrong to believe that there is more to the magic of this world? We are here, so why couldn't these mythical creatures be as well? It took a lot of hunting and obviously exploring. I found the gateway a couple of years ago, by sheer luck. I haven't told anyone, because who would listen? Who would believe me? I'm an outcast, with the ability to possess another person. Most students fear me, and their fear ensures I'm isolated. With the exception of Emory and Memphis."

Marquis nodded. "It takes a dreamer to know a dreamer. You and I aren't that different."

Nodding, Adair whispered, "It was worth it. Gortach is a seer of sorts. It can see into the future of the question the person presents to it. I *knew* the Faes have been lying to us."

Rubbing his hands together, Marquis was practically bouncing on his heels. "You do know that was our true intention for coming, right?"

Adair practically tripped over his own feet. Halting, he breathed, "What?"

# HEIR OF LIES – PART ONE

"Stories travel fast to the Isles. Even though our trading routes have been cut off since Nei's father, Briar, was ruling, word still got to us. We are rovers after all, and gathering secrets is like our oxygen." Marquis grinned. "Anyways, my dad was curious about why Briar cut off the Shattered Isles from his oldest daughter. Before he was usurped and killed, it was found out that Roque was keeping some very dangerous secrets from prying eyes."

This time Adair motioned him to continue. "It's not a coincidence that we are here, or that there have been horror stories of dark creatures ravaging Kiero. It's true my dad is here to build an alliance with the Faes, but not before finding out the truth. We are buying time. Didn't you ever wonder why I didn't go with my group? I have been assigned the key role of finding out if Kiero is *worth* our alliance."

Marquis beamed at him, and adrenaline coursed through Adair. He choked back his relief and a strangled laugh. "And what do you think so far?"

The prince stopped, looking at him dead in the eyes. "That, right now, that place is built on a warped dream, overrun with lies and deception. That the good intentions have been lost in translation. Your father is proof of that."

A moment passed. Running his hand along his mouth, Adair started walking, weaving through the towering forest. Ice cut through his veins, vicious and unrelenting.

*His* father. The traitor.

The unhinged man who was never satisfied. Did he find what he looking for? That would make him feel fulfilled in his life? If he would make the world bow to his rage, would he look back and feel happy? Knowing that he had filled his years, breaking him with his anger and his violence. That he had left his best friends, forcing their world back into a split balance. To choose sides.

What side would he be on?

He was an outcast in the Academy. He was torn in his family. When the time came, where would his allegiances lie?

"Hey! Adair." Marquis was practically chasing him, grabbing his shoulder and making him stop. "I didn't mean anything by that. I'm sorry."

Chewing his lip, Adair looked up at the sky, where the golden hues spread across the clouds like gold flecks, dusting and shaping the sky. His anger, his confusion, his *hurt* rushed up to him.

"Adair."

With burning eyes, he snapped, "Look, it's fine. I'm fine. Let's just get back, okay? I have a lot to do."

"Adair!" Marquis cried behind him.

He didn't stop, didn't turn back. This prince was just like everyone else, using him to get what he wanted. All this time, he was a *fool*, believing that maybe, just maybe, they had more in common than they had both thought.

He had *no one*. Emory turned to her family and now claimed her *birthright* - her father, making her choose. Adair was alone in this.

Roque feared him and his ability. He had been delusional to think that he ever had a place in the Academy. He had always been kept on a leash, entertained because of Cesan's relationship.

But now?

Now, it was time he accepted that his future was in *his* hands. And it started by finding out why Roque was hiding this so-called Book of Old. And why he needed access to the ancient power. Pulling his jacket closer, he nestled into the darkness curling around his heart and the echoes of those soft voices coursing through him.

"*Yes. Yes. Yes.*"

Marquis followed beside him, shooting glances every now and then out of the corner of his eyes. Adair never faltered, staring straight ahead and falling into his silence. With each passing second, with each footfall, his certainty grew into a concrete form, small at first, but then it exploded through him, sharp and consuming.

He knew where his alliances lay. He had always known it; he just wasn't able to face his own truth. They lay with *him*. Not with the Academy. Or the Faes. Or his parents.

What were his best interests in a world that was being ripped apart by the politics of kings? The thought grew and grew, and as Adair walked, for the first time in his life, he envisioned a different future.

Hours bled away as they walked in silence. The afternoon grew hot and heavy, both boys having to tie their jackets around their waists. The sun soaked into their skin, Adair's neck becoming hot and itchy. The towering trees had begun to thin, leaving the memories of Gortach deep within the forest, locked away.

"It feels so much longer walking back to our reality than escaping it," Marquis stated.

Adair raised his eyebrow at the prince, not replying. Deeper and deeper, his thoughts ran into those hidden crooks and crannies of his heart, into places he fortified with a barrier. Preparing for *his* reality. One where it wouldn't involve him and Emory as a team, preparing for a future where the Academy would have been theirs. One where his small reprieve of friends wouldn't exist.

There was a murmur of sighs on the wind as it ruffled through the leaves, making Adair's heart beat a little faster. Looking around, nothing seemed amiss or different. The overlaying songs of the forest were in full play, from the gurgling streams to the small animals running in the distance.

Adair stopped, his blood turning to ice. He whispered, "Marquis."

The prince stopped, huffing. "Oh, he *does* exist. Welcome back to the land of living."

"Something is wrong."

Narrowing his gaze slightly, Marquis's deep green eyes reflected flecks of gold in the afternoon light. Looking around, he shrugged. "I don't see anything. What do you mean?"

Adair wiped his clammy palms on his pants, trying to steady his nerves.

Everything looked normal, but there again, on the wind, the whispers became clear—and sharp. Filling with *screams*. They shivered down his spine, clambered into the walls of his consciousness. They were the piercing pain through his body, the agony in his heart. His feet carried him, even though every fiber of his core was ignited.

He heard Marquis cursing behind him, following closely, their pounding footsteps charging across the forest floor. He ran so hard, the trees blurred around him, and his tunnel vision overwhelmed him. Again, those screams echoed all around him on the wind, in his mind. The once calmness of the forest seemed to ripple, and flickers of nightmares ignited around him. The daylight was gone. And the darkness awaited him.

Vicious claws grabbed at him. Within the forest, luminous eyes blinked from behind the tree trunks and brambles, Adair caught glimpses of huge serpentine bodies and hairless skin. The monsters snapped their teeth, jumping from their hiding spots, wanting to capture him. To tear, to rip, to consume him.

Running harder, his chest burning, his breath coming out in wheezes. He was running blindly into the night, his arms hitting the trees, fresh blood running down them. There was only him, Marquis disappearing on a distant memory. He was alone.

"*Adair.*"

Shuddering to a stop, he grabbed his temples, shutting his eyes quickly, not wanting to see them. Willing them away.

"*Adair, you are almost home.*"

Tears streamed down his face at the cool touch, and he was frozen. Cool fingers tipped his chin, and his eyes opened. Their pale arms, their elongated limbs. Their empty sockets, their pinned back smiles. Their long black hair blended into the night as they circled around him, murmuring in hushed tones.

"Who are you?" Adair asked.

The one closest to him tilted its head, weighing the question. "*We are like you. Trapped in a world, in a place you don't belong. A place that is dying. I have seen your heart, Adair. I have seen your dreams and your fears.*"

Again, she placed a hand over his heart, his wild beat thrumming as she breathed down his neck.

*Too close, too close,* Adair thought wildly.

"And they are *mine.*"

The surroundings around them melted away, the screams fading to a pulse in the back of his mind. All he could take in, all he could make out, was her. There was the cackle of flames, and Adair blinked.

Flames roared all around them, uncontrolled and devouring everything they touched. He couldn't feel the heat or their burn as they licked his skin. The creature giggled before him whispering, "See? *They won't hurt you, can't hurt you. This darkness, this endless destruction, is what you crave. In all its beauty, and in all its might.*"

"No."

She curled her thin fingers into his collar bone, her voice echoing in his consciousness. "*It's time you accept the darkness in you. Stop. Fighting. Us.*"

And with that, she pushed him back, surprisingly strong. Stumbling, he fell into the roaring endless fire, the flames crackling hungrily. He couldn't tell where the fire began and ended within him; the bronze hues turned inky black.

"ADAIR!"

*The black flames, turning his heart to ash.*

"Mate, come on!"

*The flashes of a world remade. The fear. But also, the greatness. It was all him.*

"Do not die on me!! STRATTON!"

*And him, sitting on a throne of bones.*

The slap across his face was hard and unrelenting. Dots danced in his vision, and Adair took in a huge inhale, his lungs burning for air.

"Oh, thank the Black Sea." Marquis sat down hard on the ground, shaking his head. His freckles stood out like their own constellations against his deathly pale skin. Blinking, the treetops and the clear afternoon sky came into focus, and Adair realized he was on his back, his limbs splayed around him. His tongue was swollen, dried blood along his lips and underneath his nose. His whole body felt like it had been chewed and patchily put back together.

Lying there, he was stunned, unable to piece together his reality and what had happened. A few minutes passed before he could manage to sit up, rasping, "What happened?"

Marquis choked out a laugh. "Oh, what happened? You mean you saying something was wrong, then freezing and convulsing in a fit the next second… oh and then the screaming? I tried to help you, but I couldn't and your eyes…"

"My eyes what?" His voice sounded unfamiliar and worn.

Marquis shook his head, and when he looked at Adair, his eyes were wide and full of fear. "They were pitch black. Any trace of you was gone."

Goosebumps rose on Adair's arms, and he couldn't think of anything to say to the prince. He barely understood it himself. His legs were shaky, but he stood slowly, dusting off his pants. Chills raked through him, and he donned his jacket, popping the collar. He couldn't meet Marquis's searching gaze as he started walking.

"You've got to be kidding me," Marquis said.

In two strides, the prince crossed the empty space between them, grabbing his shoulder and turning Adair to face him. "You have to tell me what is going on."

Adair pulled back. "I don't have to tell you anything."

Hurt flashed across his face, and Marquis threw his hands out to his sides. "Why?"

Adair snapped. Pushing his finger against Marquis's chest, his voice shook as he said, "Because you are no different than them. You're only here to find out what you need. Not because you want to be."

Adrenaline coursed through him, his anger stifling.

"Adair, calm down," Marquis said.

With shaking hands, he started walking again, a thousand unsaid things hanging between them. Marquis followed him at a distance, his features darkening with every step. Adair didn't look back again.

When they made it back to the Academy, the sun was starting to dip into the horizon, the tinges of dusk painting the sky in a brilliant array of colors. Adair paused for a moment, observing the Academy, the courtyard, the hive of a school that had been his home for as long as he could remember.

Marquis brushed past him, shooting him a raised eyebrow before making his way back to his crew. Adair sighed, knowing he should have explained more of what had happened, of how he was feeling.

Tightness constricted his chest, and he took a step forward, the words forming on his tongue, wanting to call the prince back, before that clear voice rang out to him, "Adair!"

Emory threw herself from the rock ledge that was their spot, flying down the hill to him. She barely glanced at Marquis as she ran by. Her ebony hair was unbound, and she wore a long black jacket and loose pants. Emory's tied up boots smacked against the ground, hard, and she was breathless as she came to the forest's edge.

"I'm so glad you're okay."

Tinges of pink blossomed across her cheekbones, as she searched his face, her mouth frowning delicately at his wounds and dried blood.

Closing his mouth, he looked at Emory. Usually, his pulse would race being this close, the endless possibilities of them dancing on his imagination.

Walking past her, he started the climb back to his room and some much-needed sleep.

"Hey, Adair!" She grabbed his hand, pulling him back to face her. Worry crinkled lines at the edge of her eyes. "Where have you been?"

Shrugging out of her grip, he buried his hands deep in his jacket pockets. His mouth felt dry, and he looked at her, *truly* looking at her, and he couldn't muster any words. The silence dragged between them, becoming more uncomfortable with every second.

"Adair, say something."

"I have to go." The words escaped him, clipped and dry, and turning, he could practically feel her bouncing after him.

"Adair, talk to me."

Spinning on his heel, he asked, "About what, Emory? What do you want to talk to the traitor's son about? How your future is brimming with promise and mine...mine is..." he sputtered, feeling heat rush up through him.

Hurt flashed across her face as she spat, "I can't choose my family any more than you can! I have been worried *sick* about you! You haven't stopped for a second to think that I have possibly come to explain myself? To apologize? That I haven't been waiting for hours?"

He ran a bloodied hand through his hair, his heart pounding viciously against his chest. "No. You were perfectly clear before."

With narrowed eyes, she jabbed a finger at his chest. "You listen to me, Adair Stratton. I am sorry for what my dad told me, but I can't control what is happening in this world! We are surrounded by things that don't make sense, surrounded by secrets and lies and darkness and now a potential war!" She paused. "But after you left, I talked to my Dad, and I will not go through this without you beside me. He is reconsidering."

She beamed.

# HEIR OF LIES – PART ONE

His nails bit into his palms, hidden from her view. "No."

"What do you mean *no?*"

"I mean, stay away from me. I want nothing to do with you or your family. I don't need your charity. I don't need your friendship. I. Don't. Need. *You.*" He had contorted, losing himself in the churning anger inside him.

Emory paled with every word, her eyes brimming as she said fiercely, "You don't mean that! You're my best friend."

He cut the last strand of himself loose as he smiled coldly. "Yes, you will find that I do mean it. Leave me alone. You're better friends with those two Mixed Bloods."

Her mouth hung open, and Adair turned back to the school.

*What had he done?*

The insult cut deep. Mixed Blood, a term from Roque's father's reign. People who were not of a superior birthright and had "tainted" abilities. People like Memphis, whose parents were desolates. People like Brokk, who had no idea about his past or where he came from. Even people like Emory, whose ability was an anomaly considering her parents.

Trudging back up to the Academy, in the dying sunlight, he knew there was no taking back what he had said. He glanced back once, Emory still frozen at the bottom of the hill, tears rolling down her cheeks.

Coldness swept through him as he wrenched his gaze forward, his bitterness filling him. She had chosen her life. It was time he chose his own. What scared him most is that he believed she should have chosen him. All those years of shared secrets, of stifled laughter, of whispers, of their dreams, of their fears whisked away with the promise of a crown.

He swallowed hard, the tightness in his throat searing. It was time.

The Academy was no longer his home, and he intended to show the world its secrets.

The edges of his vision were tinged red. Adair was frozen, staring at his door with wide eyes. Time seemed to collapse in on itself; his hands shook violently at the deep red slash across his bedroom door and the insults cut into the wood.

*Traitor.*

He stepped closer, the red paint looking like blood in the dimness of the quiet hallway.

*Follow your father to his death.*

His bruised hands brushed the knife marks, his tears quietly trickling down his face.

*Monster.*

A strangled noise slipped from him, and he looked around, wondering which of his classmates had done this. How long had they thought this? Just waiting for the opportunity where no one would do anything about it. When hate would override humanity.

*Get the hell out.*

It was amazing the power that words held. Either wielded within yourself or by other people, it didn't matter when you started to believe them.

Grabbing the doorknob, he took a deep breath, twisting it a little too hard. Then everything was chaos. Sharp sirens rang through the intercom; a dull flashing light coursed down the hallway. Doors flew open like a beating drum as students poured out, their confusion clear. Over a decade of familiar faces, staring at him cruelly as they passed, their sly smirks and cutting judgments made Adair's ability course through him like a shield, tempting to crash through every single mind. Just for a second, they could feel how he felt.

"Out of my way! NOW!"

Roque barreled down the hallway, pure panic etched across his face. Pushing students out of the way, Emory chased at his heels, shooting Adair a glance as she passed him. He didn't think his feet carried him after them, fear making everything vivid, but he ran, dreading the worst.

# HEIR OF LIES – PART ONE

At the end of the hallway, the doors exploded open. Nei stood in the last of the daylight, the dried blood stains over her fighting gear; Memphis, Brokk, and Alby supported themselves beside her.

In the distance, a blood thirsty howl echoed.

Roque ran to his wife, not caring there was an audience as he grasped her face in between his hands. "What happened!? Nei!"

"Sarthaven has fallen."

It was a choked whisper, but it sent ripples throughout the students and remaining teachers. Adair stopped, making himself flush against the hallway as he watched Emory collide into Memphis, hugging him tightly, and then hugging Brokk.

Roque paled. "Cesan?"

Nei nodded, her voice growing stronger. "And Bresslin. Our company was led into a trap. I was the only one to survive. The city itself, Roque... It is overrun by dark creatures that he is controlling. They are killing desolates and anyone who defies them."

Silence.

"We were followed," Nei added.

Roque snapped his attention past her, to the towering forest bathed in golden light.

Another howl sliced through the air.

"Where's my dad?!" Marquis pushed through the throng, his emerald hair standing on end, as he stared at Nei, his voice cracking. "Where's Tadeas?"

Their heads bowed, not meeting the prince's gaze.

Paling, Marquis folded in on himself, repeatedly saying, "No. no."

There was a clambering of hooves in the distance, and Marquis snapped his head up, pushing past them. Adair followed him, coming to the entranceway.

On the horizon, a horse galloped toward them, frothing at the bit, Tadeas clinging onto the reins, his pale green hair unbound. Behind him a creature born from darkness followed. Hunting him. Its long black body twisted and moved at such a pace; Adair couldn't fathom. It roared, catching up to the King of the Shattered Isles.

Nei was shouting commands, the remaining teachers of the Academy filing up beside her, the senior students jumping in line, abilities cracking to life. Marquis was saying something to him, but he was entranced by the monster, and he couldn't look away. It was like a siren call.

"*You.*"

He started walking slowly down the steps, the voices of the Academy fading away.

"*I see you.*"

His ability flowed into his heart, into his mind. The creature twisted to the left, forcing Tadeas to turn sharply. Herding him toward the forest.

Running now, sweat dripped down the back of Adair's neck. Throwing his body weight, he hurled himself over the rock ledge as his ability exploded through him, rippling out from him. Right into the monster's mind.

The creature stopped and twisted violently toward him. It bared its teeth almost in a sickening smile at the new challenge. Adair dove deeper, into the sinew on the creature's bones, breaking and shattering the walls in its consciousness.

Charging toward him, the ground shaking from the force, he gritted his teeth and ripped against the resistance, so that he could attain control, but he slipped and was slammed back.

"*You cannot win against me.*"

With furrowed brows, he threw everything he had, barreling down, latching on, and tearing. The creature roared; Adair was almost to it. He could see its gleaming orange eyes, salvia dripping from its teeth.

Tadeas galloped past him, and Adair held his ground. It snapped.

He plunged, transporting, as he was suddenly in control of the monster's body, looking at himself, pale and bloodied in front of him. From this perspective, the world was a bleak place, no color, no light, only the bloodthirsty yearning for destruction. He willed the monster to stop, his sides heaving, as he took in the charging lines of the Academy. Nei led the assault, the ground churning from her anger; Brokk shifting back into his wolf form; Memphis and Emory running down the hill. And Marquis held back, staring at the creature, knowing that Adair had beaten them all to it.

Students spilled out, fire and ice, lightning and gas cracking to life as abilities readied.

*"You will not kill me; we are of the same..."*

Adair made the killing blow with his ability, shutting down every major organ, every nerve, every vein, obliterating it until he was slammed into his own body once more.

The monster dropped dead at his feet.

Loosening a breath, the world tilted, and he slowly turned. Everyone had stopped, staring at him with wide eyes. The world tilted, and he collapsed, losing himself into nothingness, whispers chasing him away from the light. Purring and coaxing him into the darkness.

# CHAPTER TWELVE

## Brokk

"Now who can tell me the practical uses for these plants? Mr. Foster?"

Brokk came to attention, Nei looking at him with soft eyes, the rest of the classroom seemingly half asleep. Two days had passed since they had come back to the Academy. Everything— and yet nothing—had changed.

Clearing his throat, he said, "If they are boiled, the steam becomes airborne poison."

Wyatt chuckled from the back far corner. "Maybe we should gather up the lot and use it against Stratton's dad."

Laughter rippled, as Nei quieted the room, "That is quite enough. You know the rules, everyone. Let's stay on task." She nodded then, saying, "Yes, Brokk, you are correct." She continued to drone on about how to counteract and heal themselves against this gas, but Brokk lost interest.

Shifting in his seat, he angled his body slightly and looked out of the corner of his eye to where Adair stared out the window, looking gaunt with dark circles imprinted underneath his eyes. He was a world away from them, from this classroom.

Brokk ripped his gaze back, staring blankly at the notes in front of him. He was still in shock when Roque ordered classes to resume until the funeral tomorrow. And that after, Stratton had a bloody *reception* scheduled. To award his bravery against the dabarne that he had killed.

He gripped the desk's edge, trying not to break it in half. The school was on lockdown; no one could go anywhere without

# HEIR OF LIES – PART ONE

supervision, and absolutely no one could go outside. Emory assured him it was the best thing to do in a time of crisis, but Brokk wasn't so sure. Going through empty actions while the Faes and Tadeas were locked away scrambling over how to deal with the situation at hand felt pointless.

The bell tolled lazily as everyone jumped to life around him, practically running out of the classroom. Quietly collecting his books, Brokk groaned as he stood, his joints popping and cracking viciously. A gentle tug across his mind made his eyes widen. Again, it was small at first, but then Memphis's voice rattled against the walls of his consciousness. *"I need you here. Quick."*

Trying to act normal, Brokk gave Nei a weak smile before following his classmates out, a lot of them in pairs, their discussions low and intense. A lot of friends had been lost. A lot of people Brokk had grown up with, in an instant, they had become a memory.

*"Where are you?"* Brokk made the thought concrete, knowing his friend would hear him.

Images flew through his mind instantly, and without hesitation, Brokk quickly complied, his feet carrying him to the small library he had visited countless times. He quickly slipped in the room, shutting the door behind him to find Memphis was bouncing on his heels, looking at him with wild eyes.

"Memph, are you okay?"

Shaking his head, his smooth voice filled his mind once more, *"No. Quick. Just trust me."*

Brokk froze, unsure of what his friend wanted him to do. Pinching the bridge of his nose, Memphis swore low under his breath, starting to pace.

"Memphis, what is happening?"

Stopping, Memphis looked at him, his eyes out of focus. He was listening in on another conversation. Memphis grabbed his arm and closed his eyes. Brokk felt a strong ringing fill his senses

141

and then he was succumbed, Memphis projecting what he was hearing like their own private intercom.

"Are you threatening us?" Roque's voice was low and dangerous.

A man laughed, cold and unyielding. "On the contrary. I have come today to warn you that your efforts will be pointless. What is left of the capital to accept your new title? My clan has seen Sarthaven, and it is full of creatures from your worst nightmares, breeding in the shadows and ripping every soul apart. Except Cesan and his company. We barely made it here safely. So, I have come today on our way back to the Risco Desert to tell the one thing I do know. He is preparing to march on you, Roque, with an army not seen before by men."

Silence fell heavy, and Tadeas whispered, "I have to go back to the Isles. I didn't come here to die."

"You will leave us in our time of need?"

Tadeas seethed. "I have lost some of my best men on the efforts of this allegiance. How many more? Me? My son? What will become of the Isles then, with no one to rule it?"

Roque slammed his fist onto the table. "What will become of Kiero if you leave? Please, Tadeas." The desperation made his voice crack.

Sighing, Tadeas gruffly asked, "What can we do against an impossible army? How do we beat it?"

The raider chuckled. "That is for you to figure out. Maybe it's time to consult some of our own myths long forgotten by the likes of you. Maybe the only way to win this war is to consult magic."

Tadeas laughed. "Magic? You've got to be kidding me?"

But Roque paused, and the raider implored, "The King of Kiero seems to know what I am talking about. But work swiftly. You might have days."

Brokk almost threw up as Memphis severed the connection, and they were thrown back into the present. Memphis rubbed his temples, breathing deeply, and Brokk knew his friend was barely holding on to his control.

"Memphis, what is *happening*?" Brokk repeated.

Memphis followed his agitated movements as he whispered, "There are no desolates that survived. Brokk, my parents..." His voice broke, and he stopped, just as Memphis's face crumpled.

He crossed the space in two strides, bringing his best friend into a tight hug. "I know. I'm so sorry. I'm so sorry."

He kept his voice soft, and Memphis completely broke down, the loss of their world crumpling down around them all. It would seem Cesan was making sure it would be a fight of might against might.

Minutes passed until they finally broke apart, and Memphis asked, "What *can* we do?"

Running a hand through his hair, Brokk weighed the situation. "Right now, I say we make it through the funeral. After that, we can start digging."

"And if we don't have enough time?"

Brokk looked his friend square in the eyes. "Then we fight for what we believe in. If that's still the Academy, then we do what we can."

A heavy silence settled in between them, and Memphis groaned. "I hate it when you're right."

"I know." He smirked, clapping him on the back. "Now, come on. Don't we have the same class next?"

Brokk turned and stalled, his gaze lingering on a worn black book. Dried blood stained the pages, and it looked like it had been shoved back into place.

"And what are you doing here?" He grabbed the book, the worn title staring back up at him, *Myths of Kiero*.

Intrigued, he flipped open the old pages, the book naturally falling open to a worn page, and as Brokk read, his eyes widened with every word. Looking up at Memphis, he whispered, "I think I found our first lead."

Memphis walked over, peering over his shoulder. He soaked up every word, and when he was finished, he whispered, "Do you think it's true?"

Brokk smiled wolfishly. "There is only one way to find out. Meet me in my room tonight at midnight."

The corners of Memphis's mouth turned down. "What about the lockdown?"

Brokk winked. "You truly think I haven't discovered an alternate route by now? Just be there."

Filing out, Brokk tucked away the old book with the rest of his things, adrenaline thrumming through his veins. They walked through the bustling hallway, toward an afternoon of listening to Professor Smet drone on about the history of Kiero and the trading routes developed over the years. Which to say was pertinent, seeing as their trading partners were the Shattered Isles.

Looking at Memphis, Brokk's heart sank. He had never had a family to lose, except him and Emory. He had fantasized about what his parents would be like, look like, but they were never a physical thing he *had*.

Memphis's skin was ashen, his bloodshot eyes squinting against the bustle of the Academy. Every step was too quick, every movement jerky. Brokk didn't know what he could possibly say that would make this situation easier. So, he said nothing at all, as they navigated the hallway.

The ringing of the bell sounded, and Brokk scooped up his books. All hour, his mind had been at war, a constant battle of trying not to think too much of the losses that have torn open their country. If Cesan was openly killing and slaughtering desolates and anyone who refused to join his cause... Cold fury twisted in his gut.

Not to mention his upcoming plan to sneak out of the Academy when they had just managed to escape a battle a few days prior. Every turn, every waking moment, all he saw was bloodied bodies and monsters. Pain waited for him in his heart and mind.

# HEIR OF LIES – PART ONE

Nodding to Memphis, the unspoken promise lingering between them, Brokk wouldn't give himself a moment to think about the horrors they had all recently endured. His feet carried him out of the classroom, navigating the hall with ease. Classmates nodded to him as he passed, a hero's stamp branded on him, Memphis, and Alby ever since they had returned from the Battle of Nightmares—or so he was told that's what people were calling it.

Sighing, he turned the corner, dappled light filtering into the building making the interior seem softer—more welcoming—than it ever was. Swallowing, he rapped on the door, trying to still his heart when it swung open.

Emory blinked up at him. "Brokk? What's up?"

Darkness lined her eyes, her skin dull and pale, her ebony hair pulled in a messy bun.

"Hey, Em. I was wondering if you would be up for a walk?"

Questions hung in her emerald gaze as she appraised him. "Sure. Give me a second."

The door clicked shut as internally he kicked himself. Did she wish Memphis had been on the other side when she opened it? Maybe his best friend had already sought her out, finding his own reprieve from what they had gone through.

Exhaling, the door opened once more, Emory adorned in a black collared jacket and high leather boots. A jeweled knife was buckled around her hip.

"Where were you thinking?" she asked.

"I need to talk to you. Come on."

Before he could think this was a terrible idea, he grabbed her hand, warmth traveling up his arm, as he led her outside. The sun welcomed them; the warm breeze unseasonably warm for the end of summer. Drinking it in, Brokk let go of Emory's hand, trying to keep his voice level. "Up for a trip in the woods?"

"Brokk, we can't. Whatever you have to say to me, you're going to have to do it here." She shrugged.

"And when did you start caring about the rules?"

"When people started dying." Her tone was equally as icy, and he shook his head.

"This was a bad idea. Sorry to bug you, *princess*." His words were hostile.

Emory stepped back. "Do you have a problem with me now, Brokk? Whatever it is, get it off your chest."

Standing in the courtyard, there were so many things he wanted to say. That he was sorry for not telling her the truth about the secret he carried. That he wished everything could go back to normal between them.

Tension hung heavy, like a live wire.

But most of all, he wished he could tell her about his darkest secret. That deep in the night, his heart revealed his greatest wish these past years.

And it was her—had always been *her*. To taste her lips, hold her against his chest, feel her heart beat in time with his own. He was unconditionally in love with her, and for a fleeting moment he had the impulse to tell her everything. But now, being with her, his best friends face swam in his mind  the fear of losing Memphis made him bite back every word.

Shooting fear clambered through him as Emory pointedly looked at him, daggers in her eyes.

"Just forget it." Gruffly, Brokk dropped his books, shifted in one motion, and galloped toward the trees, blood pounding, heart roaring. The coolness of the forest washed over him, as he tried to empty his mind, not looking back at Emory once.

# HEIR OF LIES – PART ONE

# CHAPTER THIRTEEN

## Adair

Sitting in his bedroom, Adair realized the days had little meaning anymore. Ever since arriving back at the Academy, he felt hollowed out. Every second, every breath, his heart sank a little deeper, his thoughts consumed by one thing. His obsession.

To find this Book of Old.

After he had killed the creature from Sarthaven and passed out, Roque and Nei had moved him so that he awoke in their office, bloodied and bruised, but there with them. Their pale faces stared at him, filled with fear and awe. Adair clenched his fists, remembering the discussion. How they were so *proud* that he was standing up with the Academy even though both of his parents...

He had blocked out most of the conversation after that. But sitting there, as they bantered on, the room around him seemed to bend and move like the ocean until Adair was staring at one fixture in the wall. It seemed to pulse, a strange glow seeping around the edges, a deep green. The mist spiraled and churned toward him, making his pulse thrum.

Blinking, he was entranced but pulled himself back to the conversation. He had nodded and thanked them graciously, saying that he was honored to be a part of this with them. How, of course, he had thought his parents were wrong. Reassured, he had left them, claiming he needed rest and had made his escape.

The first thing he did before heading back to his room was to get rid of the book that had led him to Gortach. The Faes wouldn't be looking for it, especially in the common library. If he was honest with himself, he didn't care who found it, it would only lead them to their death.

A day had passed since this, and he could practically hear the chilling whispers of those demons that haunted him endlessly from his nightmares. They clambered to him through the walls of the Academy, relentless.

"Find me. Find me."

Through his classes, through the night, they called to him. He went through the mandatory day, floating through his classes, his mind constantly calculating how he would get back into the Faes' office. How he would claw and tear through the walls, destroying and consuming everything until he found it. He could practically taste that same ancient magic oozing through the walls, and he *wanted* it.

Adair blinked, looking at himself in the mirror. His bedroom was more chaotic than usual, books and clothes littering the floor. His skin was deathly pale, bruises flowering almost every inch of his skin, dark circles underneath his eyes. Taking in a shaky breath, he started to unbutton his loose shirt. A dull pain throbbed along his chest, a constant reminder of what had happened ever since those monsters had touched him in his nightmares.

One came loose. And then another. Slowly, he made his way down the line until the shirt floated to his sides, and his breath hitched.

At his heart's center, a circle the size of his palm had risen to the surface of his skin. The inky blackness moved with each heartbeat, and tendrils spread across his skin. His throat burned as he grappled at his skin.

What was reality and what was nightmare? The two bled and blended together without any recognition until he didn't know what to believe anymore.

He swiped his hand across his chest, as if the movement would clear the blackness from his skin. Sweat dripped down his nose and his eyes flicked to the back of the door. Licking his cracked lips, he buttoned up his shirt.

# Heir of Lies – Part One

He wouldn't wait any longer.

Crossing the room, he slipped out, the door closing behind him. The Academy was still, curfew having already passed. A shiver rippled across his skin when he heard the light footfalls of the security patrolling the hallways. Looking to the right, at the end of the hallway, a dull green light caught his eye. It seemed to ooze from the interior of the walls. The corners of his lips turned up in a sly smile, and he took a step toward the light. The light blazed, cutting into his senses.

Weaving deeper into the Academy, Adair followed the light, his blood pounding in exhilaration as he let every other thought go. He had only one purpose, to find this Book of Old and be the undoing of Roque and Nei Fae.

Moving with stealth, Adair slipped into the shadows.

# Chapter Fourteen

## Brokk

Slipping the worn book into his bag, Brokk tightened the straps on his backpack. Donning his jacket, he asked, "Ready?"

Memphis nodded once. They wore practically matching outfits, which was their training gear. Lightweight and water resistant, the jacket and pants were a matte black material. Perfect to blend in with the night.

Nodding, Brokk took in a deep breathe before slamming his fist into his bedroom wall. Call it paranoia—he didn't care. In the recent years, he had secretly constructed his way out.

Emory had told him how complex the Academy was, and Brokk had tapped into its hidden passageways. He covered his mouth, muffling his cough as concrete dust floated up to him, his broken bones in his hands healing swiftly.

Before them, a dark spiraling tunnel was splayed before them, diving down into the darkness. Cool air rushed up to meet them, filled with the lingering smell of damp earth and rain.

Raising a pale eyebrow, Memphis appraised him.

Ducking into the tunnel, Brokk's voice echoed. "You know you can tell me every once in a while that I am right."

"Oh, is that so?" Memphis quipped.

They started their walk, the dampness and darkness overtaking everything. Slowly, the room faded away, along with the Academy.

Brokk's fingers trailed the walls, the weathered planks supporting the roof and sides from caving in. It had been a semiformed tunnel, one that he had spent endless sleepless nights carving out. Working through his frustrations, his fears, his dreams. Holding those feelings close and heavy to his heart for years, Brokk had come to a realization: the men who ran the Academy were controlled by one factor - *greed*.

Brokk's voice was absorbed into the density of the tunnel, just barely a whisper, "Have you ever seen the rest of Kiero?"

He could feel Memphis tense behind him. "No. Not since I came here."

"Do you ever wonder why we are trapped here?"

His footfalls thudded behind him. A beat passed. And then another.

"Sometimes, I wonder if being trapped is an illusion. We could leave any day, but out there, in the world, I think in some aspects of it, we will always be trapped. Trapped in judgements and preconceived ideas of what happens at the Academy. Of who we are. People are afraid of the power we have; some see us as weapons. Cesan has just proven that point by destroying the capital, so the dream of the Academy hosting Kiero's golden warriors is gone. Fear traps people, and there is no escaping that," Memphis responded.

Brokk chewed his lower lip. "But that wasn't our fault,"

"No? If the Academy didn't exist, where would we be now?"

Brokk snapped, "That sounds like a declaration of someone who is giving up. I'm not saying that the foundation is wrong. I'm saying that it's up to us to find out exactly what the intentions are now."

"I'm not giving up," Memphis said to Brokk's back.

Smiling softly, Brokk replied, "There's my stubborn friend."

Continuing their climb, the moldy tunnel twisted softly and gradually. Brokk shifted his pack, his mind wandering with the possibilities.

"I remember the sea," Memphis whispered suddenly.

Brokk stumbled but didn't say anything. They didn't talk about their past much.

"I remember the smell and the salt crusting on my skin. How the waves looked during a storm. How they looked when the sea was still, like glass. My dad and mom ran a small bakery on the outskirts of our town. I remember walking along the shoreline and thinking that there was nowhere else that I ever wanted to be. Even though I was young, I understood that much." Memphis paused before continuing, "I feel like every word they threw at me that day is true. That I am a monster. That we are all monsters. That this school is just breeding madness to be a sharpened weapon, and now, it's unleashed upon the world."

Brokk stopped, turning to face his friend. "We are *not* the monsters. Cesan and his beliefs...he is the one proving your parents' accusations true. But he doesn't define us."

Memphis started walking, brushing by him. "What? We're suddenly the renegades? The dashing underdogs?"

Rolling his eyes, Brokk followed. "No, you prick. We are just utilizing our freewill of investigation. To find out exactly what is worth fighting for now."

That got a true chuckle from Memphis, and he said, "I hope you're right about this."

"That's the beauty of life, my friend, you will never know until you try, if it's right or not."

The ground started to elevate, coming to a small opening. Smiling wolfishly, Brokk slid ahead of Memphis, finding the worn handholds. Using his upper arms, he lifted himself up, scaling the rickety ladder with ease. One final lift and he pushed his shoulder through a rotting door, and moonlight greeted them.

Spilling out onto the grass, he helped Memphis up, and they were consumed.

The cool night breeze brushed against their skin, and Brokk took in the forest surrounding them. During the day, the forest was ordinary, bustling with life. But in these moments with dappling moonlight painting definition and obscure shadow, he believed that anything was possible. That maybe Stratton had found something about their world that had been long forgotten, hidden in darkness.

By the art of deduction, Brokk knew Stratton had placed the book there. On Gortach's chapter, the old paper was blood stained and weathered, old notes scribbled in the side from years ago, initialed A.S.

Looking to the east, Brokk inhaled deeply, raising his eyebrow at Memphis. "Ready?"

"Lead the way."

They started walking, heading for the heart of the woods. Whatever lay ahead, they had until dawn to find their answers.

The hours slipped by into the still night, and the moon climbed higher into the sky, illuminating their way. Sweat trickled down Brokk's temple, and he whispered, "Okay, so according to this, to access the seer's gateway, we present it with the blood of the questioner."

Memphis paled, looking to him.

Steeling himself, Brokk flipped open a small knife from his jacket pocket. "Right," he mumbled more to himself than Memphis.

Sucking in a breath, he stared at the blade's edge. The sharpness of the weapon winked back at him, almost mockingly.

*One. Two. Three...*

It bit in hard, splitting his flesh. Blood welled and pooled as he hissed through his teeth as it dripped to the ground. The ground shuddered beneath them, and his blood absorbed into the earth.

Jumping back in surprise, they watched the trees bow before them, forming an intricate gateway, a blood red ruby adorned on top.

"It actually worked!" Memphis's voice sounded distant and in shock.

The archway ground to a stop, and Brokk blinked hard, making sure he was seeing things correctly. Where a doorway should have been, the space remained empty, and singed edges revealed a cavernous room. The floor was jet black, and an odd ember floated a few yards in front of them, flaring with fiery hues before winking out.

"It seems Adair didn't disappoint me." The voice was deep and ancient, a dead calm making each word ripple with malice. Squinting into the darkness, Brokk saw nothing until two luminous silver eyes appeared, glaring back at them.

In his panic, everything seemingly slowed. Memphis lunged to his right, scrambling for his sword. The ground shook with the sheer force of the predator's weight as it charged them. Ice gripped Brokk's senses, and he was frozen, watching this creature emerge from the shadows.

"BROKK!"

Cursing, he dropped his pack, shifting in one motion. Only to see exactly what Gortach was. In this form, his heightened senses picked up what his human ones couldn't. Everything was sharper to him in the night, maybe that's part of the reason he preferred it to the daytime.

He took in Gortach's sickly body, its strong and multiple limbs propelling it forward. Brokk noticed its rotting skin flying off in chunks as it ran. Snapping its razor-sharp teeth, Brokk recoiled from the smell that collided into him—the stench of death.

Howling, Brokk charged toward Memphis, and his friend ran, swinging himself onto his back as they took off into the night, maneuvering through the trees faster than Brokk thought possible. A roar sounded behind them, followed by the thunderous crack of splitting trees as the ancient creature tore after them.

"What did we do?!" Memphis yelled. Brokk could taste both of their fear as the same question coursed through him. Leaping over a fallen tree, the earth quaked, throwing his weight forward. Growling, he didn't stop, fear flickering so many thoughts all at once but one seared through him.

# HEIR OF LIES – PART ONE

*Adair.*

Snapping his teeth, he swiveled hard to the left, and Gortach suddenly appeared by their side. It lunged, missing them only by a hair width.

"It stopped!" Memphis shouted and twisted, looking behind him.

Flattening his ears flush against his skull, Brokk heard a ripple vibrate through the air. And the forest went completely and utterly still.

One howl sliced through the night. Then another. And another.

His paws pounded against the forest floor, his nails digging into the earth and ripping away from it. A cold whipping wind suddenly battered against them, thick snowflakes sweeping through the trees.

Ducking, he couldn't stop.

They had sought the truth and had unlocked another war just waiting for them. Snowflakes, dense and unyielding, continued to drop from the sky in masses, like diamonds.

"Snow? It's the end of summer." Memphis blinked against the magnitude of melting flakes hitting his skin. His hackles stood on end as Brokk heard the sound of footfalls from behind them. In his wolf form, he could feel the shudder of the earth, as whatever came for them drew closer.

Tree trunks started to crystalize and freeze around them as the temperature started to drop. The once earthy bark became smooth and encased, the glimmering surface blending in with the storm that transformed the night in a harsh winter landscape before their eyes. Everything around them became white. Brokk sniffed as deeply as he could, trying to pick up their scents to make sure they weren't heading in a circle, going in the wrong direction.

He was met with nothing but the frozen tang of winter.

Slamming to a stop, he threw Memphis off, shifting back in a single motion.

"I've lost our scents. Also, that monster has unleashed an army behind us."

*Shit.*

Memphis was immediately at his side. "We have to keep going, Brokk. Come. On."

He took a step back, readying to shift again, but a solid sheet of ice formed in front of them, thick and impermeable. Brokk slammed to a stop, and the boys watched as the wall of ice flowed all around them, closing them in and reflecting their shocked faces back at them, distorted and gleaming.

His breath was ravaged, but Brokk already had the knife palmed in his hand, as he and Memphis came into a defensive stance, their backs flush to one another. The wind howled viciously, and Brokk shivered, his breath coming in puffs in front of him. The moonlight reflected off the snow-covered forest floor, illuminating the definition of the landscape more.

Nothing stirred.

His palms were so clammy, they turned stiff and frozen from the dropping temperatures. But there, to his right, was a flicker of movement, and Brokk bared his teeth.

From the night, Bresslin Stratton materialized. Her skin was pale, her hair drawn back. Locking her gaze on them, she smiled softly, her eyes empty. Gortach appeared by her side, as well as the sound of hundreds of scraping claws and silver eyes staring back at them.

Brokk's hand started to tremble as Bresslin stepped forward, unsheathing a monstrous sword, the edge dipping in toward the middle of the blade, creating twelve wicked looking teeth along its edge. His mind unraveled the history from their weapons class: The Curse, it was called. A blade embodied with unbreakable teeth, while also capturing the opponent's blade, destroying it.

The snow crunched under her leather boots. "Well, boys, it seems we find ourselves at a crossroad."

# HEIR OF LIES – PART ONE

The rumbling snickers of her army sounded all around them. Memphis tensed against him, and Brokk clenched his teeth so hard the pressure was overwhelming.

Bresslin raised an eyebrow in mock shock. "Oh, nothing to say? No words of great chivalry? I'm slightly disappointed."

The snickers transformed into full blown animalistic chortles, and Brokk's cheeks flushed.

Behind Bresslin, Gortach rumbled, "Why not start with the shifter? He drew his blood and unleashed me. We owe him our deep gratitude."

"Is that so?" Bresslin assessed Brokk, and he wanted to fade away underneath her stare. Jutting his chin out, his lips pressed in a thin line.

"Well, it does seem to be our lucky day. I assume this is yours too?" She held up his worn pack, and in her grip, the book, Myths of Kiero, was clear to see. Brokk swallowed hard. Bresslin's lips split, showing her gleaming teeth in a pointed grin. "Oh, do we *ever* have much to talk about."

Sauntering toward them, the ice thickened, and the snow howled until all they could see was her cunning smile. Her voice drifted on the wind, "The Academy is done. It's time for you to decide which side you stand on."

"We are with the Faes." The words erupted from Brokk almost like a guttural growl, and Memphis shifted uneasy behind him.

"Really?" Bresslin appeared in front of them, and Gortach trailed behind her. Their reflections flashed in the flush metal, wide eyed.

"And here I was, willing to give you two a break to join our ranks, even given your status." Chortling, Bresslin moved closer. "You see, *boys*, I think it's very unfair that such power can be born from nothing. Especially you, Carter. Weren't both of your parents desolates outside the capital? I dare say we took care of them."

*No.*

Brokk watched as those vicious words crumpled his best friend, fracturing his control. Memphis lunged, screaming, "What did you do?"

The edge of the sword dug into Brokk's throat faster than he could register. Bresslin tutted, her breath hot against Brokk's cheek as Gortach lunged to Memphis, his long fingers closing around his throat, pinning Memphis to the ground. His choked screams bounced off the ice around them.

"Don't move another muscle, if you want your friend to live," Bresslin demanded.

The blade pressed harder, and swallowing, he felt the small incision cut and heal, cut and heal. His hands trembled, and blood trickled down his skin. Gortach froze, and Memphis drove his foot into Gortach's stomach. Breaking free Memphis rolled, ice slicing through his clothes. Brokk watched Gortach's gaze narrowing. Brokk knew Memphis was throwing every ounce of his ability into the fight, but it wasn't enough.

Roaring, the ancient creature charged and slammed into Memphis. He instantly crumpled onto the ground.

Memphis's scream tore through Brokk just as Bresslin's fist connected with his gut. Wheezing, he doubled over, and she followed, whispering into his ear, "This is just a taste of what is coming."

She slammed the pommel into his temple. Dropping to his knees, dots dancing in his vision, ice tore through his pants, skinning his knees.

The blade caressed his cheek, trailing down his chest. Memphis was screaming, the sounds like a dying animal.

Bresslin smirked. "This seems like a good place to start."

Blade met blood, and pain encompassed his world until it was all he knew, all he could taste and breathe. And he lost himself in it.

### HEIR OF LIES – PART ONE

# CHAPTER FIFTEEN

### Adair

There was something strange hanging in the air. A shimmering, tangible energy that quaked the ground with each step he took, each breath, every longing glance behind him. The tang of magic and promise clung heavy around him, making him tremble with anticipation.

Adair would no longer hide.

Sweat slid down his nose as he peered around the corner. The hallways were empty, and he had avoided all contact with the patrols so far.

At the end of the hallway, the smooth oak doors of the Faes' office stared back at him, that light seducing him, gliding around the frame of the doorway, curling and unfurling with an elegant grace.

Stepping forward, he heard his soft footfalls, his breath catching as he closed the space in strides.

"Adair?"

Emory appeared behind him, stepping out of the shadows, worry etched into her every feature. She wore a loose green shirt and fitted pants. Every day that passed, they were both growing into the people that could carve the world. She stepped closer. "What are you doing?" Every word was pronounced.

He faced her, feeling his lips turn up slowly. She blanched, stopping as she took him in, sensing that something was different.

"Why, Princess, you shouldn't grace me with such a late visit." His voice sounded alien, even to himself. Smooth, silken, and full of mockery. Her face darkened, and she stood taller, as she strode closer, striking him fiercely across the cheek.

"Listen, whatever you're going through, whatever this *is*, just talk to me, Adair. This isn't you. I want my best friend back. I *need* him back. *Please.*" Her chin wobbled, her eyes brimming, and she reached out to take his hand. "I know what the other students say. I know what you have heard. You aren't like your father, Adair. You are so much *more.*"

He stalled, tilting his head, searching every detail of her face, noticing the tears streaming down her cheeks. Running a hand through his hair, he whispered, "You're right."

He stepped closer, and she radiated light. "I am more." He felt that power stir in him. "You could have been as well."

Fear sparked in her eyes as every ounce of her blood drained from her face, and she lunged at him, trying to latch on, to drain him of his ability. He had always been faster. Emory crumpled as he slashed through her defenses, shutting them down and knocking her unconscious. Gently lowering her body, licking his cracked lips, he whispered down to her still form, "I'm sorry."

Adair continued down the hallway, leaving her behind. The light flared and exploded, like thousands of his own personal constellations, the smooth edges of the captured light forming hundreds of orbs, glistening like polished emeralds. It stole his breath away when they parted, forming his own personal walkway, and as he passed, they ebbed, dying slowly. His heart was pounding, and he could practically feel the heaviness seeping through his bloodstream, curdling him until he was only the darkness trapped within him; that had marked him.

Reaching the heavy doorway, he turned the handle. It swept inward seamlessly. Roque looked up, startled and wide-eyed, as he looked at Adair, bewildered.

Shutting the door quickly behind him, Adair didn't miss a beat. "Sorry for the interruption, Your *Highness*. I was hoping we could talk?"

# HEIR OF LIES – PART ONE

Sighing, Roque murmured, "Please, Adair, come in. And don't worry about the titles. I doubt by this point there is much of a country left that will recognize me as their *highness*."

His adrenaline stirred, and he took a seat, trying not to stare at the pulsing wall behind Roque, practically screaming out to Adair. "Oh, really?"

Roque barely heard him, his focus on the map laid before him. His eyes roamed frantically, as he whispered to himself, "We need more time to reunite the borders with the Risco Desert and the raiders there before heading into another war. The North is our only ally with Sarthaven fallen."

Adair swallowed hard, feeling that familiar tug of his ability climbing through him. "My father won't grant any more time than what we have already had."

Roque raised his gaze, squinting at Adair. He smiled, his voice surprisingly soft as he said, "The time to act is *now*."

A hunger engulfed Adair so fiercely he didn't have time to act before his ability shattered through him. Gripping Roque's forearm, the King of Kiero was frozen, his mouth gaping noiselessly as Adair rampaged everything he was. He had always imagined what breaking into a desolate's body would be like. It was a sick fascination he had. His ability was what made him feel strong first and his character followed.

As his grip tightened and his talons ripped and shredded through Roque's memories, it was like *he* was the siren, and Roque was sailing toward his deadly rocky shore, frozen and entranced.

Years flickered through his mind, bright and sharp. He shifted quickly until Adair found what he was looking for. The memory lurched through him.

*Nei clutched his arm as he slammed the hammer into the concrete and brick wall, "Roque, can you just listen to me for a second?"*

*Roque paused, thrusting the weathered book into her grasp. "What is there to talk about, Nei? I should have never made this secret society in the first place. I thought I was protecting Kiero in keeping the secret that there are other worlds connected to ours. I thought I was ensuring peace by creating the Original Six, by meeting with each world leader to negotiate politics. Now, I have helped create the one thing that could end us all."*

*She tenderly rested her hand on his arm. "We cannot have it here. The world of Daer has betrayed us. This time, we must do something. Instead of hiding the artifact, let's destroy it."*

*Roque choked out a laugh. "How, Nei, do we begin to explain that Damien Foster has made treaties of peace with these worlds under our command? It sounds insane. Illegal, and insane."*

*She rebuttaled, "The world is defined by a lot of things: Magic. Power. Love. Status. But it is the people who shape it. It once sounded insane for me to marry a pompous prince who I thought knew nothing about sacrifice. You proved me wrong. Now do the same for me. Prove that you aren't acting out of fear."*

*His hands shook, stalling, then he looked up; his eyes filled with sorrow. "No. It will stay here, hidden until the time is right. No one will know. Not even Cesan and Bresslin."*

*Nei's face darkened, her light demeanor vanishing. Her lips pressed into a thin line, and she said nothing as the wall crumpled, and Roque started burying the book within the walls.*

Adair was slammed back into the present, staring at Roque Fae. Heat flushed over his entire body as his grip tightened. "What did you *do*?" Roque paled as Adair pinned his ability sharper and deep. His pulse raced faster and faster as he demanded, "What is in the book?"

"I don't know what you're talking about," Roque rasped, his lips starting to turn blue, his skin greying with every second.

"I highly doubt that," Adair said, then slipped from his body.

When he used his ability, usually it was like circling around the consciousness before assessing his obstacles, and then he would land the blows where he wanted. This was striking with his will, and he gripped every nerve, every ounce of the king's physical anatomy until he commanded every ounce of it.

# HEIR OF LIES – PART ONE

It was like snuffing out a candle, backing the other soul into a corner and keeping it in check. They moved as one toward the wall, and looking through Roque's eyes, he could see the light calling them. Calling *him*. He moved, Roque's memories telling him that it was surrounded by magic, shielded by it. It was created by the professors, and out of their loyalty, no questions came. They moved, and the wall transformed for the only person it would.

Roque.

Gold infused pillars appeared before them like smoke, shimmering but not fully solid. Not fully real. In between them, a small shelf was created, and an ordinary weathered book lay in the middle.

They stepped closer, and inky words sprawled in the air before them, appearing from nothing.

"I can be fickle, yet strong.

Attained, yet used,

Desired, yet shunned.

What am I?"

Pausing, Adair impatiently read through the riddle. Shifting through memories, he knew if he answered wrong the consequences would be dire. Roque fought against him, his feeble attacks laughable, and Adair sunk him deeper in the folds of his ability. As that darkness tightened around him, drowning them both, the answer became clear, and Roque faded into nothing.

Smiling, Adair still controlling Roques body, whispered, "I am the truth."

The words disappeared at his deep voice, melting and dripping away any shield, laying the book bare before him. The light disappeared, the essence that had drawn him forward, whisking away with the gold pillars in a cloud of sparkling mist.

"*Adair,*" those familiar and icy whispers sounded.

Excitement trickled into his stomach.

"*Adair.*"

Reaching for it, Roque's hand shook. The voices cooed, wrapping around him, comforting yet still foreign. The world vanished behind him, and he barely breathed as he picked it up.

The front cover flipped open, the pages flailing wildly in an unseen wind. Smoke stirred only the spine and started to ooze out of the book, circling him. Breathing heavily, Adair watched as his veins and skin were drenched in the same smoke, one trailing after the other, a cosmic pull. Uncontrollable and undeniable.

The power of the book collided with them, and the world exploded.

Shards of smoke flattened and crystalized into pools of black shimmering mirrors that made up his surroundings, as he freefell through space and time. Capturing glances, his reflection showed him in his true body, his jacket flapping wildly and his unkept hair. Choking back his screams, he fought gravity, plummeting faster, his eyes burning from the wind.

Deeper and deeper, he fell, his hands grappling for *anything* to hold on to. To stop. Faster and faster, he was pulled, the mirrors intensifying around him. Distorted flashes of himself were splayed in them, his wide eyes and mouth open.

But then in the darkness, those pale faces and sickening smiles reflected at him, so fast he barely thought he saw them correctly. But all around him, captured in the flawless surfaces, those creatures that haunted his waking moments followed him down into the darkness.

Gritting his teeth together, he pressed his eyes closed, tears seeping from his lids as he plummeted. The wind howled all around him, and sharp giggles tainted them, making a sick orchestra climbing and crashing around him. Always, they played just for him.

His breath wheezed out of him, his eyes flying open. Underneath him, the light curled around his body, weaving together likes vines, cradling him. Choking on his panic, a manic laugh bubbled from his lips. Patting his body down, he was in one piece.

# Heir of Lies — Part One

Beneath him, the light started to pulse once more, a soft and comforting heat flooding through him. On shaking legs, he stood slowly, and the light unfurled. Before his eyes, a beautiful and intricate staircase formed, leading him into the unknown of this place.

Magic hung heavy in the air, and Adair paused, looking up into the darkness. Back to where he had come from.

Straightening his jacket and popping his collar up, he breathed deeply, wrenching his gaze forward: to where a world of mystery and enchantment sparked to life before him.

The staircase had solidified, its curving rails inlaid with a deep green hue, the staircase itself, having bled out any color, turning it into a shimmering black. Embers floated around him, silver instead of fiery tones. They spun lazily through the air, creating the illusion of a starry sky, each constellation blinking into existence.

His steps echoed as he walked, slow and unsure.

"Adair Stratton, it is a pleasure to finally meet you." The voice was smooth and commanding, filling with promise.

"Who's there?" His voice was surprisingly steady, and he was thankful for that. Internally, he was quaking, the shards of his old self and life ripping away, fading.

Reaching the bottom, his boot hit the floor, and a hissing filled his senses. Twisting, particle by particle, the stairs dissolved, floating up to become one with the shadows around him. Swallowing hard, he forced his body to move forward.

"It is not so much *who*, but what." The voice shook through the marrow of his bones, steady and resilient.

"I've had enough of riddles for one day, thanks. Where am I?" His questions echoed, bouncing off walls unseen to him.

Instead of answering, before him the ground tilted, and he slipped down. Finding his balance, Adair steadied himself, his eyes adjusting to the pristine light emitting from the pool before him. The surface was so still, it looked like glass. Below, the water crystals made up the bottom of the pool, their defined edges emitting a dazzling display of colors: greens, golds, blues, reds, all sparkled up at him as he lowered himself onto his knees before its edge. He was enraptured.

"Come closer, to find your truth."

Complying, he leaned forward, blinking down at his reflection. Then, the water churned, plunging him into darkness as the crystals winked out. His breath came fast, and he couldn't rip himself away. Before him, in the swirling waters, a world formed that he didn't recognize.

Flames consumed everything, whisking away the capital, the Academy. Everything he had ever known was gone.

"Sometimes, Adair Stratton, we find ourselves at a crossroads unsure of which direction to take. I see your heart, and the fracture running through it. Of the fear, and hate, and desire. The world is spinning out of control, and it is time to find your purpose. Look closer."

The scene changed, the ashes clearing, and Adair blanched as he realized he was looking at himself as a man. A city made up of stone and light bustled around him, and people passed him radiating kindness and respect, bowing their heads, their murmurs igniting his heart. *"My King."*

The world before him exploded, showing a flourishing, rich place filled with discipline and trust. Because of him. *For him.* He hungrily drank every detail in before it faded into an inky blackness once more. He panted in the darkness, whispering, "Is this true?"

"This world can be yours and more, if you want to accept your fate. Claim what is yours, Adair. The Faes have hidden us out of fear of power. Your parents are blinded by rage." The voice paused. "But you, you are different from them all."

The crystals flared back to life, and Adair stared down at his hands, the inky swirls staining his skin; tainted by darkness. He curled his fingers, clenching them into tight fists as he whispered, "What would you have me do?"

"For a price, you will have access to unlimited power, unseen by this world. There will be forces working against you if you choose this, but together, we will be unstoppable."

Scrambling back, he watched the water begin to rise, forming the outline of a man.

"I have been locked away for centuries, waiting for the right person to come along. I was sealed in this book, my wielders wanting to poison this world, wanting to destroy it. They are using all the forces they can raise to work against me." The crystals flared brighter. "I wish to purge this world, not destroy it. Cleanse it, and then allow it to flourish. For true magic to rise again."

Adair watched the water churn, and he shook his head. "How is this possible? You're *magic*?"

"Ancient, but essentially yes."

Gaping, he was speechless. From the shadows, giggles formed, and the four figures he was all too familiar with strode slowly toward the pool, gazing at him hungrily.

"And your friends here? Who are they?" he asked.

The water flickered, the form moving, gazing behind at the creatures.

The voice sighed. "These are echoes of my once masters. Bound within my magic, they are like ghosts. Unable to hurt you, but stubbornly present."

Their giggles crawled toward him, making him shiver. Rubbing his hands together, he realized that the inky smoke had started to churn on his skin.

"They marked me." Adair's voice was hollow as the magic rippled in the air, stirring.

"You and I, and even the essence of them, are all connected. There is no turning back now, Adair. Follow the path that we both know is true."

He stood, looking all around him in wonder. It was a flicker of recognition of that pull of gravity that had brought him here. The darkness that he always thought he should hide, that worked against him... Maybe he had been wrong all these years. Maybe the forces of this world had been leading him here. To this moment.

Air hissed between his teeth as he exhaled, and he murmured, "And the price?"

The shadows pressed in, the pool dimming, and the whispers closed in. It was laden with heaviness as the ancient voice replied, "Blood for blood. The price to access your power is to spill the blood of those who have hidden us here. You must destroy the Faes."

Ice ran through his veins at the lust in those words. Adair opened his mouth but then closed it tightly. A humming filled the air, and he could practically taste the endless possibilities. He stepped forward. "And how is this power worth it?"

Laughter echoed around him. "Anything you desire will be yours, Adair. Raise a city, raise an army. It will be endless. This book contains unlimited knowledge and unlimited resources and *power*. You will remake this world."

His hands trembled, and Gortach's previous warning clung to him. He took another tentative step. "And I will be king?"

"Yes."

Adair's cheeks flushed, the thrill surging through his stomach. He was so close to the pool. He stood taller, his mind racing, giving in to who he was...what he was, and always had been.

This time, he wouldn't bow to anyone else.

Without hesitation, he stepped down into the pool, the water sloshing. "I will do it. I will end them."

The light died at his words, and Adair dove into the cool water. Whispers exploded through his mind, unrelenting and sharp, as the water turned black.

*"You are ours, Adair. Ours."*

Pain shocked him. It felt like his bones were shattering and splintering, his stomach turning to molten. The taste of ash filled his mouth, and screams echoed around him. *Was that him screaming?*

# HEIR OF LIES – PART ONE

Being dragged deeper, an unseen current ripped at his clothes. Water clogged his senses, filing in through his nostrils, spilling in his mouth. His lungs burned, igniting, begging for oxygen. Dots danced in his vision, and he flailed, screaming, "Help me!"

No one answered.

He succumbed, stilling his body and mind to the pain, to his fear, and he leashed it. Water filled his lungs, choking him. Steadiness filled him, intoxication of power coursing through his soul. Onward, he was dragged down, the pressure popping his ear drums, until beneath him, the crystals flared a deep crimson red.

Roaring filled his senses, as the water started spinning and spinning, the cyclone raging against him. His body contorted, twisting and splitting, and he was pulled violently up, tearing through the water. For a moment, he was suspended in the air, choking and dragging in wet breaths.

Then, he crashed down.

Wind howled around him before he slammed onto hard sand, his ribs cracking. The water was gone, leaving a coolness in its wake. Coughing and sputtering, water spewed from his mouth as his lungs desperately took in oxygen. He was sodden, and shakily, he raised his head.

He was in a small, clear space, the wet sand hard beneath him. Fresh bruises had already started to form from the fall, and wheezing, he stood. All around him, the crystals radiated, bathing him in light. The ground beneath him shuddered, and he turned. Behind him, on the opposite edge of the pool, stood a shadow of the magic, the shadow's voice was laced with anticipation when it spoke.

"You and Adair, will be one."

The air trembled as the ancient magic roared around him. Panicking, Adair stumbled back as he watched as the shadow before him yawned, stretching wide, turning opaque. Adair couldn't move, his breath caught in his chest as he watched the gleaming crystals dim, turning black as night.

And then they exploded.

Flying back, his head and back cracked against the hard shards, nausea rocking through his body. Sticky warmth crept down the back of his neck. Cursing, he tried to sit up and was thrown back again by another shock wave, the shards of crystal turning to dust before his eyes, the particles clogging his throat, coating his skin.

"*Adair.*"

Gasping, he sat up; they were waiting for him. Those familiar pitiless eyes, the edges of shadows clawing toward his heart. Coughing, the iron taste of blood filled his mouth, oozing out of the corners of his lips. Pale hands grappled at his chest, his clothes, pushing him back and holding him still, their faces barely visible in the darkness. He watched in horror as that looming darkness stirred and shot forward, slamming into him. Inky dust particles bled and sank into his skin, in his mouth, into his soul.

And he was met with a pain he had never known before.

Screaming, he felt the tendons in his neck rip, his limbs flailing, fighting against the ancient force. Laughter rattled in his consciousness, and he was slammed back.

His body was flush to the wet sand, and he bared his teeth as the voice commanded, "Do not resist me."

Whimpering, his core was ignited into fire, and everything he knew shattered and all he knew was this. He watched as the magic of the Book bled into him, grain by grain, shadow by shadow, wriggling under his nails, rippling under his skin. He felt each pump of his heart battling against the rushing heat in his veins, pumping faster and faster and faster.

The magic splintered through his chest, and he roared in agony, bowing against his invisible restraints. Coos and whispers circled around his mind, filtering through every thought and every memory with hesitation, and he felt the stain of blackness seep into every single one of them. The darkness swept through him as quick as flames, the magic binding and securing itself deep within Adair. The world started to spin on its axis as gravity gave way once more, and he was falling again.

# Heir of Lies – Part One

His entire world had no rhyme or reason as the magic ravaged him, swelling and crashing repeatedly. The wind howled, and he was drowning in ash and malice that took over him. Centuries could have passed, or maybe it was just an illusion of the drawn-out seconds. His breath evened out from the wet rasps of his lungs to smooth fluid breaths. The heat within him dulled and cooled, leaving him hollow. His muscles, previously having been ripped, bruised, and bloodied were filled with newfound strength. His cracked skull and ribs knitted together and mended, the blood drying off his skin.

His eyes flew open, adjusting to the dull light around him instead of the midnight he had grown accustomed to. Lying on his back, the study was a newfound perspective, the bookcases and table coming into focus. And Roque, unconscious, was sprawled next to him.

"*The Book, Adair.*"

He stood, grabbing the worn leather from the floor, and a welcoming warmth spread through his fingers at the touch. Straightening his jacket, he caught his reflection on the mirror as he slid the book in his pocket. His skin was pale and drawn, but his eyes were pitch black, no definition, no dimension. Just empty. Crossing the room, he quietly stalked toward his reflection, every movement sharper to him.

The glass fogged with his breath as his gaze roamed, drinking in every ounce of him. Or *them*.

"*Finally.*"

Adair furrowed his brows at the strong voice settling within. Flexing his fingers, he brushed the glass, smearing the mist.

"*Finally.*"

Shaking his head, Adair pushed the magic back, wrenching his gaze away. He was in control. Crossing the room, he knelt by Roque's side. "Now. What should I do with you?"

"*Kill him.*"

His pulse purred with the calling, his bloodlust rearing its ugly head. Swallowing, Adair quickly formed a plan.

"*You promised us, Adair. Kill him.*"

This time, it was the voices from his nightmares, their sharp, chilling words shivering down his spine. He leaned in closer, his hands starting to shake. Roque's pulse was weak, his irregular heartbeats flickering against his jugular.

"*Do it now.*"

He breathed, "If I'm ending a kingdom, I want to do it smartly."

Looking up, the trace of dawn bled into the sky, washes of pinks and golds smearing across it in bold strokes. He rubbed his jaw. "The funeral is in a couple of hours. I need some answers first, and there is only one way to do that."

Looking down at Roque, Adair's plan slowly started to piece together. The dark magic pulsed in his blood, as the voices drawled, "*If you betray us....*"

Clenching his jaw, he whispered to himself, "I know. Just trust me."

"*Until Roque and Nei Fae are dead, the power will remain dormant.*"

Rolling his shoulders, he murmured, "That's exactly what I am hoping for."

Adair worked quickly and steadily, and by the time the sun crested the horizon, his plan was set in motion.

# HEIR OF LIES – PART ONE

# CHAPTER SIXTEEN

## Memphis

The sun blazed over the horizon, illuminating the world into clear brilliance. Sunlight kissed the forest, sharpening their landscape. Blood oozed slowly and thickly from Memphis's mouth, as his head hung limp, his hair unbound, staring at the ice encrusted ground. Each snowflake lying delicately on the ice, the swirls and twists of each, mesmerized him as he stared, pink slowly staining the peerless white. The cool weight of the silver handcuffs and choke collar dug into his bruised skin, and snippets of the night flashed through his mind.

Bresslin's fists connecting over and over with his flesh, breaking him. Brokk screaming in the distance, having been taken away by Gortach. The hours had blurred with his pain of what had happened.

His family, gone. Years of him dreaming of what he would say to them, what his parents would be like. Making the trip back to their cottage by the sea and forcing them to see he had changed. He had always been, and would always be, their *son*. And the hope of them becoming a family again was brushed away in the matter of a few words. In the matter of a war that his parents were defenseless against.

Tears slipped down his frozen skin, his breath coming in forced drags. Cutting pain rippled through him, making him wince. He was sure some ribs were broken.

"Well, well, I have to say. I am surprised of your resilience."

Lifting his head weakly, Bresslin stalked toward him, her hawk eyes cutting into him. Daggers flashed against her black leather pants and knee length boots. Her blood red cape flowed behind her, her armored chest glinting.

"I will *end* you," Memphis promised.

She smiled, flashing her brilliant teeth as the air churned behind her, the monsters and creatures born from darkness creeping behind and closing in on him.

Their yellow and orange eyes, their twisted long bodies, their blackened flesh and long snouts. Some had wings; some were as tall as trees. Some had fangs that jutted out below their jaws. Prowling toward them with lithe predatory grace, their talons sliced into the ice effortlessly.

Bresslin lowered herself, her breath hot against his face as she purred, "No, you will not. You and Brokk can't seem to wrap your heads around the fact that things are unfurling, have been for years with much planning, years of waiting for the right moment to act. Years of gaining the Faes' trust, so they would be exactly in the position they are in now. Scrambling for a broken crown when they can't even see the war coming right for them."

"Through the means of dark magic!" Memphis sputtered, blood dribbling down his lip.

She unsheathed her blade, stroking the steel along his jawline. "Our means, though of power long forgotten, have been most successful." She grinned and straightened, addressing the prowling monsters behind her, "Shall we go for a stroll with our guests? I do believe we are late to a certain funeral."

The answering roars and pounding of clawed paws collided into him, vibrating to his core. Bresslin twisted back to him, pulling at the long chain attached to his collar. "Now, you will be coming with me, Mr. Carter."

The heaviness of the chains bit into his skin, every ounce of the contact leaching him of his ability until the familiar buzz in his mind was nothing more than just an imprint, an empty hole carved into his chest.

# HEIR OF LIES – PART ONE

Yanking the end, his neck snapped in whiplash, as she demanded, "Now."

Memphis felt the sharpness of claws slice against his wrists, cutting shallowly as two lumbering dabarnes unlocked his chains from their icy confinements. Their breath was hot and heavy on his neck, reeking of decay. His shoulders screamed in protest as one loosened, and then the next. His hands fell heavy to his sides, and he staggered up, slipping on ice. Chuckles resonated around him as he straightened, clenching his teeth.

Smiling wolfishly, she ordered, "Bring the other."

Memphis focused on Bresslin, and she winked. "He is a little worse for wear. Gortach's methods...are thorough."

Lunging, he snarled at her, and she whipped the chains, making him bow. "I would not try that again." Yanking him up, she dragged him behind, the snow and ice cutting into his numb limbs.

On the far side of the clearing, Gortach came into view, and Memphis's heart dropped into his stomach. Brokk was dragged behind, unconscious. Blood and bruises flourished every ounce of his skin. Dark and polished claws sprouted from his knuckles, stuck in transition, his usually short cropped golden hair was bloodied and ragged.

"What did you do to him?!" His scream sounded far away, like he was yelling underwater.

Gortach tilted his head, his stare unyielding, and Bresslin nodded. Like the pumping of blood, the hundreds of dabarnes started pounding their feet against the ice encrusted ground, the pounding growing and growing.

Striding forward with Memphis in tow, she yelled, "For years, you have hidden in the darkness! For years you have been forgotten because of the manner of kings! We live in a world where Mixed Bloods are protected, yet such raw and ancient magic is crushed, killed, and shunned. Well, I want to change this."

The monsters bared their teeth, low growls rippling amongst the ranks as their excitement grew.

"For years, my husband and I have waited, gathering information and resources and building their trust. For years, we have bowed, but no longer. The Faes are weak, their dreams, dissipating. The time for magic and ability to rule is now. What have I told you all?"

"All is might!!" they roared back, the ice shield cracking behind them.

She grinned toothily. "*Exactly.*"

Spinning around, she unsheathed her sword, dragging Memphis behind.

Bresslin started running, Memphis breathing raggedly as the shield exploded. The dabarnes roared, galloping behind them. Smoke oozed from their movements, then darted forward like inky comets, weaving as chunks of ice smashed against the ground. They broke through, the sunlight fracturing through the remaining ice, splashes of colors dappling their skin.

Sweat rolled down his nose, as they gained momentum, cutting through the forest. Snowflakes started to fall once more, blanketing the heaviness of the end of summer with a biting cold.

Ice followed their trail, as they rushed toward the Academy.

He watched the winds roar, his chains leaching his energy with every passing second. Ice encrusted the world, freezing it in this moment, with war raging toward the last remaining thing he cared about in this world. Bowing his head, he could do nothing but run, the metal tearing at his throat.

HEIR OF LIES – PART ONE

# CHAPTER SEVENTEEN

## Adair

They were gathered in the courtyard, the morning light spilling onto the pale stones. Nei clutched Roque's arm, unaware that Adair inhibited her husband's body. Emory sat beside her, still, her flawless skin pale against the promise of the new day. Her gaze flickered amongst the crowd, searching.

Silent tears ran down Nei's face as Adair stood looking out at the transformed courtyard. Rows of long benches had been set out; black roses trailed along the backs of them. At the back of the courtyard, a podium waited framed by the archway. Behind it, the rolling hills splayed until it met the forest's edge in the distance.

The Academy watched his every move. Students, teachers, all were completely unaware that Adair was still adjusting to Roque's body, his own resting in the hidden tunnels of the Academy. His disguise was impeccable. A predator amongst the grieving sea.

Walking, the students and teachers of the Academy were a sea of black clothing and sniffling tears. Feeling their eyes burning into his back, Adair came to the podium, a torch flickering and waiting for him, a small fire pit to his left.

Lowering the torch, the fire was lit, the smoldering flames crackling a deep indigo. Adair looked to his right, spotting Tadeas and Marquis talking quietly amongst themselves. Adair's heart lurched painfully at the sight of the young prince. He wanted to yell at Marquis to leave, to make sure he was spared and not caught in the crossfire of Adair's plan. His mind scrambled, the whispers pressing heavily against his consciousness.

*"You are wasting time."*

Adair raised his gaze, sweeping over the crowd, curling his hands into fists.

*"Destroy them, and all your desires will be fulfilled."*

Gulping, the voices hissed at the edges of his mind, snapping and clawing at him. The wind tussled his hair lightly, a crispness clinging in the air.

Adair bowed his head, his low voice rumbling as Adair spoke with Roque's voice, "Today, we mourn a great loss for our school. The students, teachers, warriors from the Shattered Isles fought valiantly against dark forces our country has not seen before. The capital has fallen, and we are spinning into times tinged with darkness. Yet we stand unified and take today to celebrate the lives of our loved ones, our friends, and our colleagues. For they will live on within our memories and will never be forgotten."

Tears spilled down the faces of most students, the faculty sitting rigid, grief paining their faces. The flames roared behind Adair as a hush fell over the crowd once more. Pulling out the crisp parchment, he cleared his throat. "We remember today, Professor Iasan, Professor Ida, Collin Greenbay, Aedian McMulian…"

The list went on, and Adair read through each inky name scrolled in Nei's fine print. Each word, each beat felt like ash in his mouth. Finally, reaching the last name, he turned, gently placing the parchment in the flames, the paper instantly dissolving.

He watched for a moment, entranced as the ink bubbled and peeled, fading into the coals and smoke. The scraping of chairs slammed him back into the present, and Adair boomed, "Now, let us reconvene in the dining hall and pay our respects."

Murmurs spread amongst them, some people lingering by the flames, whispering their goodbyes.

# HEIR OF LIES – PART ONE

Adair quickly caught Tadeas's eye, the king making his way toward him. Chewing his inner cheek, he dipped his head. "Tadeas."

"Roque. You spoke well. I am grateful for that, for our fallen from the Isles."

Marquis followed them; his eyes cast down as they headed toward the Academy. Tadeas eyed the crowd. "You can rest assured that your secret is safe with me during this uneasy time."

His voice was quiet, and Adair raised a dark eyebrow, feigning innocence. "It will remain safe. I swear that to you. But Marquis and I will be returning to the Isles. You will always have aid with us, but we need to recuperate after our losses. With my entire fleet, we can bring Cesan down." He cleared his voice gruffly, stalling to clasp his forearm.

"I will have your passage readied at the port. Go back to the Isles and let our allegiance be known. Your trading routes are free, all I ask, *King*, is to not leave Kiero in the dark. Go home. Grieve your losses. We will be in contact soon."

Tadeas bowed. "What about Cesan?"

At the mention of his father's name, Adair darkened, his ability throttling Roque within his dark rage. "I will deal with Cesan and make him answer for what he has done."

Marquis stalled behind his father, his eyes narrowing, and for a moment, Adair thought he saw a flash of recognition in those emerald eyes. Just as fast as it had occurred, it vanished, and Tadeas looked to his son. "Well, we will take our leave after some of the feast then."

"I will have your horses prepared for your journey," Adair—Roque—said.

Nodding, they walked back into Academy, the sun rising higher in the sky, the smoke curling up to meet it.

Delicious scents churned through the air: honey and dates, sweet tangs of the freshly baked fruit and nut bread, the spices of mulled wine. Adair sat back at the head of the table, taking in the dining hall. Nei had outdone herself.

Deep green vines churned along the edge of each headboard of each seat, deep blue blossoms flowering as the chatter rose. The intricate petals curled, flecks of silver catching in the shades. Shimmering above them, a haze of golden mist recreated the look of a sunset twinkling above crystal water. It was flawless, every color deep and rich, as they dove into the celebration planned to last well into the afternoon and night.

Chewing on the soft warm bread, Adair sighed, his gaze briefly drifting above, a small crack barely visible where his true body lay.

"Dad, can I talk to you for a second?"

Startled, he turned to face Emory and cleared his throat gruffly, his heart hammering and his mind scrambling. Would she detect the shadows churning within his eyes?

"Brokk, Memphis, and Adair are all missing. Adair and I...we got into a bad fight last night, and he was heading to talk to you. What happened?"

*What happened, indeed?* Adair thought.

"Emory, I wouldn't be too worried. Adair is feeling a bit...lost. He just came to me seeking counsel last night... When was the last time you saw Brokk and Memphis?"

She chewed her lip, whispering, "At least a day ago."

His mind spun. Foster and Carter had a bad habit of keeping tabs on him. If they were digging, then they would be following his same path for answers about what exactly the Academy was hiding.

Gently smiling at Emory, he said, "I will make sure to find them."

*They were already too late for what they were searching for.*

She beamed. "Thank you."

"Emory?" Adair snapped his attention at the sound of Marquis's voice.

# HEIR OF LIES – PART ONE

Marquis stood behind them, his emerald hair disheveled, his hands buried in the pockets of his ebony jacket. At the far side of the hall, chairs and tables were screeching back, the pounding of drums beating through the crowd as people gathered.

They had started the Kedshima, a traditional respect paid at funerals. It was the dance of abilities. Emory looked at the young prince, tilting her head. "Marquis?"

"Would you...erm...I mean would you do me the honor of being my partner?"

Her gaze also trailed to the siren call of the pounding drums, of the partners gathering and standing across the room from one another. With a dark spark in her eyes, she dipped her head. "It would be my pleasure."

Adair sat back, watching as Emory followed Marquis through the throng of people, the drums picking up speed, pounding in double time. Taking a deep swig, the taste of crisp berries and taunting spices filled his senses. The world seemed to slow as Marquis bowed low, Emory returning the gesture, and then they walked to opposite sides of the room.

Nei grabbed his hand, squeezing gently. "With those two, it ought to be a show."

The drums stilled, and then Adair recognized Wyatt, as he roared, "Let the Kedshima begin!!"

Beautiful chaos ensued.

The drums picked up in an alluring tempo as abilities exploded. Adair watched as the hall was transformed. To the far left, a young student ran toward her partner, dodging the fire that flared and roared from his palms, dropping to her knees as leafy vines exploded from her, meeting the flames, becoming an entanglement of ash that exploded around them. To the right, Wyatt and Jaxson gravitated around each other, grinning wolfishly as Wyatt disappeared and reappeared, Jaxson multiplying himself by the minute.

Fire met ice, ice met ash, and stars erupted from the clash of might that shuddered through the room. Adair's pulse thrummed as he watched, entranced, yet unable to do anything when Emory became the predator she was born to be before his very eyes.

Her dark hair was swept back, and she walked toward Marquis, a slight smile splayed on the corner of her lips. He tilted his hand, mischief etched into his features. He clapped his hands together, and it was like they were transported to the heart of the Black Sea. Thunder rolled as the wind picked up, and water crashed toward Emory, black and churning, with one promise - to *consume.*

Running full tilt, Emory aimed straight for the middle of the mighty waters spouting from Marquis's palms. Adair saw her plan unfold, but he also knew Marquis's secret and his advantage. Emory was hoping to reach the prince through the waters because once she had contact with him, the game was over.

She had no idea she was running straight into a giant shield.

Emptying his glass, he stood, hearing Nei's distant questions fade behind him.

The other partners had stepped to the sidelines, the drums continuing to pound, rattling their souls. They all watched as the contained waters from the Prince of the Shattered Isles roared toward their princess, both parties emitting a calm confidence, each thinking they had the upper hand. Adair watched Emory succumb to the waters, crashing into them and submerging herself. Her arms were powerful as she swam, cutting through the water, only to find herself trapped in a massive roaring orb. Her brows furrowed, confused at the sudden wall she was met with.

Marquis smiled, whispering, "Game over, Princess."

Dropping his hands, the orb stopped, crashing Emory to the ground in a sputtering mess. Claps and roars of approval pounded through the room, as Marquis mock bowed. Emory looking half-drowned, laughed while still lying on the ground. Her clear voice cut right through his heart.

# HEIR OF LIES – PART ONE

Adair stopped, exhaling hard, not realizing he had been holding his breath. The room filled with chatter, with laughter, with light and love. He could feel Nei's gaze burning into his back, and he was about to turn slowly when he heard it.

The room seemed to dim, everyone fading to the background. The boisterous and alluring scents and glamor of the party swept from his mind.

"Adair. Adaiiiir. They are coming."

His heart faltered as the smell and tang of winter filled his senses. The roars and echoes of bloodthirsty cries climbed through his mind, the promise of death lingering on his tongue.

"They are coming."

The ancient essence that was locked around his heart stirred, images cutting through his mind. The forest crystallizing into a world of ice, his mother swiftly leading an army not seen by man before.

And the Academy, sitting, waiting, as the icy world raced toward them.

"Act now, Adair. Or die with them."

His heart hammered against his ribcage, and Adair was certain it was going to break through his chest, shattering him. A trickle of sweat ran down his neck, tickling his skin that had flushed both hot and cold.

"Roque, darling, are you okay?" Nei's voice was tentative, and as Adair turned, the darkness roared within him.

A slow smile splayed on his lips, and Nei backed away, her softness gone as she looked at him. The drums and laughter spun around them, the rest of the Academy oblivious to the shift of energy, her panic bleeding into her features. His blood felt like it was on fire, and he turned, locking eyes with the Prince of the Shattered Isles. Emory was walking toward him now, his sarcastic jabs lost to him as Adair mouthed one word to him, "*Run.*" Marquis's skin paled.

The world shuddered beneath him, as Adair started screaming. Everyone paused, looking to their King who crouched down low on the ground, writhing in pain.

"*Adair, you don't have to do this. Please,*" Roque's voice cut through his mind, and he growled, clenching his teeth. "*The Book of Old only has one motive, one reason for existing.*"

The pain stopped abruptly, and Adair stood, shaking, and whispered to Roque, "To *end* you."

The killing blow was crippling and unyielding, and Adair obliterated everything the acclaimed King of Kiero was. His bones turned to ash, his blood boiling and his nerve endings exploding until he dropped. And the magic that was slumbering within Adair shuddered through him with such a crippling force, it was like diving into the coolest water, wiping away any weariness, any pain, any confusion, any weakness. It filled his heart with purpose and his ability with strength and melded into everything he was.

And blackened his soul.

Adair ripped himself from Roque's lifeless body in churning black smoke. Crossing the space, he hurtled toward Nei. She was flung back as Adair collided with her, his dark magic soaking into her veins, charring and burning. Blistering rage consumed Adair, as he felt her major organs shut down, the dark magic consuming her. In mere seconds, Nei Fae was dead.

Separating himself from her body, Adair was flying upward in the inky smoke.

The screams rose and fell, building with every second as Adair's eyes flew open. In the cool darkness of the tunnel, he lurched forward, dry heaving. Looking down at his arms, his pale skin was streaked with blackened veins.

Vibrating, he clawed at his chest, ripping his shirt until he saw the monstrous burns exactly where his heart was, his skin raw and swollen. The world spun, and he reached for the familiar depth of his ability only to be met with a wall.

"Finally."

# HEIR OF LIES – PART ONE

The voices caressed and overlapped in his mind. They were the maestro, and now Adair was the instrument, bowing to their commanding hands. Heaving again, he emptied his stomach, as he was pulled down into the depths of his consciousness.

All the hope and beauty that the lustrous magic showed him before was gone. He felt himself collapse as their claws sunk themselves into his heart. Images flashed through his mind, cruel and sharp and unrelenting. Adair was sucked into the memory, and it charged through him.

*Roque Fae looked around the room, raising a dark eyebrow to the two beautiful women seated to his left. "You're sure the room is protected?"*

*The woman chuckled. "Roque, after all these years, you still doubt us?"*

*An uneasy tension rippled across the room, and sighing, Roque sat down, his features softening. "No. I don't. Forgive me."*

*The women shook their heads gently, and snapping their fingers, a white light seared down the doorframe. Making sure no one could get in or out. Nei gently clasped his hand underneath the table, squeezing it, and Roque continued, "What should we add today?"*

*The flickering eyes of the couple lingered on the two dark haired women at the end of the table. Their deep brown eyes were filled with an infinite void that also filled their world, which was foreign to Roque.*

*Roque chewed his cheek, looking to the man across from him. Damien Foster was the epitome of strength, from his dark hair to his rugged features. They had known each other for years, each meeting bringing quaking memories of pain with them.*

*Damien was rare, and that was saying a lot among their world. A man who could find and travel amongst worlds? A man who had woven together these meetings, bridging culture, strength, and magic and defying the laws so that they all could sit here. Roque looked at the glistening book in the middle of the table, filled with secrets and spells from each world. Each leader that consisted of the Original Six added to it each time they met, so the integrity of their cultures could be preserved.*

*It hadn't been easy learning that there were other worlds connected to Kiero. Damien Foster had discovered the channels in using his abilities,* like lifting a veil to show them the truth. Damien had bartered with his life and made sacrifices to get people to listen. To show them the opportunity of an alliance that was woven across time and space. One that Roque and Nei tucked close to their hearts, shielding from their country.

Roque unclasped his hand from Nei's, and the fey from Daer cleared their throat and said, "It is our turn."

Roque stated, "And what will you be addressing?"

For a moment, they didn't say anything but tilted their heads slowly, an identical smile blossoming on their faces. Their whispers made the end of his hair stand on end. "Magic not heard of before by your worlds."

Looking at the book, it drifted toward them, scraping against the table. Meeting their outstretched hands, the cover flew open, pages churning wildly under their touch. The others shifted uneasily.

The fey looked at each other, their lips splitting into sharpened grins. Soft green light flared from under their fingers, soft and alluring. For a moment, the scent of moss and warm spices filled the room. Strange and vivid, beneath their bony joints, images flared, materializing in the book, as their eerie voices whispered to the pages in a language foreign to them all. The sharp and guttural words wove, the notes hanging heavily around them, sharp as any sword and calming as still water.

The world within the pages was beautiful and cruel, and the world of Daer was shown to them, the only way they could understand. Of towering castles, born from rock and gems, hidden in forests so ancient Roque couldn't fathom their timeline. The rivers ran black, the intricate flowers blooming to ash. Of a tale of a court that had once ruled within the kingdom, breathing life into magic, breathing hope and truth into its people.

Only to be destroyed.

The imagery flashed, turning cold. The emerald haze of the paradise vanishing in a pull of smoke, and the very lights within the room seemed to dim. Black roses ruled over the once majestic castle, and the crumbling brick showed the weathering of time. Where once beauty flourished, a harshness had fallen over the world and the fey that lived there.

Roque cringed as the echo of screams resonated within his mind and looking more closely at the book, he saw that timeless world burn, the

# HEIR OF LIES – PART ONE

*faeries* churning and changing into something else entirely. With smooth inky hair and empty eyes, the four women bowed before the King sitting on the throne of carved bone. It was peerless white, the contrast so great it was like the last star in a blackened night.

The courtroom was empty, besides them. The king wore thick armored plates, his blade glistening as he spun it rhythmically in his palm, his eyes sharp and golden, scar tissue roping around his neck in silver webs.

"For years, we have lived in this shell of a world. It is time to change that," the king said.

Bowing their heads in unison, their whispers overlapped in haunting tones, "We will not fail you, our King."

Standing, they clasped dark green emerald gems and, forming a circle, started chanting in the same sharp guttural tones, their plain white robes fluttering around their bony knees. In a flash of emerald light, they were gone, leaving a scorched ground in their wake.

The king started to chuckle at first, then rolled into a deep laugh. The Oilean were born from the heart of darkness itself, and as his trained assassins, they would rid this new-found world of everyone in it, leaving the magic for their own taking.

Just as they did with this one.

The King of Daer looked to the crumbling ceiling and dreamt of the carnage they would make, and he knew he would wait until the day came that the Oilean would connect their worlds. And finally, he would be able to scrounge new lands, filling his starving soul, feeding his magic. He would be able to get his revenge.

Until that day came, he would wait. And he would be ready.

Gripping the blade, the King of Daer, also known as Declan, sent it soaring to the opposite wall, the hilt thrumming with magic. It collided with the stone and exploded, the sword vanishing with the impact in a cloud of smoke, the debris crashing around the room.

The king smiled as the sword materialized back into his palm, fresh and glinting, as he stared at the absent space where the wall was. Beyond that, the roars of his kingdom beckoned to him. Where the rolling forests once stood, a sea of white greeted him, and the hollowed-out bones of the previous fey staked in the ground like delicate art.

Smoke churned in the shadows, and he knew his people could taste the longing of magic lingering in the air, on the tip of the scales.

And so, Declan sat back and waited.

The vision disappeared, and Roque gagged from the backlash, their magic having pulled each of them into the memory. He looked up slowly, his pulse stuttering.

The book was pulsing, and a deep humming filled the room. Looking up, the moment hung in between them like an eternity. Where once sat the exotic fey, now sat demons with empty eye sockets, long ebony hair framing their pale skin. Their lips were pulled and pinned back, revealing sharpened teeth. Tilting their heads in unison, a giggle escaped their lips before the room exploded in a fury of chaos.

The lights flickered, sending the room in a disarray of splintered movement. The Oilean stood, their facades gone, their magic exploding from them. The very shadows seemed to deepen, whispering dark terrible things as cracks of ability filtered around them. Damien roared forward, his blinding light raging against the night.

"Damien, NO!"

But he looked back to the group, just as the Oilean multiplied, the four of them circling around him, and he whispered, "The channels are closed. They cannot get back."

Screams met with the guttural sounds of the fight as the creatures sunk their teeth into his neck, and the darkness overtook him, leaving nothing but ash. Screams multiplied around the room, and he looked to Nei, her panicked eyes searching his own, both thinking the same thing.

What could they—a desolate and a healer from the Shattered Isles—do?

Giggles filled the room, bouncing around them and their consciousness. Hands found his in the darkness, warm and strong as Aine's voice tickled against his ear. "My daughter has removed the seals on the door and is gone. Do not let me down, Roque."

Brilliant ice blue light filled the room as Aine stepped forward, the Queen of the Windwalkers said, "You want them? You will have to get through me first."

The Oileans' joints popped sickeningly as they scrambled forward. "Ah yes, Witch Queen. Witch Queen."

# HEIR OF LIES – PART ONE

The explosion threw them back, Roque's head cracking against the wall with a sickening thud. Spots danced in front of his eyes, and in the flickering lights, Roque watched as Aine became the very substance of her power, colliding with the smoky darkness of the Oilean. Squeezing his eyes shut, tears burned beneath his lids at the sudden blinding flare of light.

Heat scorched his skin, becoming too hot, as Roque screamed, preparing for the end. When the lights flicked back on, the heat died with it.

The lights flicked back on.

Coughing, Roque stumbled forward, his voice rasping, "Nei...Nei!"

"Here. I'm fine. I'm fine." His wife lay across the room, looking shaken but unscathed.

With ringing ears, Roque stood, any trace of the Oilean and Aine gone; the scorched ground and the ashes skittering around the room were the only trace of what had happened. The room tilted, but Roque walked toward the table, the blackened book pulsing with light, the surface of the wood completely singed underneath it.

"Roque, no! Can't you see it?"

Nei was before him in a second, pushing against his chest, shielding him from the work they had cultivated over the years, the work that would change the face of their culture, for Emory, for Kiero. The book that contained spells from worlds of Langther, the windwalkers, Daer, and the fey, and he had been the commander behind such an expedition. A desolate, orchestrating the most influential artifact Kiero had ever seen.

Now, all of it was destroyed in a second.

He seized her forearms. "Nei, I have to see it! All our work..." he trailed off, and tears slid down her face.

"They destroyed it. I can...sense it. It's dark magic. It's not safe. We must get rid of it! Roque listen to me. The channels are destroyed, closed. It's over. But those faeries tainted it. They may be gone; they may not be. But their magic is a siren call to them. A weapon. And dark magic only calls to its master."

*The stirring of the Academy sounded behind them, and his mind was freefalling. Clenching his teeth, he said, "No. No, we will hide it, and until we can understand it, we won't destroy it."*

*Nei paled, stepping away from him, shaking her head. "Aine's and Damien's blood is now staining our hands, and you would have us keep it?"*

*There was no trace of the rest of their society having disappeared with the Oilean. No blood stained the floor. Ash was the only trace left, floating gently down to the ground. Roque looked up at her.*

*"Yes, we are going to keep it. We don't even know what we are dealing with yet. All those years of forming this group will not go to waste. The whole point of this group was to prepare and compile a history of each world's culture and magic, a peaceful agreement to bridge foreign allies with Kiero. To pass down to our children so they could live in a world not in arms with one another."*

The memory became washed out and dull, churning until Adair's settings become clear once again. Curled up on the tunnel floor, cold sweat soaked through his shirt, clinging on the inside of his jacket.

"You see, we did have one purpose."

Shivers racked through him, making his teeth chatter as the voices cut through him.

"For your greatness, Adair, we needed your body to act as our vessel. Together, we will be unstoppable."

Tears slid down his dirtied cheeks, and he pushed himself up onto his knees, whispering to the darkness, "No, please no. You promised me, if I did this, if I k-killed them, I would be free. I would be more."

"You already are."

They attacked relentlessly, tearing through his mind, through his ability, through his memories. His secrets and fears, all dissolving as he was pushed under, drowning in the old magic burning through his veins. It was like having his oxygen cut off, everything becoming fuzzy except for the last desperate attempts to remind himself of who *he* was.

# HEIR OF LIES – PART ONE

Laughing with Emory as the sun set, the golden light brushing the world in a soft luster.

Walking through the courtyard at night, the rest of the Academy asleep, but when the stars erupted in the velvet sky far above, tracing constellations, leading his heart and his mind to every untouched adventure that awaited him. He would lie on his back, boots crossed over his legs, the bench cool underneath him as the hours slipped away, directed by his imagination, and reality would shatter him.

All that ever mattered was that one day he would break out of his confines, and he would discover exactly what the world had to offer. Because each day that disappeared and Adair was taught about the mythology, the history, and the mystery of Kiero, a piece of him died because he wasn't experiencing it.

Adair snarled and clawed and threw himself at those memories, at the burning desire to hold on. As fast as they came, they were gone, and the walls of his reality disappeared as well. The room was much like the one before, the curling stairs plunging down into the cavernous room. He stepped forward, his footfalls echoing and falling alongside his panicked breaths. Down and down, he walked. Sweat collected in his palms, as he clenched and unclenched them.

Finally reaching the bottom of the stairs, he turned, a soft silver light bouncing against the slick walls. A pale hand stroked his cheek. The touch froze him and broke down every barrier he had, laying him bare. Every dream, wish, hope, longing that had ever taken root within him was gone.

Until he felt nothing.

Until he *was* nothing.

"Adair."

Tears fell as his lip trembled.

"*Don't be afraid.*"

He felt their nails dig into his jacket, pulling and pushing, and he didn't know what *his* reality was anymore.

The Oilean hissed in pleasure, clawing at his chest, at his arms, pushing him further and faster back. Stumbling, his gravity tipped, and the wind was pushed from his lungs. His fingers started to burn, the heat spreading viciously up his arms, binding his legs, surging through his chest. It splintered and pulled him apart, and all he could do was watch in horror as all around him dark spears sprouted from the ground, shuddering around him and growing taller and taller.

And that darkness that had been waiting for him, greeted him with open arms, pulling him close, forming a cage. Flipping onto his side, he dragged himself closer to the bars, and watched the four figures lower themselves to eye level.

"Now, you will understand your freedom."

"NO!" he roared, fighting against his confinements, and as their figures grew distorted, the shadows climbing and consuming, the lights were extinguished. Everything went dark, and he spiraled.

The first thing that he heard was the relentless pounding of hundreds of footfalls above him. A sharp ringing filled his ears, and blinking, he realized he was on his back, arms and legs splayed out. Disoriented, he looked up at the tunnel's ceiling, dust floating down through the semi-darkness, lightly coating his face and clothes.

Stretching, he slowly stood, brushing himself off. Screams echoed around the Academy; the tunnel's walls seemed to move as shocks shuddered down them. To his right, frost had slicked the walls, creating a distorted mirror. Tilting his head, he looked at his reflection in the ice.

A pink flush had crept into his cheeks, and for the first time in years, he felt *alive*. Leaning closer, the ice misted from his breath, and he took in his sweeping black hair, but he paused as a slow smile tugged at the corners of his lips. He took in his eyes next. His pupils widened, bleeding in the now black iris around them, all flecks of the dark brown gone. All traces of *him*, gone.

A deep chuckle passed through his lips, and he tentatively traced the outline of his features, growing more distorted with every second. Flicking the melted droplets off his fingertips, he murmured, "It's time."

Clenching his fists, he slammed it into the ice, and the impact should have shredded his skin and his knuckles, leaving a bloody print. Instead, the cracks split through the ice, racing up and through the sheets, and ice fractured around him. Adair flexed his unharmed hand, grinning viciously.

The ground shuddered beneath him and looking up, his hair stood on end with anticipation. The temperature continued to drop, and his breath outlined in front of him as he looked onward, to the war that raged above him. He could practically taste the ancient magic spurring through the Academy because it was the same that coursed through him, a gravitational force that wouldn't let him go, *couldn't* let him go.

And he would answer it.

Bowing his head, his body became magic and smoke, and soon, he was flying, cutting through the physical barriers of the school.

He was no longer a man, no longer just Adair Stratton.

The voices purred inside him, coaxing him onward, as he became destruction, chaos, and rage. He became the monster they claimed he was, the fear that was whispered behind his back.

And as he raced to escape the tunnels while, inside, Adair battered against his confinements, screaming, unable to do anything but watch as the magic sealed him within, overpowering and enhancing him.

He burned with one desire.

To end the Academy.

# CHAPTER EIGHTEEN

## Brokk

For the first hour, he had screamed, gut wrenching wails, as he heard the Academy get ripped apart, stormed by Bresslin's forces. There was no rhyme or reason to their destruction, and the smell of smoke and the harsh tang of winter cut into his face, as his head hung limply, the sounds of war clashing around him.

The metal bit into his wrist, a steady drip of blood slowly seeping onto the ground. He no longer wanted to hear the dabarnes shatter through the icy courtyard, the screams rising and falling. The Academy was caught completely unaware by Bresslin's rage.

*"First, I will make you beg."*

He cringed against the memory, slithering through his mind of Gortach's sick whispers.

*"Then, I will make you bleed."*

A whimper escaped him, and he clenched his eyes shut.

*My name is Brokk Foster. I will not break. I will not break. I will not break.*

He repeated this over, trying to shut out the increased sound of concrete being smashed, the roars of the dabarnes, the screams of the residents of the Academy. The singing of metal against metal, of ice crackling over everything, alive or not. The ground shuddered, and he was sure the world would split apart from the forces clashing together.

"Brokk."

# Heir of Lies – Part One

He squeezed his eyes tighter, and for the first time, he let his mind wonder what it would be like just to drift away from their government, from their politics. Like the raiders had done. And the Shattered Isles. Leaving Kiero to battle over an acclaimed crown.

"Brokk!" Defeatedly wrenching his gaze, he squinted through his non-swollen eye at Memphis, cringing at how true Bresslin was to her word. Memphis's wrists and ankles where melded into blocks of ice, his body stretched taut, blood running down his arms, the chain collar tight around his throat. They were on the outskirts of the forest, left broken and beaten, their torture listening to their home falling into ruin, seeing enough but not all.

"We have to do something." Memphis's voice cracked.

"If you have any plans, I would love to hear them," he rasped.

"So, we just give up, stay strapped to a block of ice? Brokk, Em is in there,"

"Don't you think I know that? But what *can* we do against a bloody army of demons!"

Memphis's face grew ashen as he spat, "We can *try*."

*Try*.

Brokk wanted to laugh. How many years had he spent *trying*? Trying to figure out his past. Who his parents were, why they didn't want to keep him. Trying to live up to the expectations of the Academy, to grow up to become Kiero's guardians.

But he had tried to stay true to his heart and what he knew was right, and that's all he could ever want.

Looking at the world around him, the hush of the forest snow was encrusted and timeless. His gaze drifted to the Academy, the smoke starting to curl up toward the sky. Was he ready to try, to potentially *die*?

His heart slammed against his ribs as he licked his dried lips. "Memphis, you know you can be a prick, right?"

His friend grinned. "On occasion."

Groaning, Brokk shook his head. "If we die…"

"Most of our plans could end with that option. They haven't yet, and today, I have no intention of breaking our luck."

Fear filled every ounce of his soul, but he knew he wouldn't forgive himself if he caved. For himself and for Emory.

His eyes frantically ravaged the forest, looking for anything that could help them. A crack exploded in front of them, and he cringed and desperately whispered, "Please. Help us."

He had spent his lifetime in these woods. A lifetime of endless nights. The pounding of his paws against the earth, the moonlight carving his path, all his fears and worries stripping away. It was those nights that he shifted, and the symphony of magic and mystery filled his senses. He wasn't so oblivious to not know that he was being watched. The myths around their world, specifically the woods around the Academy, were one of legends. That before the magic was born in them, in the form of abilities, their world was divided.

It was said that the woods were a sacred place, defended by Warriors who once lived in the lost city of Nehmai. Immortal fey whose magic could surpass wildest daydreams, and they would protect their border against the darkness breeding in the magic.

Over the years, the myth turned into many variations, saying that the Warriors had disappeared, sacrificing their magic into the very bowels of Kiero, seeping into the air, the trees, their food, their *bodies*.

And as such, people born with abilities came about *naithe*—or blessed. At first, it started as a gentle murmur, children born from parents of no abilities, and it spread through Kiero like wildfire, tainting what started out as awe into madness. He didn't believe that they were *chosen*, but the myths of the Warriors curled around his heart, tucking it away, and only allowing himself to hope on those nights in the woods, that they weren't gone from their world.

Maybe it was futile, but he had no other ideas, and as he whispered those words into the icy wind, he clenched his eyes shut, his heart lodged in his throat.

For a moment, the very world seemed to hold its breath, the clashing of the war raging beyond them.

"Brokk."

He froze, straining against his imagination, but there again on the wind, his name was whispered like a gentle caress. With a racing pulse, he allowed his senses to float beyond him.

"Brokk, find a way back."

Fear tore through his chest, but he couldn't stop himself, as he dove into his ability. At first, he was met with nothing, the enhanced metal having neutralized him. But there, underneath that void curtain, a flickering ember pulsed, straining to be there.

He did not falter as he slammed into it, and the world exploded.

Catching a glimpse of Memphis, who was looking at him, waiting for an answer, then fractured light erupted around him, and Brokk was falling. His scream ripped through him, and he was blinded by the swirling of light but also of memories. It was like standing on a hillside, watching the world spin into rewind, time having no meaning anymore.

"*They will think all is lost.*" Brokk dove toward Bresslin's voice, not fully understanding what this part of him was, but he trusted it. Because he trusted himself.

"*And they will watch as we destroy everything they love,*" Gortach grumbled. "*You aren't afraid they are more powerful than you think? Especially the shifter?*"

*Bresslin smiled. "The only way they could get out of their restraints is if they knew the spell protecting it, wouldn't they? It would be impossible for them to know that saying* ceol *would transfer the energy consumed by the metal back into them."*

*Gortach rumbled a laugh as Bresslin brandished her sword in front of her. "It's time."*

Brokk felt like he was being wrenched back, diving back into that sea of endless blinding light; the energy crackled around him, and he could *sense* it, the currents raging around him, and he was falling again.

Howling wind surrounded him as his eyes flew open, forcing himself to take in the scene. Brilliant slashes of gold, silver, and blue dove around him, like waves crashing against the shore, flashing and roaring in their spectrum. He was afraid but also mesmerized as one voice above all the rest stood out, "*Brokk.*"

Brokk dove toward the echo of Emory's voice. She was his anchor, leading him back into reality. She was in trouble—and Brokk would be damned if he let anything happen to her, today or any other day.

Emory had *known* he had this...this time-traveling ability. In his heart, he had known but had always pushed it away, not allowing the part that he didn't understand to dictate his life. A sharp ringing filled his senses, and the light fractured and splintered once more, and he was slammed back into his present body. To a gaping Memphis by his side.

"What the hell..."

Brokk said, low and harshly, "*Ceol.*"

The metal shuddered to life, the collars vibrating against their throats, and Memphis cursed by his side, putting most of his vocabulary to shame. Heat flared along his wrists and his throat, as the shackles fell, allowing his ability to stir once again.

His ebony claws slid back into his skin; his canines clicked back into his gums; and his body was no longer stuck, half shifted and broken.

Running over to Memphis, he murmured "*ceol*" and as Memphis fell, he turned to face the Academy, the smell of decay and the sharp tang of metal consuming his heart, as he shifted back to his wolf form.

Brokk was not one to take being chained like an animal lightly.

*My name is Brokk Foster, and I will not break.*

Shakily, Memphis came up to his side, his hand resting on his golden fur. "After all is said and done, you are going to tell me how you knew..." he trailed off, not able to find the rest of his words, his bruised face swelling with every second.

Brokk knew what he wanted to say but couldn't, and he growled in response.

"My thoughts exactly." Memphis climbed on his back, whispering in his mind. *"To war?"*

*"To Emory,"* Brokk thought.

Memphis climbed on his back, thinking aloud, "I don't have any weapons."

*"You are a weapon."*

And then they were running.

Breaking through the tree line of the forest, Brokk dodged viciously as a dabarne rolled in front of them, covered in thick vines, wrapping and growing, as Brokk recognized the first-year student who fiercely assaulted the monster, sweat collecting on her brow as she concentrated, the ground shuddering.

Flinging his weight forward, he pushed off his haunches, cutting through the air, and caught the knife sailing through the air directly at her back. The blade broke in his jaws.

The courtyard raged around them, students attacking the army of hundreds, the darkness pushing in on them from every side, every angle. Screams overlapped through the ice, ash, and blood. All around him, bodies dropped beneath ebony claws, through razor sharp teeth and ear-splitting roars.

"On your left!"

Spinning, Brokk watched Memphis launch himself off his back, meeting the charging sleek body, its elongated nose pulled back over its teeth. Landing hard, he felt the wave of energy leave Memphis, and then it froze, hissing viciously.

Brokk threw himself at the creature's throat, ripping out its jugular as it thudded to the ground, cracking the ice with its weight.

Fire blazed behind them as Memphis sprinted toward Brokk's back, and a first year charged the line, fearless.

Brokk galloped, and Memphis flung himself on him, and soon, they were weaving through the battle. Gripping his fur, Memphis raged against the creatures' minds, each wave like a shooting arrow landing a killing blow.

Everything was spattered with gore; bodies of his fellow classmates were lying on the snow encrusted ground. Wave after wave, the dabarnes' attacks were relentless. Bleak shock coursed through Brokk, trying to register the war around him, that they were *losing*.

Suddenly, a dabarne appeared to his left, its inky talons moving too fast for him to jump out of the way, as it connected with his side. Talon ripped through flesh and fur, all the way down, exposing his rib.

Brokk's vision dipped as he almost passed out from the pain. Relief came as he healed, but he tripped when the dabarne took its opportunity to attack. Rolling, Memphis was thrown off, and the beast snapped at Brokk's throat with ferocity. Kicking his back legs to connect with the dabarne's gut, Brokk threw the beast over his body, forcing it to roll.

Gaining his footing, Brokk lunged toward the enemy, but Memphis was already there, blood trickling down his nose as he snapped the dabarne's neck with his mind. Running back to Brokk, Memphis clambered on his back once again.

His muscles were on fire as he galloped, twisting and jumping through the remains of the courtyard, and he wanted to stop, he wanted to throw up, he wanted to scream.

"NO!" Bresslin's voice cut through the fight. Pushing faster, Brokk's nails clawed into the ice as they scrambled up the stairs, the force of the army charging behind them.

"Get inside now!!!" Memphis roared to the remaining students, and the cries as they tried to follow broke Brokk's heart. He couldn't look back as he charged through the open doors. Memphis slamming them shut behind them.

Brokk shifted back and threw up, the force and sting of the acid burning his throat.

"Brokk, we have to go now. Find Emory. No one else made it."

The hallways of the Academy were eerily quiet, the lights flickering faintly. The pounding outside grew, and all Brokk could do was stare at the floor.

# HEIR OF LIES – PART ONE

Looking up, he met Memphis's gaze, dead in the eye. "You have to find her. We will never out chase them. I can hold them off for as long as I can... but *find her*."

Memphis crossed the space between them. "And what, leave you to die? You've got to be kidding me. Now is not the time for some noble sacrifice!"

Brokk could feel the force shiver up his spine, into his bones. "You have to." Not looking back, he shifted and then exploded through the oak doors. The wind shrieked, snow stinging his eyes, and he howled, the sound ominous and haunting.

"*Run, Memphis.*"

He launched himself forward, landing heavily at the base of the stairs. Shifting back, he quickly picked up a discarded sword, gripping the hilt as he strained against the storm.

A sword slashed down toward his chest, missing him by a hair's breadth, as he raised his blade to meet it, sparks flaring between them.

"You are becoming more annoying by the minute, *Mr. Foster.*" Bresslin pushed against him, making him bow as ice ran up his forearms and up the blade. She smiled. "You are only hindering the inventible. But I am curious to how you and Mr. Carter escaped your restraints."

He didn't answer, as he ducked, slicing at her shins and making her step back.

She mused, "You never were one for many words, were you? A pity, to end up like your classmates after all."

She charged, slamming the blade down, and his arms became numb from each block, the vibrations crawling up his skin. She was relentless, as the gleaming edge carved and dove toward him, missing him only by an inch. The storm picked up as he slipped, and then rolled as Bresslin's sword cracked through the ice with ease. Right where he had been.

Charging, he connected with her waist, and they rolled, Brokk trying to pin her. Her boots connected with his chest, and he was sent flying. Shifting as he landed, his claws dug into the ice,

201

screeching with the impact. All around them, in a tight circle, the dabarnes watched him, drool dripping from their maws, their yellow eyes eagerly waiting for the command to end him.

"Enough. Do you really think *you* could win against us? This is so much bigger than you could ever dream, little shifter."

His growls cut low and deep as he took the first step, his hackles raised, baring his teeth.

She shrugged, taking him in. "You have a valiant heart; I will give you that much."

Pushing off and thundering toward her, his heart broke with every footfall.

Bresslin smiled, and she snapped her fingers, the storm ceasing. The snowflakes hung in the air, transcending gravity, gleaming like diamonds in the afternoon light. Each intricate pattern was amplified as the sun touched the defined edges, shining like stars among the carnage.

Flattening his ears, Brokk faltered when Bresslin whistled merrily. The ranks of demons split - they created a pathway of savagery, and his world tilted as Gortach loped down toward him, Emory chained and in tow behind him.

Shifting back, Brokk sprinted for her, roaring. Fear encompassed him at the sight of Emory, bloodied and chained. It sent him spinning and seeing red. "What did you do to her?" he screamed as Bresslin prowled around him, assessing his reaction.

Bresslin tutted. "I take offense that you think I would chain and beat our beloved *heir*. I have other means to get my hands dirty. This was all too easy, betraying Nei and Roque who trusted Cesan and me to blindly follow them. Why share in the wealth when we could seize an entire kingdom from them?" She rolled her eyes. "And this legendary school is laughable. None of you have known true loss, pain. No one here was prepared for the weight of war, even with your abilities. Coddled children aren't soldiers, even if you were all told you are." She smiled, bright and sharp. "You have lost; the Academy is fallen. Your heir was found trying to flee, to leave you all to your fates."

# HEIR OF LIES – PART ONE

Gortach had reached them, and Emory would not meet Brokk's gaze. Silent tears slipped down her cheeks, and Bresslin grazed the sword's end underneath her chin, forcing her to look up. "I was very upset to see someone had beaten me to the pleasure of killing your parents."

All he saw was red.

His fist slammed into Bresslin's stomach, his left connecting with her jaw in a sickening crack. She laughed darkly, spitting blood as he stood there. Brokk's chest heaved, and his mind reeled with what she had just said.

"Ah, I finally touched a sore spot. Yes, it's true, the *King* of Kiero is dead, along with his weak wife. It is finally time true leaders step up to the task of ruling this country."

Emory's chin wobbled, but her voice was strong. "My parents were not *weak*."

Gortach snapped the chain attached to her collar, wrenching her back, and Brokk could not resist the current of wrath that burned in his blood.

His world was one of tooth and claw, of instinct and reaction. The ground shuddered underneath him as the dabarnes lunged at him, Bresslin giving the order with the swipe of her sword. Emory was pulled back, screaming his name when he charged toward her, straight into the heart of darkness itself.

Sharp teeth pierced and ripped into his haunches, but he leapt, missing another set of talons swiping at his heart.

The dabarnes were fast.

But he was faster.

There were maybe fifty in front of him, the rest falling behind. He snarled as they stomped their feet in dominance. Emory was maybe ten yards away. The creatures bared their teeth, racing toward him. Pushing faster, his surroundings becoming a blur.

Five yards.

The thick torso of a creature slammed into him, crushing the wind of out of chest, pinning Brokk to the ground, almost at the forest's edge. Its teeth snapped at his throat, but sinking his back talons into its hide, he pushed down, slicing clean through.

Rolling, he leapt over the body only to be met midstride by talons sinking into his haunches and teeth into his shoulder. Brokk's howl pierced through the air. He was almost at the woods.

All he could smell was the blood and decay dripping from their jaws. Panic settled into his chest as his body felt drained from healing repeatedly, as the monsters around him feasted on his pain. Sinking their talons into his side, his ribs cracked and shattered underneath their pressure. He thrashed, the vital drive to survive thrumming in his blood. All that he saw was gleaming teeth as they closed in on him, his howls tearing through him.

*No, no, no!*

He felt the shudder roll through the ground first. The dabarnes stopped, raising their heads, distracted by something or someone else. The group hissed around him, wrenching their gazes from their killing blow. Ears twitching, he craned his neck and caught a glimpse as the doors of the Academy exploded off their hinges. Adair stood in the doorway, smoke curling around him.

At first, he just stood there, his mother and the army thrown off as he looked at the ground. Fear lurched through Brokk when he heard the throaty chuckle.

Adair looked up, grinning, and the world erupted into mayhem.

# HEIR OF LIES – PART ONE

# CHAPTER NINETEEN

## Adair

Adair bowed to the dark magic commanding him, and it was intoxicating. The winter wind bit at his skin, but he didn't feel the cold. He didn't feel anything. The shattered doorframe lay around him, and for a moment, he couldn't breathe, as he stared at the blood-stained stairs, and the carnage of monster and students sprawled around him.

The smile tugged at his lips as he looked up to the hundreds of dabarnes, tilting their head, assessing him. And *what* he was.

"It was such a waste, their power."

The voices curled around his mind, burning into his heart. He honed in to the one person that would answer for this.

His mother moved through the ranks with a lethal ease, her voice breaking over her ranks with cool indifference. "Adair."

In the confines of his mind, he was pounding against the bars, shattering apart, screaming, *Why did you do this?*

The air stirred around him, and the ice started to melt underneath his feet.

"I will admit, I'm surprised you're still alive," Bresslin said.

*You don't mean that; you don't mean that; you don't mean that.*

Ice tore through his veins, and he could taste the power lingering beneath his skin, tasting it on his tongue. "Your father and I had every detail planned meticulously for years."

*Mom, please, no. Don't do this. Not you. Not everyone.*

"You are weak, have always been ruled by your heart, and couldn't see what we were doing before your very eyes," she continued.

The energy exploded from his chest, suctioning the air in tight around him and then expanding, the remaining windows shattering behind him from the force. The army was flattened from the impact, shards of ice and glass cutting into their hide. Bresslin was bowed, a shield of ice flaring up around her. Walking down the stairs, the wind picked up, and he shivered in pleasure.

"Enough," she growled, ice cracking, jagged shards breaking apart, becoming long spears churning slowly in the air.

All of them were aimed at his heart. She roared to the army around her churning restlessly, "NOW!"

Not one moved.

The magic within him hummed and thrashed until the energy was too much, his body withering and overpowered.

Letting go, the world erupted into flames.

Brilliant, emerald fire roared around them, enclosing the army and his mother in the flames and bending to his will. He paused at the edge of the ring, his heart pounding against his ribcage. He saw his mother yell, the words lost to him as the spears of ice sliced through the air. A flicker of movement at the end of the courtyard caught his attention, and Gortach slithered in the shadows, a slim shadow being dragged behind it.

The fire hissed as the water evaporated. Gortach was pushed from his mind, and all he could think about was the scene in the dining hall, remembering what he had started.

And what his mother finished.

It was like wings took flight as his soul filled every single one of the dabarnes, his command cold, smooth, and unbreakable. He breathed, walking around the flames as they towered toward the sky. In the middle of the courtyard, Bresslin now fought for her life, the dabarnes attacking her ruthlessly under Adair's command. Steel flashed as Bresslin wielded the Curse with lethal precision, but it would never be enough.

Adair dove into that pool of magic, and then he was flying. The black smoke swirled around him, choking his senses, until he materialized at the end of the forest, his eyes scrounging the tree line.

*Where is she; where is she; where is she?*

"Adair."

Just the sound of his voice sent him spinning, as Adair slowly turned, exhaling hard. Marquis was covered in blood, his jacket and shirt ripped, his chest heaving. His hands shook, the bloodied sword trembling in his grip.

"What have you done?" Marquis asked him.

He slowly rolled his neck, the bones cracking, and he purred, "Marquis."

*Run, Marquis, run*, Adair thought.

Dropping his palms, the emerald fire pooled in Adair's palms, the flames reflecting in Marquis's gaze. He coolly regarded the prince. "I hope you have been enjoying the change of pace. Now, you have two choices: join me or die."

Marquis's face paled, but defiance sparked in his eyes. "If you want me, come and get me."

*No.* The thought resonated deep in Adair's core, a part of him wishing his friend was already sailing across the Black Sea—far away from him.

The fire flew from his palms with great force, but the prince rolled out of the way, his hair singeing.

As they circled each other, Marquis said, "This is not you, Adair. You can stop this. We don't want to live through a war in our lifetime."

Fire flew from his palms. "It's already begun." Raising his eyebrows, Adair flicked his wrists, the flame overtaking Marquis's now feeble attempt to overthrow him.

Closing the space between them, Adair ducked as a wave of water crashed down on his head. Charging forward, his fist connected with Marquis's jaw, and then gut. Marquis doubled over, wheezing. Adair laughed darkly.

"Your abilities are useless, Marquis. The fact you can neutralize power doesn't matter anymore. You are not a shield against me, and you are sure as hell not special." He grinned. "Kiero has never seen a force like me before. This is your last chance, Marquis. I would rather not kill you. Bow to me, be my second, and we can take this world together."

Pain briefly flared in Marquis's eyes. With shaking hands, he snapped, "I could never stand with you and accept the war you are bringing down on us all. This isn't your future Adair. *Please stop.*"

Adair's bloodlust thrummed in his veins as he shook his head. "That was the wrong answer, I'm afraid."

Water roared from the prince's palms, and Adair plunged into the new power coursing in his body. He could feel the endlessness of the magic. No more limitations held him back. His heart begged for mayhem, and he would make sure to satiate his soul with it.

Pushing forward, Marquis's wrists snapped, broken. His scream was guttural and animalistic as the blood bubbled from his lips. Dropping to his knees, Marquis panted, "They took her you know. Emory. They're all dead. I tried to protect her. I tried to get her out." He shook. "My dad and I survived. We got out through the tunnels, but Emory tried to follow us before Bresslin's army captured her." A pause. "Are you ready to have Emory's blood staining your hands, Adair? Will you look back on this day and be proud of the man you are becoming?"

Adair shuddered, the fire moving up his arms as he licked his cracked lips. Groaning, he pushed back against the darkness, and for a second, *he* broke through the cages as he roared to the surface, breaking through.

Clutching his head, he stumbled back. "Get out of here. *Now.*"

Marquis faltered, trying to get up, supporting his wrists. "What?"

"Marquis, *run!*"

Those inky claws hissed and snapped, dragging Adair back down, down, *down.*

"*You should not fight what you are, Adair.*"

# HEIR OF LIES – PART ONE

He was rocking back and forth on his heels, tears slipping down his cheeks, the reality of his situation slamming into him. The world tilted on its axis, and all he could smell was the blood, smoke, and ash, clotting his throat, coating his skin. His mother's screams died on the wind.

*"Stop resisting us."*

Adair bit his lip so hard blood filled his mouth. He had relished in how it felt to overpower and rip Roque apart, slowly and deliciously, feeding off Roque's fear, knowing his secrets and knowing that he had never done enough. And he had *enjoyed* killing him. After him, each life he took was like oxygen to embers, sparking and catching until he was an inferno.

*Emory is dead. She is gone.*

Painfully, the magic burned through his mind, through his blood, making him retch, his bile mixed with blood. Falling to his knees, the frozen earth beneath him crunched. Adair's fingers scraped along the ice; his nails should have ripped off from the force, but his skin remained flawless.

Howling, his anguish cut through the woods and the emptiness of the Academy.

*"You are ours."*

The pain he experienced before was nothing, *nothing*, compared to what seared through his body now.

A cold sweat coated Adair's skin in a glistening sheen as the magic pulsed faster through his veins. Fire ignited first in his arms, racing down to his torso, chest and legs. His heart palpitated as his bones felt like they were turning to dust, and Adair's screams begged for relief.

Voices bounced around his mind, but they weren't memories. They weren't anything at first, just soft whispers, echoes of places and people that he had once known. Of the secrets he had learned, the knowledge of men and their lies, of broken crowns and hidden truths, of the madness that cultivated it all.

*"You will do our bidding to remake this world."*

The vision sharpened, and Adair stood, looking at the still pool of water, afraid to go to its edge. A dull throbbing ached in his temple as he shuffled toward it.

*"We will do great things together. Rid the world of this weakness. And start to purify the magic."*

Staring at the water, the surface rippled as his quick breaths hit the surface. Inspecting his reflection, he stared back at the shadows curling before him in the water, deep purples and blues ribboning below the surface with every second.

It was there, at the edge of the pool that Adair saw what truly had overtaken his body. His reflection shimmered, skeletal bones jutting out beneath his parchment like skin, his eyes scooped out, his smile strange and unknown. There was no humanity left—he had become the nightmare.

Whimpering, he scrambled back, but the water continued to churn, the pond lapping at the edges as the shadows crawled toward him, slick and persistent. They rushed and crashed at him, blotting out any light, and overtook him, covering his legs, his arms, his torso, his eyes until that's all that was left of him.

Adair drew in a deep breath and, not for the first time today, he woke up, lying on his back. Blinking, the sky took on an odd filter, hazy and unclear. Sitting up, he dusted off his jacket, eyeing the edge of the forest. All that stared back at him were the trees encased in ice, the downy flakes of the snow coating the world.

Standing, he turned, staring at the skeleton of the building resting on the hill and the hundreds of creatures coming at him.

Slowly, Adair stood, dusting himself off. Looking back toward the Academy, he walked to the army of monsters now at his disposal. Cutting through the ice and leaving the forest behind, ashes skittered amongst the fallen.

A dabarne loped to him, its long snout flaring as it smelled Adair. "You are not like the other. Not even the man and women who set us free from our cage. Who are you?"

Taking in the gashes on its hide, its rippling muscles and unyielding eyes, Adair slowly walked toward it, placing a hand on its mammoth shoulder. Growls rippled throughout the army, but the dabarne watched as blackness ran down Adair's arms, flowing through his fingers and flaring underneath his palm. Flesh started to knit itself back together, sealing the wounds, and he could feel that same magic stirring in the monster's heart.

He lowered his hands and bellowed for all to hear, "I am your KING!"

It was like watching grass flatten against the wind, as the dabarne in front of him bowed the front half of its body, the army following suit. As they all bowed, the air around him crackled, and he drank in the sight.

Behind the army, in the broken courtyard, a ring of ash lay, a lifeless body in the middle. His gaze skittered over the woman indifferently, but glinting in the rumble, her sword was beside her, its cruel edges and duel blade with sharpened teeth. Striding through the lines, the army's answering roar echoed around him, and he drifted through the ranks like a ghost.

Reaching the middle, he picked up the blade, gripping it in his hands. It was heavy, the hilt cold. Looking up to the Academy, Adair raised the blade in the air, his yell more guttural as his army whispered and chanted throughout his mind.

"*Our Dark King rises; he rises; he rises; he rises.*"

His world was filled with inferno and rage as the Academy ignited in emerald flames. Lowering the blade and turning, Adair said, "I think it's about time we pay the capital a visit, don't you?"

There were ear-splitting roars rose around him, and Adair grinned viciously. His blood thrummed; his skin rippled with goosebumps. He could never get enough of this intoxicating elation. Nothing would ever be enough for his hunger. He would walk to the ends of the world and take and consume and never feel satisfied.

As gravity left him, his army galloped behind him, their footfalls like rolling thunder shuddering across the world. He was consumed by magic and smoke as he shot across the sky like a celestial body, and for the first time in his life, he knew exactly where he belonged. He dove and twisted, his dark soul consumed by power, and he left the ruined scene behind him, allowing the Academy to burn until it was nothing more than a scorched memory.

HEIR OF LIES – PART ONE

# CHAPTER TWENTY

## Emory

In a split second, her world had crumbled around her. The girl who was worried about her first crush, bored of waiting for her future to begin—she was gone.

The metal collar constricted around her throat, and she choked, her breath coming out in labored wheezes. The monster was dragging her deeper into the dark enchantment of the winter forest, constantly looking behind, as if expecting to see the army born from darkness chasing at their heels. If she was being honest with herself, she did as well.

Dried blood coated her skin as she looked at her chained wrists. Was it only a few hours ago that her mother was reminding her to be on her best princess-like behavior in front of the King and Prince of the Isles? That they were honoring the teachers and students that had been killed in a celebration of life? Tears brimmed her eyes, and she felt the panic claw up her throat, thick and fast, as her world and mind spun.

They were gone. *Gone.*

Stripped away from her, baring her soul for all to see. She forced her feet to move as the sharp slashes of betrayal cut deeper and deeper into her heart when she replayed what had happened.

She had tried to escape with Marquis when the killing had begun. One moment, he was helping her up. The next, the screams shattered through her, and then with a sweep of darkness, the lights had gone out, and Bresslin Stratton had exploded into the room, commanding the army of demons that had rushed in behind her. She wielded the Curse, her sword, with such finite skill, the massacre had been a blur—but the Academy never had a chance.

She relived those final moments repeatedly. Emory was in so much shock that she couldn't move as the screams rose around the dining hall. Marquis had grabbed her hand, dragging her, yelling at her, and all she heard was a sharp ringing slicing through her; all she could feel was the sensation of her body leaving the ground and Marquis's comforting warmth radiating through her.

He was the only person Emory had ever encountered that she could touch without her ability draining a person's life force. It was anchoring amongst the chaos. Almost comforting.

Tadeas had bellowed to Marquis, "This way, hurry!"

They had cut across the space, and her stomach churned repeatedly. The darkness closing in on her.

She was having a panic attack, the cold sweat clinging to her body, and she couldn't breathe, couldn't get away from the sounds of her friends and family being slaughtered around her, of forces that she didn't understand playing against her. Of her parents' best friends destroying the dream they had worked so hard to build, to achieve *peace*.

They had almost reached the King of the Shattered Isles when pain flared up her calf, and she was ripped away from Marquis.

"Emory, NO!!!" Marquis screamed.

Her head cracked against the ground, and she dug her nails into the cool floor, trying to stop. Her nails scraped against the concrete, but it wasn't enough to stop her, and she was quickly ripped away as she screamed.

Her captor's magic shivered through her, clouding her mind, clogging her senses. The creature's power was ancient as it shivered through her veins. Twisting her body, Emory slammed her boots hard against its chest.

Lashing out, punching and clawing, screaming in frustration. Decayed flesh connected with her jaw, slapping her head back, and stars erupted in her vision. The cool snap of metal froze her as she felt the collar lock around her neck and wrists. A flame flickered in between Emory and the monster before her when she was wrenched to her feet.

"Well, look what I have here."

This *thing* was born from the eternal depths of darkness. It had saggy grey flesh, a menacing silver gaze that bore into her soul. The creature loomed over her in a skeletal stance, tatters of rags clung over its lower abdomen. It smiled, and Emory cringed.

The rest played out before her in flickering moments as she fell into shock. The chains were spelled, neutralizing her ability, and she was dragged through the war of the Academy. Warm blood dripped down her leg, as they wove and wove until they raced through the tunnels and hallways, breaking through to the courtyard. It was chaos, the charging assault of the remaining students being torn through and ravaged.

This world was made from ice and blood, and she was ensnared.

The creature cut through the edges of the fight, growling to her, but she didn't hear a word. It could have been minutes or centuries, but one voice brought her slamming down into reality.

"Well, it would seem we meet under unlikely circumstances." Bresslin Stratton circled her with a hunger burning in her eyes.

Emory lunged, the chain snapping her back as her body was whiplashed.

"You will want to keep that fight for as long as you can. You will need it." With that, she had turned back to killing everything and everyone Emory loved: her home and her future.

And all she could do was watch. For the first hour, she had fought, pulling and snapping at the chains. The second, she had stood there, as ice and ash floated through the air, clenching and unclenching her hands until she ripped into her palms. The third, the doors exploded, and her heart nearly burst out of her chest when she spotted Memphis and Brokk in the throng of the fight. She collapsed to her knees as student after student fell, the storm raging around her.

*They are not dead, not dead.*

Then the storm had stilled, and the creature tugged at her chain, growling in pleasure. He lumbered forward, and her body complied, the metal digging into her flesh. Jutting her chin out, she stood tall as they walked through the army of rotting flesh and gleaming eyes. Creating a pathway, the monsters awaited command, their gazes following them hungrily. She practically growled back, but her heart plummeted when she saw why the contagious tension rippled amongst them.

Brokk locked eyes with her, screaming words that she didn't register. All she saw was his golden eyes burning like molten: the grief, the rage, and determination. The world bled away, and it was only them. She saw in him everything that fiercely coursed through her.

It was the briefest of seconds before he ripped his gaze away, and everything crashed around them. She swayed when he shifted, fear immobilizing Emory as she watched Brokk charge the army. Her screams were lost in the chaos as she lost sight of him. She couldn't lose everyone she loved.

The chains snapped back, and the creature rumbled, "You are coming with me, little heir."

Swiveling around, she slammed her boot down on the creature's leg, her calf screaming as the wound tore open even more. She threw her body weight backward, pulling toward Brokk. He was lightning streaking across a stormy sky, and she cried as he was closed in, his fur covered in blood. She became feral when he stumbled. The binds that held her to her humanity untethered when he fell.

"NO!!" She was spinning into that eternal blackness that clutched the edges of her world, dragging her down. There was a crack like thunder, and she snapped her head up, honing into the completely obliterated doorframe of her home. Adair stood there, looking out at the courtyard with a bored indifference.

And the world exploded into flame.

Being wrenched back, she clawed at empty space as she watched her best friend turn into someone she didn't recognize. She looked to the creature as he forced her to stumble after him.

"We have to go back!" she cried. "I don't care if you kill me, at least let me save my friends. Please."

It stopped for a moment, flashing her its grotesque teeth. "You really don't know? Your friend back there, he's the reason your parents are dead and is the reason that the darkness that once held the world will rise again." She balked, and he laughed, tugging her harshly. "As I said, that is our cue to leave."

They plunged down the rolling hill, and she swallowed hard against the bile clawing its way it up her throat.

*No, no, no.*

The forest loomed before them, looking like a city carved from ice, and as they ran into its cover, all she could smell was smoke and ash.

Blinking away the memory, Emory sucked in a deep breath, and took in the forest around them. Shivering against her shock and the bitter cold, her fingers turning blue, her mind desperately tried to plan.

With chattering teeth, she asked, "Where are you t-taking me?"

"Back to my lair."

"What are you?"

It snapped at her. "An ancient creature that has been long forgotten. I have been trapped in between time, waiting for this day to come. Usually, I take a blood price to feed my magic. I'm sure you know little Fae, that our power is always a give and take."

Her mind raced as she pieced it together, the only creature she knew from myth that took a blood price: A seer and exchanger of truths.

"*Gortach*," she whispered.

"Clever girl."

Emory was sure early hypothermia had set in, her limbs becoming more sluggish with every second and her mind diving into the betrayal.

*Adair killed your parents. He killed your parents.*

Licking her cracked lips, downy flakes of snow shook off the trees, drifting lazily on them. One landed on her nose, melting; the icy droplets turned pink from the dried blood, and tears slipped down her face.

Why didn't she try harder to reach through to him? To make him explain what was going on. Each day, he had become more withdrawn; each day, he had pulled further and further away. All along, he was the nightmare. The threat. She steeled her heart at the truth. If Gortach didn't kill her, Adair would.

The snow crunched underneath their feet, and they wove through the trees, deeper and deeper into the heart of the woods. Hours must have passed, and they were lost to what was happening. It was an amazing effect, how entering the forest was like entering another world, everything peaceful and quiet when outside its confines the world was being ripped apart.

Stumbling, she landed on her knees, throwing up in the same moment. Tears stung her eyes from the force, the foul acidity filling her senses.

"Get up!" Gortach scowled, but she couldn't move.

The iciness of the snow held her, and she bowed her head. Tremors raked her body; she was frozen.

"Pathetic human, move!" He pulled as she fell face first in the snow, ice shards tearing her skin.

That's when she felt it. The sharpness in the air, the churning of energy. Gravity left her, and in a flash, she was being held up against Gortach's chest, his inky talon pressing against her throat, poised to end her.

Vomit and blood covered her, and she swallowed, her gaze roaming the empty woods. The wind picked up, blowing more

# HEIR OF LIES – PART ONE

snow off the branches as Gortach rumbled, "If you want her to live, reveal yourselves!"

It was a split second before Memphis stepped out from the dying light, his blonde hair matted and stained as he hollered, "NOW!"

The snow around them shifted state, turning into water. The wind became savage, and the trees bowed as the water rose and rose, gathering into a roaring wave. Emory saw two figures behind the water, their green hair shining. The wave crashed down, and they both succumbed, drowning on land.

The water crashed against Emory, knocking the wind out of her chest. She was dragged down with Gortach, the chains binding her, the metal collar cutting off her oxygen. She felt his talons rip through her clothes, clawing at her back. Frantically kicking her legs, she tried to swim up, her chest burning. Her lungs expanded and expanded, her ribs straining against the pressure.

Water filled her nose, and panicking, she opened her mouth. Water filled her lungs in searing pain. Dots filled her vision, and she was dragged deeper, the chains pulling her down, down, *down.*

All she could see was the dappled water as the afternoon light filtered through it, and Emory knew she was going to die. The thought filled her, and weakly, she kicked her legs again, fighting against every fiber in her body. Flashes of memories came to her, her parents' voices ringing in her mind, the last words they ever spoke to her. And she fought.

*"You will learn that greatness does not come from a country's acceptance, or even a crown. You will see, Emory, that greatness comes down to a person's decisions and what they choose to stand by. Even when every odd is against them."*

Fire burned through her, and she wondered if Adair thought he was on his path to greatness. Darkness pulled at her, and she clawed toward the surface, any surface. There was a flash before her, imploring green eyes, and a strange guttural voice that yelled, "Ceol!"

Pressure was loosened from her wrists, from her neck, and she felt her body suspend in the water, floating up. Hands frantically clawed around her waist, and she was surging upward, through time and space. Maybe this was what dying felt like, a freedom, a fierce peacefulness. Her eyes were closed, and she felt herself climb, up, up, up.

Until she broke through, and freezing air assaulted her.

Eyes flashing open, Marquis's face filled her vision, his forearms pressuring hard down on her chest. He hissed in pain, his wrists bound in makeshift splints, and she gazed at them, wondering who had hurt him.

Sputtering, he rolled her onto her side as water spewed from her lungs, and she dragged in painful breaths. "Good, Emory. Listen. Breathe. Listen to my voice and breathe."

More voices circled around her.

"Memphis, will you shut up? He just saved her life."

*Brokk.*

"Oh, and you're so trusting, all of sudden, when we all almost died for them!"

*Memphis.*

"Will you both be quiet? We don't have long."

*Tadeas.*

Relief coursed through her violently, and she coughed up more water, shivering from the freezing water that soaked her clothes.

"Emory, you have to lie still for me for a second, okay? We have to get your clothes dry." Marquis's voice was soft, and she closed her eyes, exhaustion crippling her.

Her best friends argued around her, not trusting the prince. She didn't understand why. Over the course of the last couple of weeks, Marquis had a steadying force from just being himself. He had never pushed her like Adair had. He had never confused her like Memphis did. And so, she lay still as a roaring wind sounded all around her, and she was lifted from the ground. Her world became a spinning entity. The wind was warm, like she was standing on a coastline bathing in the sun. She spun, faster, faster, *faster.*

# HEIR OF LIES – PART ONE

Until gently, she drifted back down, finding her feet underneath her. Her hair was tangled and wild, but she opened her eyes, swaying slightly as she croaked at the disheveled prince, "Thank you."

Marquis dipped his head and stepped back when Memphis shot forward, gripping her in a crippling hug, whispering in her ear, "I thought I had lost you. I thought you had…"

His voice was thick with emotion, and she hugged him back. "I'm here."

Breaking from his hold, she looked at Brokk, looking rough but nonetheless alive. "How did you all find me? I saw you fall Brokk… And Adair…"

"We split apart because someone wanted to be the hero of the day," Memphis said, raising a pale eyebrow at his friend, "but it didn't take me long to figure out you weren't in the Academy. I used Brokk's secret tunnel and headed for the woods. That's where I found Marquis and Tadeas."

Brokk cut in, "Adair has some control over the army. I knew Gortach had you, and I barely got away, but I did."

Piecing the rest together quickly, she looked over her shoulder, the suspended roaring orb of controlled water churned behind them, the limp body of Gortach floating within it. Shivering, she looked back at the group. "Thank you. I owe you all my life."

Tadeas looked to his son before moving toward her. "Emory, we have to get back to the Isles. Right now, this country is lost to the Strattons. You can all come with us, find sanctuary there."

Chewing on her bottom lip, she looked to Brokk and his gaze darkened. Her heart dropped into her stomach, but she knew she had to hold firm.

"Thank you, Tadeas, but no. Protect the Isles, and I will call on you." She stuck her hand out toward him. "For all our sakes, I hope you will keep your promise to come to Kiero's aid when we need you."

He shook her hand firmly, his voice gravelly. "We will uphold our end. You will always find sanctuary on the Isles. Where will you go?"

Her pulse jumped, her heart battering against her chest unevenly as she whispered, "Into hiding."

Nodding, he bowed to them. "There are dark times ahead. I hope that we will all meet again on better terms."

Marquis mimicked his father, wincing against his splintered wrists. He caught her eye and quirked a smiled. "I'm glad you're not dead."

She chuckled. "Yeah, same to you."

He shuffled, uncomfortable, but in a clipped tone whispered, "If you see Adair again, don't immediately try to kill him. He is still in there, I think, despite what he has done."

Anger licked at her heart, confusion and frustration battering against her will. Bowing her head, she said, "I can't make any promises."

His face darkened but Marquis dipped his head. "Until next time, Princess."

And with that, the King and the Prince of the Shattered Isles turned their backs. Marquis faltered, before looking back at Emory. His emerald eyes flooded with emotion, as the winds shifted. The orb Marquis had created suddenly crashed to the ground, but just before it hit, it burst back into its downy snowflakes. The snow drifted lazily, like it had its own mind, curving and blanketing the world in its wintery state once more. Her throat became thick, and sincerely hoping they didn't die, she turned back to a scowling Memphis and a pale-looking Brokk.

Memphis stepped forward, *seething.* "Why didn't you agree? What do you think is left for you here?"

"Memphis Carter, my parents just died back there. Our home has fallen. One of my closest friends just betrayed..." she faltered and sucked in a shaky breath. "Do you honestly have the nerve to think I would let my parents dream die? For nothing?" Her voice cracked like a whip, and Memphis pressed his lips into a thin line.

Howls cut through the air, falling and climbing over one another in a haunting tremble.

Whipping around, she searched the fading light. "We don't have much time."

The howls grew behind them, sounding too close, too fast.

"Brokk," Emory said.

It was just his name as a whisper, but she could feel his tension crackle like lightning behind her.

His voice was husky as he spoke, "No. Absolutely not. We are in this together. We have always been in *this* together."

The wintery winds blew around her, as Emory steadied her breath. This was her home— her *kingdom*.

Turning around, she drank in the sight of Memphis and Brokk. The Academy had been their universe, where their friendship had bloomed.

Her heart stuttered at the thought that she would never be able to truly tell Memphis that she dreamed of them being together. And Brokk. How could she ever put into words that he was like the sun to her, radiating happiness.

Love wasn't always clear, wasn't always intimate, but that didn't mean it wasn't there. It was shown in their support; the boys in front of her had almost laid down their lives to find her. It was the fact it killed her to imagine her life without them. Love was their adventures, their bonds, and loyalty. They had found each other in this life—they would do it again. They were her best friends, and that bond could never be broken.

Lifting her gaze to meet Memphis's, her pulse stuttered, his ice blue eyes cutting into her. Chewing the inside of her cheek, her words felt bitter as she said, "Adair killed my parents. Do you really think he will stop until any threats are out of his way? The entire school is gone." Pausing a moment, Emory gathered her thoughts. "I will not let everything whither into nothing. My parent's dream of peace can't die because of Adair Stratton. I need time, and Kiero will fall under his madness for a time. Until we can fight back."

Memphis scoffed. "You wish to disappear, but to be brought back? Impossible. Where could we hide from his army?"

Emory locked eyes with Brokk, lips pressing thin. How could she ask him to do such a thing? But Adair wouldn't stop, and the Fae lineage had to survive. She would take back Kiero—*she had to*. Memphis's gaze flickered between them as his voice dropped into a dangerous whisper, "What do I not know?"

The howls climaxed, and she could practically see the dabarnes' gleaming teeth, how they ripped flesh so easily. How in hours, they had demolished some of the strongest people in Kiero.

The time was slipping by too fast. The army could be upon them at any moment, Adair leading them.

"Brokk, I am begging you. *Please.*" Her desperation bled into her words.

"You do know that I barely understand it myself? That this *power* in me is unstable."

Emory threw her arms out. "I think you understand it better than you know, but you are afraid to give into such a strong ability."

"Yeah, I am. Our world literally just entered another war that we barely understand because of forces rushing against us. We just *lost* our friends, our home. I almost died; Memphis almost died; you almost died. Our only safe passage just left because you are banking on *me* to do something I'm not even sure I can do."

The cold air formed into fog as she exhaled hard. "I get that you are scared. I am too. But you didn't see Adair. Didn't see the look in his eyes as he saw his own *mother* and destroyed her without batting an eye. Gortach..." she waved her hand at the lifeless body. "...a seer who only knows the truth assured me that Adair is the reason this is happening. I lost him weeks ago, and no one, especially me, saw the change because we were all so wrapped up in what was happening around us! About kings and queens and a legacy!"

# HEIR OF LIES – PART ONE

Tears were streaming down her cheeks, and her voice was hoarse as she jabbed a finger into his chest. "Brokk, you can get us all out of Kiero. We can be safe—you, me, and Memphis together. Like it always has been. *Please.*"

The snow drifted down around them, the afternoon bleeding honey-colored light, and if they were suspended in this moment forever, it would be chaos trapped in the breathtaking beauty of their world.

Brokk was visibly vibrating, and he swore, turning to slam his bloodied fist into the nearest tree trunk. It exploded, bark splintering around them, disappearing into the drifts. He didn't turn around, but his words came out like poison, "Something happened when Bresslin had us. Whatever this is in me, I have always felt it there, but I don't want to be *more*. I think you would all be scared, too, since being a shifter puts people on edge. But to also..." he paused then whispered, "but to also have the power to manipulate time. To jump through it."

Memphis tensed, looking at his best friend as Brokk turned to them both, a darkness sweeping through his features. "It's torture to feel that *alive*, when all I want is a shot at a normal life. A shot of feeling peace. But this, this is more of a beast than my other form. And I have no idea why it has to be me."

Roars thundered through the air, shattering their illusion that they were alone in the woods.

"But I do know two things for certain. That for you, Emory, I will go to the ends of this forsaken country to keep you safe. And that your parents..." Brokk's lips quivered as he snapped through his anger and welling sadness. "...even though I don't understand why this is happening, I trusted their dream. I trusted what they wanted Kiero to flourish into, and it's not this. It got twisted with their secrets."

Memphis was so still, he looked like a statue carved from the ice around them.

Her heart welled, and she pled, "Then keep their dream alive."

Focusing on Memphis, Brokk nodded. "I can do this. Jump through time, to keep her safe. But will you stay with me?"

Panic flashed through her. "What do you mean?"

She looked to Memphis, whose face had turned grave. He ripped his gaze from Brokk and looked like a ghost as he walked toward her.

Emory whispered, "Memphis?"

Palms tingling, her breaths came in quick bursts. She could practically feel the ground underneath them quake, the distant army closing in on them. Her pulse flew unevenly, sweat collecting at the base of her neck, as she absorbed Memphis's pinning gaze.

She flicked her eyes to Brokk, and he nodded once.

Memphis was before her, dissolving the space between them. His voice was gruff as he leaned in, his breath hot against her cheek. Both of his hands cupped her face gently. "I love you. Please, just never forget that."

Ice ran through her veins, and the world dropped away. Her stomach felt like it was being ripped from her, and she had the illusion of warm hands supporting her. Labored, sickening wails were echoing around her... Or maybe that *was* her.

The forest became a blur, the ivory bleeding into everything, leaching it all of color. In the distance, a voice bounced toward her, like cutting through a fog.

"Em, hold on."

And then, her world cracked into thunderous light. She was falling, the wind roaring around her, but she felt another presence, and she knew she wasn't alone. They spun and spun, brilliant golds, greens, and blues fracturing around them like diamonds, blazing like embers. Ice ruptured through her, numbing her, until she was tearing through a sea of light.

The golds bled into silvers, curling and twisting like liquid metal. The blues and greens softened into teal, and it reminded her of crashing waves. She wasn't sure she had ever been to the ocean. The thought struck her violently, and she tried to twist, but gravity pulled her down faster, her hair tumbling around her.

# Heir of Lies – Part One

Where was she? Where had she *come* from? Who had she been?

With each thought, she spun faster, dislocating her sense of self, until there was the sweet scent of damp grass and the trickling warmth of sunlight on her skin. Her body slammed against the hard ground. There was a whisper of words, his soft voice dying, and then there was nothing but pain. Nausea and throbbing raked through her, and she was distantly aware of the world churning around her.

She was greeted blissfully by the darkness with open arms, and she knew no more.

# CHAPTER TWENTY-ONE

### Emory

"Miss? Hello?" a woman asked.

"Do you think she is dead?" a man responded.

"Will you shut *up* Aideon and call *911?*"

The two voices bantered around her. There was a pause, and then a series of clicking as the male voice, Aideon, spoke smoothly, "Yes, hello. My wife and I are pulled over on Gore Road, just outside the city, where a young woman looks to have been beaten and is unconscious."

Another pause.

"Yes, visible wounds, dried blood, bruises. Okay, thank you, and yes, I will stay on the line."

The padding of soft feet sounded further and further away.

She felt the cool tickling of grass underneath her, a soft wind brushing across her face. Unfamiliar sounds whirled around her, all too sharp, too fast, and too much. Groaning, her eyes fluttered, catching snippets of the scene around her. A piercing blue sky and downy clouds. The woman beside her, her blonde hair tumbling around her shoulders, her features pinching with worry. A strange shaped box was behind them, pulled off to the side from the winding paved pathway, crawling with more people and some form of...carriage?

Coughing, she shut her eyes again, feeling dizzy.

# HEIR OF LIES – PART ONE

The woman's voice was gentle when she said, "Hold on, sweetie. It won't be long now. Everything is going to be okay."

She didn't know what she meant, but she was happy to lay here while her body radiated pain. Emory drifted on the sea of sounds and smells circulating around her. Concentrating on breathing in and out, she was comforted by the rattling wet sounds of her lungs dragging for breath. She winced, her eyes flying open when a piercing, wailing noise sliced through the air.

The man, Aideon, stated, "There's the ambulance and the police. Is she awake?"

Her heart clawed faster at the strange words. *Ambulance? Police?* Tears seeped from the corners of her eyes, burning as they trickled down her cheeks.

There was an intense squealing and then chaos erupted. Overlapping voices collided around her, questions being shot every direction.

Flinching, Emory tried to get away as another man and woman came into her view.

"Can you tell us your name and how you got here?"

Squinting, Emory took in the big white box with red flashing lights blinking on it. They carried a strange bag; the man took out several tools, and she bared her teeth in a feral way. Heart pounding as they came closer, panic immobilized her.

*My name.*

The world spun.

*What is my name?*

A spark bloomed in her chest, becoming an inferno.

"Emory Fae. Emory Reia Fae." Her voice sounded a thousand miles away.

"Can you tell us what happened?"

Trying to sit up, they responded, coming too close to her, too fast.

"Get away from me!" Emory said roughly. Her mind churned, pulling and tugging at strings with empty endings. What *had* happened? She was met with a brick wall. Who was she? Another wall. Where was her home? Her family?

Strong hands and a soothing voice pinned her, "You are going to be okay."

Her screams grew louder, her nails biting into flesh helped to ground her. She was feral, trying to bite, snap, do anything. There was a sharp prick on her arm, and in an instant, the world fell away in blanketed nothingness.

She dreamt of the woods. Towering trees, weaving a canopy of brilliant leaves. The green leaves were starting to turn color, the tips curling, golden hues and fiery reds and oranges changing the summer into the comforting blanket and refreshing air of fall.

She stood, looking up, breathing in musky tones. The dappled light danced across her features, and the corner of her mouth pulled up. Looking down, her feet carried her into the unknown. And that was the biggest adventure.

*Crunch, crunch, crunch.*

The leaves crinkled beneath her, and her simple black pants and deep green shirt flowed in the gentle currents of the wind. As she traveled deeper, the leaves and the light casted her in a golden haven, the vibrancy taking her breath away.

Golden, like a burning sunset. Golden like *his* eyes.

She scrunched up her nose, her mind bending and falling with the thoughts, her heart picking up its beat. The world around her flashed, the leaves dropping off the trees, ice racing along the trunks and branches.

In the distance, screams and howls mixed into a haunting melody, and she was frozen. *Golden, like his smile.* Swallowing hard, unable to catch her breath, the smell of smoke filled her senses. *Like his heart.* The wind howled, blustering around her, sounding like a pack of wolves baying at the moon. Her hair stood on end, but she wasn't afraid.

"Em."

# Heir of Lies – Part One

It was that voice, familiar yet unknown. Smooth and entrancing. Dark and enchanting. Slowly looking over her shoulder, at the icy landscape encasing around her, a figure stood in the shadows, his features blurry, but the sword glinted in his hand, and behind him, smoke oozed around him like gas, dancing toward her.

"*You will come for me.*"

She couldn't react, couldn't move, as that darkness rushed toward her. A pulsing green light cut through the shadows, the man watching as it overtook her.

His dark voice commanded, "And you will be mine."

Emory bowed to it, to him, as her world became nothing more than the shadows and his voice luring her into that void.

Emory woke up, screaming. Blood curdling, heart wrenching screaming. Strange tubes were in her nostrils, draping down her body and taped to her arm, and a persistent beeping sounded beside her. The room was small, drapes cornering her in on the bed, shielding her from the world—or the world from her. Sweat clung to her aching body, as the dream quickly faded from her mind.

She tried to hold on, to *remember*, but as the room came into focus around her, the dream left, leaving her breathless.

"Oh, good. You're awake. Sweetie, how do you feel?"

A woman appeared, holding papers on a board, looking at the instruments around her, her analyzing eyes roaming over Emory as she took notes.

Emory tilted her head, taking in her loose brown hair and kind eyes, her white shirt and plain blue pants, giving no indication of where she was. "I feel...sleepy," her voice rasped in a gravelly tone.

"That would be the sedation wearing off." She flipped the page of the board she held. "Emory Reia Fae, is it? That's a beautiful name. Can you tell me your age? Or where your home is?"

Swallowing, her throat constricted. "Thank you. And, um..." She closed her eyes, trying to fight off the burning panic rising in her. "I'm fifteen years old. Turning sixteen."

The woman nodding, smiling softly.

"I don't know where my home is. I don't...remember anything else."

The corner of the woman's mouth turned down. "That's okay, sweetie. Emory, you're lucky to be alive. You have been in the hospital for a week and were in a coma. It's not abnormal when your body has gone through...well, extreme circumstances, and your MRI was showing a lot of stress to your brain. It's not abnormal to experience amnesia. Or memory loss."

She blinked, the words falling around her, not making any sense.

The woman continued, "I'm your nurse, but we need to take it slow. The police have released a report with your information, so your family will know where you are. Let's just get you feeling better, okay?"

Tears slipped from Emory's eyes, and all she could do was stare at the nurse, her mind scrambling.

"What are these *things* around me? What's a hospital?"

The nurse tensed, tilting her head. "Darling, what do you mean?"

"I don't know what these things are! A nurse, a hospital! Where am I?" Her voice climbed several octaves, and she succumbed to the panic. The nurse pressed a button, and coolness spread through her veins. The world tilted once more.

"Emory, breathe. You are going to be okay. Everything will be okay."

The nurse and room started to dissolve and bleed away, becoming blurry. It was her fading whispers that filled her. "I don't know where I am... I don't know..."

# HEIR OF LIES – PART ONE

Her words carried her to a place where nothing was focused, and she drifted, lost amongst the current.

# Chapter Twenty-Two

### Emory

*Two Months Later*

"Emory, you will need to talk to us for this to work."

Emory stared down at her hands, memorizing each detailed line and crinkle of her skin, not wanting to look up at the woman posted across the desk from her. Her hair was tightly bound in a perfect bun, her black wardrobe too stuffy and too perfect. The folder lay open on the table, the sheets rustling against one another with each turn of the fan.

Two months had passed since she had been found. Each day, Emory felt her conviction to find out the truth of her past dissolve until it was nothing more than a whisper in her heart. She had learned the hard way that people scoffed at talk of other worlds and cryptic dreams, shrugging it off as trauma or escapism from the "accident".

Nurses. Social workers. Therapists.

They all looked at her like she either had two heads, or with such a dark pity, it made her want to throw up. Or punch something. And the more Emory learned about this world, she dreamt that she *had* lived a fantasy, that maybe, just maybe, she was destined not to fit in here. Any notion that didn't fit the mold was discredited without a moment's breath.

"Emory?"

# HEIR OF LIES – PART ONE

Exhaling hard, she wrenched her gaze up to meet her imploring eyes as she wearily said, "I already told you everything. Repeatedly."

"Honey, it's okay to be scared to tell the truth."

She swallowed her retort and went back to staring at her hands. The woman sighed. Emory set her resolve, and her silence was unrelenting. The seconds turned into minutes. The minutes into hours.

Finally, the social worker grabbed the papers, her voice soft when she said, "I will leave you with this question. How does thinking of your family make you feel?"

Snapping her eyes up, she looked at her hawk ridged nose and her sharp eyes. Emory's nails dug into her skin. "I don't *know*."

The woman's face crumpled, and Emory watched as the worker collected her papers. "You know you can call me anytime you need."

Emory watched as she left, leaving her card behind on the table. The door clicked, and she loosened a shaky exhale, holding her head in her hands.

Sweat collected at the base of her neck, slowly trickling down her skin. The walls seemed too close; the air too hot. It had been sixty days. Sixty days of confusion, of frustration. Tears burned, brimming in her eyes as she shut them, gnashing her teeth together. She had danced along the edges of her mind, diving into that empty carved out hole in her heart.

It wasn't that she didn't give them an answer.

It just wasn't the answer *they* wanted.

And with the truth screaming at them in their faces, she was turned away, deemed unfit, labeled and tossed to the side for examination. Footsteps sounded in the hallway, and she wiped angrily at her eyes, composing herself as the door swung open and revealing a grumpy looking Lourie.

"Well, are you ready?"

Her chair screeched back, as Emory stood, nodding stiffly.

They left the social worker's behind, coming into a poorly lit hallway. Continuing in silence, Emory followed her, her heart dropping with every second. There had been no trace of who she was, no trace of *anything*.

Naturally, she was put into what she learned was foster care, and Lourie had come into her life. As her foster mother, she was thrown into a repetitive schedule of daily scowls and the dullest life possibly imaginable, waiting as she was dragged through therapy and different medication line ups.

Lourie threw open the door, and the crisp wind hit them like a wall. The tinges of fall peeked through the world, painting the horizon in golden and fiery hues. Lourie's car was parked at the curb, and Emory faltered, breathing in the heady scent of change flickering through the air.

The city was a kingdom of grey and, at the heart of it, a labyrinth of cement. But on the outskirts, a wildness bred, gatherings of looming trees, the bulk of dark woods. The leaves crinkled in the breeze, their blazing colors flashing as they were ripped from their branches. Her pulse thrummed, and she stared, that thread in her gut pulling her into its hold.

In her dreams, the woods were a place born from fire and ash, of ice and secrets. Of shadows that chased her, *called* to her.

Not only did Emory feel peace but a deep longing in the forest, and she allowed herself to dream another world waited for her, called to her. It was there that reality fell away and so did every other barrier, and she felt a lingering hope that she had belonged somewhere else. A place that she had a family, that she had called home.

But always when reality crashed into her, she awoke to blurring images, to the taste in her mouth of longing. But nothing more.

"Are you *coming*?"

She honed her gaze with narrowed eyes at an eye rolling Lourie. Heat flared through her, and taking one deep breath, she took a step forward. And then another. Closer and closer to the car, her fate sealed with an iron hold.

## Heir of Lies – Part One

But her heart soared, settling into the darkness of the wilderness, of the unknown, and she knew that maybe, just maybe, she wasn't lost at all.

# Chapter Twenty-Three

### Emory

*Six years later*

The lights in the movie theater dimmed, and Emory shivered, pulling her button-down jacket tighter around her. Grabbing her pop absentmindedly, she took a big gulp, the mixture of overly sweet and fizzing sugar, calming her nerves.

The previews jumped to life in front of her as his warm voice tickled her ear, "This one looks good!"

Internally groaning, she wanted to roll her eyes at her well-groomed date, Kane. From his sweeping dark hair, to his deep eyes and really, *really*, good sense of humor, she should have been in heaven.

Moore, her co-worker's voice, sliced through her mind, "*Give him a chance, Em! What's not to like, super-hot and he reads?!*"

Internally, she cursed her best friend for convincing her to step away from her well-loved reading chair and, more importantly, her *routine*. First, she would make a cup of tea, put on her worn sweatpants, and reality bled away as she lost herself in realms of fantasy.

The movie had started rolling, and settling in, she chased Moore's voice out of her mind, reassuring herself that she *should* be happy. Her dating life had been hit-and-miss, mostly meaning, she wasn't interested. But Kane was nice, a decent guy, and if she was being honest with herself was not *that* hard on the eyes.

She dug into the popcorn, the salty, buttery masterpiece filling her senses, and she pushed every thought from her mind.

The dark tones of the instruments sprung to life, setting up the perfect tone for the horror movie she had chosen to see. Settling in, she was transported as the movie pulled her in, and she was lost.

A half hour later, she was chewing on her nails as the two main characters booked their weekend away, lost in the mountains. Kane leaned closer as her heart raced, and every instinct screamed in her that this movie was terrible, that the characters were one hundred percent going to die.

She loved it anyways.

She felt him lean in, his breath tickling her neck, and she tensed. He stalled, awkwardly staying half leaned in, as they watched the carnage unfold. She stuffed her face with another handful of popcorn, wishing that she hadn't listen to Moore, and her guidance to look put together for tonight.

His hand slowly and gently brushed her knee, and she almost choked. Taking this as an encouragement, Kane leaned in, searching for her neck, her cheek, her lips.

"Kane, can we just watch the movie, *please?*" Her voice was smooth and clipped, coming off cold. In the semi-darkness, she saw his brows furrow, but his voice was gentle, "Yeah, absolutely."

He settled back into his seat, and the tension in her chest uncoiled. She took in a shaky breath. Not a lot made her nervous, not a lot set her on edge, yet when it came to dating, it completely unraveled her, but it wasn't because she wasn't interested or that she didn't want a companion.

Her eyes flicked briefly over to Kane, immersed in the movie as the music climbed, building the perfect tension just before the chaos. She chewed her lower lip as she brought her attention back, her heart pounding against her chest. She just hadn't found the person that she thought would be worth taking the chance on.

The movie passed in a blur of blood and dark twists, and when the lights brought the theater back into life, she stretched happily. "Well, that was what I needed in my life."

Kane raised his dark brows in question and got up silently. Her heart sank, as she followed, putting on her knee length jacket, her ebony hair braided back, her leather boots buckled against her jeans. They left the theater, and she caught glimpses of herself in the stainless-steel patches against the wall, her golden eyeshadow bringing her emerald green eyes to life, her bloodstained lips flawless against her pale skin. She internally swore at Moore and her makeup skills.

Kane turned around before they exited to the parking lot. "Look, Em."

He nervously ran his hands through his hair, and she cut in before he could continue, "Thank you for tonight, Kane, really. I'll text you later?"

Before he could gather his thoughts, she quickly hugged him and then turned her back, walking toward her car. She pushed through the doors, the cool summer air licking against her face. She nearly always dressed like she lived in a constant state of fall, even though during the day, humidity clung heavy in the air, slicking everything with condensation. She shifted through her shoulder bag, found her jingling keys, and the light beep of her car sounded to her left.

Her mind was on autopilot as she looked up to the clear night sky, searching for her answers. *Any* answers.

As usual, the shimmering stars blinked down at her a million miles away, taunting her. Sighing, Emory opened the door and got comfortable. Throwing her bag onto the passenger seat, she had the inclination to pound her forehead against the steering wheel. She decided to start the car and make her way home instead, her mind throbbing painfully with knowing exactly what Moore would say.

# HEIR OF LIES – PART ONE

She started the engine of her Honda, pulling out of the parking lot. Picking up speed, she turned onto the street and raced beneath the streetlights, the city that was so much like a cage flying past. But like most things in her life, she had grown accustomed to it.

"Oh, come on!" Emory seethed, her keys stubbornly sticking in the lock.

She wrenched them to the right, and the doorknob eased underneath her grip and swung open. The low lighting from the lamp had been left on, casting her apartment in its warm glow. She smiled, throwing her coat and bag on the well-loved couch, the grandfather clock ticking soothingly amongst her stuffed bookcases. Her phone buzzed distantly, but ignoring it, she walked down the hallway, kicking off her shoes and letting her hair down in one motion.

As the night grew longer, thunder rumbled in the distance, the promise of summer storms lingering in the air.

Her phone buzzed again in the living room, and she knew Moore had been waiting up. Her friend would have to wait until the morning.

Shimmying out of her jeans, she put on a worn baggy t-shirt and flicked off the lights. Outside her window, lightning streaked across the sky, illuminating disjointed shadows and structures before plunging them back into darkness. She flopped on her bed, her blankets molding around her body. Groaning, she soaked it in.

Having her freedom for the last three years had been pure bliss. This was all she ever wanted. No more pushing from Lourie, no more families looking to adopt her, no more of anyone shaping her into someone she didn't want to be.

She knew she came from *somewhere*, where people knew her, her past, her family. And until she figured out what had happened, she would dictate her future. It was no one else's decision.

The rain began to fall, and it lulled her into oblivion.

Like usual, she dreamt of the forest. The lush canopy of leaves, the world around her blooming with life, and, of course, the alluring secrets hidden in its heart. Her face broke into a wolfish grin as she whispered into the air, "Are you here?"

The wind tousled her hair, the towering trees filtering a soft light, and she stepped forward, abandoning all rational thoughts, all aspects of reality, waiting to hear his voice. A voice that was the warm brush of calm, of reassurance, of home. At first, as a teenager, she thought of him as her guardian. A spirit amongst the living, only meeting in her dreams. It was a delusion, yet very much a reality to her.

The first time, she had woken shaken, the world was churning. Emory had thought she would never see these woods and him again.

The second time, she wished to never wake up. It was an intoxication, an addiction of being high and far away from her reality, and she desired it. *Needed* it.

But as the days blurred to months, the months to years, he had never left her and had always called her back. Back to the earthy reprieve—and to him. It was here, she felt safe. It was here, where fantasy took over.

"Emory."

Shivers ran up her spine, curdling her nerves into mush. Exhaling, she turned slowly and took him in. They had to be around the same age, his long blonde hair tied back, his strong angular face hiding secrets and temptations tucked within the corners of his mouth. Her gaze roamed, uncontrolled and blatant, working from his jawline to the crook of his shoulder. His loose shirt clinging to the edges and valleys of his muscles. He radiated, and it was all for her.

# Heir of Lies – Part One

"Emory."

He strode toward her—everything else faded away. Dream, reality, she didn't care about the definition. Her feet carried her, not faltering as she closed the space between them. His strong hands cupped her face gently, securely, the warmth from his fingertips flushing her skin. Resting his forehead against hers, she closed her eyelids, breathing in the scent of fresh rain and mint.

"Em."

*No, don't say it. Please. Do not say it.*

"He is coming for me. For us both."

Eye lids fluttering open, Emory took in his ice blue eyes. A snap of a twig sliced through the woods, and a nervous tittering rippled around them. He froze, and she could practically taste the tension rolling off him.

"Memphis," Emory whispered.

*Snap. Snap. Snap.*

She was thrown backward, and the world was devoured in flame. The fire towered above her, eating away at the trees, the lush leaves. She could taste the ash, clogging her throat, blinding her, tickling her skin like she was standing in the eye of the storm.

Rolling, she tried to stand, to scream, to escape the turned nightmare. Golden eyes flashed through the haze.

"*Run.*"

Memphis's voice hooked into her mind, her heart, the very marrow of her bones. Teeth flashed as his screams grew desperate and terrified around her.

"*Em, run!*"

She wheezed through the smoke, her lungs searing, her vision spinning. The ground shook behind her, and she pumped her arms faster. She flung herself forward until gravity left her. Her teeth sank into embers and dirt. Spitting and coughing, her flesh burned, but she tried to stand, to keep going. Sharp claws ripped through her pants, shredding skin and muscle. Bile clawed up her throat, as she was dragged backward, screaming.

Being flipped on her back, she expected to see a monster. Instead, a man smiled down, and the flames crackled hungrily around them, the scenes dancing in her eyes.

His golden eyes narrowed, and he leaned in closer, like a lover's embrace. He whispered, "Emory." From his knuckles, smooth inky talons ripped free. They stroked her legs and sides, trailing along her shoulders. "Come back to me."

Her scream lodged in her throat, as the man's hand shifted to a giant paw before her eyes. Locking her eyes with golden ones, a wolf hovered over her now, thick golden fur shimmering like molten. Growling, its muzzle pulled back revealing glistening teeth. Snapping its teeth, Emory screamed as the world tipped and disappeared.

Her body was soaked in sweat, and her skin prickled as she tried to still her racing heart. Her room took shape under the blanket of the night, thunder rolling ominously. Her tongue felt thick and swollen, as she got her bearings. Her legs were tangled in her comforter, her hair sticky and slick.

*Breathe. Just breathe.*

Looking to the walls surrounding her, lightning flashed, illuminating everything before plunging them again in the darkness. Her pile of laundry, assortment of books, her mishmashed dresser. No trees. No thicket of woods. No two men. One, a mystery, a gravitating lull that pulled at her. The other, a killer. A monster.

She shuddered, frowning as she pulled her sheets closer around her. It was just a *dream*. One she had in variations since she was a teenager. Always ending the same. Always in blood. In fire and ash.

Groaning, she pulled the sheets over her head, lying back down. Thunder rolled, growing in tempo, and Emory squeezed her eyes shut, hoping she could get more sleep, and thanking the forces in the universe that she was off tomorrow. She drifted, piercing eyes and soft murmurs chasing at her heels, trying to lead her back, and she allowed them to.

# Part Two

## Dark King

# HEIR OF LIES – PART TWO

# CHAPTER TWENTY-FOUR

## Memphis

**Six Years Prior**

Memphis just stared at the empty space where both of his best friends had been. The snow, the ice, and the howls seemed a world away as his hands trembled and tears streaked down his skin. The shock of what Memphis had done pierced through his heart. He had *wiped* Emory's memory; he had felt her entire sense of self disappear. Pacing, bile seared his throat, and the aches in his bones and bruised and bloodied skin roared in pain, but he couldn't stand still.

What had he d*one*?

Mind reeling, the air around him churned, as if being sucked in on itself, only to expand, blasting energy backward, as Brokk reappeared, swaying.

Memphis surged, spittle flying from his mouth as he demanded answers. "Is she safe? Brokk?!"

"She's safe." He looked down at his shaking hands.

Memphis swore, looking at Brokk as he swayed, and relief flooded through him. He closed the space in between them in two seconds, his muscles constricting as his fist flew, cracking against Brokk's jaw and snapping it backward. Blood stained the white snow, and Brokk swore, swiveling back toward him. Ebony claws sprouted from his knuckles.

"This is really a priority right now?"

Memphis was unhinged, and his voice rose serval octaves, "How long?"

"How long *what*?"

"Have you been lying to me?"

Spitting on the ground, Brokk jabbed his half-formed claws into Memphis's chest. "Memphis, how do I explain something I don't understand? That I never wanted? How can I tell you about a part of myself that I fear most above anything? I didn't tell *you* because I didn't want to admit it to myself."

"That's not answering the question." Memphis's voice was a whisper, and Brokk growled. Memphis knew they had to go now, but the world had stilled, and it was just them. Just this.

Brokk was shaking. "Our world is falling apart. Adair is waging war. Emory is on a different *planet*, and all you care about is that I haven't been telling you one secret? *One*?"

Memphis snapped, "Yes, I do care because we have always been able to trust each other. But everything is a lie. Emory knew. Why didn't you think to tell me? And now she won't know anything, thanks to me. Not you. Not this world. Not me."

"Emory found out by chance, Memphis. I never wanted her to know. Never."

The words hung between them, as their silent argument did before. Memphis was reluctant but knew Brokk was right. He normally was.

"She can't live a life that is always torn in two. She would never move on, never fully experience what that life would offer her. Is that what you want?" Brokk asked.

"I want her to be here. I want us to be together," Memphis said.

Brokk stalked up to him, spitting in his face. "What, so she can die? Stop whining and look at the reality. Adair can hunt her down, manipulate her, and use her like he did with Roque and Nei."

Brokk shoved his chest hard, and Memphis said, "Get away from me, now."

# Heir of Lies – Part Two

"No, for once, here's the ugly truth, Memphis. She didn't feel the same way that you do. Your image of your relationship and life together will never be what she wants. As one of her best friends, trust me, I know. She had a crush on you, and you have been in love with her for years."

Both of their chests were heaving, Memphis's ability churning with his anger. He was ready to tear through and obliterate something when the pieces became blaringly clear. How many times had Brokk used this powerful ability? Did Memphis even truly know his best friend?

"Get away from me. You have been controlling this situation all along. Have been controlling *her* all along. Me too."

Brokk scoffed. "You've got to be joking, right? Memphis, *no.*" He shook his head, stepping closer.

"Get away from me."

The ground shuddered beneath their feet, their impending doom clawing closer. Memphis stared at the sky, ashes floating and cascading down at them, overtaking and blotting out any color that lingered there. Looking past Brokk, the first line of dabarnes roared toward them, their festering skin and bloodied teeth coming into focus.

Fear curled into Memphis's heart—all along he thought he could be a savior of the Academy. Now, there was no guarantee that he would ever see Emory again, or that they would survive this day.

Shifting his weight, he turned, his decision steeling in his heart.

Something heavy slammed into his temple, and the world spun into a giant mass. He saw Brokk's face, his eyebrows knitting together as he whispered, "Hold on. Please."

Memphis dropped, his body colliding with ice, and he was plunged into oblivion.

# CHAPTER TWENTY-FIVE

### Adair

Landing on the ground in a plume of smoke, Adair's fingers dug into the dirt, as the sun broke over the horizon. The smoke settled, curling around his feet in black and purple hues. The brisk morning air collected dew, and as he rose, small puffs of mist flared in front of him.

"My King?"

The dabarne's voice brushed up against his mind, and the creature prowled to his side when he stood. It was a question and a recognition, and Adair bared his teeth as he fixated on the city in front of them. They had traveled through the night, groups of his army breaking off, Adair feeling the shifts of energy like stars streaking across constellations, creating a beautiful serenade of screams that followed him from below.

His fire. His carnage.

He rolled his neck slowly, bones cracking. Sarthaven and his father waited for him down below.

A distant thought tugged at his mind. Once, a lifetime ago, this city had been his lifeline, his hope to explore and to create. Swallowing hard, the thought dissipated, as another thought filled his mind, the magic ripping through his bloodstream, building and building.

"I go in first, alone. Cesan is mine."

# HEIR OF LIES – PART TWO

Approving roars and cackles rippled behind him as he unsheathed the Curse, his reflection shimmering in the steel, distorted by blood.

Looking up, he stalked toward the city that once was said to bustle with life, flourish with culture. It was the heart of their country, where trading routes were established with the Shattered Isles, where the first King of Kiero sat on his throne, where the monarchy was built and then destroyed.

Now, red and black smears stained the ivory towers. Adair shivered, clenching his blade tighter as the first wall of magic hit him like a breaking wave against a rock.

Smoke curled, floating above the streets, and he could hear the distant cries, the shuddering roars.

*So, not all the dabarnes came to the Academy.*

His footfalls were soft against the dirt, the late summer air humid, making his clothes stick. The homes and towers curled up in the sky, and as he drew closer, the true might of the city unfurled around him. Excitement surged through him when he approached the blackened gates, the curled metal creating beautiful designs reflecting a night sky.

The tang of magic intensified, as a guttural growl sounded behind the gates when they slowly opened. "And who are you?" a voice asked.

Slow steps sounded, and the owner of the voice came into view. Adair stood still, raising his eyebrow in cool composure. Inside, he blanched, ripping against his confines, sickened yet unable to watch, unable to do anything.

It resembled a human, but its grey skin was now decaying. Its blackened eyes took him in, the bone structure poking violently out from its skin, no muscle mass holding anything strongly. Its hair hung limply, leeched of any color, and the color was the same as bone.

Adair didn't answer, and the creature shuffled toward him, sniffing, tilting its head. Its voice turned grating, "Once, I dreamed of being like you. Like *him*..." It motioned to behind at the city. "Born into a world with no ability, no power, no status, watching the world thrive with magic. And all my life, I could do *nothing*." It smiled, which was more like a grimace, showing a mouth empty of teeth. "Until now."

It bowed its back, this creature that once had been a desolate, screaming shrilly as spittle flew from its mouth, and it charged toward him. The magic rippled out, the creature thinking it was powerful, that it was enough to destroy *him*.

Adair stood, chest heaving. A fire burned through his veins, consuming him. His anger, his lust, exploded through him, fusing with his magic, as Adair smiled darkly.

The creature was maybe a few paces from him, its eyes bulging, completely overtaken by the madness of the magic raking through it, feeding on it.

It leapt through the air, and he ducked. Slicing up, the blade cut through flesh, and the body hit the ground with a heavy *thud*. Panting, Adair bowed, not caring that he had been showered with blood, placing his hand on the ground, and the earth quaked. The dark magic flowed down his arms, pooling into his palms. Dropping to connect his hands to the earth, the ground shuddered as it caved in, splintering toward the city.

Adair was running, following his magic. The buildings around him shuddered, and his magic flared as every single standing architecture cracked, blackness running through them like a spider web.

He stopped; his shield surrounded him as the city crumbled down around him. Screams were crushed, roars silenced, and the world was one of dust and bone.

The dust settled in the rubble, and Adair flicked his shield down and then began running again. The streets were winding, the once bustling roads deserted, the gore of war staining Sarthaven. Pumping his arms harder, Adair flew deeper into the city, knowing his father would be waiting for him. Or at least he certainly hoped.

Adair raced, gritting his teeth, pushing harder, leaping over rubble. Both his ability and the dark magic worked together in unison. The magic cleared his path, burning and destroying, all the while he could feel his ability webbing out in the city, searching for his father. He would not hesitate ever again to take over Cesan's body.

His surroundings were a blur, and he was vaguely aware as he turned, a clear view of the Draken Mountains stretched up to the sky, and in the middle of the courtyard was Cesan. Adair saw Cesan's eyes flick up toward him before all the cement rubble rose and shot at his father under Adair's command.

Snarling, Cesan flicked his hand, the rubble turning to dust before his eyes, skittering around him. "You're not the only one who has learned new tricks, son."

The ground quaked, and Cesan grinned, his cloak floating around him. Resting above his brow was an inky black crown, the base made up of bones, the spires jagged. Huge vines shot through the ground, racing up to ensnare Adair, but he cackled, fire exploding from him with such force, Cesan staggered back. A wall of green flames circled Cesan, and for a second, he was entranced by the inferno. A second was all Adair ever needed.

Roaring, the flames split as Adair charged through them, and Cesan unsheathed his blade just in time, sparks flying from the steel as they met. Twisting, Adair slashed at his knees, his chest, his arms, forcing Cesan back toward the hungry flames. Rolling away from the fire's edge, Cesan attacked with magic, the force slamming into Adair.

*Bow to me.*

Cesan seethed. "Never," he spat, and Adair abandoned everything, and the only thing he succumbed to was the darkness within him.

He was relentless, moving inhumanly fast, his blade an extension of his arm, slashing, cutting the back of Cesan's knees, and Cesan faltered, blood running down his calves.

Panting, Adair slammed the pommel of the hilt into his father's back, bones cracking from the force. He prowled around him, years of rage thrumming in his veins. All the times he made him feel small, worthless. All those secret meetings filled with blood and bruises. The hidden tears, the betrayal.

Stopping in front of him, Adair plucked the crown off his head, twirling in it between his fingers.

His voice was low when he said, "You know, I never told anyone what you did to me. You taught me to hate myself, that I was never worth anything..." He crouched down in front of him, slamming the sword into the dirt. "...and I believed you."

Cesan's gaze raked the sword in Adair's grasp, recognition flaring in his eyes. "You have your mother's sword."

Adair licked his lips. "I enjoyed killing her almost as much as I will relish in killing you." Standing, Adair tossed the crown aside, and the iron melted before Cesan's eyes.

Adair dove into his ability, the world leaving him. He was nothing but never-ending bloodlust, and he tore through the false king's body, ravaging it of any power, leaching that same magic that burned through him.

And he took it all.

Slamming back into his body, he watched the lifeless Cesan crumple in front of him. The inferno stilled, disappearing into pulsing embers. For a moment, all he could do was stand there. The power that raked through him was intoxicating and never ending. He trembled, and he completely lost himself.

The *him* that was caged, that was fighting, was dead, nothing stirred in him except those alluring voices, and they chanted one thing to him, *purred* to him in pleasure and ecstasy.

*Dark King. Dark King. Dark King.*

Grabbing the Curse, he sheathed it, turning to his army of dabarnes. They reminded Adair of wolves, now his pack, ready to hunt for him—to kill for him. Before him, the hundred of dabarnes bowed, his army that was born from nightmares.

"Anyone who is of ability and wants to join my forces can. Rid the world of its weakness, rid the world of the doubt, of the lies. There is one king now, and they will either bow, or they will die," Adair said to them. The roars were shattering, and Adair screamed over them. "We are the future!"

# Heir of Lies – Part Two

Adair looked to the mountains and grinned, the thought spreading through his ranks. "Bring anyone who wants to rebuild this world to the Draken Mountains. My kingdom will be born there. Go. But tell no one of this location. *Ever.*"

The army roared, galloping through this city of ruins, and pleasure raked through him. He knew they would spread through the country like a plague. Soon, the world would know his name. *A mad, dark king.*

Adair started walking toward the Draken Mountains, and he was remade. Everything was a distant detail, and he was his power.

*"Listen to us, and you will be unstoppable."*

The smoke curled around him, and he took off, cutting through the air, less of a man and more destruction. It was seconds before he was standing before the face of the mountain, and giggles sounded in his mind when he rolled his neck.

He flipped his palm over, and on the opposite hand, a dark green talon replaced his nail. Cutting deep and slow, his blood welled, dripping onto the dirt. Placing his hand on the cool stone, he dragged his flesh over it, tiny splinters of rock entering the wound. Stepping back, Adair looked at the blood red slash and grinned madly when the stone turned to dust under his blood, creating a doorway.

*"All of Might, our Dark King."*

Alone, with the chilling voices of the Oilean curling around his mind, Adair stepped into the center of mountains, and didn't look back.

# CHAPTER TWENTY-SIX

### Brokk

Running deeper into the woods, the two monsters closed in on their heels. Froth collected at the corners of his mouth, and he wanted to stop. He wanted to give in. Memphis's shirt was in his mouth; his friend was unconscious and thrown across his back, the bloodied fabric the anchor between them.

Stumbling, he pushed harder, his quaking muscles drained of energy. Flashes went through his mind, leaving Emory, their idea of growing forces against Adair. Memphis crazed and broken. He knew his friend wanted to leave, but he couldn't let him, no matter how mad they were at each other.

Even though Memphis could be annoying and stubborn, he loved him.

A day had passed since Emory left, since the fall of the Academy. It was a long night of endless running; the once comforting blanket of night turned against him, harboring screams and breeding nightmares.

Brokk leapt over a decaying log, his back paw catching, and they were both flung forward. They landed hard, and Brokk swayed to stand, looking at his friend who didn't stir. Snarls sounded behind him, and he knew he couldn't run anymore.

# Heir of Lies – Part Two

He turned, sides heaving, as he took in the two circling dabarnes. They snapped their teeth, daring him to prove their dominance wrong.

His hackles rose, and he dove down deep into his motivation for staying alive. And then he charged, his growls guttural and deep. They clashed, claws ripping fur and skin, spittle and froth flying. Brokk sank his teeth deep into the rotting flesh, choking and gagging. He was body checked, flying violently as the second dabarne caught his throat, dragging him down.

Its teeth held him, any movement on his end would tear through his flesh. The second one prowled up to him, saliva dripping from its maws, and Brokk understood that he wouldn't stand a chance two against one. He needed to fight now.

He flattened his ears, his growls intensifying, as he prepared to twist his body from the dabarnes pinning grip. A flicker of movement flashed to their left, and a wild scream cut through the woods. A young girl charged at them without hesitation, without fear.

He was in awe of her courage and stupidity.

The dabarnes stalled, and Brokk felt the energy surge through him as he shifted back, slamming his fist into the creature's jaw, teeth flying onto the ground. The girl was pale and covered in dirt, her electrifying blue hair unbound. A small curved blade flashed as she sunk it into the side of the dabarne, and it screamed.

He parried, shifting back, and threw everything he had left in him at the wounded one to their left, and with a crunch of bones, it dropped. The girl practically growled at the other one, but another scream tore from their right, and the three most unlikely people Brokk ever thought to see ran past the trees.

Alby. Wyatt. Jaxson.

They threw themselves at the monster, blades sparking, the wet thud of steel into flesh, and Brokk shifted back, dumbfounded. Once both forms were still, they chortled, relief flooding into their voices.

"Brokk! You guys are alive?" Jaxson exclaimed.

"Who's the girl?" Wyatt asked.

"No one else survived. Alby hid us, but then we heard howls and followed them," Jaxson continued, talking over Wyatt.

Overwhelmed, Brokk ignored the questions and turned to the girl. "Who are you?"

Jutting her chin out, she said, "Bryd Reit."

"Why are you out here?"

"My town..." her chin wobbled, "...was destroyed by those creatures. I was one of the only survivors to escape. The rest of my fellow villagers, those who didn't perish, left with them on the promise of glory with the Dark King."

A heavy silence fell over them, and Brokk raised his eyebrows to his friends, all of them knowing exactly who the Dark King was. She locked eyes with Brokk.

"Please. Help me."

Running his hands through his hair, Brokk exhaled. "As long as we are out here, we are targets. Where can we hide? Somewhere Adair won't find us."

Alby croaked, "I can hide us, until we figure it out,"

"No, look how drained you are already! I'm not having your death on my hands as well."

"I can hide us," Bryd spoke calmly.

They all turned to her as Brokk whispered, "*How?*"

She smiled and spoke to Alby, Wyatt, and Jaxson. "Please. Stand still." She concentrated, and Brokk almost dropped to the ground in shock, as one second he was staring at the group, and the next all that remained were the woods.

Bryd lit up at his expression. "I can cloak anything, for any length of time. I can hide us, if you will have me."

The group returned, and tears slid down Brokk's face as he broke down, completely and utterly. The last twenty-four hours caught up with him, and he just cried, raking breaths dragging in as he caved in on himself.

His heart broke as he thought of Emory a world away, and he silently promised himself he would cherish her safety until the day he died. He wouldn't let her parents' dream die, no matter how far they had drifted themselves. He saw his purpose sharply then, and he choked down laughter as he stood, legs shaking and taking in the spitfire in front of him.

"Yes. We will have you," Brokk managed to reply.

"Excellent, as long as you aren't a group of murderous psychos, this should be great."

Brokk really laughed now. "You're safe. We are what's left of the Academy."

"Like *the* Academy?"

"The one and only."

She nodded, lost in thought, before she whispered, "That's where we should go, probably."

*Back to the Academy?*

He mulled over the thought before nodding slowly. "It would be the last thing Adair would expect. What do you say, should we go back home?"

Their swearing and catcalls were answer enough, and Brokk limped over to Memphis, scooping his still unconscious friend up.

They slowly made their way back home.

# CHAPTER TWENTY-SEVEN

## Adair

*Two years later*

Standing on the shoreline, the Black Sea crashed, the mist and salt coating his skin. His hands shook as he clenched the parchment in between his hands, the words branding themselves in his mind.

*Marquis Maher* was now the King of the Shattered Isles.

Yelling, Adair incinerated the letter in his palm, the scorched paper catching in the wind and floating like ash.

"*Calm yourself, our King.*"

"Is this what you wanted? After everything? To share *my* reign with a King from across the Sea?!" he yelled to the open air, to the wind and the crashing waters.

"*You know you and your people need his resources.*"

Adair paced back and forth, Marquis's words bouncing in his mind: *Go to war with me and lose your trading routes my father upheld with you. Cross our waters, and I will kill you.*

Adair sent emerald green fireballs rocketing out from his palms, just to watch them flare, then hiss and die as they hit the water. He envisioned they were Marquis, and it calmed his racing pulse. Wrenching his gaze, he turned, popping the collar on his black jacket, and walked back to his kingdom.

# Heir of Lies — Part Two

He entered the woods, deep purple leaves and moss creating an illuminating light. The woods circled the Draken Mountains, the beauty here unlike anything Adair had ever seen.

One that captured the essence of shadows.

Hisses and growls followed his footfalls, and yellow eyes flickered to life, watching his movements. The Noctis Woods—better known by his people as the Heart of Midnight—was a refugee for ancient dark magic. It was his reprieve, a place where he could just be. The foliage of leaves casted a brilliant dappled light, and Adair looked up. Across the sea, Marquis thought he had him shackled, backed into a corner.

Adair chewed on the inside of his lip, his answer forming in his mind. Whispers from the shadows pulled at him, but in a flurry of mist and shadow, he was flying.

In seconds, he passed through air and stone and materialized in his court room. His throne was inky black, bones carved into it, and Adair stared at his loyal guards, smiling viciously.

"It would seem we are supposed to show our allegiance to a new King across the Black Sea." They shifted uneasily, and Adair snapped, "Parchment and ink, *now*."

They scrambled, and Adair chewed his cheek. His dark gaze flickered back as he was handed what he needed, and nodding, he started his letter.

"Marquis..."

He wrote eloquently and without hesitation, and knew his old friend would come to trust him again over time. And until the day they didn't need him anymore, Adair would convince him he had bowed to their agreement.... Only to sink the knife in his back when he dared not look.

His low growl of laughter erupted from him, bouncing around the room, as beneath them, their kingdom grew, because to his people, he was their safety.

His guards bowed their knees around the room, as he wrote, softly weaving lies, sinking his claws deeper into everyone he could. Adair would never live in a world where there was opposition of another resurfacing. He would kill all flickers of defiance against him, starting with Marquis Maher.

# Black Dawn Rebellion

# CHAPTER TWENTY-EIGHT

## Brokk

*Six Years Later*

Sweat rolled down his spine, making his black armored chest plate feel suffocating over the top of his black shirt. Kieroian steel was an impregnable iron, one they were lucky to get their hands on to fuse in their protective gear.

The night was bleak and all-consuming as Brokk Foster looked to where he knew his best friend and Commander were hidden. Weeks of tactical planning and training brought the soldiers of Black Dawn Rebellion to this moment.

The slight tremor in his hands was the only sign of how he was feeling. Pressing himself closer to the mossy ground, Brokk breathed in the sweet smell of dewy grass. There was a snap of twigs, and the group went rigid, frozen in the shadows. Laughter filled the forest air as four men with blood red sashes placed brazenly across their chests walked into view a few hundred yards away. They quipped at each other, totally relaxed, their voices sounding like a constant buzz.

Blood thrummed in Brokk's ears, and his heart pounded wildly. The seconds felt like centuries until finally he saw a flash of silver, and Memphis's smooth voice filled his mind, *"Now."*

# HEIR OF LIES – PART THREE

Brokk didn't need to be told twice. Springing from the ground like a demon from the darkness, he pulled his curved twin blades out in front of him in seconds as he cut them off. The group stopped in the pale moonlight, exposed.

He tauntingly greeted, "Evening, boys, sorry to interrupt your rounds, but I dare say, you're a little close for comfort to our home. Convenient for us though..." He twirled the hilts in his hands. "...we wanted you exactly here."

The leader of Adair's men took a daring step toward Brokk. Smirking, he readied his blades, and in a flurry of movement, his friends dropped from the tree branches that had camouflaged them. Dressed all in black, their weapons brandished in front of them, the Black Dawn Rebellion acted.

Nyx Astire was a flash of purple hair as she froze one guard in her telekinetic grasp, slitting his throat before he could react. Blood spattered her as she lithely moved on to find her next victim. To Brokk's left, Jaxson and Wyatt threw their knives, not even having to use their abilities to slay their enemy. Brokk charged, eyes fixated on the two guards that broke away from the fight.

The familiar popping and breaking of bones shivered through his body as animal instinct took over, and the wolf inside him did too. The ground shook from his colossal paws, golden fur rippling like a beacon in the night. His growl rumbled like thunder, and for a split second, he forgot who he was. All that mattered was that he took his targets down.

Paws shredded fabric, bone, and sinew as Brokk ripped apart the soldiers. The screams died in the night, and flicking off his emotions, Brokk did what he was trained to do. What they had *all* trained to do in the six years Adair Stratton had become the Mad King.

Shifting back, trying to calm the elation of how good that just felt, Memphis snapped him out of his glorified moment. "Brokk! Come here."

The last guard was openly crying now, forced to his knees, hands shaking behind his head. Brokk almost felt sorry for him. *Almost.* Up close, he was much younger than Brokk thought, fear replacing the guard's bravery now. Memphis's icy blue eyes cut into his, and he didn't have to say anything for Brokk to understand.

Telekinetic or not, his friend wore his heart on his sleeve. They were all on edge, and who could blame them? Six years of hiding. Six years of losing this war. Brokk swallowed back his thoughts, wearing his mask, one of confidence and anger.

"W-who are you?" The guard's voice squeaked out several octaves higher than it should have. Nyx kicked him in the gut, making him gasp for air.

Her thick purple hair was pulled back in a high bun, revealing Nyx's uncanny ability to have stone cold features. Her violet eyes flashed, relishing in the man's pain, her slender figure ready to kick him again. Nyx had been recruited into their cause when Alby found her in the northern Arken Mountains, her community destroyed by Adair.

Nyx flicked her gaze to Memphis, her lips curling up as she took in her boyfriend and Commander who crouched down in front of their prisoner. His long blond hair was tied back, revealing his severe features.

They all bore scars, some more visible than others.

"It's your turn to listen. We are your worst nightmare. If you don't comply with our demands, you will die. If you co-operate, you will return home with a message to your king."

Brokk didn't think the man's face could go even paler. Memphis took a thick blindfold out and, in a gruff manner, tied it over the guard's eyes. Nyx looked to Alby who looked to Wyatt and Jaxson. Brokk put a hand on Memphis's shoulder, squeezing lightly before slinking behind the prisoner, smelling his defeat.

He whispered, his voice hoarse in the man's ear, making him jump, "The Academy is very much alive. I promise you, we are sick of hiding in the shadows." He chuckled. "Besides, I'm sure your *king* would like a reunion after all these years."

# Heir of Lies – Part Three

# Chapter Twenty-Nine

## Memphis

The traces of dawn bled through the tree line as they pressed through the forest, Brokk bouncing beside him, and the rest of his friends wearing smug smirks. It was a huge win for them to finally get one of Adair's men. The Mad King had an uncanny ability to have his soldiers slip through their fingers.

Memphis's head spun from the anticipation of information they could finally get their hands on. The first and most important thing being where their friend was hiding after all these years. They were all tired of playing cat and mouse.

*We have to move or raiders will be picking us off one by one.*

Panic clutched his heart at the thought, as Memphis yelled, "We have to hurry!"

Their hostage grunted as Jaxson shoved him faster, Memphis focusing on making it out of the woods, to where the Academy lay hidden. The trees started to thin, soft rolling hills coming into view. His entire body felt numb as he ran, cursing under his breath.

The group followed tightly around him, always staying in formation and never faltering. Always prepared for the worst.

Breaking from the safety of the woods, Memphis frantically reached out with his ability, the tendrils of his mind expanding. "*Bryd, we're back. Take down your barrier!*"

Sprinting full tilt, a shimmer of light reflected with the rising sun, and the empty field before them unveiled a deeper truth. The building was vast. Over the years, the Academy had shifted in looks with their rebuild with kieroian steel.

The once old bricked school was now a world of metal, the only substance that would keep them protected against Adair's assault of dark magic. The broken archway leading up to the chiseled stone steps were cracked and worn. The windows had been reconstructed and barred with iron. The once oak doors now stood ripped off the hinges, two rebels standing guard, the heavy iron door shimmering behind them.

The Academy was once a place where dreams were supposed to be nurtured, a school to master one's ability. And *now*, the building was more of a cage, having been transformed over the years as more rebels joined. To the east, their lookout tower stretched up toward the pink wash clouds as the sun rose.

For six years, they had hidden, buried deep in the earth, while Adair Stratton ensnared Kiero in a future bathed with death; a reality filled with fear.

Their group bounded up the stairs, slowing to give curt nods to the guards, the shadows dancing in their eyes as they took in The Mad King's sigil blazed across the man's chest.

Reaching the door, Memphis pushed down hard on the handle, revealing a dark hallway. Ushering his team in, he took one last look at the scenery before him. Nyx strutted by him, the guards warily following her. It was to Memphis's understanding that his girlfriend had beat most of the rebels in their fights, earning herself an unhealthy amount of goods in weapons and clothing. But most importantly to her, a reputation of fear.

Memphis soaked in the thick rolling forest, and to the east, the skeletons of the Ruined City peeked out. Concrete and ghosts were all that was left of the once thriving Sarthaven: *The city*

## HEIR OF LIES – PART THREE

*beneath the stars.* Behind that, the Draken Mountain Range looked ominous as ever, piercing the clouds.

Sighing, he slammed the door, closing them in the darkness.

It was disorienting and freezing as always, and Memphis blinked hard as his eyes adjusted. Excited hooting and catcalls exploded, and the founders of the Rebellion danced around him. Memphis was just about to tell them to remember themselves, but Nyx pranced in front of him, violet hair blazing, and pulled him in fiercely for a kiss.

Her lips were hungry and demanding, and his body bowed into hers. Warmth spread through him, pooling in his gut, and he grabbed her face in between his hands. Her breath was fast, and closing his eyes, Memphis lost himself to her wild, fearless energy. Her tongue parted his mouth, the lingering taste of spiced berries dancing along his senses. Every nerve sang as he pulled her closer.

The night had been long, the stakes high. They all deserved to savor the victory.

An awkward, "eh-hmmm," sounded behind them. Breaking apart from Nyx, Memphis saw a petite girl with electric blue hair. A huge smile broke over his face, and he motioned Jaxson to bring their prisoner forward.

"Bryd, as always, thank you for keeping watch for our return to the Academy. Where should we put our esteemed guest?"

Taking a tentative step forward, Bryd inspected the soldier, her eyes widening as she saw Adair's sash. The lanterns on the iron walls behind them glowed as she smirked, "Cell fifty-five is empty, Commander."

Wyatt and Jaxson didn't wait to drag the guard forward. They followed Bryd down the winding hallway.

The Academy was swarming with life, rebels barking at one another, murmuring, "Commander," as they passed Memphis. Nyx squeezed his hand, her consciousness brushing against his, her voice filling the cavities of his mind. *"You need to eat before you deal with that. Let's go get breakfast."*

Squeezing her hand back, they made their way down the hallway.

The Academy consisted of a hive of passages and levels, the dining hall the heart of their headquarters. Reaching the rusted elevators, Nyx pressed the worn button, the doors sliding open. Stepping in the iron cage, they were sealed in and then dropped into the ground, the air howling around them as Nyx laughed, their hearts in their throats. It was a fast way to chase away his tiredness if even for a second.

The gears grounded to a halt, and the cage slid open. Nyx practically dragged him along. Fifty tables were full, and the roar of noise washed over them, the men and women talking excitedly. News spread unnaturally fast, which was a side effect of pooling humans with a varying amount of abilities together.

Sitting down at an empty table, Nyx pouted. "Someone is especially grumpy for such a productive night."

Memphis focused in on her with furrowed brows. How did she not understand the burden that sat on his shoulders? Of what they would all have to face—and very soon. Of how close they were to confronting Adair. If they learned of his location, then it would only mean a march. After all these years.

*Years of you being afraid*, he thought.

Shrugging, Memphis pushed the doubts down. "Just the usual stuff."

She arched an eyebrow in disbelief before leaving to get their food. Memphis wanted nothing more than to continue his way to their room and catch a few hours of blissful sleep. But above all else, duty called.

Nyx returned with small bowls of fruit and bread, which they both devoured in silence. Finishing, she gave him a curt nod, and they got up, both knowing what came next.

The cells were located on the same level as the dining hall, so it wasn't far to go until the stood outside a door labeled, *Fifty-Five*.

# HEIR OF LIES – PART THREE

Brokk was already there, along with Alby whose fiery red hair and spattering of freckles was much too alive for their dreary scene. Having been with the rebellion from the beginning, he rarely talked about his past, but Memphis knew there had been no word of the survival of his hometown, Pentharrow.

Excitement and dread ran through Memphis like a live current, and he murmured, "Let's go."

The cells were basic, and small strange runes encircled them on the walls. As soon as they stepped in, they took in the guard, whose blood was already running freely, thanks to Wyatt and Jaxson. Bryd stood in the corner, a silent observer.

"You two have been busy during breakfast," Memphis said.

Jaxson grinned as he multiplied in the already small space, showing off his ability. "Even so the bastard won't talk."

Sitting in the chair across from the guard, smoothing his jacket, Memphis blatantly stated, "You have obviously chosen not to comply with our wishes."

The guard spat blood at his face. "Adair will finish you once he finds out you survived."

Scoffing, Memphis leaned in. "And how will he? Your men are dead, and you have no idea where you are or how you got here. I would say it's in your best interest to tell us where Adair's been hiding all these long years." He deliberately paused. "Where. Is. His. Kingdom?"

Interlocking his long fingers, he waited. A flicker of doubt sparked in the man's eyes, as he took in his words, his façade slipping.

Nyx stalked toward the guard with lithe grace. She grasped his cheeks, locking her violet eyes on him, whispering, "You will tell us where Adair is. Now."

The guard convulsed in pain, a silent battle going on between them. Memphis watched in silent horror, knowing exactly how much pain Nyx was assaulting on his consciousness. Blood started to gush from his nostrils like rivers, and Memphis barked, "Enough."

267

Gasping, the guard slouched forward in his restraints. Memphis leaned toward him. "Are you ready to tell us now?"

Silence met them like a wall, and Memphis nodded to Jaxson and Wyatt. They bounced, but the man cried, "Wait. Wait." He looked to Memphis, then said quietly, "The Draken Mountains."

Nyx froze as if she'd been slapped. His heart pounded at an uneven rhythm as he choked out, "As in *the* Draken Mountains? Past the Ruined City?"

The man was laughing now, blood bubbling from his lips. "Those are exactly the mountains I am talking of. We have built another society in the mines. One which is clear of Mixed Bloods."

Spitting in his face again, Memphis's resolve broke. "I dare you to say that again traitor. Mixed Bloods? How can you even say we are different when we live in a world of super charged abilities? Adair is a power-hungry madman. One that caused this war. We are just trying to end what he *started*."

The guard was laughing uncontrollably, not listening anymore to a word that came out of his mouth. Spit flew from the guard's mouth in a disgusting display, and Memphis stood up, looking to Brokk.

His second-in-command stood with him, sadness welling in his golden eyes. Memphis stretched out his hand, Brokk passing him his curved twin blade. He grasped the hilt and turned to the guard, whispering, "I'm sorry."

Thrusting the blade forward, the man choked, and the light drained out of his eyes. When the guard died, Memphis turned to the group, his voice flat, "We meet in Command in a half hour. Be ready."

Filing out with Nyx, he gripped her hand, the tremor shaking through his body. Nyx squeezed his hand back, as she led him down the hallway toward his room. The heaviness in his heart lifted, when they reached his door. Opening it, Memphis walked in, Nyx quietly following.

"You did what you had to, Memph. Don't mourn those who don't deserve it."

# Heir of Lies – Part Three

Turning, he closed the space in between them. "I know it's what I had to do, and that is exactly why I acknowledge every life I take. I never wanted to be in this position—to lead a rebellion."

Brushing his blood-stained hands against her cheek, Memphis leaned in. "But I have to say, having you by my side always makes it easier."

He brushed his lips against hers, lightly at first, but then his tongue hungrily parted her lips. Her hands moved with practiced precision, unbuckling his armored chest plate as it clattered to the ground. Fire burned through Memphis's veins, his body begging for *more*. Nyx kissed him back with equal vigor, shoving him roughly toward the bed, "You're a smooth talker, Carter. It's one of the many things I love about you."

His breath caught as he lifted his shirt off, revealing his defined and scarred chest. Nyx's violet eyes glowed mischievously as she prowled toward him, and they lost themselves in each other before they had to go back to meet the others.

# CHAPTER THIRTY

## Brokk

The waves of nausea crashed into him, and Brokk sat tensely next to Memphis. Sitting in Command, the clamor of shouting echoed around the small room, overlapping and cutting each other off as they tried to find a solution.

Except Brokk and Memphis had the solution, and they had kept it hidden for the last *six* years.

Slamming his fist hard on the table, Memphis seethed. "We can't allow Adair to destroy us. Look what he has already done to Kiero. His armada is vast, the dabarnes ruthless. The darkness that has bred into our country is too much for us to stand a chance. We have no edge, and if we show our hand, he *will* destroy us."

The room fell silent, ghosts of the past playing behind all their eyes.

Memphis pressed on. "We have his location, and we need to flush him out. We started this rebellion on bare bones, with nothing more to support us than the bonds of friendship, and our hope that, together, we could win against his forces. The question isn't the Rebellion's ability to fight. I don't doubt your spirit, or heart." He looked at them. "It's about being smart enough to know that we cannot overpower Adair. His ability is too great. That leaves us with the question about how we approach this situation."

"There is no one left to stand up to him," Nyx said. "The monarchy was built on the Faes' name, but who is left of that

# HEIR OF LIES – PART THREE

line? Emory is *gone*. Being a leech, she would have been the last person who could overpower Adair. To have the power to steal someone else's ability just by touch... I have to say, I am jealous of that fact. There is no one to oppose him other than us. We are the only hope Kiero has."

Just at the mention of Emory and her family's name, Brokk's gut twisted, palms becoming sweaty. Black dots spotted his vision, and a deep roaring filled his ears. He gasped, "Excuse me."

Pushing his chair back, he scrambled out of the room and into the hallway, gulping in the damp air. The shuffle of feet and the clicking of the door was Brokk's indication to look up at Memphis, his arms crossed over his chest.

Whispering with venom in his voice, he said, "Pull yourself together, man. It's too obvious that something is wrong."

Standing, the world tilted, and he shook his head. "We have to tell them. It's been too long, and nothing is getting better. It's time to make a difference. *She* could be our difference."

Memphis countered, "You don't think I realize that as well? How is everyone going to react when they find out their leaders have kept this a secret for six years? There will be an uprising. That we saved her while we entered a war. How do we explain that rationally?"

"The Rebellion will see reason. We start with the team, and then go from there. We start with our friends. We owe them that much," Brokk replied.

Memphis ran a hand through his hair, dark circles under his eyes. Loosening a breath, he said, "We do this together."

"Always."

Keeping a firm hold on his churning breakfast, Brokk reentered Command, knowing when he came out, everything would have changed.

Brokk and Memphis finished telling the truth about what happened six years ago when the Academy fell. What they had done to save Emory Fae.

Brokk looked up to meet Nyx's gaze first, but she looked like she was about to kill Memphis. Venom churned in her gaze, and Brokk noticed her palming her knife she gripped in her lap.

The rustling of scanners and screens that kept surveillance disrupted the tension. They had kept up a lot of the technology the teachers of the Academy had created, but their world had reverted with Adair waging war, instead of progressing. Brokk tried to ignore the buzzing and read each of his friend's expressions but found nothing but hatred in their features.

The bitter taste of guilt coated his tongue, and for the hundredth time, he reassured himself it was his only choice to save Emory Fae. Even if it meant that his existence had turned into one of torment—that he had become a soldier, that he had killed more of Adair's men than he would like to tally up, that everything he had done since that fateful day in the woods was for her.

"How could you do this?!" Nyx suddenly screeched, pushing her chair back and seething. Jabbing a shaking finger into Memphis's chest, she said, "I trusted you. This is not something you keep to yourself, Memphis Carter. *I trusted you.* By fire and flame, you are saying that while Kiero fell, towns have been destroyed, and thousands of people have died, Emory was ensured safety because of you two? You both have betrayed us to save *one* girl."

Nyx was trembling, tears glistening in her eyes as she locked her violet eyes onto Brokk. Wyatt, Jaxson, and Alby looked at them skeptically, their frowns and darkened expressions were answer enough.

Addressing the room, Memphis whispered, "I'm sorry. We both are. But this *can* change our chances. From Adair's point of view, I don't think there would be anything more challenging than Emory returning from the dead. We use her and the Fae name to be the face of this Rebellion, and we finally end Adair.

# HEIR OF LIES – PART THREE

Emory is the heir of Kiero, and it's time for her to return, to reclaim her throne. We have no other option."

Nyx rolled her eyes. "Well, doesn't that just sound like the perfect fairy tale. The long-lost princess finally home to free her lands. Only, she saved her hide to leave the rest of us to suffer. Not very noble, from where I am standing."

Memphis's face darkened. "You can be mad at my faults in this and in my decision to keep this from all of you, but Emory would have been killed if she stayed that day."

Nyx flipped her purple hair over her shoulder. "Call a meeting. Tell the others. Go on an ops mission, bring her back, and then maybe I will not end you, Memphis Carter."

Memphis flushed a deep red, not getting the last word in before Nyx stalked out of the room haughtily.

The others followed, not giving them a second glance. Memphis turned to Brokk, angry. "Well, that went *fantastic*."

Rolling his shoulders, Brokk ran a hand through his hair. "You have to understand their point of view, Memphis. We both have betrayed our rebellion—our *family*—with this secret. Let them navigate their emotions while we bring Emory back."

Brokk's stomach twisted then at the thought of seeing her again. Gone was the gangly fifteen-year-old he left in the throes of another world. She would be twenty-one now—a *woman*. Would she even recognize the man he had become? Would there be an undertone of memory, even though Memphis had taken them away from her? Heart cracking, Brokk pushed the thought down.

Sighing, he watched Memphis flush a deeper red. Standing, he said, "Call the alarm in an hour. Until then, take a moment to gather yourself. Then we will leave."

Walking out of the room, Brokk navigated down the hallway. People surrounding him were just blurs of colors.

It only felt like yesterday that she was there, laughing beside them. That he would get lost in her emerald eyes. That they were attending classes and the worst stresses in their life were navigating her parents and their politics.

But now, Emory would be brought back to a world on fire. To one of her best friends now a Mad King while himself and Memphis lead a rebellion to *kill* Adair.

Time could change a lot of things, but as Brokk pushed past the sea of people clad in black, he knew nothing could ever prepare Emory for that. He hoped desperately that the woman a world away would remember him as he once was. That above all, she would remember the depths of their bonds of friendship and forgive him for the choices he has made since.

"Please proceed to the dining hall. Please proceed to the dining hall...."

Stomach twisting, Brokk lined up to enter the next elevator heading down to the dining hall. Numbly stepping in, the grate slid shut, and he was dropped into the ground. The wind howled, and he tried to prepare himself.

When they came to a grinding halt, he realized the dining hall was nearly full already. Stalking in between rows of familiar faces, he took a seat at the nearest table. Brokk scanned the crowd near the front; Nyx's purple hair reflected against the lanterns' glow. As if feeling his gaze, she turned her head, locking her eyes on him.

Her mouth was set in a grim line, and she slightly tipped her head toward him. They all knew from this moment on everything was going to be different.

As if on cue, Memphis walked out, stopping to take in everyone. He was dressed in a pale blue shirt and black pants, his lace up boots shining. Brokk could read his friend in a second, the inner turmoil evident from the slight quirk in his nose, his pale eyebrows knitted together.

"Good morning." Memphis's authoritative voice quieted the bustle in the room, and he clasped his hands in front of him. "Firstly, I am sorry to take you all away from your tasks but thank you for coming. As always, I applaud you on the combined efforts

# Heir of Lies – Part Three

to overthrow Adair. As you all know, we formed this rebellion to form a sanctuary to anyone who has been terrorized by the Mad King. We are here to heal and gain our strength, so we have a fighting chance against him."

He paused and the room hushed further.

"As a group, we have accomplished amazing feats, but we have all lost too much over the years. Every person in this room has trusted me without question, has taken me as their leader. All of us have been working toward one resolution, to reclaim our world." Memphis paused again, his voice echoing in Brokk's mind alone. *"It's time."*

Sighing, Memphis continued out loud, "I have not been entirely honest. In fact, I have lied to protect a secret that was never mine to keep. For this, words cannot begin to express my regret and guilt."

Stony silence resonated throughout their friends, their family. Brokk's heartbeat thumped in double time, his stomach dropping.

"Years ago, there was a girl with an unusual ability. Her name was Emory Fae. She was also one of my good friends and the rightful heir to Kiero. You may have heard about her untimely disappearance, about her death at the war of the Academy. This is a lie. Six years ago, she came to Brokk and me for help, and we agreed."

Brokk felt like their eyes boring into him could set him on fire.

Shifting uncomfortably, Memphis pushed on. "Adair had already slaughtered her parents. Had broken the Academy and the peace Kiero had found during the Faes' time. He was planning to kill her to end the royal family. When the time came, I erased her memory, and Brokk...well..."

Standing up, Brokk ran a hand over his buzzed hair. "I have the ability to manipulate time. I connected to a channel, to another world, and brought her there, left her there for protection, so that when the time came, and Kiero needed it most, Emory Fae could return and claim what is rightfully hers."

275

Anger licked through the hall in a ripple of a thousand whispers. Brokk back-pedaled fast. "It's not as specific as you think. I can only go through channels I have connected to before. I can't go back and change history."

Nodding, Memphis continued, "We saved Emory and transported her to a place called Earth. She has no recollection of us, or of this world. We were selfish. But we intend to bring her back. I will restore her memories and, being a leech, means that she can *steal* abilities. If we can get her near Adair, she has a chance of ending him with his own ability. She is the only one who can help us win our war. She will be the face of Black Dawn Rebellion, and returning to her rightful place as heir, we will have a chance. We use her to stop Adair."

Memphis was driving a knife into his heart. Brokk knew this was a tactic. Memphis had to hold the rebels together. Brokk would save her a thousand times over and never feel *regret* for doing it. His Commander only saw his guilt.

Adair was the cause of Kiero falling into ruin, and the blame laid on him alone. If Emory had stayed, there would be no chance…no hope.

Shouts rattled off the walls now, as accusations were thrown at them. Black Dawn had digested the news, and looking around, Brokk realized their words would mean nothing. It was up to their actions now.

Memphis exclaimed, "I promise you retribution. I promise you a free land. It is time to act, and if you will still have me, we will do this together."

Pure chaos broke out.

Yelling filled the dining hall, and Brokk wanted to dissolve into the wall.

*Betrayal. Betrayal. Betrayal.*

His blood sang with the word, and he began to weave around the tables and the accusations. Making his way up to Memphis, their plan hardened his heart. Looking out at the defeated faces, the anger rolling in at them from the group of people he considered family, hurt him.

# HEIR OF LIES – PART THREE

Gripping Memphis's forearm, they both looked to Nyx, hoping that she could settle the rebels. The voices turned to white noise, and Brokk took a deep breath, feeling the pieces click into place like a puzzle. There was a deep pull in his gut, and he let go.

The world they knew shattered into light, and shimmering ribbons of silver and gold washed the channel. The howling wind reverberated around them as they freefell, Brokk's heart lodging in his throat. A thousand voices echoed around them, their words muffled as Brokk and Memphis fell. Brokk felt the connection, the web, and he followed it, drawing closer to Emory.

It could have been centuries or seconds that passed, but in another explosion of light, they slammed down into grass. Brokk let go of Memphis and threw up in one motion. Acid pricked tears in his eyes, and staggering, disoriented, the sounds and scenery slowly came into focus.

They were in a strange forest made of tall trees and a grey cement path twisted through it, opening to a field. Beyond, a small stream bubbled over the many rockfaces. The noise was another matter completely. There was a constant beehive of activity, peoples' voices the crescendo throughout it all.

Memphis shook his head, eyes instantly narrowing. The sticky heat of summer clung to his dark military clothes, his Commander's shirt looking incandescent. Turning slowly, he registered what Memphis was staring at. A young woman in overly flashy clothing had stopped on the path wide-eyed and frozen at the sight of them.

Before Memphis could start battering about Emory, Brokk asked in a smooth voice, "Excuse me, but could you tell us where the nearest town is located?"

She squinted at him in suspicion, saying, "You're in it. The nearest street is King Edward."

Waving a hand to her left, Brokk dipped his head in thanks, towing Memphis with him.

Seething, Memphis asked under his breath, "Why didn't you ask her if she knew about Emory? Are we even in the right place?"

Brokk snapped tensely, "Of course. Once I travel a channel, it's set in my system. I wouldn't have been brought anywhere else. But look around you. Look at us. I don't think anyone would tell us even if I had asked. We're a bit rough around the edges in comparison to this world."

This world that wasn't ravaged by Adair or magic. Brokk could feel his ability draining with every step—they didn't have long before their abilities would deplete in this world with no magic. They had to move fast.

Around them was a maze of cement and roaring metal machines. Wires were strewn from pole to pole as they followed the grey path. Casting their eyes down from the stares of passersby, it was unlike anything they had seen before. Chemical smells mixed with the stale air assaulted them.

Memphis whispered, "Well, this is overwhelming. I can trace through people's consciousness to track her. I just need time."

Brokk nodded his head, trying to choke down his fear. They should have stayed in the forest away from prying eyes. Heading back to the cover of the trees, he motioned to Memphis. "C'mon. We're drawing too much attention to ourselves."

For the first time in his life, Memphis didn't argue, and they made their way back to the woods.

Dark clouds rolled in the afternoon sky while they stalked down the grey path once more. The forest had provided them with a couple of hours to gain their bearings. Both men had felt it, their abilities being stretched too thin in this world.

Brokk wrung his hands, asking for the hundredth time, "Are you sure?"

Memphis curtly replied, "For the hundredth time, yes."

When it came down to it, it had only taken Memphis a couple of hours to find the thread of Emory's actions and trace her back

# HEIR OF LIES – PART THREE

to where she lived, which was a small three-story building, thankfully, not too far from their primary location.

Jealously pierced through him. This safe world was only fleeting. Brokk wondered what Emory's life was like and how they were about to change it.

Thunder rolled from above them, and the clouds took on a green hue as lightning flashed in the distance.

"We have to hurry," Brokk said.

They ran, twisting and curving around buildings and people. The humidity was suffocating, sweat rolled down Brokk's body, and Memphis motioned to his right.

"Over there," he said.

Crossing over to a bigger grey path where blaring screams echoed around them, they dodged the speeding machines.

Pushing forward, they swept toward an older man walking toward the brick building, and Memphis whispered, "Watch this."

The man stopped, clearly confused, and slowly reached for his pocket, withdrawing a key. They caught up to him, and his eyes took on a milky quality as Memphis whispered, "Walk. Unlock the door. You didn't see us here."

It was as easy as that. Brokk sprinted, Memphis following behind him.

*Emory. Emory. Emory. Emory.*

Heart surging, his feet carried him faster as they spiraled up the staircase.

Memphis said, "I got the door!"

Stepping into the building, the hallway was darkly lit, the staircase in front of them old and worn. Ominously, Brokk and Memphis lithely moved up the stairs. Reaching the third floor, Memphis stopped in front of a door that read one hundred and seven and grabbed Brokk's arm, stopping him.

Suddenly, the light source cut, plunging them in complete darkness. Brokk heard the lock springing free, the door creaking open under Memphis's command.

Raising his eyebrow, Brokk muttered, "Learned some new tricks?"

Memphis whispered back, "I've been practicing."

Stepping into the room, Brokk froze, his breath slamming out of his chest when he spotted a silhouette at the end of the hallway of the apartment.

The woman stilled; her green eyes luminous as lightning flared in the windows behind her. Long black hair trailed past her shoulders, her petite frame, lean and healthy.

Emotion tightened his throat, and he whispered, "Em."

Her scream echoed throughout every fiber in his body, and she sprinted to her right, grabbing a small device, the screen lighting up underneath her touch.

"I'm calling the police right now. Who the hell are you?" Emory yelled.

At their non-response, she ran back into the room, and a book flew past his head. Both Brokk and Memphis ducked from the continued assault of items.

"Em!"

"I swear if you take another step..." Her voice was low and commanding. She didn't get to finish her thought because fear flashed in her eyes, and her face drained of all color. Her body crumpled; Brokk rushed forward, catching her before she hit the floor. The strange device skittered on the floor, a voice ringing out from it as Memphis came up beside Brokk.

He stepped on it, destroying it beneath his boot as he said, "I just placed her former memories back in. Her mind couldn't handle it; she will come around in a couple of days or so. We have to get back to Kiero. Now." A smug expression crossed Memphis's features when he took Emory in like a prize.

Lifting Emory in his arms, Brokk tried to compose his racing pulse as he also gripped Memphis's arm. Each time, it was easier to fall into the pull of the current of energy. The world cracked and dissolved into a million pieces but, at the same time, into nothingness. Freefalling, he held onto his friends, wishing he could just freeze this moment a second longer to feel her body against his.

It was a reminder that she was real, and that they had succeeded.

They were bringing her *home*.

Blood poured from his nostrils. Pressing his sleeve to his face, Brokk sat down, pinching his nose. Emory was still unconscious and sprawled across the forest floor. They were back on the outskirts of the Academy.

Memphis paced back and forth; his brow furrowed. "We are too exposed; we have to get back to the Academy, Brokk. You can rest there," Memphis snapped at him, his agitation obvious.

Stemming his bloodied nose, Brokk asked roughly, "Memphis, what's your problem? We have succeeded, Emory is home. No matter what we are walking back into with the rebels, I have dreamt of this day for the last six years."

"Oh, I can imagine you have, Brokk. Now let's go before a dabarne or a raider attacks us. We are letting our emotions cloud our judgment," Memphis stated, darkly.

Pressing his lips into a thin line, Brokk gave a brusque nod.

Traveling by the channel left him irritable and drained. Anger curled around his heart. He risked just as much as Memphis had. Without him, Emory wouldn't even be here. Brokk's emotions were on a tight leash, feeling as if any moment he would lash out. Using his ability had its limits, and he needed to rest. He saw it as an exchange of energy and strength to be able to accomplish something others have only dreamed of.

Standing, he made a move to lift Emory, but Memphis protectively moved in front of her.

"I have to be the one to bring her in. We both know that." His voice was just a whisper as Brokk squinted at him. Shaking his head, Brokk left him, making his way back to the Academy.

Tension swelled inside him, but he was too tired to start a fight. Memphis following suit, cradling Emory in his arms.

Time was a mysterious thing. What only felt like a couple of hours on Earth, an entire day had passed back at the Academy. Brokk spotted Nyx stalking back and forth like a predator about to pounce.

Giving her a slight nod, her gaze grew distant when she took in the sight behind Brokk. In Memphis's arms, Emory hung limply, pale as her hair swayed with the rhythm of his steps.

"Is she dead?" Nyx asked.

"Just knocked out. Memph restored her previous memories. It will take a couple of days before she will be awake, he thinks."

For once, she didn't snap back at him with a snarky reply. "I have reached an agreement with the others. We stand with you both, moving forward with the new plan and *her*. Everyone is still having trouble with the logic behind saving her life but letting ours fall into this mess. Luckily, you were both young, and you have done enough to redeem yourselves since then. People will forgive you, in time. But never forget, Brokk, that now she has to pay the price."

Patting her shoulder, Brokk maneuvered to the door and on toward his beckoning bed. With one last look, he reminded himself Emory would be there when he awoke, no longer a long-lost memory. Opening the iron door, he wondered how long Byrd had left the Academy uncovered, not hidden by her ability.

Stepping into the hallway, he was met by its emptiness, and he made a mental note to ask her if any of the raiders or Adair's men had seen them.

*Shit.*

His head was pounding, the metallic taste of blood running down the back of his throat as he tried to stem the flow. His feet carried him as he stumbled toward his room. Down the hallway, he turned left and then right; he was greeted by his all too familiar grey washed door. Pushing it open, he saw a small bunker, a desk with books, and scattered papers floating around.

# HEIR OF LIES – PART THREE

Pinned up above his bed was a small illustration. Its edges were burnt, smudges of dried blood spattering it, but it was drawn by Emory, one of the first things Brokk had found when they returned all those years ago. It was a piece of her that had turned into his most prized possession. The portrait was rough, but him, Memphis, and Emory were clearly depicted, laughing and carefree.

Brokk walked to the picture, running his thumb over the worn paper, before he collapsed on his bed and sleep overtook him.

*Running through the woods, Brokk heard the ambush behind him following closely. The volley of arrows thudded into the tree trunks, and he ducked, clutching the weapons in his grip. He just had to make it to the Academy border line, where Alby and Wyatt were waiting for him. His raid had gone smoothly—the burnt down village providing weapons and charred clothing the rebels could salvage.*

*Sprinting, Brokk ducked as the next wave of arrows came far too close. Thirty of Adair's soldiers ambushed him, and he barely escaped with the goods. Pushing faster, the scene changed, the woods around him becoming ice incrusted, snow drifting down all from the now black clouds.*

*Stalling, Brokk looked behind him, the soldiers disappeared, and he was alone.*

*"Brokk Foster."*

*A cold sweat coated his body, as Brokk slowly turned. Adair stood in front of him, his black clothes soaked in blood, his mother's longsword, the Curse, grasped in his hand. A blood red cape was clasped around his throat, his eyes pitch black as Adair said, "You have failed. Do you know I relished in your friends dying screams? That each life I took, you couldn't do anything to stop it. And now, I have come for you."*

*He couldn't move, fear rooted him in place. Adair stalked toward him, the snow falling heavier. Coming face-to-face with him, Adair breathed, "Goodbye, Foster."*

*Brokk felt the steel slice into his gut, cutting through muscle, blood spilling. Dropping to his knees, he tried to stem the flow of hot blood staining the peerless snow, but his vision dipped, and the last thing he heard was Adair's laughter as he died.*

Awakening from the nightmare, Brokk's scream was lodged in his throat. His room came into focus, the ice-covered forest fading away, Adair with it. Voices of the past whispered to him, bloody swords cutting through his memories.

The nightmares had always been bad. He was too full of secrets and war for them not to be. Every morning, he said his silent mantra, *I will get through another day,* and like every other day since Adair proclaimed himself king, he made himself get up.

Sliding out of bed, the morning light spilled into his room through a tiny window which he was lucky enough to have. With the previous day's events fresh in his mind, he made himself presentable. He could feel the dry blood cracking on his swollen face, and staggering to the washroom, he washed it away, the clear water running pink in the sink.

Glancing at his reflection, short golden hair stuck up at odd angles, his buzzcut growing in inhumanly fast. Toned muscles roped down his arms, two scars along his abdomen where a dabarne had torn into his flesh years prior—an injury that even his ability couldn't heal. All boyish features had longed disappeared, leaving no softness behind.

It was finally time to reclaim their land. Adair had taken too much for far too long. Whistling, he put on some worn black pants and a grey t-shirt, slid his boots on, and made his way into the hallway. It was a quiet morning, the distaste of their current visitor obvious. The few rebels Brokk saw on his way to Memphis's suite kept their eyes glued in front of them, ignoring him blatantly. He had a lot of mending to do.

Sighing, he limped toward Memphis's office, which thankfully was only a couple of doors down from his own.

# Heir of Lies – Part Three

Approaching the similar grey washed doors, he hovered, waiting a moment. He could hear soft voices from within, whispering back and forth fervently. Rapping his knuckles against the door twice, Memphis opened the door, looking like he hadn't slept at all. Pale blond hair was slicked back into his usual ponytail, sporting the same black leather he wore yesterday. A shadow crossed his face, and stepping back, he let Brokk in.

"How is she? Is she awake?" Brokk asked.

Nyx stood in the corner of the room. "She's coming to all right."

"Nyx, please." Memphis glanced at Brokk, he spoke to him privately, "She has regained consciousness much sooner than I ever thought possible. Nyx has been the only one with her so far, and you can guess how that is going. I say we go in together and see how much has come through. I am guessing a lot of the memories will still be unclear to her yet, so let's go easy on her okay? As far as she knows, we have just abducted her from her home."

He had the urge to roll his eyes. He *knew* that. Nodding anyways, he followed Memphis down the hall, his heart slamming against his ribcage. Maps and an assortment of books littered the floor, and Brokk was mindful to step around them. Memphis had never been clean, but Brokk kept the thought to himself.

Stopping at a black oak door, Memphis turned the doorknob. The door swung open, and they walked in, Memphis leading. Emory sat in the middle of the bed. Her green shirt and black pants were disheveled, her long hair was over her shoulder as she slowly took Memphis in. Anger lit up her green eyes as she demanded, "Where am I?"

For once, Memphis was at a loss for words; mouth hanging open, he scrambled. Brokk stepped into view, Nyx following. Brokk was about to begin to assist him in trying to explain this. But in a second, Emory's face darkened, her reaction instantaneous.

Charging at Brokk, Emory screamed, "You!"

Dumbstruck, her scream cut into his core as he easily sidestepped her attack.

Memphis screamed, "Brokk, leave now!"

His body followed the order, his mind reeling. Walking out of the room, the door slammed shut behind him. Rooted in place, he listened for the after effect. Silence greeted him coldly. Frozen in place, he tried to calm his shaking hands.

*Why would she want to hurt me? What just happened?*

Closing his eyes, he counted to ten, steadying his emotions. It killed him to do so, but he backed away from the closed door and left the suite in hopes to find Alby. To try to make his friends understand his actions were the first step and to put back together the foundation they worked so hard to make.

# HEIR OF LIES – PART THREE

# CHAPTER THIRTY-ONE

## Memphis

The scream tore through his mind, and Memphis watched Brokk stalk out of the room, his hurt plain across his face. Glancing at the now panting Emory, her anger dissipated to confusion once more. Her movements were impatient when she perched on the edge of the bunker, cradling her head.

"Emory? My name is Memphis Carter. Do you know who I am?" He could feel Nyx's eyes burning into his back.

Emory peeked up at him through her fingers. "I'm not going to answer that until you tell me where I am and why I am here." Her voice was like crystal, smooth and commanding. The voice of a *queen*.

Guilt tinged in his gut, and he chose his next words carefully. "I realize what this is going to sound like, and that it's insane. Brokk and I brought you here to *our* world. This is the Academy—our home. You came from Earth, but this world was your home first. Kiero. We grew up together. Your parents built our government, and a school called the Academy. To us, you are rightful heir to their lineage."

Her mind was like walking on ice, too much pressure at once and it would break. Memphis had to dance around the edges, especially to protect what he had done. Softly, he asked, "How much do you remember?"

Her eyes were daggers, and she stood up. "Why should I remember this place? This world? You're telling me that you just kidnapped me and transported me to another world? *This isn't freaking Star Trek!* It feels like my mind is being split into two, I remember my life—going to work, my apartment, my friends—but now..." she winced. "Now it's like someone has drawn back the stage curtain, and all these broken memories have come into play. I see myself as a little girl, and instead of being raised in an orphanage, I'm with parents. And we had abilities...like supernatural abilities. Which just proves that I have lost it, or you have obviously drugged me. So, if you're going to kill me, then just do it."

Memphis blanched from the pure venom in her tone.

"*Show her,*" Nyx's quiet voice resonated in his mind.

Memphis stared back at Nyx, narrowing his eyes. He could gently feed more memories to Emory, it was the only way to make her see the truth.

Reaching toward her, he placed his palm against her temple. Her skin was cool and soft, and he could feel the adrenaline rushing through her.

"Get away from me, *now.*" Her voice hitched as he stared into her eyes, and he entered her mind. Her consciousness was a tornado, unforgiving and pure destruction. Memories, images, noises swirled around her mind, battling to find the truth. Each one trying to find its place once more in the timeline of her two very different lives. It was like dropping a pebble into an ocean. Memphis watched his added memories fight against the tide of her consciousness. He relived every moment with her.

*Brokk hugged Emory tight, messing her hair. She playfully punched his shoulder.*

*They poured over books long into the night, Memphis smiling at her concentrated expression.*

*Memphis levitating glasses in class.*

*Brokk shifting into a golden wolf, playfully barking.*

*Her parents, their classes together. And... Adair, quietly in the shadows, watching and waiting.*

# HEIR OF LIES – PART THREE

Everything abruptly went black. Furrowing his brow, he tried to retreat when Emory's breath began to be labored. Eyes rolling into the back of her head, the whites showed as a slow trail of blood trickled down her face.

Panicking, Memphis reached out for Nyx's help. It was as if they had been shut in a soundproof room, his own thoughts muffled. He watched as Emory's body went ridged, and then a flurry of activity sparked, and all Memphis could do was watch and listen.

*Emory tucked herself into bed, the soft glow of her cell phone lighting her room. Her head sank into the familiar curve of her pillow as she drifted off into sleep. Of course, it wasn't long until her dreams took over.*

*She found herself in a dark forest, the trees thick and dense. Bouncing on the balls of her feet, she took off at a slow jog, her breath coming in puffs.*

*"Em... Em... Emory."*

*A soft voice called out to her, as a figure with long blond hair stepped out of the shadows. She ran to Memphis. The name felt like home. With arms wide open, she collided into his chest, burrowing her face in the crook of his arm.*

*"Em, help me." His eye silently pled, then the world erupted into flame.*

*Screaming, she tried to reach out to him, but all that was left was smoke and ash. Choking, she blindly stumbled. Every time was the same. Tears streaming down her face, she sank to the ground waiting. He would come.*

*"EMORY!" Her head snapped up, and focusing, she saw Memphis moving toward her. She didn't wait. Pushing off from the ground, she propelled her body forward, running as fast as she could. She saw the knife glinting in the filtered light, his golden eyes dead as Brokk stalked toward him.*

*"NO!"*

*But it was always too late. She locked eyes with him, and he smirked, revealing his pointed teeth, Memphis's blood dripping from the knife.*

She awoke–her scream caught in her throat. It had always been the same nightmare for as long as she could remember. Trying to still her *shaking hands, she frantically glanced around the room, as if for the hundredth time, she could save this mysterious man, but she was alone.*

Memphis came out of the vision with her as fast as it came, Emory's body lying on the bunker, convulsing.

"What happened?" Nyx surged forward, grasping Emory's body and turning her on her side to avoid further harm.

"I... Nyx..."

*This was going to end them.*

Nyx didn't wait for him to sort out his thoughts. "Hold her legs down for me, will you?"

Numb and at a loss for words, he complied. Minutes passed before the episode subsided, Emory becoming still once more. Her skin was ashen, drained of any color.

"Is she okay?" Memphis asked, meeting Nyx's deadpan glare.

"Minor injuries. She will be fine though. I am more interested in the fact that a couple of minutes ago, I couldn't access her mind or yours. *What happened?*"

He could physically feel the heat rolling off her body in anger, radiating waves. He licked his lips. "I planted a few more memories trying to make some things clear, like we didn't abduct her! Her mind Nyx...it's at war. Things are becoming clear to her in snippets. Not all at once. She has some idea of who we are." He shuddered. "In her memory, we were trapped in a dream. Her dream. Brokk and I were in it; Brokk was different though. He was her nightmare."

"Why would she be dreaming actively about you two six years later, if you cleared her mind so she wouldn't remember who she was?"

Casting his eyes toward the floor, Memphis was reliving a moment that felt like a lifetime ago.

"Memphis Carter." Nyx seethed at him, and he felt her energy expand outwards, toward his mind.

"No!"

Throwing up his mental guards was a slap in the face to her, and cringing at the impact, Nyx staggered back. In the same instant, his bookcase started to shake, a cracked brown book started to float leisurely toward him. She caught it in a fluid motion, eagerly reading: *Dreamscapes: A Guide for Telekinesis's*

"I never thought..." he scrambled.

"You never *thought* what, Memphis?" Her voice was a dangerous whisper.

"She is one of my best childhood friends. After I saved her, I studied how to place memories and images in another receiving party's dream subconsciousness. I was fifteen and only tried a couple of times. There were too many unknown variables at play. She was in another world, for instance, and I didn't even know if it would work..." His voice trailed off in the obvious answer.

Nyx's face contorted, as she spat, "Don't insult me, Memphis! Childhood friends? You are *in love with her*. I'm not blind, and neither is anyone else. You are going to condemn us all by being blind." With a flick of her purple hair, Nyx strutted toward the door. She threw back one more remark at him, "I have to start my watch. You can babysit your *dear* friend here."

With a click of the door, she was gone. Sinking into the nearest chair, Memphis was lost in the impossible. There was one key element he had kept from Nyx, but it seemed she knew all along— when it came to manipulating a dreamscape, one thing ruled: emotion. It formed the shape and being of what the sender was trying to convey.

Guilt made his stomach flip. It was a child's jealousy; he so desperately wanted her to have an echo of him within her, and now, it was the only clear memory she had.

*So far.*

Angry tears stung his eyes, and Memphis chucked the book across the room. The minutes slipped into hours as he tried to figure out a way to fix what he had done. How could he explain to Brokk why over the last six years he had made sure Emory would be afraid of him- would *hate* him. In the dark corner of Memphis's heart, the answer lay- if he couldn't have Emory then no one would.

# CHAPTER THIRTY-TWO

### Emory

It was as if her body had been ripped into a thousand different pieces. Her lungs burned, begging for relief. Emory heard the soft crackle of fire. Her head was a spinning mass; it was its own continent.

Squinting, she tried to focus. Blinking slowly, her surroundings came into view. Her pulse picked up.

She wasn't in her room.

She wasn't in her home.

The metal world around her seemed to have one purpose. To keep people in. To keep *her* in. The last twenty-four hours rushed over her in a flurry of confusing memories. *Him... Memphis.* The name rolled around in her mind, familiar yet unfamiliar all at once. Her eyes flashed open, her heart thrumming with adrenaline.

Heavily, Emory sat up, trying to pull her thoughts together. For now, the room was empty, her captors gone.

*Now. This is your chance to escape.* The thought clambered through her wildly, and she acted.

Standing from the bed, Emory stumbled, her legs weak, her clothes dirtied. Breathing heavily, Emory ran to the door, pushing the handle down as it opened. Containing her surprise, she slipped into the hallway. What kind of criminals would keep their prisoner in an unlocked room?

# HEIR OF LIES – PART THREE

Walking fast, Emory pushed the thought down, keeping her head down as she tried to locate how to get out of this place. The hallway was quiet, and Emory didn't pass anyone else. It had to be late into the night, and she sent up a thank you to whoever was granting her such luck.

Trying not to run, she turned left, passing more shut unmarked doors, but slowly, the hallway slanted up. Heart pounding, her palms slicked with sweat as she tried to stick to the shadows, walking faster now. Ahead of her, doors loomed, and panic bloomed in her chest. Running now, Emory tried to hold back the tears burning in her eyes. She reached the massive doors, pulling them open, and the night air slammed into her.

Gasping, she sprinted, rushing out into the rolling field. The air was brisk, a sweet aroma hanging on the wind, the crescent moon tucked in the midnight blue clouds. Ahead, a massive forest loomed, and she frantically looked for any sign of modern civilization where she could find help.

There was nothing.

A stitch laced through her side, and her converses lost footing. Emory slammed into the damp earth. Rocks sliced through her palms as she tried to break her fall, blood welling in the cuts.

Tears slid down her cheeks as she got up, whispering, "Keep moving. C'mon."

Looking back, she expected to see the place she had been taken to, but dread pooled in her stomach as all she saw was open field—no sign of any building whatsoever.

"What the hell?" Emory whispered, fear making her thought process choppy. Sprinting again, she pushed toward the woods.

If she could at least not be captured by these psychos again, then she could find help. Sucking in deep steadying breaths, Emory pumped her arms, and broke through the tree line, not breaking stride. The trees were massive, towering up toward the sky, blocking out any moonlight.

Emory was cast in complete darkness.

Slowing her pace to a light jog, shivers ran up her arms, blood and sweat coating her exposed skin. There were no evident pathways, as Emory surged over the mossy ground, dodging roots sticking out and different brambles pulling and ripping at her clothes. Her breath came in misty puffs, as she headed deeper into the woods. The wildness of the forest pulled at something deep in her gut—she had never seen any place that wasn't touched by humans.

Shaking her head, Emory slowed to a walk, pushing down the panic as she mused aloud, "They gave me drugs and must be on something themselves—obviously I'm not on another *world*."

Dread continued to pull at her gut, Emory freezing as a branch snapped behind her. Ice shot through her veins as she turned slowly, yellow eyes glowing behind her. The first thing she saw was the rotting flesh as the serpentine creature stepped toward her. Bald, saggy skin covered the monster, its long snout and twitching ears revealing sharp canines. Snapping its teeth, its gaze flashed. It was bigger than a car, and Emory backed away slowly, not breathing. Behind it, two more yellow eyes appeared, the growls filling the forest unlike anything Emory had ever heard before.

A branch caught her foot, and she fell, falling onto her back. The creature sprung toward her, its companions following. Screaming, Emory flinched back, covering her eyes but not before a flash of silver cut through the air—the curved knife slamming into the creature's belly, black blood spattering.

The purpled haired woman ran into the clearing, completely ignoring Emory as she ripped her knife from the flesh of the monster, her left hand cutting up as she wielded a long sword, slamming it into the creature's neck. It howled as it fell, head rolling, decapitated from its body. The woman fought with a ferocity that Emory had only seen in movies as she flung herself into the thick of the battle, the two other monsters throwing themselves at her.

The ground shuddered, and Emory scrambled, shock numbing her body. She expected to see another demon about to kill her.

# Heir of Lies – Part Three

Instead, a monstrous wolf entered the clearing, golden eyes roaming over her body, before it propelled, jumping over Emory and joining the throng of the fight. She couldn't move. Emory watched the wolf take down one monster within seconds. Shaking uncontrollably, Emory gasped. She turned, sprinting away from the fight, snapping back into reality.

Crying, she had never tried to run so fast, sweat coating every inch of body, branches cutting her cheeks, but she didn't falter. Her life depended on it.

Impossibly, the purple hair woman appeared in front of her, sheathing her sword. "Going somewhere, Princess?"

"Get away from me!" Emory screamed, backing away.

"Oh, I don't think so. This can go two ways. The easy way or the hard way. It's your choice."

Behind Emory, more twigs snapped, and the golden furred wolf came up behind her. Nausea rolled through her body as Emory shook her head. "This is impossible." Her words went unheard as she watched the wolf shift to human form, revealing it to be her other captor, the man from her nightmares.

"Emory, you need to come with us. You're lucky Nyx saw you on her watch. The dabarnes are only a taste of what roams these woods."

The man had gentle eyes and short cropped golden hair. He wore a black collared jacket, pants and leather boots, reminding her of medieval fashion. Fear shot through her, and Emory tried to run, the woman sighing behind her.

"I guess it's going to be the hard way then, Princess."

Emory barely had time to register the pommel of the knife flying toward her temple, before it cracked into her skull, the copper taste of blood filling her mouth. Darkness overtook her.

Emory woke up with a raging headache, to find herself back in the same room she had escaped. Blinking slowly, she tasted stale blood in her mouth, and she gingerly felt her temple, the split skin swollen to her touch. Voices filled the room as she looked to her left, where a man with blond hair was leaning forward in an intense conversation with a freckled man with scorching red hair.

Memphis scrambled up, alarmed and surprised. "Emory, you're awake." He breathed her name, as if she might disappear.

Sitting up slowly, she grimaced when pain shot through her body.

Memphis searched her. "You're in pain."

"Obviously, I was knocked out by one of your cronies against my will," Emory gruffly said.

"You're lucky to be alive, Em. I'm not—*we are not*—your enemy. Please try and understand that beyond these walls, you will die if you try to escape again," Memphis stated.

"So what? I'm your prisoner? I would rather die," Emory declared.

Shaking his head, Memphis looked to the red-haired man standing awkwardly in the corner. Fear flickered in his face, as his body slowly started to look very much like the wall behind him.

"Alby, leave," Memphis commanded.

The man's resemblance flickered back to his own, and he left the room.

Confused, hungry, and hurt, she had little patience left. She needed more answers. Now.

Taking her into full view, Memphis sat down in front of her, exhaling hard.

Seizing her opportunity, Emory lunged across at him.

He moved with inhuman speed, catching her wrists before Emory could do any more damage. Standing face-to-face, her chest heaved, and his ice blue eyes cut into hers.

"Emory, I'm not asking you to trust me, but just give me the chance to explain. It will be a lot easier if, for the moment, you don't attack me."

Shoving out of his grasp, Emory tried not to throw up. She couldn't physically beat Memphis, for the time being, it would seem she *was* their prisoner. Rubbing her wrists, her palms tingled, and her head pounded more, a strange undercurrent of energy churning through her body. Blinking, she paced, trying to make sense of the monsters she had seen in the woods, the monsters that had almost killed her.

"What were those things in the forest?" she asked.

Memphis rubbed the back of his neck, and she couldn't help but notice defined muscles flexing with his every move. He replied, "The darbarnes are beasts under the Mad King's command. They are ruthless killers, ones that we have been fighting for many years."

"Uh-huh," Emory said skeptically as she sat back down. No matter how much logic or excuses her mind was coming up with—the fact was, those *dabarnes* were like wolverines that had met nuclear radiation.

They weren't from Earth.

Head spinning, she looked at Memphis as he sheepishly said, "I'm sorry about overloading you earlier. I just thought if you could see for yourself, you would trust us more—trust *me* more. I know words can paint pretty truths. I never thought this would happen."

He gestured to her entirety.

"Let me give you your first tour, if you're okay with that." Smiling warmly, he held out his worn hand to her.

"No. I'm good," she said coldly.

Biting his lip, he looked like he wanted to say more, but thankfully, he stepped out of the room, leaving her alone.

At first, her anger had deferred the need to nourish her body, so she sat on the hard cot, her mind running in circles of the impossibility of what Memphis had told her. The blank wall provided no answers, and every couple of hours, Memphis came to show her where the restrooms were to relieve herself and tried to persuade her to eat. Her icy responses were enough to shut him down.

In the windowless room and hallways, depression clouded her thoughts, making her body feel heavy.

It was on the second day without water that the dehydration and hunger pangs outweighed her fear of getting killed.

Opening the door, Memphis tentatively stepped in. "Emory, I'm begging you..."

"I want to eat," she cut him off.

Surprise flickered across his features, and he nodded. "Okay... okay good. Let's go."

This new world surrounding her was cold and metallic. Stepping out into the hallway, he said, "Dinner rush."

Even though evening was upon them, the hallways bustled with life. Trying to ignore the on-looker's glares, she weaved with Memphis throughout the crowd, heading toward a caged elevator. Curiosity blooming, she asked, "How many people live here?"

"There are sixty of us left, but Alby, who you met earlier, is constantly scouting for survivors. He is the only one who can go unnoticed. Other than Brokk."

"Survivors of what?" Emory asked.

Memphis's face darkened as he murmured, "Let's just get food into you first."

Pressing a worn copper button caused a chasm of clicks and whirs to sound as the gate opened, and they stepped in. Without a moment's notice, the compartment dropped, and they freefell.

A scream threatened to choke her, and her stomach was thrown into her throat.

Smirking wickedly, Memphis yelled, "You get used to this!"

Looking frantically for something to hold on to, Memphis reached out, offering his hand which she blatantly ignored. In seconds, the compartment slowed, and the door grinded open, revealing a huge cavern, its coolness washing over them. Lamps were secured on the walls, washing the room in warm light; tables and chairs were scattered everywhere. Not missing a beat,

# Heir of Lies – Part Three

Memphis led her to the far end of the room where it was a bit more private.

Grabbing her hand, she balked at the touch; his touch was warm and strong; anxiety pooled in her gut, but she didn't pull away.

*What are you doing?*

Emory tugged her hand from his grip, and he pulled her out a chair. Motioning for her to sit, he said, "Wait here a moment."

Looking around at the cavernous room, she took in the men and women that surrounded her. All wearing black, various weapons peeking from sheathes across their backs, thighs, and hips. The drawn faces revealed nothing but the bleak existence in this *place*.

Memphis rounded a corner, disappearing, and she finally crumpled. She wanted to scream and cry and possibly launch a chair across the room. Her mind reeled with questions. Not a minute later, Memphis came back carrying two steaming plates of what looked like steamed vegetables and some form of meat. Salivating, she tried not to rip the plate from his hands.

Setting them down, he took a seat across from her. Tensing, he tilted his head to the right, and Emory followed his gaze.

The woman with electric purple hair stood frozen at the elevator's doors. *Nyx, her name is Nyx,* she reminded herself of this.

Memphis shook his head slightly as she continued her way to take a seat across from a man Emory didn't notice before. His golden hair shone in the half-light, his eyes quickly flashing up to meet hers.

*Brokk. The man from your nightmares.*

Frowning at the strangeness of it all, Emory turned her attention back to Memphis. A migraine painfully pulsed in her head, threatening to break her skull, so she started with the easiest question she could muster.

"How do you get the resources to survive here?"

299

"Mostly Alby and Brokk. They can scout fast and easily without being detected. We usually do a week of collecting and hunting and wait until we run out and then repeat the cycle. We have a pipe system that collects rainwater and a water well. You can imagine, it requires a lot of maintenance. It makes for busy work, which is good."

His gaze never left hers, even as he dived into his food.

She followed suit, the food melting in her mouth. It was divine.

Memphis swallowed and continued, "We have been building the Academy to be an indestructible force. Our safety is only possible thanks to Byrd though. Her ability cloaks our entire perimeter so that if anyone comes too close, they will only see rolling hills. It's the only thing that has kept us alive this long."

A hollowness grew in her stomach, as she remembered the night she escaped, and there was no building in sight when she had left. The impossibility of it all!

Memphis's face darkened, his voice becoming clipped, "Emory, what if your entire existence, your entire life, was a lie? This is a lot to digest already, I know, but there is no easy way to put this. I will start with the facts."

Her chest hurt as she waited.

"Your name is Emory Reia Fae. Your mother was Nei Fae and father, Roque Fae. They built our government and, through that, built the *Academy*, so we could live in a world where we learned to use our powers for the greater good to help protect our country. They strove for a free world where they could watch you grow and prosper. Their dream was shattered when all of that was stolen from them."

Memphis looked lost in memory. "There was a student, Adair. We all attended school here together, but he grew to be ruthless, and above all else, power hungry. He killed your parents. He tore apart everything they had built, and he was about to end the bloodline with you. We were all best friends." He stiffened. "Brokk and I couldn't lose everything, and under the circumstances, you asked us for help. You asked us to save you. Brokk has the ability to travel through channels of time, and as you are aware, our world is full of surprises. We left you on Earth, stripped of everything you stood for... But, you were alive, and you were safe."

Unaware that her mouth had been slightly ajar for the last minute, she shook her head. "Are you saying that I have fallen into a modern fairy tale? I was the royal princess whisked away, and you and *him* have brought me rightfully home to...to what? To fight in an epic battle? To restore harmony upon the land?"

A hard glint shone in Memphis's eyes as a stillness settled over him. "You have no idea how much has been lost over the last six years. People have been slaughtered by the thousands because Adair didn't deem them powerful or useful. Families and homes forever broken... We have been trying to build our numbers to stand up and reclaim what is ours." He paused. "You always have been, and rightfully are, our leader. You have always been the key."

Emory looked at the surrounding people for the first time since coming here. Most of them were young. There was no excessive talking, no laughter. They kept on task...whatever that may be. It was very military and echoed a hollow life.

*It would explain the dreams.*

Her life back on Earth was empty as well. Brought up in an orphanage, she had few friends, other than Moore, and she took care of herself until she came of age. She had always wanted *more*. Why shouldn't she accept this life as her own?

"If this is true, will I start to remember them—I mean my family? My past?"

Memphis's face softened. "It's hard to know how your memories will come back to you. If I was to take a guess after the other night, they will sort themselves out in spurts, one coming clear at a time. It could be weeks, months, even years for everything to start to make sense. *But I can help you.*"

She almost didn't catch the last sentence, and she snapped to attention as he uttered it, unexpected heat flooding her body.

Memphis leaned forward, urgency coating his words. "Emory, from the beginning of history, magic has been present in Kiero. Centuries ago, there was a capital called Nehmai were fey flourished, their magic blossoming across the land. The Warriors, an elitist army, protected the city from the darkness that tried to ravish Kiero. The great war of this world saw the city and the warriors destroyed, and the myth goes that their magic bled into the land, reblooming in humans in the form of special abilities. Your family was one of the strongest I have ever known, and your ability will help us have a chance against Adair. No one else can do what you can."

*My ability. What is he talking about?*

Shock rippled across her skin, making her hair stand on end.

Holding out his hand, Memphis said, "Let me show you what I mean."

It sounded insane. Every girl dreamt of a handsome mysterious man from her dreams saying that she was *chosen* for something to liberate their world. But she wasn't one who trusted easily—or wasn't softened by good looks. But her one weakness was curiosity.

With fire in her heart, she shot Memphis a hard glare before reaching out her hand, interlocking her fingers with his. Nothing happened at first, and a flush crept up her neck at the thought of noting how warm his hold was, making her uncomfortable. Then a slow, high-pitched hum started around them as everything fell silent.

Emory felt the pressure squeezing around her mind; it was sharp and probing. Then, everything exploded around her, and she couldn't help but gasp. Hundreds, no thousands, of thoughts, conversations, and memories shouted at her all at once. With her eyes wide, her body went rigid.

*"You just need to talk to her Brokk... Look at them over there..."* Nyx's voice sounded clear through the chaos, and Emory let go of Memphis's hand. Panting, her body hummed from the adrenaline rush.

# HEIR OF LIES – PART THREE

"What was that?!" Her voice was hoarse, her fingers still tingling.

"Your body will still be adjusting back, living in a world that has no magic, your ability disappeared. But in our world, the term for what you are is *leech*. If you maintain physical contact with anyone, you can use their power while they are left defenseless." He said this smugly, his blue eyes alit.

*Leech.*

She turned the word around in her mind thinking of the possibilities. Something was tugging at the edge of her mind, and she sighed. Her body ached, and her heart throbbed. She was tired, overwhelmed, confused, and apparently had super powers. Warily, she eyed Memphis. "I don't have a choice to go back, do I?"

Memphis studied her curiously from across the table. "Do you really want to go back? This is your home, *Emory*, and despite its flaws, you are the key to righting the wrongs Adair has done. Give it more than a week for things to feel right."

Before she could retort that this whole situation felt like it was leading up to stockholme syndrome, a screeching siren rang over the hall, and Memphis stood abruptly, as did everyone in the room. The reaction was an electric current running through the group as everyone stopped what they were doing.

Memphis breathed, "That's probably Alby returning from his scout. Care to join me?"

She pressed her lips in a thin line while looking at the man before her. He bit his lower lip, waiting for her to answer, his blue eyes piercing through her. His hair was tied back, and a small crooked smile started to lift the corners of his mouth. He was a stranger, and yet...yet she couldn't shake the feeling that this was familiar. She couldn't shake her curiosity about the man who sat across from her. Emory couldn't deny any of it.

She had always daydreamed of having a more fulfilling life; had spent years wondering about her parents, what they had been like, what their likes and dislikes were. Now, she just had to figure out if the information she was being fed was reality or fantasy.

With a nod, they made their way back over to the elevator. A well-mannered assembly line followed as they filed into the doors. A hand shot out to hold the doors open as Emory and Memphis stepped in. Brokk gently tipped his head toward them just as the doors shut, and they shot up, her heart dropping into her belly from the motion.

Sucking in a breath, she tried to hold on to her food. A smooth hand wrapped around hers, and she glanced at Memphis, a slight smirk on his face. He gave her a reassuring squeeze and let go quickly when they reached the top. Stepping out, Emory noticed a flash of golden eyes as Brokk fell into step beside them.

"Memphis, Emory." Brokk nodded. His voice was gruff and clipped, a shiver running along her spine in response.

She had no *proof* that she shouldn't trust him...other than her dreams. For six years, she was lost to his anger and betrayal, and now that they had met in the flesh, she couldn't shake her unease. She mimicked his earlier response and tipped her head toward him. Right now, she couldn't trust anyone.

Memphis whispered quietly to Brokk, something she couldn't hear, and Brokk answered, his fists clenching.

"Boys will be boys." Nyx slinked beside her, distracting her from trying to catch the conversation happening in front of her.

Holding out her hand to Emory, Nyx smirked. "We haven't been properly introduced. I don't count the other night when you almost got us all killed. I'm Nyx Astire. Our rebellion apparently needs you, but time will only tell what you are made of, Emory Fae."

Each word dripped with sarcasm, as Emory met her gaze head on. "I didn't ask to be brought into this."

Nyx chuckled. "Oh, I know that to be a lie. You asked six years ago to leave; now these are the consequences."

Bristling, Emory changed the subject and asked, "Black Dawn, how did you guys choose the name?"

# Heir of Lies – Part Three

Nyx's violet eyes narrowed, and her mouth twitched, but to Emory, it seemed more like a flinch. "Adair has stripped our world of any *peace*, any *balance*. For years, we have been planning, hiding, and waiting for the day we had the upper hand, had a card he wouldn't be able to read, to foresee our moves, so we could stand a *chance* of survival.

No one besides Brokk and Memphis knew you were alive. We have obviously found out otherwise.

Every single person in this room has watched their entire families and friends die in an instant. We have seen things you couldn't even imagine in your worst nightmares. We have been forced into a life where we get fleeting glimpses of happiness and hope in our dreams, only to awake to a world burnt of it.

We swore that when it was time, we would rise as strong and fast as the dawn but with no mercy, no empathy, a blackness in our hearts so Adair could feel, if only for a second, an ounce of what we have felt.

That time has come, and as you will find out, *you* are our upper hand."

Emory was left speechless, and Nyx, with a hollowness reflected in her violet eyes, pushed past her.

*A world stripped of humanity, and she was to restore it?*

A knot twisted in her stomach at the thought.

"Nyx can come on a bit strong sometimes, but her heart is in the right place."

Memphis appeared at her side, Brokk now lost in the throng of people ahead of them.

"She seems lovely."

A throaty chuckled resonated from Memphis, and Emory couldn't help but smile herself. After a few minutes, the group reached a deep grey door and stopped in front of it, Memphis turning the knob to go in. Nyx, Brokk, and Emory followed. Maps were scattered on a small round table, coordinates and a rough map of Kiero hanging from the wall and in the half shadows.

Three people waited for them. Memphis swept his arm out. "Emory, may I introduce to you Wyatt, Jackson, and Bryd"

She took them in, trying to smile. None returned the favor.

*You will find out you are our upper hand.* Nyx's voice echoed in her mind as she took the nearest seat, Memphis and Brokk on either side of her.

Nyx perched herself several chairs down, glaring at her the entire time.

"Where's Alby?"

Brokk searched the group, waiting for the answer.

"I sounded the meeting." The young girl with electric blue hair leaned forward, *Bryd*, her voice was choked. Dread filled Emory's stomach. A strained silence followed.

Memphis's face drained of color as Brokk asked again, "Where's Alby?"

Bryd twisted her ocean hair, murmuring, "I was on watch. Alby had gone a couple of hours before to do a quick scout of our perimeter, to make sure there was no new movement. Brokk had also gone out prior, but Alby seemed focused on finding Brokk when he talked to me. He wasn't prepared for them to be so close... He was alone, and Adair's scouts outnumbered him. They took him."

Tears threatened to escape as Bryd leaned back. Emory's own breath picked up as they all took in what this meant.

Nyx stood up, shoving her chair back, whispering, "We move forward with the plan. Alby is tough, and he has prepared as we all have for this situation. He *will* hold on..."

"If he is still alive..." Wyatt cut her off.

Nyx locked eyes with Wyatt. "We will not give up..."

"Enough!" Memphis cut in, his fist slamming into the wooden table. Anger sparked in his eyes, and he continued, "We have to stick together. This is what Adair *wants*—for us to dwindle into nothing. We are as prepared as we will ever be. I agree with Nyx. We move forward."

# Heir of Lies – Part Three

Wyatt pushed his chair back, throwing out his arms. "Well, we have the element of surprise, mate, that is for sure. Is she prepared to take on what moving forward means?"

Shaved head and arms covered in swirling tattoos, Wyatt locked gazes with Emory. She set her jaw stubbornly, not backing down from his stare. She was glad she had all their attention.

"Memphis has been trying to help me piece together my past. I know what me being back means to you. I also know that everyone here has lost their homes, friends, and families. Their lives. I was saved so I could help you now, and that is exactly what I intend to do."

"You know *nothing*, girl, but your spirit... We can work with that." Wyatt nodded.

Tension rolled off both Memphis and Brokk as they filled her in on exactly what her returning to Kiero would mean. Everything blurred together after that.

One second, they were in Command, the next she was being led down the hallway into the weaponry room. Longswords hung from the wall, a variety of knives and armor hung on the adjacent wall. Emory froze, not knowing what to do with herself, and Brokk sidled up beside her.

"Hey," he said softly. His voice was a low baritone, as smooth as honey.

"Hey. I never thanked you for saving me...but thank you," Emory replied.

"No thanks needed. I understand why you tried to run. You have no reason to trust us or what we are saying is true. I get that. This all must seem like we are the villains, doesn't it?"

Emory didn't reply, cold running through her veins as she looked up into his golden gaze.

Awkwardly shifting his weight, Brokk changed the subject, "I can help you navigate the armory, if you would like?"

Before she could reply, Memphis walked up to them, a black chest plate and sword in hand. Eyeing Brokk, Memphis cut in, "Emory, you will need these."

With shaking hands, she fastened the chest plate over her black shirt, trying not to throw up. She had changed out of her clothes from Earth, leaving them smelly and folded beside her bed. Sheathing her sword, she looked at the rest of the group who looked like demigods.

Gasping, she reached out to Memphis. "I can't do this. I can't even fight."

Looking grim, he said. "Em, we will do the fighting once we find the group of raiders. The plan is for word to get back to Adair so he will know that you are alive and with us. That we are fighting back. After that, word will spread fast enough to finally ignite this war. You are our spark."

Tightly curling her fists, Emory exhaled. Swallowing the lump in her throat, she nodded.

Stalking out of the room and down the hallway, rebels bobbed their heads at them in respect.

Chills ran down her body when they reached a clad door, and Memphis pulled the iron handle. The dusk was serene, purple hues painting the sky. A smell similar to honeysuckle clung on the air, and Memphis barked, "Brokk, you take up the rear. Nyx, you're with me. Em, in the middle. At a jog."

They set off, and Emory stared around her in amazement as she took in their world in the fading light. It was rugged and wild, forest taking up the horizon for miles. They entered the coolness of the trees' shade, and Emory looked back, surprised to see, yet again, nothing but rolling hills behind them.

Out of breath, she said, "Absolutely amazing."

One girl had done that. One.

Brokk shimmied up beside her, looking amused. "It's even more impressive being from the outside looking in, isn't it?"

Emory quickly looked ahead, paying attention to where she was putting her feet and didn't answer him. Brokk nodded, falling back as she ignored him, granting her space. She knew she was being irrational, but she didn't trust him.

Sweat slicked her body as they pressed further and further into the woods, the ground rolling with each slope.

# Heir of Lies – Part Three

Emory took deep gulps of air, the ancient forest creating shadows and tricking her eyes at every chance. It was full of mystery, something born from myths, and she felt a distant tug on her memory of familiarity. Of *home*. Sometimes, even when memories were foggy, it was as simple as a scent or the emotions associated with seeing and revisiting a place that Emory knew what Memphis had said was true.

She felt the ties in the wind, the trees, the gurgle of a stream in the very ground beneath her feet. She felt the history around her come alive, and it ignited her as well.

All of this was, of course, shattered with the simple twang of a bow.

A growl ripped from behind her, making Emory shuddered to a stop, and a gigantic wolf flew over her, catching the arrow mid-flight and snapping it in half. Memphis and Nyx drew their blades in fluid motion, charging the group in front of them. Emory`s mouth was hanging open in shock. His golden fur rippled with his bulking muscles, and molten eyes locked in with hers. He snapped his massive jaws, as if saying, "Move it."

With shaking hands, she drew the small curved blade from her thigh, running after the group. Her body and mind were numb. Surely this was a dream? A nightmare? The point when reality and fantasy started to bend and bleed together? Hyperventilating, her palms tingled. The group in front of them consisted of three men, all with long black hair braided back, blue ink staining their skin. The deadness in their eyes stopped her short.

"Well, well, well. What do we have here? A band of misfits?"

His crew laughed, and Nyx snapped at them, "To say the least."

Nyx was liquid fire as she charged the raider, throwing her knife, the steel cutting through the air and finding its mark in the raider's heart, as he dropped dead. Pulling the knife from the body, Nyx ran on to find her next victim. Flames jumped into the remaining raiders' hands, and they didn't waste another second with pleasantries.

Fire roared and twisted around them, Memphis leaping from the flames. Nyx narrowed her eyes, knives flying from her hands faster than humanly possible. Brokk lunged, only to be blocked and forced back with a wall of wildfire. His growls felt like thunder when he snapped his enormous canines at them. Emory violently shook as she watched the fight.

Whoever these raiders were, they were powerful. So, in that second, with no one noticing her, Emory slinked back amongst the shadows and waited for her opportunity. Memphis and Nyx had one raider, and Brokk fought off another. Her heart pounded with each breath, and she hoped she was right. That the power and electricity in her veins wasn't lying to her.

The man was forced back, coming closer and closer until Emory lashed out, grabbing his forearm. She had dropped her blade at this point, and instantly, her world shifted and changed. It was like the flood gates finally opened, and her whole body electrified, her blood was boiling.

Raw, undiluted power flushed her cheeks, and she swore in disbelief, looking at Memphis and Nyx, her eyes burning red like embers in the night. The man sagged against her touch, and as she snapped her fingers, flames danced from fingertips, coolly kissing her skin. The other raider's mouth hung open, and he whispered, "Impossible."

Sending the flames toward him, she said, "My thoughts exactly, if I'm being honest with you."

Brokk pushed him down, his paw holding him in place. Memphis said, "Now, boys, there are only two of you left, and we find ourselves at a crossroad. Either you can comply with us, or you will not like the result if you don't. We have a message we would like you to spread amongst your clans in the Risco Desert. As well as making sure Adair's soldiers find out."

By this point, the raider's eyes rolled up into his head, and she continued to consume his power. His friend took one look at them and desperately said, "We're listening."

Memphis clapped his hands together. "Excellent! Please tell anyone you meet that the Academy lives, and our rebellion is marching upon Adair. And most importantly, that our *Queen* has returned. If they would like to join our cause, then they can meet us on the outskirts of these woods. We will find them."

Letting go of the man, he dropped like a bag of rocks. Brokk growled down at him, and Emory was sure he had pissed himself. Lifting his paw, the man scrambled toward his friend, dragging him away and not looking back once. Memphis gleefully looked at her, but in that instant, Nyx shoved her against a tree, her knife pressing against Emory's throat, "What are you playing at?"

She shoved Nyx back, exhaustion clouding her mind. "I don't know. I followed my gut, and that's where it took me. It looks to me you were lucky that I did that."

Nyx barked a laugh. "We were doing just fine without you, thanks."

"That's not what I saw."

Her violet eyes flashed, and Memphis quickly intervened. "We accomplished what we came out here to do. Now, let's get back to the Academy in one piece, yeah?"

Nyx sneered at her and took off, Brokk by her side.

Memphis came up to Emory, squeezing her hand. "You did great out there. Now, let's go home."

She looked into those ice blue eyes, and from her overwhelming anger, shock, exhaustion, fear, and adrenaline, it was all she could do to nod and put one foot in front of the other as they navigated the forest together.

Her new room was bleak and small. Emory's head pounded, dots dancing in her vision. Cupping her hands over her eyes, Emory took in deep breaths. This was her reality now. A war zone. A long lost princess. A savior.

Hot salty tears leaked between her fingers, as she tried to make sense of her thoughts. Of her life.

A knock sounded at the door, and she jumped, scaring herself back to the present. Clambering, she quickly wiped her cheeks and shuffled to the door.

Bryd stood outside, waiting meekly, not quite looking her in the eyes. "I thought I would come for a proper hello. I know how it feels to lose your home, and to be swept up in the business here." She smiled weakly, finally looking her in the eyes. "Plus, we girls have to stick together."

Emory choked out a teary laugh, hysteria on the edge of it. She assessed the younger girl. "It's Bryd, right? How old are you?"

"Seventeen. I joined the rebels shortly after ...well, everything happened. I was eleven at the time."

An awkward silence followed, and Emory tried to find the right words to say. Instead, Emory stepped out into the hallway, shutting the door behind her.

Bryd quickly changed the subject. "It looks like you need some fun. Want me to show you the ring?"

The hope in her voice trapped Emory in a corner. "Sounds good."

They wove further down and down the halls, Bryd not ceasing to talk the entire way. Emory nodded, trying to match the other girl's enthusiasm.

Finally, they reached another iron door that looked identical to the rest. Behind closed doors, though, it was revealed to be a cavernous room, jagged pieces of metal closing in a tight ring where two figures were in a deadly dance, weapons flashing through the air like lightning. Emory recognized Memphis's flash of blonde hair as he ducked and parried his opponent's attack. The brute laughed, the laugh booming around the walls, his tattoos gleaming like freshly spilled ink.

Bryd excitedly explained, "We designed this room to test our training. No abilities are allowed; we are stripped bare to our strength and skill."

Emory gripped her forearms with white knuckles. "So like Gladiators?"

Her eyebrows rose. "Like *what*?"

# Heir of Lies – Part Three

Emory murmured, "Never mind."

"Anyways, they don't stop until one of them yields, and then they switch out with their partner. In this case, Memphis and Brokk are against Wyatt and Jaxson. Whoever's team defeats the pair wins along with bragging rights. Which between these four is a bit of a sensitive subject."

The crowd surrounded the gleaming metal roared in approval when Memphis got Wyatt in a chokehold. Emory curled her lips in disgust; it was barbaric that this was their form of entertainment. Wyatt threw Memphis over his shoulder like a rag doll, and Emory looked away, focusing on the figure standing along the edges, his golden eyes revealing nothing, his bronze hair now freshly buzzed.

Her heart basically dropped into her stomach when he met her gaze and nodded slightly. She looked back to the ring, feeling a blush creep along the back of her neck.

Adrenaline made her hands shake, and dread pooled in her stomach. It didn't make sense to have such an irrational fear, but there was something about Brokk she couldn't shake. There had to be a reason she had nightmares about him being a ruthless killer, but she wasn't about to find out the reason.

Bryd pulled excitedly at her sleeve. "Memphis just yielded so..." She was cut off by the scream of the onlookers now as Memphis leaped over the jagged ring, and Brokk replaced him with ease. It was a lithe grace only a predator would have, and Brokk quickly made Wyatt sweat by engaging in a fast boxing match. Their fists were a blur, each hit calculated and strong.

Bryd continued a personal commentary on the match, but Emory left her new friend alone, making her way to Memphis who was slouched on a bench. Sweat slicked his skin, and his eyes bright and alert as he watched the fight.

"You find this fun?" she asked. Emory's voice was much curter than she thought, and Memphis looked up at her in question.

Blood trickled down his split lip. He shrugged. "Everything we do here has a reason, even on our off time. It's encouragement and constant learning that makes us stronger than Adair."

Her eyes trailed over his toned muscles that were evident under his shirt, her thoughts faltering. He cleared his throat. "You have to remember no one wants it this way. We are dealing with our situation the best way we can."

With violence.

Blood and vengeance.

Emory's heart sunk, her own blood running cold. She missed her home, her life. But knowing that all these people have known nothing other than cold iron walls and a constant state of war, that there was no softness here, no escape... Her heart thudded with a new-found determination that there had to be a way to help all of them rebuild their lives.

Looking to Memphis, she spoke softly, "I'm going to call it a night. See you tomorrow?"

Before she could leave, he stood, capturing her hand, lowering his lips to her skin. The kiss was soft and quick, and he locked his eyes blue eyes with hers, whispering back, "I've waited six years to hear you say those words. Sleep well, Emory."

Memphis left her then to her own flustered self, Emory keenly aware that even from the ring, Brokk had his eyes locked on them the entire time.

Emory turned, leaving Bryd to watch the rest of the fight, feeling Brokk's gaze burning into her back until she was back out in the hallway. Loosening a breath, she made her way back, trying to push both Memphis and Brokk from her thoughts.

The next day proved harder than she thought. Black and purple bruises flowered her skin, and her hair was a matted, sweaty mess. She needed a shower. Or ten.

Walking to the small closet, she opened it, being met with an array of black shirts and pants, jackets, one pair of leather boots, and an unnecessary amount of knives all donated by Nyx.

# HEIR OF LIES – PART THREE

Sighing, Emory looked to the small pile of her possessions from Earth: dirty jeans, a green t-shirt, black high-top Converse, and her iPod that she forgot was in her pocket.

Her stomach twisted as she donned herself in the rebels' clothes, doing up her boots before opening her door. The hallways were already teeming with rebels. Emory joined the flow, trying to get her bearings and remember where Command was located. She had no idea what time it was, or if she had overslept.

Spotting swirling tattoos, she yelled across the crowd, "Wyatt, wait up!!" Maneuvering through the crowd, she breathlessly met him. "Morning. Where can one grab a shower in this place?"

Crossing his arms, he stood his ground. "Shouldn't you be with Memphis, preparing?"

"I won't be any use like this." Emory stubbornly matched his stance.

He sighed, practically rolling his eyes. "Come on. But you will be fast, and then I will personally take you to Command."

She wanted to kiss the man.

The showers, it turned out, weren't too far away from her room, the metallic tones of the room making everything shimmer. Wyatt had been clear; the showers were on a timer. She had fifteen minutes to feel human again.

It was the most blissful shower of her life. Steam curled around her, washing off layers of dirt and dried blood. There was a compressed bar that looked like soap in the stalls that Emory vigorously scrubbed herself with until her skin felt raw. The lingering aroma of citrus and rose lifted in the steam as Emory made a mental note to ask Memphis who or where he got the soap from. Her mind slowly rejuvenated, and with her body clean, she stepped out, drawing the curtain back and wrapping a towel around her. Emory quickly found out she wasn't alone.

Standing in front of the mirror, Nyx swept her violet hair up into a ponytail. Emory froze, water dripping onto the cold floor. Nyx's slow smirk made Emory's skin crawl.

"Well, well, well. Princess, aren't you looking radiant this morning? Any big plans for this fine day?"

Emory quickly grabbed clothes outside the stall, assessing Nyx. Venom leaked from her; she was like a snake about to strike its prey. She crossed her arms, "Training with Memphis, or that's what I've been told."

Nyx bared her teeth, mocking, "Of course. But maybe first, I could show you the ropes. After all, time is ticking."

It was a challenge, plain and clear. Emory should back down and go with Wyatt. She should follow her orders, but it wasn't in her nature to comply that easily.

Emory shot back, "Of course. What do we do about Wyatt waiting outside those doors for me?"

Nyx threw Emory supple leather boots. "Get dressed, and then we leave the way I came in. Wyatt is stupid to think he knows all the tricks of this place."

Nyx sensing her unease, raised her eyebrows. "Is there a problem?"

Oh, was there *ever*. The black gaping tunnel in the wall appeared after Nyx had pressed two loose bricks. She had explained it was a vacuum tunnel that connected right to the ring. Emory gritted her teeth and swallowed down the urge to be sick.

Stepping in front of Nyx, she said, icily, "See you down there."

Crouching down, Emory tucked in her limbs and sucked in a gulp of air. She threw her body weight forward into nothingness. Free falling at a dangerous speed, the wind howled around her as her body was jerked left, right, left, right. Her scream was stuck in her throat, eyes unable to shut, and suddenly, a hissing noise sounded and another opening made itself visible.

Emory was spewed out, flying, metal jagged teeth that surrounded the ring below her as she slammed into the ring, bones cracking, black spots entering he vision. Nyx wasn't far behind, hooting, she flew out of the chute, all powerful grace as she landed nimbly on her feet. Emory scrambled up, quite sure now her wrist was either broken or badly sprained.

"What is wrong with you?" Emory asked.

Nyx cocked her head in fake innocence. "*Tsk, tsk*, Princess, don't be sour. You agreed to it. Besides, that is good practice for your nerves. You will face worse things in the coming weeks. Now, since we don't have weapons, how about some hand-to-hand combat practice?"

Emory gnashed her teeth together. "So you have another chance to further surprise me? No thanks."

Nyx circled her lazily. "Now, believe what you want, but I am here to help you. I'm not living in some fantasy that you would be prepared to even live in this world, let alone survive it. In physical strength and ability, you are a newborn. So, are you ready to change that?"

The few rebels that had been down here attending to the room had now gathered around the ring.

Trying to still her heart, Emory said, exasperated, "No."

Nyx threatened, "You're going to have to be."

It happened in slow motion to Emory. Nyx swung out her leg, trying to sweep Emory's feet out, making her jump while anticipating this, and Nyx connected her fist with Emory's jaw. The crowd leered at them, and Emory fell, the copper taste of blood filling her mouth.

"Get up," Nyx growled, pacing with predatory fixation. This wasn't a training lesson. This was personal.

Emory's legs had turned to jelly, and she failed to find her feet. Nyx moved too fast, peppering her with a swift undercut to her jaw, slamming a kick into her gut. Emory fell onto her back, blood flowing down her face from her now split lip. The world spun, as white hot anger flared within her.

Rolling, Emory lunged and grabbed Nyx's ankle, pulling her to the ground. It felt like time freezing but also jolting faster all at once. Nyx didn't struggle at all. It was ice and fire running in her blood when Nyx's power seeped into Emory. It was raw and wild, and Emory, with a thread of fear, realized that she liked it. Nyx had gone limp by this point, her eyes rolling in the back of her head.

Voices screamed at her through her consciousness, making Emory release Nyx, her entire body shaking. With the connection broken, the telekinetic powers started to fade, leaving Emory broken and panting on the ground. Nyx had paled to a scary shade of white.

"What, by flame and fire, is happening?" Memphis's voice boomed across the room, making everyone freeze. For the first time, it would seem, in her life, Nyx was speechless. Anger flashed in Memphis's eyes when he took in the state of both on the ground.

Coming to the edge of the ring, Memphis whispered to Nyx, "Nyx. Get her out. Now."

Slowly helping Emory up, she nodded to a bystander. "Jake, if you will."

The young man with ashy hair and a grim stature flicked his hands, and gravity didn't seem to exist anymore as they floated over the sharpened edges of the ring. Nyx nodded at him and limped toward Memphis, Emory swaying behind her. She needed to sit. Now.

Listening to her body, she slumped down on the cold floor, aware of the argument roaring in front of her.

"What were you thinking?" Memphis fumed.

"They needed to see what *she is*. She is human, and she is weak."

Memphis yelled now, spittle flying from his lips, "Just weak? Because when I came in, she wasn't the one unconscious. You need to go, now. Report back to what you're supposed to be doing."

Nyx looked like a fish out of water, gulping for air. Mouth closing and opening wordlessly, she finally turned a deep shade of red and stalked out without a second glance at them.

Memphis held out a hand toward Emory, pulling her back to a standing position. The world tilted, and he said, "Come on. One foot in front of the other. I'll get you patched up."

# Heir of Lies – Part Three

Blood roared in her ears, and she leaned into Memphis, allowing the world to take on a warped perspective.

"*Breathe, Emory. Breathe.*" Memphis's voice cocooned around her mind.

Emory looked down at her shaking hands, trying to register what had just happened. Every minute took her closer to a tight knit web of emotions and betrayal she didn't ask for. It wasn't her fault she had been rescued, nor was it her fault for being brought back. She was trying to pick up the pieces and learn the secrets of her past for herself, not simply accepting what was thrown at her.

In the two weeks that have passed, each day, she was being morphed into a version of herself she didn't think was possible. In a world that shouldn't exist. But she had chosen to try and was learning exactly what that would cost.

Her world took a drastic dip, and Memphis hurriedly brought her around another corner, supporting her aching body. They came to a smooth iron staircase, but instead of being dark silver, it was an incandescent white, making it look like it was carved from ice.

Memphis noticed her staring and said, "Some kieroian steel can be manipulated with heat to achieve this color. We are lucky Jaxson listened in class all those years ago."

Their footsteps clanged around them like bells tolling, marking every second. She could feel his gaze boring into her, and looking up through her lashes, she murmured, "I'm okay."

Coming to a full stop, he said, "You're okay? What about me? What about Nyx? Emory, what were you playing at? Nyx is just *looking* for an excuse to have it out with you. You are far too important to me for you to put yourself in these situations without me around." Memphis clenched her forearm, fingers white.

Her eyes locked onto his hold. "Memphis, let me go. Now. I'm not some lost kid for you to control. I can make my own decisions."

He stepped back. "Decisions that will land you hurt or worse? Emory, I will not lose you again."

"But you can't keep me in a cage, Memphis! I'm not your property and never have been! Stop treating me like your pet and *show* me that I am your equal! Show me my world. I want to see all the parts of it, good and bad, but I won't from behind these walls. Let me try to understand what you have lost, so I can understand just exactly what I am fighting for."

Memphis stepped closer, his breath hot on her cheek. "You don't understand."

Emory threw her arms out. "No, I don't. Allow me to learn. I can't hide down here forever. I have gotten one afternoon, Memphis, one day to get out."

She knew she had hit a nerve when his jaw tightened and eyes narrowed. Several seconds passed in silence until he stiffly said, "Fine, okay, fine. But we are swinging by the infirmary and the armory, and that is nonnegotiable."

She couldn't keep her elation in place, even through her wounds. "Even though we are weapons enough?"

Memphis picked up his pace. "We aren't weapons against everything that is out there. And besides, you will be of no use if you're beaten half to death."

She couldn't argue with that. Up they climbed, Emory noting Memphis's furrowed brows, his lips turned down, as the tensely continued in silence. They made it to the top of the staircase where a closet of a room was located on their right. Memphis ushered her in without a word and quickly set to work grabbing an arrangement of jars. Emory took a seat and tried to stifle her groan but was failing terribly.

Finishing, he held a strange dried root in front of her. "Eat this, and I'm sorry in advance about the taste. Thistlewood is one of the oldest healing roots in Kiero. Your mother researched its properties; she was a wonderful healer, he said, all this while not quite meeting her gaze.

# Heir of Lies – Part Three

Emory tentatively took the grey root from him, popping the whole ting in her mouth, chewing fast. She tried not to wince as a harsh heat swept in her mouth and throat as she ate it.

Crouching down in front of her, he rested his hand gently on her knee. "Emory, look, I'm sorry. I shouldn't have gotten mad. A lot of that is between Nyx and me and has nothing to do with you." He took a steadying breath. "And you were right. You deserve more. You deserve to pull your weight, to know the truth. I've spent so long knowing you're the heir and being bred a soldier that I was blinded by my duty to keep you safe. And we have been hiding for so long, I grouped you into that rule. I'm sorry. Can we start over as friends?"

Heat flushed her cheeks, taking in the man in front of her with his heart bore on his sleeve. A thousand doubts flooded through her unexpectedly. Was he only playing another card in the game? But to get to the truth, she had to take her own risks. To play this game, she had to be just as daring. And she didn't have many offers of friendship as of late. Eyes watering from the thistlewood, Emory smiled. "Of course."

He patted her knee, standing up. Memphis had been right about the root. Almost instantly, a cooling sensation swept over her muscles, her dizziness gone.

Revitalized, Emory followed suit. "Any idea about where we are going?"

"Now that, I am going to keep a surprise. Ready?" He beamed.

Nodding, they re-emerged into the windowless hallway, setting out again.

"So, my mom was a healer?"

"The best to be found. Not only was that her ability, but she was the most knowledgeable person I knew. She always had more love for her research than she did in politics, but once the Academy started, she made it a priority along with your father. She had a heart of gold, your mom did."

"Why start the Academy then?"

The corners of his mouth turned down. "There was a lot of unrest along the borders, especially between the Shattered Isles and Kiero. People using their abilities for worse, or not knowing how to control them. The Academy was the start of a school that would help protect the land and its people with gifted students. Its main purpose was to help people like us so their power wouldn't consume them."

"What went wrong then?" Emory asked.

Memphis murmured, "The need for power. And that's the hardest to understand. Looking back, no one saw it coming. I found out after, that it had been rumored that your father was keeping an artifact of ancient magic. Something that, if wielded, would make you unstoppable."

Her blood ran cold. "And Adair has it?"

Memphis peeked at her. "How much do you remember, Emory?"

She shrugged. "Right now? Nothing. It's more like I feel a connection to things I see. Like the forest, that stirs up a lot of feeling."

Memphis nodded. "You have to take it in a day at a time. You must understand, we did what we all thought was best. Adair was our friend. He was one of my best friends. But to him, there were more important things. His family name and the never-ending lust to be the best. He believes that anyone who doesn't have a strong ability is not to be worthy of a choice."

Chills snaked down her spine, her mouth running dry as Memphis continued, "After your parent's death, and after the Academy fell, the world changed. Adair's wrath spread through Kiero, and people either joined his kingdom or he killed them. When it comes to you and Adair, you have always had a target on your back, Em."

Emory stopped dead in her tracks. "What do you mean?"

Memphis cleared his throat, not meeting her eyes once more.

"Memphis, *what?*" It came out more as a plea as she pulled him toward her, stopping him.

# HEIR OF LIES – PART THREE

"It was well known that Adair always had feelings for you. On your fourteenth birthday, he had it planned to move on these feelings. His family and your family had been close and, honestly, were two of the most powerful family names. He had always believed you two to be destined."

"But I rejected him?"

Memphis didn't have to say anything more but looked at her with hollow eyes.

Emory looked down at her shoes. "I rejected the now Mad King, who once believed that we should have ruled Kiero together."

Memphis sighed. "That's exactly why you hold the most power over him. Not only does your ability trump his, but you are the only person who can reach him. He has never let you go, Emory."

Ice settled over her heart, strong and unveiling. She stared down the hallway as she walked, processing everything. Memphis followed more slowly, giving her space.

She whirled around. "Why did I say no to Adair? It sounds like we were really close." Her heart thundered, her gut twisting.

Memphis's gaze roamed over her face, lips, and trailing. His silence said enough. His *look* said enough. Heat crawled up her neck, and she pushed forward, not knowing what to say.

*Did she have feelings for Memphis once?*

If that was true, she had left him to love a ghost, a memory. Pushing the thought down, Emory didn't know what to say. There was no time to dwell on what could have been if she had stayed.

Memphis clearly sensed her discomfort and, thankfully, broke the silence. "We'll just pick up some bows. We have a bit of a walk ahead of us." A small twitch sneaked out the corner of his mouth, and she sighed internally.

*It wouldn't be awkward.*

The armory was located at the end of the hallway and was like an iron cave. Rows upon rows of steel blades, armor, and bows hung neatly. Coolness washed over them, and Memphis instantly lit up when he started rummaging through a small carved chest, murmuring to himself.

Emory stood, surveying his back as he looped strange clear goggles and straps over his arm. "What exactly do we need these for?"

Chuckling, he winked over his shoulder. "You asked to see all the parts of Kiero, and though seeing every inch of it is impossible right now, I can show you something beautiful."

*Something beautiful?*

Several minutes of collecting items later, a slender bow strapped over her shoulder, and a quiver full of arrows, they left the armory. Memphis held the goggles, looking like a kid on Christmas morning.

As they walked, Emory looked at the building around her. Patches of older looking brick peeked out from below the windowsills.

"You guys did a lot of work here," Emory stated.

Memphis shot her a look. "After Adair took the throne, not only was Kiero ravaged by looting raiders and the dabarnes, but the countryside was assaulted with waves of unexplainable destructive magic. Gases that have wiped out cities, explosives that have destroyed whole forests. Alby has observed it while on his scouts, so over the years we have reinforced the Academy with lots of kieroian steel. In case we are in line with one of these attacks, it will protect us. The metal absorbs the impact, making it stronger."

Chewing the inside of her cheek, Emory nodded. "That's reassuring."

Reaching the end of the hallway and at the elevator, Memphis pressed a worn button and glanced at her. "Emory, what do you see when you look around you?"

"A war zone," she replied.

"But, past that? Past the loss and the hiding and the divide, what do you see?"

# HEIR OF LIES – PART THREE

Mulling this over, clasping her forearms, the gates groaned open in front of them. Stepping in, Memphis closed them in as they were propelled above ground.

"I see love and friendship, and strength."

Memphis nodded. "Three things Adair will never truly understand. To have lost everything but have the hope to rebuild the future is the strongest weapon in the world. We hid you so that you could reclaim your throne and help us build that world."

Goosebumps rose on her skin, guilt sinking in her stomach.

Memphis caught her expression. "Emory, it was all our choice for you to leave. The people need their rightful leader. They need *you*."

His fingers tenderly lifted her face to meet his gaze. "We all need you."

Her stomach did a double flip, her nerves singing. Clearing her throat, she took a tentative step back. "It's hard for me to understand what exactly I will need to do."

Memphis chuckled. "Emory, you are our hook. Adair himself hasn't set a foot outside of his kingdom since you left. He sends his cronies out to do his dirty work. We are in a warzone between them and the raiders. But if we can draw him out with you, we have a chance to engage him. A chance to *end* him."

"So, I'm just supposed to let more people die for me?"

The elevator groaned to a stop, and they were hit full on with sunlight. Emory closed her watering eyes as Memphis opened the gate. The hot afternoon air was like a wall when they stepped out.

"You can't look at it like that."

"But that's the truth! At the end of the day, people have lost— and will lose—their lives because of my parents' mistakes, and in turn, because of my mistakes!" Her voice rose to a panicked yell, and Memphis cocked his eyebrow.

"It's the price we have to pay, Emory. Your parents built a government they thought would ensure peace. Whatever they were hiding was for good reason. It wasn't their fault, or your fault, that Adair unhinged that."

Emory planted her feet firmly in the grass, narrowing her eyes at the solider in front of her. "And why wait so long to try and change things?"

Memphis's face darkened. "Adair is playing with dark magic. That mixed with his ability is lethal. If we would have tried to overthrow him, we would have died."

Emory bit back her retort, sensing the conversation was over.

Exhaling heavily, she started to walk, Memphis on her heels. The forest splayed in front of them drew her forward with every step. The warm breeze encircled her, making her blood pound. The heavy scent of earth, sweet pollen, and dust pulled at her senses and pulled at her memories through a fog.

*Home.*

She chewed over the word, and the new meaning it now held. She had a family. A mom, a dad, a lineage. Overwhelming her, it all came crashing through her façade, through her fake sense of calm. She had left her home and people that had loved her. People she had loved. And now, they came face-to-face as strangers, to rebuild, to grow. How could she grow if she didn't even know who she was?

Panic bloomed in her chest, as her mind spun. Memphis came up beside her, tentative and too burly to miss. "Em?"

Emory Fae. Heir. Traitor. Coward.

Clenching her fists, nails pinching her skin, each thought dug holes into her heart, searing it. She needed to forget if just for a minute. Her muscles responded first, feet bounding as she turned and left Memphis behind. Pumping her arms hard at her sides, syncing her breath, she ran. Memphis's surprised cry echoed behind her.

Sweat prickled her skin, her legs burning, and her surroundings became a blur. Breaking through the forest line and interrupting her stride, Emory wove in between the trees, the speckled light glittering. Branches and spindly trunks created a catacomb around her.

# HEIR OF LIES – PART THREE

A matching crunch sounded behind her, and Memphis side swiped her. He was fast. He pulled her waist hard, and she didn't have a choice but to side roll messily into the dirt and leaves before her. The bow dug into her back, and she clamped down her jaw in complaint. Her head smacked hard, and stars danced in her vision.

"What are you playing at?" he breathed huskily, his eyes slits and chest heaving. Her tongue felt thick and dry in her mouth. Memphis continued. "I brought you out here on the promise I would keep you safe. To keep you safe, we must stay in a team. To stay in a team, I would advise you not running at a drop of a hat. We are in raider territory. Always remember that." He held her gaze, allowing the words to sink in. He exhaled, his warm breath tickling her face. "Now can I let you up? I'm sore from the ring and don't feel like tackling you again."

Emory nodded, and he stood up, offering her his hand. Truly, she couldn't help herself smirking up at him. "You're out of shape, old man." He balked confused, and Emory winked. "Memphis, it's a joke."

Shaking her head, they walked through the woods, trying to catch their breath, and Emory listened to the gentle wind sing each sigh, the sound stripping her worries away one-by-one.

Memphis strapped the goggles on enlarging his eyes and blond lashes. Truthfully, he looked like an extremely fit bubble fish. Emory squeaked, trying to cover her laugh as Memphis bantered on. They had walked for hours, either in silence or careful conversation, knowing they had both pushed each others' boundaries this afternoon.

Finally, they reached a clearing, the thickets of trees thinned, and sloping grassland greeted them. Strange purple and black birds chirped and swooped down in a graceful dance around them as they entered. In the middle of the clearing, a large still pond awaited. Emory walked toward it and had to do a double take, making sure her eyes weren't tricking her. The rose gold water swirled and churned before her like a frosted mirror. Emory was entranced. "What is it?"

Memphis was radiating, making his features light up. "This was founded and named by your mom. Welcome to clearing Monenta, it means 'the clearing of lost memories'. Your mom used to come here to work on her research and study the waters. I thought you would want to see it."

Emory nodded, muted by the beauty and fascination of these woods. That's when Memphis handed her a pair of goggles and, with a wicked glint in his eyes, asked, "Ready to explore?"

Beaming back at him, Emory grabbed the goggles which suctioned to her face when she adjusted the strap. She peeked over at the Commander, just as he peeled off his thin black shirt, revealing the dips and valleys of his chiselled chest. Pink scars rippled in the afternoon light. Too many for her to take in at once.

Memphis looked up to meet her gaze, and mortified, she jerked her head forward. Heat pulsed off her body. *Get a grip on yourself.* Taking deep breaths, Emory felt heat flare in her cheeks. Looking back at Memphis, she asked, "Will we keep our weapons?"

"We will, just follow my lead." Winking, Memphis surged forward, dragging her along with him.

They jumped, plunging into the cool water. Initially, the shock stung her skin. She dropped further, toward the bottom, her eyes closed. A hand brushed her cheek, and her eyes flew open. Memphis pushed a strange triangle cone toward her, motioning to put it over her mouth. Her lungs were already complaining for oxygen, so she didn't hesitate. Instantly, the fabric molded to her skin, and beautiful clean air met her lips.

She couldn't help but be delighted as she exhaled, and a school of bubbles escaped from the spout. It was like a portable oxygen tank, and this realization made her relax, so she took in the hidden world around her.

Memphis swam lazily, looping and twisting, the streaming light capturing his fluid grace in front of her. He looked more at ease in this aquatic world than she had seen thus far. Long pale green reeds encircled them, growing from the clearest gold sand Emory had ever seen. She swam forward, kicking her still booted feet as a school of long eel-like fish cut in front of her. Her limbs were flayed out in every way as she tried to get away, her breath coming in short bursts.

The fish eyed her cautiously, their grey skin looking dull against the backdrop of their home. Memphis flashed her a quick thumb's up, motioning to them: *They were okay.*

She gently treaded water, taking them in more closely. Memphis reached a hand out to the fish closest to him, brushing its scales lightly. That's when their world exploded into an array of dancing colors. The school encircled Memphis, swimming laps around him, each fish seemingly glowing, their grey skin dissolving.

Hundreds of shades of colors danced on their skin, bathing them in a rainbow of light. She gasped, utterly entranced by the display. Memphis dove toward her, grabbing her hand once more, and they swam deeper into the lake, the fish following and roping around them. It was like being in a pearl, a crystal world hidden from prying eyes.

They swam for several glorious minutes, her body becoming more natural in her weightless state. Memphis's blond hair billowed out in front of her as they stopped suddenly in front an oddly shaped tunnel.

Mischievousness danced in his eyes as they plunged toward the darkness, and she didn't have time to protest because they were sucked in, leaving their new friends and their glorious light behind.

For a second, she was disoriented, not knowing where her body began and Memphis's ended, as a current surged from behind them, pulling them deeper. The silken blackness dulled gradually, and the walls came into view, the sand providing a soft glow from beneath them.

It looked like they were in a worn cavern, strange markings etched all around them. Emory couldn't quite make them out because they suddenly plunged down, her yell caught in her throat. She squeezed Memphis's hand so hard, she was surprised the Commander wasn't wincing in pain. Darkness blinded them again, and her stomach lifted to meet her throat at the sudden gravity change, the current gone.

Floating, Emory squinted in her goggles, trying to make out the shadows. She let go of Memphis's hand and swam forward just as an iron voice rang out.

"Who dares disturbs us?"

The bone pommel was luminous as a blade met her throat, pricking her skin, and she tried to back pedal; Memphis was behind her, and she rammed into his bare chest.

Through the shadowed water, two luminous eyes shone back at her, slowly revealing who the voice belonged to. Pale white hair floated around his strong upper body, his muscles taunt from holding the sword. Strange tattoos swirled on his skin, the same markings they had seen before on the walls. Emory's eyes trailed down his skin until her gaze stopped where his human body changed to that of a fish, deep blue scales glinting back at her. Two huge incandescent flippers propelled him forward as the merman repeated in a dangerous whisper, "Who dares disturbs us?"

Memphis squeezed the back of her arm as he swam in front of her. She was frozen, and the merman took in Memphis with furrowed eyebrows. Memphis had stilled, staring at the creature intensely. It dawned on Emory that the two were having a private conversation just then, as the merman's eyes constantly flickered over to her, assessing.

Her hands shook as the merman slowly lowered his weapon after several painful seconds and swam to her, coming face-to-face.

"So, Emory Fae, you have finally come to claim what is rightfully yours?"

*What was he talking about?*

# HEIR OF LIES – PART THREE

Panicked, she looked up to Memphis who nodded his head. This was a test. Memphis had purposely put her in this situation. Forcing her to trust him. She looked into the merman's pale grey eyes and nodded.

He smiled wickedly, revealing pointed teeth. "If you can retrieve the heirloom, you may keep it." He waved her forward, past Memphis and into an even darker tunnel. Emory's heart rammed against her chest.

An *heirloom*. Searching within herself, she had to find the strength to get back the only piece of her family. A stubborn determination slowly started to build as she looked to Memphis.

He was solemn but intense, as if waiting to see if she would back down. It was probably stupid of her not to.

She swam forward, taking deep breaths. *You can do this.*

The mouth of the tunnel swallowed her, and she didn't look back. An oppressive silence filled her senses, and she had to squint to see five feet in front of her. But she pressed on, goosebumps covering her skin. Slick rock surrounded her, and the once golden sand was now black. Her gut was screaming at her to turn around, that this wasn't right, but she pressed on.

Swimming around a tight corner, she avoided the jutted rock's edge, but that's when Emory felt it. A change in the water that felt like charges had been turned on, creating a pulsing electric current. Stopping, she floated, listening intensely. Nothing. Her breath came in sick huffs, panic chewing at her. She hated the darkness.

The strange pulsing current started faster like her own personal tribal drum calling her and beckoning her closer.

Slowly, she turned her head to look ahead and was met by sharp gleaming teeth, saggy green skin, sparse inky hair, and eyes that were opaque. The creature sniffed at her, creating bubbles between them. Instead of limbs, it had long tentacles and crawled toward her, snapping its teeth. It had caught her scent.

Frantically, Emory clawed her hands back, reaching for her bow. The creature cocked its head at the movement. The nightmarish specimen lashed out, moving far too fast for her human eyes to take in. Slimy tentacles wrapped around her midriff, tightening around her, and she was reeled in. Kicking and screaming, Emory tried to escape, but it only made the creature hold tighter.

The only problem was that no one could hear her.

Its blind eyes swiveled side-to-side as an ancient voice rattled, "Your scent...is one I recognize...from long ago...when these waters...were considered...sacred. Who...are you?" Each word was drawn out and dragged as if the monster wasn't sure if she was a friend or foe. Again, it cocked its mostly bald head at her, waiting for an answer. The blasted oxygen masked was in her way though, and she couldn't move, couldn't breathe.

"Noooo? That's...a shame. It has been...a long...time since...a warrior swam...these tunnels. I will be...sorry...to end you."

*No, no, no!*

More tentacles wrapped around her legs and arms, binding them and her will. This was it. Emory stared at its gleaming teeth, its rotting skin, and she was pulled down toward her death. Closer and closer she came until its long eel like tongue caressed her cheek, tasting her. She was truly sobbing now.

Cringing away, Emory pressed her eyes closed, saying a silent plea, and then a blaze of light warmed her eyelids, making her world a pale red for a second. Then she was dropped.

Eyes flying open, she saw the creature hissing at the light around them, backing away in the shadows and its algae like skin peeling as if it had been burned. She hung suspended in the water, and Memphis emerged in her vision, his bloody hand pressed against the wall, millions upon millions of carvings acting like personal suns swirling and dancing in sync.

His eyes were wide and panicked, his chest heaving as his voice rang through her mind, loud and clear, *"Behind you there is a chest where that thing was. Grab it now!"*

She swiveled and spotted a beautifully engraved small chest, practically blending in with the sand. Diving, she willed her muscles to move, taking deep gulps of oxygen. Her fingers wrapped around it, and she was surprised it wasn't bigger than her palm.

A roar cut through the water, making it ripple, and Memphis mentally shouted, *"Hurry!"*

Cutting through the water faster than she thought was possible, Emory was about halfway to him when the Commander let go of the wall, and they were spun into inky darkness. Disoriented, she faltered but familiar arms wrapped around her and dragged her with him.

*"Swim, Emory, swim!"*

Her muscles were on fire, burning and cramping. There was another roar from behind them, but they climbed upward out of the cave's mouth. That was too close. An earth shattering bellow shook around them once more just as they shot out of the tunnel.

"Thieves!" the merman shouted. He had waited at the entrance, sword pointed at their chests.

Memphis turned to face him, his body taut, and the only indication of him taking action that Emory could see was a twitch of his eye, and then the merman's grey eyes rolled in the back of his head and he dropped, unconscious. Gripping her hand, Memphis yanked her hard, climbing toward the currents and to their escape.

What had that thing been? Her revulsion and shock caught up with her, making her stomach churn. The current caught their bodies, shooting them up and through another darkened tunnel. Fear pierced through her, her imagination running rampant, and she waited to feel the tentacles wrapping around her once more.

She had almost *died*. Memphis had willingly drawn her down there like a moth to a flame. He had risked her *life* to gain whatever was in the box.

Upward and upward, they spun, as her anger grew. Right about when she thought she was going to be sick, they were spat out into the calm lake, golden sand and all. Memphis didn't falter and cut through the rose gold water, climbing for the surface.

Emory only focused on the dappled light and the whirling clouds of the clearing. She forced her limbs to comply. Water rained down around them when they burst through, resurfacing. Ripping the mask off her face with a giant squelching noise, she gulped in the refreshing air. Letting go of Memphis's hand, she paddled for shore and lifted herself on the grass. Blissful solid ground met her, and she breathed in the sweet scent of the dirt and grass as she rested her cheek on the ground, her legs still emerged in the water.

"Do you still have it?" Memphis's voice sounded like sandpaper. He was resting beside her.

"Have it? Oh this? This box you nearly let me die for? Yes, why in fact, I do have it." Pure venom filled her voice as she lifted herself up onto shore, throwing the goggles to the side.

Memphis rose up to meet her, droplets of water running off his skin. "You don't understand."

"Oh I don't understand? I think I *understand* perfectly. That you led me into a trap to get something you have wanted for years!"

Birds flew out, squawking from their hiding places when her voice rose several octaves.

"Yes. I knew the chest was down there. I knew about this place because I found your mom's diary in her old office. I knew that this chest was meant for you, to help you! The mermen inhabit this water, but that other thing…I had no idea. If I did, I wouldn't have brought you down there."

She wiped water from her eyes angrily, blinking hard. "So, you admit it was a test? You admit you brought me knowingly into danger?"

Memphis stepped closer, the corner of his lip lifting. "If I didn't believe you could handle it, we wouldn't have come here, period. I respect you, and I thought you would want whatever it is your mom left you."

Shaking her head, she clenched the chest to her palm and exhaled. "Yes, I do. I just wish you hadn't lied to me. That's not how you will win over my trust, and just so you know, that is *not* how most people choose to relax."

# HEIR OF LIES – PART THREE

Memphis chuckled. "But don't we make a great team?"

She hesitated before she murmured, "Maybe. Now put your shirt back on." She tossed him the light fabric. "Let's go back so I can look at this from the safety of my bunker."

Pocketing the small chest in her soaking pants, they walked back into the slumber of the forest.

They made it back to the edge of the forest line, to the rolling hills where the Academy was hidden. Memphis leaned against a tree, poised and skeptical. "So, was that enough to satisfy your curiosity?"

Lifting her eyebrows, she retorted, "No, but it will do for today."

"Excellent, because I'm starving." Pushing himself upright, she was just about to make a snarky comeback when a twig snapped from behind them.

They both spun in unison, Memphis reaching and drawing his bow in a fluid motion. Emory followed and, with shaking hands, drew her bow taut. The horizon was clear, but it wasn't until five figures dressed in forest green fell from the trees, landing gracefully, and stood.

Memphis barked, "You have a second before I shoot."

The closest figure to them stalked toward them, declaring, "You are losing your touch if you didn't notice us until now. Besides, rumor has it, you need our help."

Memphis's stance relaxed slightly, but he didn't lower his bow. "What clan are you from, raiders? Is this a meeting of acceptance, or a promise of another war?"

The man lowered his hood, revealing his bronze skin and hooded eyes. His group followed closely; weapons drawn. "We are from the Blood Dust clan. Naturally, you have to understand I can't tell you where that is located, or I will have to kill you."

"Naturally," Memphis said, smoothly.

"Is it true you and your, uh, army are taking on Adair? With the heir?"

Memphis grinned. "You might recognize your future queen when she is standing right in front of you... Are you with us, if we *were* planning such a thing?"

The raider's eyes lazily found her and looked most unimpressed. He stepped closer. "You're telling me that this *girl* is the key to your freedom? I would reassess your plan." He shrugged. "Also, we came to kindly remind you that we answer to no one. The lands we inhabit are ours, and no one else. We will bow to no queen."

Memphis pulled the bow string tighter. "Then you will fall with Adair."

Emory looked between the two groups, divided by her claimed regency. She lowered her bow. "What if I promised that you would remain free on your land? That you wouldn't have to answer to me as long as you promise to help us in this fight."

Their leader cocked his eyebrow. "How can we know that you would keep your word?"

Memphis shot her a warning glance, but she pressed on. "Your land will never be free as long as Adair is on the throne. At the end of the day, you have, and will continue, to answer to his actions. You help us now, and you ensure you keep what you want most. I'm here to help rebuild my parents' world, not one born from flame and ash."

A quiet unease rippled throughout the group, and the raider turned his focus on her. "You have quite the mouth on you, Emory Fae. Maybe you are telling the truth, and maybe you aren't. Time will tell."

He spun his knife in his hand, eyes returning to Memphis. "As for you, *Commander*, we decline your offer for now. We will continue to watch, but I'm warning you. If you seek us out again, it will be the last thing you do. If we decide it is our fight, then we will come."

Before Memphis could react, the raider sent the blade sailing through the air, and with a twang, finding its mark in the tree

# Heir of Lies – Part Three

beside Memphis. The raider sounded a sharp whistle, and they took off, scampering off into the cover of the trees once more.

Memphis loosened a shaky breath, lowering the bow.

"Well, that went well," Emory said.

Memphis grabbed the blade out of the tree, smiling. "They will come. Raiders never leave a token of good favor."

Emory scoffed. "These dynamics... I don't think I will learn them fast."

"Raiders are fickle. They wanted to test us, too. To see if we are a threat to them." Memphis strapped the bow on his back and sheathed the blade.

Emory waggled her eyebrows. "Aren't we?"

"Let's just get back." Memphis kicked at the ground, rolling his eyes.

It felt like a flutter of wings brushing against her consciousness, as she was pulled into a memory.

*Memphis crushed Emory against his chest in a massive bear hug.*

*"Memphis get off me!" Emory shoved him back, grinning crookedly.*

*"Em, you are the best. Thank you for not telling anyone."*

*Exhaling, Emory looked at one of her best friends. "Memph, it's not my place to tell anyone you are getting private tutoring with your ability."*

*Eyes glowing, a flush filled his cheeks as he hugged her again. "Still, thank you."*

As fast as it had come, the memory left, leaving Emory breathless. Over the last few weeks, snippets had come to her, most of it meaningless information but had solidified the echo of Memphis Carter within her. He was stubborn, was manipulative, had a taste for danger.

But wasn't she as well?

She looked to the horizon, where the setting sun dipped in the sky. Brilliant golds and oranges bled into the sky, and the forest was painted with golden light.

Together, they walked back to the Academy, side-by-side and in happy silence.

The necklace fell out of the chest with a clang. Emory had sprawled out in her bunker, staring at the chest and working up the courage to open it.

Tentatively, she scooped up the thin silver chain, gazing at the beautiful amethyst gem with flecks of gold dust layering it. Her hands started to shake when she saw there was the tiniest of notes folded neatly in the bottom. As if reaching for the most delicate of feathers, she lifted it out and unfolded it.

*For you, my dear. To remind you that you are never lost.*

Her mother's handwriting was thin and beautiful. Emory soaked in the words before her: *To remind you that you are never lost.*

Pride and fear shot through her simultaneously. This had been her mother's, held by her, touched by her. She dropped the note and sat on her bed in silence, not quite grasping the beautiful gift. Had her mom known that she would be in danger? Why else hide a family heirloom?

Groaning, she dropped her face in her hands, not wanting to face her reality.

A sharp knock sounded at her door, and she stood, electrified. In a daze, she grabbed the necklace and clasped it around her pale throat while she walked to the door. Opening it, she asked, "Yes?"

Wyatt stood in front of her, thick arms crossed in front of his chest. "Well, isn't that a pleasant way to greet someone. Hello to you too, Princess."

Sighing, she mimicked his stance. "What do you want?"

He grumbled. "I'm to take you to the library to enlighten you on a history lesson."

That got her attention. "I didn't know there was a library."

Pressing his lips together, he waited.

Rolling her shoulders, she closed the door behind her, and the pair took off down the hallway.

Wyatt tried to make conversation with her. He talked about his turn in the ring with Jaxson and how, "The git had multiplied

# HEIR OF LIES – PART THREE

and cheated his way through," about him tracking the raiders, about what he ate for dinner.

On and on and on, he rambled until Emory stopped him. "Wyatt, why are you trying so hard to be nice to me? Why now?"

Scratching the back of his neck, Emory caught more detail of his tattoo: a sun beating down on the forest, deer like creatures with huge antlers and wings climbing out of the shadows through the air. In inky swirls, three women cupped crystals in their palms. The detail was beautiful.

"I didn't like you because I thought you wouldn't be able to survive this world or wouldn't accept it. I told Memphis that not only did you have to prove to yourself that you are strong enough, you had to prove it to the rest of us as well. Now that you have, I would like to get to know you, if that's okay with you."

She turned a flaming beet red. Wyatt. Burly rough and tough Wyatt had accepted her. He playfully punched her shoulder.

"Don't let this go to your head, though. The others will take time, especially Jaxson and Nyx."

*Nyx.*

She cringed internally at the thought of the other woman who was fueled by her inner fire. She hoped that their paths didn't cross soon.

Onward they walked, and she was at a loss for words, which Wyatt seemed to understand.

The library, it turned out, was on the same level as her room. The door was like every other in this metallic world, and Wyatt pushed it open, motioning for her to follow. The room was dark with one bookcase. The dreary walls were covered in maps, painting a visual picture for her. A very small desk and two chairs lay at the center.

It was small, but it was the coziest place she had seen here yet.

Wyatt pulled a worn black-covered book from the top shelf and gently said, "Sit."

She gracefully accepted, her battered and bruised body complaining about her earlier activities that afternoon.

"This is the last copy of the History of Kiero," he said, bitterly. "It dates back to before your parents were married. Memphis thought reading this might help your memories become clearer."

She eagerly reached for the book, Wyatt holding it just out of her reach. "I will advise you to absorb what is here, but remember that this time, our future is ours to write."

He held her gaze and then gently laid the book down in front of her. Standing, he took his leave. "I have to go check on Jaxson. I will be back in a couple of hours."

His words were already background noise to Emory as she gently opened the fragile cover. It was apparently the day of gifts.

She eagerly looked to the first sentence and was swept away in the story about a magical kingdom that was divided from the beginning. Of how her parents' marriage was part of peace treaty between the Shattered Isles and Kiero that would help stop slaving in Kiero and unite the borders and ensure all their resources would still be produced and sold. Of how they built a democratic society to ensure everyone felt they were equals, that they had a say about how their towns and government should be run. This had worked for a while, and fifteen peaceful years had followed.

Emory leaned closer, her nose practically touching the pages when she reached the part that introduced Adair's family. The Strattons had been her parents' best friends and advisors, it was said, and they had always thought the Academy was too soft. That the students should be taught how to use brute force and grow their abilities instead of learning how to control them.

It was only a paragraph describing the Fall of the Academy, and all that was said at the end was, "It is unknown why the Strattons' son unleashed his ability for destruction and sadly killing The Faes to usurp the throne. It is rumored the Strattons also perished."

Emory leaned back, exhaling hard. Blinking heavily, she wondered how long she had been there. Her eyes stung, and her lower back cramped. She turned to look at the door and yelled, falling out of her chair when she saw Memphis's silhouette leaning against the open door.

"By flame and fire, Emory! I'm sorry. I didn't mean to startle you."

Groaning, she stood. "You could have knocked."

He stepped closer, eyes lighting up. "I was wondering when you would notice I was there, but you seemed rather engrossed."

Her mind was still digesting all the information she had took in. She eyed the Commander warily. "Where's Wyatt?"

"He got held up with Jaxson, so I came by to tear you away. You should get some rest."

Not arguing, she made her way to the door and into the hallway.

Memphis whispered to her back, "It suits you, the necklace."

She turned to look at him with raised eyebrows. She was exhausted, sore, and above all else too tired to think about the rugged man in front of her with his mind games. "Goodnight, Memphis."

She turned her back, and he gently grabbed her hand, his thumb slowly tracing circles on the inside of her palm. Her heart stuttered as he lowered his full lips to the top of her hand, not breaking his gaze. The kiss was feather light.

Straightening, he stepped toward her, slowly. "Em," he whispered, voice dripping with honey.

A coolness settled in her stomach, and she cleared her throat. "Where is Nyx tonight, Memphis?"

Stopping, he smirked and winked at her icy expression. "Sleep well." With that, he was gone, disappearing down the hallway and leaving Emory more confused and frustrated than before.

Stalking, she slammed the library door behind her, which was all too satisfying. She made her way back to her room, not able to shake how much she liked Memphis's lips on her skin and how much she wanted to find her Commander again.

# Chapter Thirty-Three

## Nyx

The taste of blood coursed through her mouth. Nyx cracked, her emotions fueling her when she ducked as Brokk's fist swung to meet her face once more.

"You're going to have to do better than that!" she said breathlessly, knowing he was on a short fuse. She wanted him to give her his all.

Spitting blood out, Brokk lunged at her relentlessly. Her body responded: duck, uppercut, duck, right hook... There was a satisfying thud when she met her target. Brokk grunted, responding in kind to their savage dance. Minutes, hours passed; sweat poured off their bodies, both trying to find some sort of calm.

Finally, she yielded as Brokk stopped to catch his breath.

It was hours after their day had concluded, but they both needed a distraction. Brokk had finished his turn in the ring, and she had dragged him here. Their training arena was small but efficient located adjacent to the dining hall. Worn dummies with Adair's sigil blazed on their chests littered the room, and Nyx leaned lightly against one, her heart pounding.

She traced the line of her jaw with her finger, feeling the skin had spilt.

"Have some pent-up frustrations there, Brokk?"

# Heir of Lies – Part Three

His golden eyes narrowed. He stalked toward her, rolling his shoulders at the same time. "Don't be coy, Nyx. Both of us know the answer to that."

That she did. The thought of Emory left a sour taste in her mouth. Their *savior*.

She scuffed the floor with her boot and, moving centrally, began to stretch. Brokk followed suit. Nyx pulled her purple hair back with a worn band and concentrated on her breath. If Memphis had given her a proper chance, maybe the entire fate of their group wouldn't lie with a girl who had experienced nothing. They spent years scouting, planning, and gathering information, and even then, they had just found out Adair's location. Memphis held them back for safety. They were skilled, but Adair was always better.

"We will figure this out. I know you think she can't do this, but she *will*. She is a part of this as much as you and I are. It's not her fault we kept our secret from everyone. Give her a chance to prove herself, Nyx. Put your feelings aside about Memphis for the time being. He cares about you."

She glared at him, wanting to laugh.

*He cares about you.*

What should have been a comforting gesture made her insides clench. Being a telekinetic was frustrating around Memphis as he always put up a wall. And she wasn't about to forget what she heard in that one moment there was no wall. Her anger washed over her in waves and crashed down hard.

She snapped, "He *cares about me*? You are as blind as the rest of them if you think that's the truth. I have seen into his soul, Brokk, and let me correct you; he only cares about himself." She scoffed. "Also, your best friend has been in love with *her* this entire time. To the point where he sabotaged you as well."

He stiffened.

"He did dream *implants*, Brokk, so Emory would be afraid of you. So, he could have her. If you think that's love and that Memphis is doing the best for everyone, you can watch as he sends this rebellion to their grave. I'm going to find another solution other than death." It all came out of her in a breathless rush, and Brokk's face hardened further as she shook her head. "Ask him for yourself. I'm not leaving it all on the shoulders of our *queen*."

Not waiting for a reply, she stood up and jogged out of the room, trying desperately to run from the truth of her own words. Thinking of Memphis didn't hurt any less and being in the same room as him was her own personal torture. Especially when he couldn't take his eyes off Emory.

Whatever messed up relationship they had was over. Her gut twisted at the thought, already missing his touch, the warmth of his lips on hers.

Slowing to a walk, she rubbed her eyes tiredly. She needed to forget about Memphis and needed to decide what her next move was going to be. There needed to be a resolution that didn't rely on Emory.

Nyx wandered into the empty dining hall, leaving her room and the training room behind her. Breaking into a brisk walk, she wove down the hallways, her footsteps echoing into the empty space around her. Three a.m. was a quiet time, and she relished in every second.

Arriving at the elevator doors all too quickly, she stepped inside, a plan quickly formulating in her mind. It was time she took her fate into her own hands; it wasn't Memphis's choice to decide who she died for. And it certainly wouldn't be *Emory*. She was a distraction and clouded the minds of two lovesick school boys. They couldn't win against Adair. He was too strong; six years of death and hiding was proof of that.

She let her hair down as the seconds dragged on. All she saw around them was a bleak future, but at least they were *alive*. She would not risk her entire family's existence for Emory to fail.

The elevator ground to a stop, and she took a sharp right, heading toward the watchtower. Jaxson's shift was about to end, and he wouldn't question her. She quietly ran down the hallway that led to the staircase to the watch tower. Her body thrummed

# HEIR OF LIES – PART THREE

with adrenaline, and she skidded to a stop beside a closet. She needed to grab a few things - she slung a worn jacket over her shoulder and strapped twin blades onto her thighs. There were always stashes in case of an emergency.

The cold night air washed over her when she trotted up the stairs, and she pushed the worn door open.

Jaxson sat on a wooden perch, his chin resting against his hands as he stared longingly onto the horizon.

She spoke softly, "Go to bed, Jaxson. I have it from here."

Snapping to attention, he jumped slightly, not having heard her come in. "Nyx, you scared me a bit there. How are you?"

She winked at him. "I want nothing more than some peace and quiet under the stars."

Nodding solemnly, Jaxson hopped down. Before leaving, he placed a burly hand on her shoulder. "We have to be prepared not to give up hope for Alby."

His words were like a weight anchoring into the ocean floor. Climbing on the perch, Jaxson left, the door swinging closed behind him, Nyx closed her eyes. She could move forward with this. It was already too late to convince Memphis of another plan to overthrow Adair. He believed in Emory like he never believed in her.

He has and *would always* choose Emory.

Her chin wobbled and opened her eyes. There was no going back now.

She silently said goodbye to the man she loved, and her eyes searched the land stretching out in front of her. To her left were the woods, and beyond that was an escarpment of mountain terrain...and Adair. Reaching out her mind was as simple as breathing to Nyx. She brushed against a thousand consciousnesses, and a thousand whispers sounded back to her. But she only searched for one, and she didn't have to wait long.

"*Adair said to stay put! We follow his orders, and we wait. Anyone who says otherwise is breaching direct orders, and you know what that means...*"

The scouts were northeast of them, hiding out just outside the blocked perimeter that Byrd provided, and her pulse quickened. Nyx stood and, in one fluid motion, flung herself off the side of the tower. Her feet scrambled, trying to find foot holes as she held on. Once secured, she made the treacherous climb to the ground. Her muscles strained with the effort, her white knuckles shining back at her. She glanced below her and could see the grass now. *Excellent.*

Closing her eyes, she let go, her arms tucking into her chest, and she summersaulted through the air. She was nothing but freedom and the wind screaming around her. She was rage; she was power. She was no one now but this.

The ground met her quickly, and Nyx landed nimbly, her fist planted in front of her, her feet already trying to push off the dirt. She didn't wait to hit the ground running, and her purple hair swung behind her. She calculated that it would only take ten minutes for her to find them or vice versa.

Sweat slicked her body once more, her thoughts flying with the possibilities of what she was about to try. Trees blurred past her, and weaving in and out, she felt the electric pulse of Byrd's façade when she passed through it. She couldn't look back. She wouldn't. There was no room for weakness or second guesses. She saw the scouts before they saw her. Their red sashes were beacons in the night.

"Well, well, well. Lookie what we have here, boys."

There were five of them. Pale and ruthless, they had their curved swords pointed at her in less than a second.

Hands up, she responded calmly when she skidded to a halt. "I came here to talk, gentlemen."

Laughter erupted around her.

"Talk? How would you even know we were here, pretty thing?"

There was a hunger in the leader's eyes Nyx had only heard of. Narrowing her eyes and never breaking contact with him, her voice resonated throughout his mind, *"You are going to have to be more prepared next time."*

# Heir of Lies – Part Three

His face drained of color as the sword quivered in his hold. "She's a telekinetic."

A ripple of unease spread through them. According to Adair, every person with an ability powerful enough had already been recruited with him or dead. He never thought anyone would build numbers against him. She was proof they had slid through the cracks.

She didn't wait for them before she continued, "I want to speak with Adair directly. I have an offer to make him. One he will not want to refuse."

The leader asked, "And what makes you think you have anything he would even be interested in, that is other than yourself?"

Nyx's fingers curled into fists, her nails biting into her skin. "I can give him our *heir*, Emory Fae."

She flung images of the last couple of days in each of the soldier's minds; Emory's face standing out clearly in every one of them. Every single one of their mouths fell open. The silence was deafening.

She sauntered forward, cooing dangerously, "Now this is just a guess, but I think Adair would want to be reacquainted with such an old *dear* friend."

She had them. The leader already nodded his head in awe at her. "Right you are..."

"Nyx. My name is Nyx."

With adrenaline coursing through her body, she shook hands with the scout, and the six of them ventured further into the night. Nyx didn't look back toward the Academy, instead she mentally said goodbye to the rebels she had thought was her family.

Sweat trickled down her neck, pooling beneath her soaked shirt. The guards traveled at a breakneck pace; her body was numb; her muscles screaming at her to stop. But there was no stopping what she had done.

Her violet eyes flickered back and forth between the soldiers, trying to take in as much information about them as possible. She bit the inside of her cheek to still the feeling of wanting to scream. Grounding herself, assuring herself this was the right decision, she reminded herself she had no other option, and no one left to see reason. Her entire existence has been encased with secrets and heartbreak. She refused to let Memphis condemn them all.

If Adair wanted Emory, she would gladly fulfill that wish for him. Especially if it meant a parley for their freedom. One life to save them all was worth giving in her mind. Her mouth ran dry at the thought, but she would no longer hide.

She was *tired*, and Adair had already beaten them. He had no idea they had survived, but in what world did they have a chance against a disease that had already destroyed everything?

Nyx continued to walk toward her impending doom, and her thoughts galloped wildly. For the first time in years, she allowed herself to feel the raw pain she had kept at bay for so long. In the darkness, at the hands of her enemy, she grieved for the thousands of lives that had been lost. Their freedom that Adair had stripped from Kiero. And above all else, Memphis.

That pain was crippling, radiating from her core. It was like hitting a wall over and over but never being able to break through. She allowed all the memories to swallow her whole one last time. His laugh, his crooked smile, the safety she felt in his arms. Memphis had always been home to her, a prince that had brought her back and had given her life. That had made her feel normal and she grew strong with him. She tucked every moment, every kiss, every memory away close to her heart.

She clenched her jaw. She wanted to scream, to cry, to *hurt* something so that she knew she wasn't the only one who felt like this. As the group finally broke out of the forest, Nyx held her head high. She would never be able to go back, never be able to have Memphis. She had never fully had him.

# HEIR OF LIES – PART THREE

Finality struck home with her, and she walked forward, the ghost of who she used to be long behind her. This wasn't a fairy tale; she wasn't the princess who won the prince. She was a soldier who would win their freedom. Everything had a price, and facing Adair was hers. The time for hiding was over.

The sun peeked over the horizon, painting the land in pink hues. Nyx blinked, taking in the flat landscape around her. Crumbling buildings scattered in front of them, the dust heavy in the air. She had heard Alby talk about this place—The Ruined City. It was a skeleton of Sarthaven, an echo of life that once was. Miles behind it, the Draken Mountains pierced the sky, a towering wall of grey.

The soldiers slowed down, taking her in more closely in the daylight.

Their thoughts were screaming at her blatantly: *dangerous, enemy, soldier.*

She slyly lifted her brows at them. "I do hope we are getting close boys."

The leader walked up to her, his darkening eyes holding her as he pointed to the mountains. "I hope you're ready to enter a pit of snakes, rebel. If you're lying, you won't be lucky enough to see the sun again."

There was barely any light in her life anyways. She had always preferred darkness.

She held back her shock and swallowed her bitterness in one foul swoop. The life that bustled around her was Adair's *doing.* It was like entering a beehive made of stone. The soldiers surrounded her as they maneuvered through the different tunnels and caverns, onlookers stopping to get a clear look at her.

*Visitors are slim when your king uses all his energy to destroy life.*

Yet, here was a whole colony at his disposal.

Fire grew in her, begging to be released. She wanted to be free, but her reality was that she would always be shackled. She just had the freedom to choose how.

The group trudged up a winding staircase until they were outside an arched door where the soldier knocked three times. Nyx willed herself to have the strength to do this. The door swung open, and she was pulled inside to face her monster.

The throne room was enormous. Black marble pooled before her, stretching up to a ceiling, opening to the sky far above. Adair sat on a sharp throne, human bones glittering on the foundation. He quickly glanced up at them but did a double take when his intelligent eyes landed on her.

*He was a shadow of a person.*

Gaunt, pale skin. Black hair flattened. His features could have once been handsome, but now...now they seemed to contort with anger. He was just an evil man. Nothing more.

The group leader stepped forward. "My highness, this rebel has requested a presence with you regarding..."

"Regarding the return of the Fae line," Nyx cut the soldier off, and her voice was steely.

Staring right back into those endless eyes, Adair stood up, prowling toward her. They were soon face-to-face, and she remained impassive when he whispered, his breath hot against her skin, "What did you just say?"

"Emory Fae is alive, and I can give her to you. In exchange, of course, for my people's freedom, including the hostages you hold here in your kingdom."

Nyx didn't wait for him to laugh or to kill her. She charged into his mind, throwing every moment from the last forty-eight hours at him: Emory, the leading star in all of them.

The room grew silent and colder, and he didn't break his stare when he ordered his men out. Nyx's skin crawled with anticipation, waiting any moment for him to crack and attack her. Instead, he circled her, taking her all in, and Nyx had never felt more stripped bare in her life.

Stopping, he stroked her cheek. "And how do you exist? A telekinetic of your ability should be with me, not roaming freely as a rebel."

He looked amused, and it was the most nightmarish expression she had ever seen. She swallowed once and made sure every word was crystal clear. "I came from the Academy, *Your Majesty*. Do we have an agreement or not? Emory, for our freedom."

Now he laughed, and it turned her blood cold. Nodding, he held out his hand to her. His voice was smooth and alluring when he said, "How could I refuse?"

She grabbed his hand and shook it once.

# CHAPTER THIRTY-FOUR

## Adair

The rebel left escorted by his guards, and Adair Stratton ran a hand over his mouth in ecstatic awe. So, the rumors had been true then. His world spun into a flurry of emotion.

Emory Fae had survived.

She had *survived*.

The Academy had slipped through his fingers after all these years. But now, he had a firsthand way to infiltrate them, and he realized his opening to act was quickly leaving, purple hair and all. His plan formed quickly and efficiently, the whispers of his mind egging him on.

Adair shoved the door open, his voice echoing off the stone walls as he shouted, "Wait! Bring her back a moment."

She had eyes filled with fire and hatred, and as the guards dragged her toward him; she stared him down the entire way. Adair sneered; she had spirit, he had to admit.

But that wouldn't last long.

Adair could feel the energy pulse around them when he grabbed on to her and shut the door firmly behind them. Nyx stiffened; her fear so tangible Adair could taste it.

# HEIR OF LIES – PART THREE

Trying to sound sincere, he whispered softly, "Now, I don't remember you from our school years. How is my dear friend Memphis doing? And Brokk?"

It was like stepping down on glass as her resolve shattered in front of him and she grumbled, "What do you want?"

Adair's mouth filled with a bitter taste, and he let go, the human part of himself completely dissolving. He walked up to her, close enough to see her lip quiver the tiniest bit. Good. She should be afraid.

"This..." His finger stroked her cheek, leaving a black burn mark in her skin that glowed softly then dissipated. The world spun, those voices in his mind laughing now. Nyx's violet eyes glazed over, as Adair's ability took possession of her body and mind.

"*Yes*," those dark voices cooed.

Nyx was frozen; the flutter of her chest rising and falling was the only indication that she was alive. In his mind's eye, he spun what he wanted, then a gem necklace and a sword appeared around her neck and in her hands. Both were gas at first before they solidified.

"You did not get these from me. You raided them from the Ruined City."

Utterly disoriented, she repeated him in a monotone voice.

"Excellent. Our agreement is that you will go back home to the Academy. My troops will be behind you. Get them in, and your friends will live."

She repeated him again, violet eyes glazed over.

"Now go. Time is of the essence."

Like a puppet, she walked out, Adair's claws in her mind active. It was like veins pumping blood to a heart, the connection so alive and vital Adair wanted to laugh. Nyx was in there, supressed and fighting. But it would never be enough, not against them.

The voices crooned to him, praising him for what was about to happen, what he had set in motion. Nothing could stop her. The blade and necklace were laced with the same poison he had created to neutralize abilities. Though, the empty shell of Nyx wouldn't mind, not with him in control.

As he said, it would never be enough. Not against them.

The man he used to be had died a long, long time ago. No one, including himself, could bring him back. The voices pressed against his mind, suffocating Adair until only one thought ran through him. He would start by killing Memphis Carter, and then the rest of the rebels would fall.

One by one.

# HEIR OF LIES – PART THREE

# CHAPTER THIRTY-FIVE

### Brokk

Brokk cringed when the crowd around him leered at the two figures in the ring. Emory's face was in a concentrated mask, sweat dripping down her face as Wyatt lunged at her yet again.

Looking to his left, Memphis took in the scene before him. Always the figure of calm.

Sighing, he rolled his shoulders back, his stiff muscles popping. A hard thud sounded, and looking up, Emory caught Wyatt's arm. With a fierce expression, she disappeared. Wyatt's face instantly paled, and he was left helpless. A minute later, Emory released and glanced up at Wyatt.

"Again," Wyatt said, and the two of them continued their attack and defense.

"Brokk, I need to talk to you." Jaxson materialized beside him, concern dripping off him.

"What's..."

"It's Nyx. She came to cover the rest of my watch last night. I forgot some papers out there, and when I went back out an hour later, she was gone. No one has seen her since, and her room is untouched..."

Dread filled every ounce of him.

Brokk moved in a blur, his heart thudding as he headed toward Memphis. He should have kept an eye on her after their match last night, but he was left with his thoughts about how to confront Memphis about what she had said. She had distracted him, and he was selfish enough not to think about her.

"Memphis, we need to talk. It's about Nyx."

"I haven't seen her since the meeting last night, Brokk." He glanced at him and frowned. "I can't leave right now. We are alternating opponents with Emory. Time is of the essence."

"Nyx is missing. A match is more important than that?"

Memphis exhaled, shaking his head. "She can take care of herself, Brokk. We all can. How do you know she is missing?"

He filled Memphis in on the details he was given, and Memphis rubbed his face wearily. "This isn't the first time Nyx has gone venturing off. She needs space. You of all people should understand that. You should be focused on what is ahead, helping Emory and the others prepare for the fight. I need you to be focused, Brokk."

Anger flaring, he said, "No. I will not stand back while Nyx is missing and while you are too preoccupied to care! We should have scouts out; we should be *looking for her!* She was upset about you, and I'm worried about her."

Memphis snapped at him, "You forgot yourself, *General.* That was a command, not a request. You will forget Nyx, and focus."

Brokk's hands connected with Memphis's chest, shoving him backward, hard. He was yelling now as his resolve cracked, "She loves you! And you used her to keep your bed warm until Emory was back. You use people for your own advantages, Memphis, and I'm done. Nyx told me what you did to Emory, manipulating her dreams. There is only one monster I see, *brother,* and he is standing in front of me. If you won't go looking for Nyx, I will."

He was stupid for banking *everything* on Emory. His future. Their future. A month wasn't enough time, and with Nyx and Alby gone, depression hooded his thoughts. His body reacted before he could think anything through. Turning on his foot, he left the training room, not caring about the protests behind him.

# Heir of Lies – Part Three

Not caring that Emory had been frozen in the ring as she took in his words. Memphis had everything he had always wanted—power, Emory, a plan.

And it would kill them all.

Sweat dripped into his eyes, and he stepped into the elevator. Air hissed around him, and coldness ran through his veins, numbing his body. Numbing his heart.

He left the compartment, jogging down the twisting hallway, memories flying at him like bullets. Memories of the echo of a girl who couldn't even look at him now, of a family long lost, of a world that didn't exist anymore.

He barged through the door, slamming it shut. Running full tilt, he exploded in a flurry of emotion, four giant paws grinding into the earth, only propelling him faster. Scents overwhelmed him, and looking to the forest sprawling to the northeast, he galloped, leaving the hillside behind him. Leaving the Academy behind. He would find Nyx, and he would bring her home.

The sun was setting, the warm glow bathing Brokk's fur. He had been running for hours, following Nyx's trail. The forest swallowed the horizon, and he rested his head on the ground, ears twitching at scuffles of animals around him. He allowed himself to close his eyes for a moment. Only a brief rest...

The breeze moved through his fur. The soft wind curled around him, and he drifted to sleep.

*The memory shifted and dissolved as Brokk slammed into the ground, damp grass and moss underneath him. Staggering up, he whipped around, waiting. A giggle sounded in the darkness. Taking a closer look, he saw broken rock formations jutting out of the earth and green flames roaring. Squinting, he took a step closer, and the world ignited.*

*"Find us, Brokk Foster."*

*The world was drenched in ash. It swirled, filling his nose, mouth, clouding his eyes. Another giggled resonated before everything went black.*

Eyes flashing open, he was greeted by the steely edge of a blade. A growl grew deep in his throat, and he lurched up. It was late into the night, moonlight filtering only slightly through the trees. And a foreign scent filled his senses.

His visitor was dressed in a black hooded sweater, tight leather pants, and boots. His eyes flickered back to the blade. It hummed with magic, a faint blue glow pulsing from it. It was dangerous, laced with malice.

Hackles up, he jumped back swiftly, as the figure side-stepped his attack. The stranger laughed and threw the hood back. He knew that laugh. Nyx's hand stroked his head as dread filled him.

"What a coincidence. We meet here of all places, Brokk."

Shifting back effortlessly, he stalked toward her, his hand lashing out to shove her against the nearest tree, and her body cracked against the bark.

"What are you thinking, Nyx? I could have hurt you!"

Her violet eyes narrowed. "Hurt *me*? You need to brush up on your predictability." She scoffed. "I just needed time, Brokk. Why are you out here anyways? Because I know you, and I have a feeling we are looking for the same thing."

His gut twisted; his hands fell to his sides. "I came looking for you. To bring you home."

She barked out a laugh. "Home! What does that even mean now? Our entire lives our *home* has been a delusion... I joined a rebellion that has done *nothing* against the Mad King. What hope do we have if we continue to follow Memphis's orders? The hope we have of regaining Kiero back fades every single day."

Her eyes darkened. "Brokk, I am tired of hiding, tired of having my actions calculated, weighed for the benefit of our *family*. Memphis doesn't make the calls for me anymore. No one does. And I am taking my future in my own hands. Can you say the same for yourself?" She spat the words at him, the words like sharpened knives.

Each one struck true. Brokk ran a tired hand over his face. "Memphis won't change his decision. He will draw Adair out."

# Heir of Lies – Part Three

"At *what cost? Are you willing to pay his price?*" Her voice danced through his mind.

Tilting his head, he drawled, "What was the price of your new blade there?"

"Wouldn't you like to know?" she quipped.

Flicking the side of his cheek, an acute sting spread across his skin. Droplets of blood ran down his cheek, but before they hit the ground, the cut had healed. Shaking his head, he looked at Nyx, but she had already started walking into the night.

"We better get back before Memphis sends more people after us."

"I'm already one step ahead of you, Brokk."

Sighing, he fell into step behind her. She had failed to tell him how a *disguised* magical sword fell into her possession. Animals were way more sensitive to energy, and that sword was drenched with power, where as to his human eyes, the sword was just a sword.

It would seem he wasn't the only one with secrets, and he had every intention to find out what exactly she was up to.

# Chapter Thirty-Six

## Emory

Her feet thrummed against the forest floor. Her surroundings a blur. She was infinite. She was free. The wind hummed against her skin, and behind her, a throaty laugh sounded. This was a different time, the world a brighter place.

She came to a slower jog, and Brokk came into view beside her. "I will always beat you, Em. I will always catch up."

His golden eyes were molten excitement and joy shining through them. She felt a hot flush creep up her neck, and she stopped.

"And when I'm gone?"

Sadness had carved a hole into her; time had always passed too fast.

Brokk stopped beside her, reaching out to cup her face against his palm. "You will never be lost to me."

Warmth curled and spread throughout her body. Savoring the moment a second longer, before she pushed forward, racing away from her fate.

Emory awoke with a start. Sweat clung to her body, her hair sticking to her forehead. It took a moment to register a pair of eyes staring at her from across the room.

"Are you okay?"

Memphis stood up from his seated position across from her bed. Squinting, anger flickered through her. How had he gotten in her room? It was late evening, and she had come to rest before training commenced after dinner. Her calves cramped as a sweet reminder of what was to come.

# Heir of Lies – Part Three

Sighing, she rubbed her temples. "Memphis, you don't have to babysit me, and after this afternoon, I don't particularly want to see you."

"I just came to apologize. I know you heard what Brokk said. I want to say that I'm sorry you didn't hear it from me. I don't know if you remember, but Brokk and you have always been closer. I wanted to have a fighting chance against him. It was a child's jealousy, and I know that's not an excuse." Concern pinched the corner of his face in a soft gentle way, and he searched her for an answer.

She sighed again, anxiety curling around her heart. "You need to be honest with me for us to be friends. Some things are slowly coming back to me, but you can't manipulate me, Memphis. I am afraid of Brokk, and all of that boils down to *you*."

Her dreams were mostly memories—of school, her family, and Brokk. *Lots* of Brokk in fact. It made sense to her if Memphis claimed they had been close. A flush crept up the back of her neck as she tried not to navigate her feelings when it came to the golden eyed rebel. She pushed her thoughts back for the moment, focusing on the task at hand.

Almost a month had passed since she had arrived. She gingerly sat up and grabbed her black jacket and training shoes. She was ready in a second, and when Memphis extended his hand toward her, she blatantly ignored it. For this to work, Emory couldn't hate Memphis, but that didn't mean should would make it easy on him for lying to her.

Energy expanded through her palm, as she suddenly grabbed Memphis's lingering hand. Concentrating, she tested her ability out. She was thrilled when his thoughts collided with hers, "*Just talk to her, you coward....*"

She smirked at him. "Talk to me about what?"

It was as if her skin was an electric wire. Dropping her hand, a flush spread through his cheeks, and he murmured, "Your ability isn't faltering either, I see."

"Nope."

It was still surreal to her, the fact she had this coursing power throughout her body. But everyday that passed, Earth seemed more like a dream, and Kiero the place that she belonged. The facts were that this impossible world existed—despite her lack of belief in magic and far away lands.

Emory glanced ahead. She had promised herself that she would give the rebels a chance. She hadn't really warmed up to being killed by a rogue raider or dabarne. She shut the door a little too firmly behind her.

Sighing, she looked down the hallway, her heart skipping a beat, hoping to see Brokk's golden gaze. She was about to ask Memphis where the General was when it started. There was a high-pitched screeching, like nails on chalk boards, and every single person stood to attention. Memphis's color drained, and he gripped her hand hard.

"What's that?" Her voice sounded as small as she felt.

"Air raids. We have to move. Everyone, a code blue. This is not a drill!" He shouted the last bit out in the hall, and the residents of the Academy filed out toward the cells, Memphis towing her along.

The first wave hit, and Emory thought the world was going to split open. The ground shuddered, as Emory was ricocheted off balance. Memphis steadied her as they came to the cells, and Memphis opened the door, quickly getting them in and shutting it firmly behind them.

Emory trembled, whispering, "What about the others?"

Memphis slid to a seated position against the wall, closing his eyes. "They all know what to do in these situations in order to reach the cells. Adair periodically does air raids, trying to flush us out. We found out the hard way that he has concocted a gas that not only immobilizes you but neutralizes your ability. These cells are made of kieronian steel, so even if the gas gets in our ventilation, we have to wait twenty-four hours for it to flush out." He sighed. "We wait it out like the other times."

# Heir of Lies – Part Three

Memphis said this like they were discussing the weather. Sadness took her breath away at the fact they lived in a world like this.

*Because you wanted to escape to save yourself.*

The honesty in the thought struck deeply, and she sat down next to Memphis, feeling the tension and heat rolling off his body.

"What happened to Adair?"

This close, Memphis's full lashes made his blue eyes hypnotic as he stared at her, weighing her question. "He was my friend, as well, at school. Your parents shaped this world into something worth being proud of, their unconditional love nurturing us all into believing we are more than our ability. That we aren't monsters. Adair was no exception. He has started a wildfire that can't be put out, and the result of that is this war."

Emory replied, "Isn't the Academy considered strong?"

Memphis cocked his eyebrow at her. "We are the only ones left who are strong enough to give Adair a run for his money. We fight now for all the innocent lives he took, for shattering your parents' legacy. We fight for them, for their love, and for our freedom."

Emory sighed, letting his words settle in her core. Silence seemed to suffocate them in the cell as bomb after bomb was dropped above ground. In that moment, such an absurd idea struck her, she bit her lip, feeling exposed and glanced sideways at Memphis, who looked like a carving out of marble—flawless and jagged, capturing such a ruggedness she couldn't tear away from it.

She noticed the corners of his lips turning up. "What?" he asked.

"I know this isn't the solution to overthrowing a Mad King, but the rebels need something to celebrate, and that's each other. I have an idea."

Emory had his full attention now. "I think we should hold a party, a dance to be specific."

Confusion clouded Memphis's face. "Dance?"

She beamed up at him. "Seeing as we have a bit of time trapped in here with each other, I will fill you in."

Her body was stiff from sitting for a day in a stone cage, but she smiled as she pressed the elevator's button. Everyone was exhausted and was headed back to their bunkers to get some sleep. Stepping in, she could still hear Memphis's excitement about her idea of holding a dance to celebrate what the rebels have accomplished. And didn't fail to notice Memphis's eyes had never left her face.

She exhaled lightly and pressed the elevator's door, trying to ignore the pulling sensation in her gut at the thought of him. Emory knew she needed to focus.

Each day, her memories became clearer but only about the three boys she had used to call her best friends. The once nightmares of Brokk faded with each passing day now that she knew that was only Memphis's doing. She remembered them as teenagers—Brokk her confidant, her best friend that would do anything for her. And Memphis—she knew their relationship had always been complicated. But above everyone else, she had been remembering Adair Stratton. The gangly boy with dark hair and shadows in his heart who made her stomach churn.

For right now, Memphis Carter thought of her as his foolish pawn, and Emory continued to let him. For the time being, she *wanted* him to. Rubbing her eyes, she needed to find Brokk, to talk to him. She wanted clear the air between them, to apologize for being so cold with him, and in her heart, she knew he was the one who would tell her the truth about her past—the parts she couldn't remember. She needed to focus on her personal plans. As much as she liked Black Dawn, she wouldn't allow herself to be manipulated. She knew in her heart; this was only just the beginning.

# Heir of Lies – Part Three

The following day, Memphis scheduled training for her first thing after breakfast. The hours had slipped by in Emory's frustration when she couldn't find any trace of Brokk. Chewing the inside of her cheek, she looked at Memphis.

"You have to imagine you can see the ability flowing through you. It's a life force, and more importantly, it's *your* life force," Memphis drawled.

Circling around Emory, concentration pinched his eyebrows together. She huffed, frustration leaving her palms tingling. They were trying to hone her abilities to control them more. Sweat stung her eyes, and her heart dropped as Memphis stopped to look at her, saying, "Again."

His study was a small training space, but she needed to take advantage of the time she had. Books soared from their shelves, encircling Memphis before shooting out like bullets at her. Emory dodged the assault, silently thanking her karate teacher for years of classes on Earth. She spun toward Memphis, breathing deeply and trying to clear her mind as she found her mark and clasped his forearm. Pushing forward, she gritted her teeth and willed that rush of power that had been so close to the surface since she had gotten here.

Emory waited, but nothing happened.

Memphis scrunched his face as a laugh burst from him in a strangled, choking sound. Emory swatted his arm, annoyed and Memphis waggled his eyebrows, trying to ease the tension.

Grabbing her hand, he enticingly whispered, "Above anything else, your concentration will be your best friend. Dive into that well of power and allow your ability to take hold."

Sighing, Emory rolled her shoulders, and escaping his hold, she started to walk away.

Memphis said to her back, "Let's go again."

Tiredness clung to her, but Emory prepared herself. Tremors shook through her legs, as Memphis paced the other side of the room, agitated. Narrowing her eyes, anger licked at her heart. How dare Memphis alter her mind against her will.

Six years of lies, of seeing Memphis as her guardian. Her protector.

Exhaling, bitterness filled Emory's mouth, and she allowed herself to fill up with the frustration about the lies, deceit, death, and how her world had been torn apart by all of this. Memphis stilled, arching a pale eyebrow at her. Her pulse thundered when Memphis closed the space between them, fists flying.

She had never been coordinated, but fueled by adrenaline, she tried.

Her forearm blocked his hit, her flesh bruising from the impact. Her feet scuffled back, and using her core, she threw two uppercuts that Memphis easily avoided. Breathing hard, she sprinted, her arms grabbing him around his waist as they crashed into the bookcase. Her right hand grabbed his wrist, and Emory felt her ability crash into him. Memphis's face darkened, and in a flash, he slammed his elbow into her nose. Dots flooded into her vision; blood gushed down her face. Fire ran up the bridge of her nose, the pain so potent she squeezed her eyes shut, falling back.

Memphis was suddenly on her, pinning her wrists above her head. Reacting, she slammed her knee into his groin, hissing through the pain as she rolled. Memphis, for the moment, was preoccupied, trying to recover, and Emory reached for his ankle. Blood spattered down the front of her shirt, soaking it through as her ability crashed into Memphis Carter.

There was no room for guilt, for second guesses. Her anger took over every crevice of her mind, and she channeled it toward Memphis. She felt the shift as his ability started draining out of him and into her, but she pushed the fact aside, focusing on debilitating him, *emptying* him of his strength.

"Enough, Em! Enough!"

A swift kick to her gut left her dry heaving, as Memphis shakily stood, panting.

There was a strained silence before Memphis asked, "What was that about?" He stared at her like he was seeing her clearly for the first time.

# HEIR OF LIES – PART THREE

Pinching her nose, Emory replied, "I think you broke my nose."

"Pain is part of growth."

Shaking her head, Emory stood, narrowing her eyes at the rebel leader. "Always remember, I'm not someone you can trick and push around without there being consequences."

With that, she left, slamming the door behind her. Shaking she went to find Bryd, hoping the younger girl could point her in the direction of a healer. Limping down the hallway, her thoughts darkened.

If she could control what she was and master it, she could face Adair alone. It was time she fought her own battles.

That night brought on a thick blanket of dreams, capturing her in the memories.

*Emory ran down the hallway, screeching as Memphis and Brokk tailed her. She could have doubled over from laughing so hard, but she pushed faster, her black hair loosening behind her. They turned the corner, and she almost slammed straight into her father, his arms folded across his wide chest, his kind eyes shining down at her. The boys almost ran into her back from stopping so fast, and they instantly dipped their heads in respect. Her jaw ached from trying to compose herself.*

*Her father's mouth started moving, but it was as if the memory had been tampered with, and Emory's surroundings started to blend together.*

*She caught movement behind her father, a tall commanding looking man, and she focused on Adair when he came into view. He couldn't have been older than twelve, his willowy stance and long limbs looking awkward as he walked toward her. His dark hair and dark eyes reflected no kindness, only a bitter resentment.*

*"What are they doing with you?"*

*They meaning Brokk and Memphis. Emory bristled.* "What are you *doing? They're my friends, Adair. They don't need further explanation than that."*

He sneered. "Two orphaned mutts that shouldn't even be allowed here, and you have them on a leash. Put it together, Em, and you wonder why people don't take you seriously. You are a princess, not a commoner. Start acting like it."

His words stung, and the memory swirled and twisted, dissipating to darkness.

And she was alone.

The rest of the afternoon passed with an excitement that was never seen before. Emory had found Bryd who pointed her in the direction of the rebels' healer, Delane. His ability had healed most of her wounds from her training session so, now, just deep bruising remained.

News of the dance had spread like wildfire, and she leaned against the wall in the hallway, clutching the one possession from Earth she had on her when Brokk and Memphis had come. Her iPod.

Emory looked at the groups of people bustling around, carrying fabrics, tables and chairs, talking excitedly. Gripping the iPod in her palm, she just needed to find a way to create speakers. The dance was scheduled for tonight, and it was the last piece to get everything ready.

"This was a great thing you did, Emory. Your parents would have been proud," Memphis said, his stark blond hair tied back elegantly, his midnight blue loose shirt and freshly pressed black pants defining his edges.

"Thanks," she said curtly.

"Look, Emory, about this morning…"

Cutting him off, Emory met his gaze, "Look, let's forget about this morning for the time being and concentrate on what's at hand."

Sighing, he rubbed his neck. "Okay."

"Also, have you seen Brokk? I need to talk to him."

Memphis shook his head. "I haven't seen him since Nyx left, a week ago."

# Heir of Lies – Part Three

Dread pooled in her stomach. "That doesn't worry you?"

"It isn't the first time this has happened, and I can guarantee you it won't be the last. Both Brokk and Nyx can safely handle themselves. Our plan moves forward to confront Adair tomorrow—with or without them."

Heat crept up her cheeks, and she swallowed back her concerns. Nodding toward him as graciously as she could manage, she asked, "Memphis, before tonight, though, is there *any way* you can get this to work?"

The iPod gleamed in the palm of her hand, her tiny headphones wrapped around its silver body. Memphis picked it up curiously.

"I need it to project throughout the entire room," Emory said.

"How does it work?"

Showing him how to turn it on, they scrolled through her music, ranging from *Fleetwood Mac* to classical. Awe flooded his face as she chose a song, and the music played between them from the tiny speakers built into it. Stopping it, Emory raised her eyebrow in question.

"Leave it to me." Memphis nodded, taking her iPod, and disappeared down the flooding hallways.

It was just before dusk, and Emory stared at herself in the broken mirror. Earlier, Bryd had dropped off something for her to wear to the dance, apologizing since it was all she had other than her training gear. Bryd had wanted her to have it and then explained that she had made something else for herself. The black sheer overlay fabric clutched her curves, the dress ending just below her knees. The cool air made her skin prickle against the backless scoop. It was stunning. It had belonged to Bryd's mom before the dabarnes had destroyed their town. It was a work of art, how the fabric caught the light, shimmering and dancing.

Her hair was twisted into a low bun, and she slipped on comfortable black flats (again thanks to Bryd). Taking one last look, she turned to leave the bunker - she was ready for this.

Suddenly, the piercing alarm sounded in the hallway, and she heard footsteps thudding, running past her door. Poking her head out to see people running down the hallways in a blur, she saw a familiar face and shouted, "Jaxson!"

He turned around shouted back at her. "It's Nyx! She's back!"

*Just Nyx?*

Sprinting down the hall next to him, they stopped at the entrance. Memphis was already there. Nyx locked eyes with her, dirt and blood smudged on her cheeks, arms, and neck—where a gemmed silver crescent moon amulet sat. Her shirt was torn; her chest heaving like she just ran for miles.

"Where's Brokk?" The question burst through her lips, and Nyx furrowed her brows.

"He's not here? I haven't seen him since I left. I went for a perimeter check to clear my head that night and ran into Adair's scouts a lot closer to home than I would have liked. They captured me. It's lucky I made it back here. I didn't go down without a fight." She smirked. "They weren't so lucky."

Memphis exhaled and closed his eyes, bringing her into his chest for a hug.

Emory's heart gave a painful clench. "Did Brokk say anything to you before he left, Memphis? Was he upset?" Emory looked to Memphis and waited for him to answer. There was a hollowness to his eyes Emory had never seen before.

His lie was thick and heavy. "No, he was fine."

Nyx swayed a little, and Memphis brought his attention back to her, his arms supporting her lower back.

Nyx took in their clothing and asked, icily, "Am I interrupting something?"

He whispered softly in her ear then asked Jaxson to help her to the infirmary to see Delane. He complied without question, and Emory had heard enough. It didn't make sense, didn't seem like

# Heir of Lies – Part Three

Brokk. Not that she had allowed herself the chance yet to get to know him well.

The pit in her stomach grew; something didn't add up about this situation. She noticed Memphis out the corner of her eye, silently walking beside her. Reaching the elevator door, she jabbed the button.

The elevator plummeted, as they rushed downward, the free-falling sensation making her heart feel like it was in her throat.

The doors opened, and Emory stepped into the dining hall, speechless. The lanterns were set low, softly bathing the room in a dim glow. The tables and benches had been cleared, and soft roped banners wrapped the walls. Black Dawn Rebellion greeted them quietly, dressed as formal as they could, looking to her.

She might be an heir built on lies, but she was the rightful queen, nonetheless. Emory didn't hesitate. Without a backward glance, she walked to the middle of the room and spun around, coming face-to-face with Memphis, his eyes locking with hers in a fiery gaze. She held out her hand to his and nodded to her waist. His other hand wrapped too close, too low around her hip.

Breath hitching in her throat, she felt her body start to the music that erupted around them, leading Memphis into her well-learned steps. Her body was humming from how his hands felt on her skin. Her ability and thoughts rushed through her like fire, wanting to devour more. His thoughtful eyes held hers. She felt her heart drumming fiercely against her chest, and in that moment, no one else existed in the room. It was her and Memphis.

An echo of happiness crossed his face as he whispered, "Did I mention you look beautiful tonight?"

Her heart lurched, as she tried to steady her thoughts against his honey tone. Avoiding his statement, she went for a safer route. "How did you get the music playing?"

The familiar soft serenades swam around her, and Memphis simply said, "Look in my right ear."

She realized one of the earbuds was in his ear. Her shock was evident as she murmured, "It's you?"

"It's a new trick I learned for tonight. Being a telekinetic, usually I communicate to an individual. This was the next level."

Smiling, awe blossomed within her at their world. The first song ended with a round of applause, and in a second, a faster upbeat song replaced it seamlessly. Arching her body to spin away from Memphis, she was brought back—hand to chest, eye to eye. Their feet moved without thought, and her blood pounded throughout her veins. She grasped at something to say, *anything*.

Mouth running dry, she tried not to get lost in him once again. A guy had never had this effect on her before, and she felt electrified on this high. Between her anger at Memphis and the intoxication of the music, she didn't want it to stop. So, she didn't think about the consequences and, her body betraying her, gravitated even closer to Memphis, their hands still clasped.

Warmth spread through her core as Emory's senses were overwhelmed. He even *smelled* enticing. He dipped his mouth to the side of her ear, his breath tickling her skin. He swallowed nervously and rested his forehead against hers, stopping.

That's when a sharp poke stung her back, and she practically jumped out of her skin.

"Can I *cut* in?"

Emory spun around to take in Nyx, purple hair curled seductively and falling loosely around her. She still wore the same clothes she had arrived in. Nyx's hand shook as she held it out toward Memphis, assessing his clouded expression.

Emory took tentative steps back and then turned as Nyx stepped into Memphis's embrace. The image of them burned in her mind, as her anxiety clawed through her. Taking a shaky breath, Emory tried not to think about how close she had been to kissing Memphis.

Weaving through the throng of swaying bodies, the music swelled and crashed in her mind. Making it to the edge of the dining hall, she promised herself she wouldn't stare. But naturally, she couldn't help herself. She spotted the duo, Nyx

# HEIR OF LIES – PART THREE

dipping dramatically, their bodies creating their own dance. They were lithe and beautiful. Even from here, she could sense the tension.

Sighing, she swept the room with her eyes, seeing Jaxson and Wyatt bobbing in an awkward dance in front of her, and she couldn't help but smile. Both burly men caught her gaze, and Wyatt made a vulgar gesture at her. Chuckling, she moved on, the messaged received. The ambiance of the room soaked into her, as she tried to still her beating heart, her mind trailed to Brokk. Where was he? Was he okay?

Bitter tears pricked the corners of her eyes as the tiniest of wobbles trembled on her lips.

*No. You can get through this.*

She had to.

Aimlessly, she wandered, gulping deep breaths and searching for Bryd. She wanted to talk to the younger girl, finding comfort in their friendship. She circled the hall twice, not spotting her electric blue hair. Maybe she had stepped out for a minute.

The music changed to a song filled with beautiful harmonious violins, and Emory stopped to listen to the serenade. It was heartbreakingly expressive, the notes climbing and falling in a whirlwind. There was no greater comfort to her than music. Feeling better, she turned around and stopped immediately.

Memphis stood there, hands in his pockets, his hair tousled. He looked even more handsome than at the beginning of the night, which is exactly why she straightened and crossed her arms defensively in front of her.

"Emory." His voice was soft and unsure as he stepped closer.

Jutting her chin out and in a voice like ice said, "Yes? What do you want, Memphis?"

His crooked lips lit up his face as he reached out. "*You*, Em. I want you."

A deep flush heated her cheeks, and her anger led her tongue. "No, you don't, Memphis. Do you even realize that you are playing with people's emotions? Just leave me alone."

Trying to turn away, he clasped her hand. "You're telling me that I was the only one who felt what we had out there? Emory, Nyx and I are done. I loved her once, and she is one of my best friends. But..." He stepped closer, and she was frozen.

"There wasn't a day that passed that I didn't regret sending you away, making you forget. It was wrong of me to manipulate you like I did, wrong of me to not let go of you. But ever since I first met you, I was in love with you, and there was a time where you felt the same. We were worlds away for years, but the heart doesn't forget even if our mind does."

He was so, *so* close to her. She looked up to meet his gaze, her body trembling. Butterflies soared in her stomach. She should walk away and leave him with his silver tongue.

"You can just forget about Nyx just like that?"

He shook his head. "We have been over for a long time, and she knows you have always had my heart. Always."

Throwing away her judgements, her worries, she caved into the recklessness of the moment. His gaze roamed her face, searching her for a response.

Wickedly smirking, she dragged him on the dance floor, and they were swept away by the music. She shouldn't feel like this, but her heart was ignited. Every nerve in her body was on fire as he brought his hand underneath her chin, tipping her face gently toward his. Her eyes fluttered to a close, her breath ragged, their bodies creating their own tempo as they spun and spun.

His lips were warm and welcoming, her blood singing with pleasure. The world stopped when she pressed her body into his. She didn't care if they had stopped dancing. She didn't care who saw. It could have been a second, but it felt like an eternity as he gently pulled away, a low chuckle rumbling through his chest.

Her cheeks were on fire. The next song started playing a fast-upbeat tune. He didn't hesitate, and spun her around the room, gentle but powerful. Blurs of people surrounded them, laughing, dancing, the lights low and energy exploding through the room.

# HEIR OF LIES – PART THREE

Pulling her in closer, he whispered, "You have no idea how long I have wanted to do that." He grinned as she flushed an even deeper crimson.

Leaning in, wrapping her arms around his neck, his breath hot against her face, she could feel the magnitude of their energy as their lips met once again. Memphis let go of her hands to cup her face gently.

The music swallowed them whole, as they discovered their own powerful language. Selfishness ran away with how good his lips felt, and for tonight, she allowed herself to enjoy every kiss, every caress that he had to offer. Hours passed, and they danced for every second of it, laughing, talking. Wishing for more.

Sweat dripped down her neck, and she said, "I need a break, one second."

She walked toward the edge, and before Memphis was able to follow, he was swept up with his friends, laughing and dancing once again. Even just one night, all worries were forgotten.

Until it wasn't.

Emory spotted Nyx in her line of sight, arms crossed and looking predatory.

*You did nothing wrong. It was Memphis's choice.*

She wanted to say something to her. Anything that would make it right. She chewed on the inside of her lip, mulling it over and taking the other woman in. Her purple hair was now tied back in a high ponytail, tight black combat gear extenuating her perfect curves. Nyx flashed her a smirk, and Emory's blood ran cold as Nyx pointedly unsheathed her curved twin blades from her thighs and slowly stalked toward her.

In that instant, the ground started to shake, the lights flickering. Locking eyes with Nyx again, she sneered with such hunger, fear shivered down Emory's spine.

Emory quickly scanned the crowd, panic settling into her chest. She ran back to Memphis, knowing who the one person she hadn't seen tonight was. "Bryd is missing."

Memphis's face drained of blood. Mouth gaping, he looked and saw Nyx moving toward them. Everyone stared at her. The music cut. And their world exploded into chaos.

The elevator doors burst open and multitudes of black clothed figures stormed into the dining hall, all adorned with red sashes. Screams resonated around them, a sick serenade. Smoke drifted in behind the strangers, their swords glinting. Hands pushed her back, and she stumbled out of the way.

Memphis roared at Nyx, "YOU!" He barreled toward her, dodging as her sword cut at his shoulder.

Nyx panted, "Memphis, I need her!"

His fist connected with her gut with a thud. Nyx collapsed to her knees, and Memphis turned, grabbing Emory's hand, and together, they sprinted toward the hallway.

Running full tilt, they weaved around their friends, leaving them to fight alone. "It's Adair's men... I can't believe..." Memphis shook his head, not able to finish the sentence. Silent tears rolled down his cheeks as he digested the betrayal.

Nyx had led Adair right to them.

He flung the door to his room open and ran to the bookcase, pulling a novel down. The bookcase shifted to reveal a staircase spiralling into the darkness.

"You have to get out of here. Find Brokk. Stick to the woods, and don't let them find you."

He didn't allow her time to speak as he pushed her onto the staircase, making her stagger down. He shoved the novel back in place, sealing her in the darkness and sealing both of their fates.

# HEIR OF LIES – PART THREE

# CHAPTER THIRTY-SEVEN

## Memphis

The bookcase slid shut, and Emory disappeared.

Adrenaline coursed through him; everything surrounding him moved in slow motion. Nyx had betrayed Black Dawn to Adair. After all these years, Nyx had betrayed him. His friend. His once lover. The truth was black and white before him, but why did everything seem so grey?

As he ran out of his room and down the hallway back to the dining hall, guilt washed over Memphis, thick and suffocating. Maybe if he had been honest with her from the beginning about Emory, she wouldn't have made such a reckless decision.

Screams rained down, and he took in the scene before him as Memphis watched Adair's men kill his friends without mercy. Steel flashed as blood spattered on the ground, and Memphis's breath was knocked from his chest: for a second, he was transported back six years ago, when the Academy fell, and all he could register was the ashes as death rained down.

Snapping out of his panic, he forced himself to move.

"NYX!" he roared, searching for her in the throng of chaos. Luckily, living in a war ridden world, Memphis was a soldier through and through and was always prepared for the worst-case scenario. Underneath his dress clothes, he was armed to the teeth. He loosened twin blades from his forearm, and a ragged breath tore from him.

Rounding the corner, he was quickly cut off. Standing in front of him, Nyx was shaking, covered in blood.

Taking a step toward him, her voice cracked, "Memphis, you have to leave. Now."

At her words, his vision was tinged red from anger. His body was calculated as he charged at her, his blades swinging. Her violet eyes were pleading as their blades met, sparks flying from the force. They were met face-to-face before Memphis twisted away, not giving her an inch before he attacked again.

"I trusted you."

Nyx's face darkened. "And I loved you. But I wasn't going to let you end us all. The price was Emory. She was supposed to buy our freedom, but Adair lied. This wasn't our deal. You have to believe me."

Sweat trickled down her face, pain lacing across her features as Memphis's blade cut through her arm. Her words were poison to his heart. No matter what Adair promised her, she still made the decision to go through with it.

Memphis gave himself one second to glance behind Nyx as she parried his blows. In the sea of black, Jaxson had multiplied by the hundreds, trying to overthrow the soldiers.

He was the only one left standing that Memphis could see.

"Jaxson!"

His desperate cry was lost in the madness around him. He had to get to him. He had to save him.

Nyx was backing herself into a corner, and Memphis didn't wait to reach out into her mind. Filling it with screeching white noise, he watched Nyx instantly freeze, her brows furrowing before she caught on to what he was doing. He shoved forward, clenching his teeth. Nyx's face paled, and she sagged against the wall.

Turning, he ran. Buzzing filled his senses as he cut down the soldiers around him, fighting his way to Jaxson. He was almost there, but from the sideline, a soldier threw a glass bowl into the throng, sickly blue gas swirling in it.

# HEIR OF LIES – PART THREE

Memphis's heart dropped into his stomach. The glass bowl quickly smashed, and the gas cascaded out, encircling them. Stumbling he tried to hold his breath. Jaxson locked eyes with him, fear making them shine bright. He slammed back into one person; the gas was stopping the use of their abilities.

Memphis screamed as the soldier behind Jaxson slid his blade into his friend's heart. Blood pooled, and Jaxson dropped. Soldiers stepped over his friend's body, surrounding him with soulless eyes.

Still screaming, he lunged toward them, unhinged and feral. A man from behind him grabbed his hair, shoving him onto his knees, where a soldier standing in front of him quickly landed a punch to his cheek. Blood filled his mouth, and Memphis spat it onto the man's face - he *laughed*. The soldier put a knife to his throat, the steel cold against his flushed skin.

Voice laced with venom, the soldier said, "You're lucky Adair wants you and your rebel girlfriend alive. Otherwise, you would be dead for that."

Before Memphis could retort, the soldier slammed the pommel of his knife into his temple, and sharp pain shot through his head, his world starting to disappear. He greeted the darkness, allowing it to swallow him whole.

# Chapter Thirty-Eight

### Brokk

The first thing he noticed was the smell of fresh mint overwhelming his senses. Groaning, he tried to open his eyes, the dried blood cracking from the effort. By fire and flame, he was *groggy*. Breathing deeply, Brokk tried to focus on his surroundings. Objects slowly started to come into focus: a small round table, a blue teapot sitting in the middle with steam still curling from its spout. Scattered chairs and books cluttered any other available surface, and a small kitchen was tucked in the corner.

"You sure did take a turn for the worst."

A small woman materialized in front of him; she looked no more than twenty, her blonde curls cascading down her back. Flinching back, Brokk moved to get up...except his hands were bound. Fighting against the corded restraints, she smirked at his effort.

"You're not going anywhere until you and I have a little chat."

Her dark brown eyes shone playfully back at him as she poured herself a cup of tea. Clutching her saucer, she plunked herself across from him. He gave in for the moment, scowling.

"There, there! Now I get to ask my questions first, seeing as I saved your life and all."

*Saved me?*

# Heir of Lies – Part Three

Memories came back to him.

Nyx and him heading back to the Academy; it had been late in the night. Adair's men had caught them off guard.

Nyx had greeted them like old friends.

He had been ambushed.

"Trying to piece it together, eh? Your pretty friend left you for dead, she did."

Numbness spread through his body like ice as he processed what this meant.

"How long have I been here?!" his voice escalated with each word.

"Well, I found you tied to a tree about four days ago, so you count that plus these... About a week then."

A *week*.

The Academy would have been blindsided. How would Adair's men have gotten in though? Nyx could have forced Bryd to expose them, and if she was down, they sat in clear focus for the world.

His thoughts raced with the scenarios, his heart clenching with every thought. He had to get out of here. Flexing his wrists, he fought against the restraints.

"As I said, I would concentrate on answering my questions. You're not going anywhere fast."

Twirling her dainty fingers once, the slick cord tightened, cutting off his circulation. Stopping, Brokk eyed her cautiously. *Who is she?*

"We were heading back to the Academy."

She clucked her tongue disapprovingly.

"Now, now. We both know that was destroyed many years ago, and I don't like liars, Brokk, not at all."

"Is it impossible for you to think you're the only one who survived? We have built and hid our resistance... That is, until recently." He gritted his teeth together.

"No. I suppose not, but I am curious how you managed it." She leaned forward eagerly.

"How do you survive?" he countered.

She slurped her tea loudly and smacked her lips obnoxiously while in thought. Grinning, she replied, "By the art of illusion."

"Well then, you just answered your own question."

"How many?"

"We had sixty."

She deflated. "Your friend went to Adair."

He didn't answer, didn't need to.

Pinching her eyebrows together, she suddenly jumped up running to the next room. Minutes passed as scuffling and muttering came from around the corner.

"Ah-ha!" Running back, she smacked a torn weathered book in front of him.

"Now I have a story for you. You see, I obviously didn't find you by chance. I followed you. I have been following you."

His skin crawled. "Who are you?"

"Let me formally introduce myself. My name is Peyton. You see, I have been around for a long time. I have seen and heard many things, and you, my dear, are the greatest mystery I have ever known."

She waved her hand slowly in front of her, and her skin started melting off. Brokk jumped in surprise. For a split second, a white-haired lady sat in front of him, clear brown eyes twinkling back at him. She waved her hand back and her earlier form returned.

"You bring out the young part in me again, dear. It's quite refreshing."

"So you're..."

"A witch, yes, and unfortunately, the last of my line. I am a hundred and twenty years old and have the gift of taking whichever form I choose—whether it be human or not. You see, I had a dear friend once who could relate to me. Her name was Morgan, and she was a shapeshifter. She had a hard time controlling her ability. As you know, it is quite easy to lose yourself a little bit in the beast."

She sighed. "Anyway, Morgan and I grew up together, living in the same small village of Ferry, which is across the borders from

# Heir of Lies – Part Three

here. The years passed, as they always do, too quickly. Morgan was hearing whispers of a government being built to help anyone with special...gifts."

She flipped the book open, and Brokk's gaze fell upon a tattered picture of a woman leaning against a tree trunk, her dark auburn hair falling around her shoulders, her golden eyes shining sullenly.

"She had an opportunity to have a better life, one that would understand her gift, not try to hide it. She left."

Brokk's entire body went cold.

"Months passed without a word, and then one day, I was sent this."

She flipped the creaking pages, and small particles of dust floated up. Brokk leaned in, breathing in the musty scent. Another tattered picture lay in the middle of the page, Morgan laughing with a man with ebony hair and dancing green eyes.

He froze.

"This was the last I heard from your mother. She was swept up in a world that was segregated from the rest of us. Only the best, only the strongest. It's bullocks really. Look at us now." Peyton shook her head and, with a dazed expression, looked out the window, lost in thought.

"What are you trying to say, Peyton?" His voice was just above a whisper, and a small tremble vibrated through his body. He was scared for the answer.

"Morgan found *love* and look how that served her! To love Roque, who was already promised to Nei. She was *happy*. And you see, I couldn't have that, oh no. We had a promise, we did. So, I found her, watched her. Until the time was right."

She wrung her hands together in agitation as she paced back and forth, looking deranged.

"It was a year. I stayed in the woods and watched. You see, I had acquired something, something of upmost importance, which would change everything. Your mother was supposed to have it...not him...not him." She shook. "It was a snowy evening, and Morgan had caught on that I was there. She met with me. How much people can change in a couple of years, I tell you. She promised me what they were starting was for the good of Kiero, but what she didn't see was that she was already being blinded by lies."

A pause, then, "There had been whispers of a prophecy. About two children born from royalty. We had set out to stop this from ever happening. But what I didn't realize was that I had already failed. When Morgan showed up that night, with a bundle in her arms, which was a small child, I knew, yes, I knew I had to take matters in my own hands."

A cold sweat dripped down the base of Brokk's neck, but he was entranced.

"I drove my knife deep into her heart, and as the life drained out of her, it was my mistake I didn't realize I was being watched. Roque stepped out of the shadows, all pride and arrogance. Hatred fueled his movements, and he charged me and took from me the only thing I care about. He took the book, and he took you and hid you until it was time. No one knew, no one." Peyton ended with a whisper, sweat dripping off the end of her nose, her form flickering quickly from young too old.

Three thoughts surged to Brokk in that moment.

He was Roque's son.

Emory's half-brother.

He was in the most danger he had ever been in his life.

A growl ripped from his throat, and he didn't think as he changed. The binds that held him to the chair transformed in a second, erupting into slithering snakes made of writhing flames. Their beady eyes were an endless black as they circled his paws, hissing and cackling. Peyton hovered above the ground—her true form in plain sight: yellow papery skin, frizzled white hair flying every which way, eyes filled with hate. Looking down, both snakes coiled and sprung toward his legs in a flurry.

He tried to run, crashing into the chairs and table. If he could just make it to the door… Their teeth sunk deep in his skin simultaneously. A quick icy burning filled his veins, and he dropped to the floor, blood dripping from his human hand as he shifted back. His throat felt thick.

Peyton cackled above him, and Brokk tried to focus, but his world was spinning on its axis.

"You think I would let you slip through my hands again? Oh-ho! I have *waited* too long for this. Roque hid you for your life, but I needed to see what you would become. Haven't you ever wanted to know more? Haven't you wondered why you are so different?"

*Yes.*

The thought rang through his mind so clearly it reverberated in his heart, in his body. The room tilted upside down, and Brokk felt himself slipping away. He tried to hold on, a low moan escaping from him, and he was taken away with the venom into a world constructed of poison.

The steady rhythm of dripping water woke him. The room was dark, strange, and dampness clung to his skin, the smell of moss in the air. He blinked hard, trying to get a better focus. A small candle sat in the far-left corner with a long wooden table in front of it. Brokk, then, brought his attention to a small circle of eight jagged rocks in the middle of the room. Perfectly placed, they shone with a metallic green finish, glowing ominously in the darkness.

*What was this place?*

Looking up, a low cement ceiling met his gaze, and groggily, he tried to focus. The taste of blood filled his mouth, and by the feel of his right eye, it was tightly swollen shut. His breath was labored, and since his body felt as if it had been chewed through a mill, he guessed he had been there a while. His hands were tightly bound behind his back, and he rested his head against the cold wall when he registered what had happened.

So many questions screamed through his mind. He was *Roque's* son. Why had he never told him? And Emory...she was his *half sister.* Disbelief made his thoughts fuzzy as he tried to process the information.

"He's awake." A high-pitched voice echoed in the small room, snapping him back to reality.

"Who's there?" Brokk asked.

A giggle was the only response.

Fear paralyzed him, goosebumps erupting over his skin. Her laugh was an uncanny match to his dream. Peyton suddenly materialized in front of him, making him slam back into the wall.

She cackled. "Hello, dear. I was wondering when you would come around. Our tactics last time must have drained you." She smiled back at him, ruthlessly, not waiting for a reply.

"I will let you in on a little secret. I can imagine you must have *so* many questions. But unfortunately, those will have to wait. You see, I do think it's a little unfair that the *most* powerful person in Kiero only uses his abilities to save one girl. What you did, it changed *everything.*"

"What I did! The monarchy was built to ensure peace to protect this land. It's Adair that changed everything!" He gritted his teeth.

Peyton didn't hesitate; her hand was cold and strong as it struck across his face. His blood pounded up to his skin.

"You stupid boy! Haven't you realized by now that what is happening is because of mistakes made from the past? Roque was never destined to have access to the power he did, and it is the same with Adair. Emory was never supposed to leave, and you were never supposed to be born. But alas, the world is a fickle place. The fates have been changed. The entire balance of Kiero is about to tip over, and it is entirely based on you."

She sucked in a breath before continuing. "You see, when your *father* stole the Book of Old from me, he had no idea the consequences of that. It was never mine to keep but only to be delivered back to its rightful owner. Morgan and I were promised a life of riches, and she tossed that away for love. I am now bound to a lifetime of servitude until the wrongs have been set right.

# HEIR OF LIES – PART THREE

You are not the only group fighting for the power to rule Kiero, and you will not succeed without our help."

Another giggle erupted behind Brokk.

Peyton dipped her head and, locking eyes with him, said, "Adair has the Book of Old which contains dark magic that would make your head spin. He made a deal with my masters'. You see, they enjoy these games. For taking the Faes lives, he would have access to its knowledge for a limited time. But he didn't listen to them and stashed himself away, trying to build his strength, justifying to himself that by being high of birth, it was his to keep. That it was his right to become King. And so, they waited for someone to help them achieve what they wanted. And, here we are. "

"I won't be your pawn."

"Would you rather die?"

The question hung heavily in the air, and Brokk stalled, reflecting on it.

"Brokk Foster, you are the most influential person in this game right now, and upon agreeing, I can answer any question you have. All I need is for you to say yes. Otherwise, I will torture you, and eventually, you will break anyway."

Peyton was inches away from his face, her rancid breath filling his senses. He didn't trust a single word, but what were his options? Say no and be tortured and tested on?

He stared into her eyes, searching for his answer. "If I say yes, will my friends... If they aren't already ..." He couldn't finish the sentence.

Peyton's mouth quirked, finding his pain funny. She sighed dramatically. "If you say yes, we will ensure you rule, and yes, your friends, if they are alive, will be safe. "

"Who do you serve?"

Peyton clucked her tongue disapprovingly. "Is that a yes?"

Brokk was numb as he nodded once.

Peyton shrieked in response, and a dark green flame erupted from the eight stones, dancing around their edges. Before his eyes, four ghostly figures emerged from the flames, jet black hair clinging to their shoulders, and where the eyes should have been, two gaping holes replaced them. They all wore the same simple white dress, their lips peeled back from their teeth, frozen in a permanent grimace. Their bare feet slapped the floor as they stalked toward him in unison.

It was as if he had entered his nightmare. Heart pounding against his rib cage, Brokk was helpless as they advanced on him.

*What had he done?*

The one closest to his left giggled again as they formed a semi-circle around him. Their voices were like scraping nails, and he cringed.

One spoke, "Brokk Foster, it is our pleasure to finally meet you. As our lovely Peyton has already explained, we have wanted you on our side for some time. Despite Peyton's certain...*vengeances* plotted against you, we are not involved in such trivialities. We have one ambition, and we grow tired of not being able to have full control of our actions. We are trapped here, in this room, in those stones. Our world is much different than yours, much wiser. Our knowledge was not supposed to be known here. Curiosity has always gotten the best of us. Connecting our two worlds has had dire consequences, one being losing the Book of Old. You see, some power is not to be dappled in."

Their pointed looks chilled him.

"To acquire this book would mean we would be able to go back, having the right power to do so. You see, fey rings are quite peculiar things, and it is quite a sensitive process. We are fortunate enough that your world is filled with unique magic and have been able to survive decades without any dire consequences. Which brings us to you."

They exchanged glances before another said, "You are another puzzle entirely. We have watched your progress since birth, and though, yes, you come from impressive lineage, one could say you are much more unique than that. One who can bend the laws of time. What an extraordinary gift to have at your disposal. But it

# Heir of Lies — Part Three

would very much seem a lot of it is untapped, perhaps even suppressed."

"I never asked to be different. I have barely used it!"

"Exactly." They spoke in unison; their voices overlapping and creating a sick melody.

One sighed then said, "You don't crave to use it for power. In fact, if we have a firm understanding, you wouldn't want this power at all if you had the choice. But what if we could give you that option?"

They had his attention. Staring into their lifeless faces, their white smirking demeanors, he treaded lightly. "And what would you propose exactly?"

"You bring back the book from Adair, and we will free you. Not only that, but we will help you kill the Mad King."

*Nothing is that simple.*

"You're telling me that you can end what we have been fighting for *years* if I say yes— guaranteed?"

They all nodded their head simultaneously.

His heart ached. Uncertainty was the only thing he had known in his life, of his past, present, and future. To perhaps allow the sliver of hope that things could be different was poison.

Faces flooded his mind: Memphis, Alby, Bryd, Nyx...Emory. His family. Wasn't he prepared to go to whatever ends it took to allow a promise of a life worth living? One without death, fear, and loss. Isn't that what he had always wanted? This was his only solution. However uneasy he felt about this situation, Brokk couldn't say no.

They knew this.

Taking a steadying breath, he set his jaw stubbornly. "You give me your *word* that you will follow through with your promise."

*He couldn't give up hope. Not yet.*

"Then it will be done."

The one closest to him pulled out a long-curved silver knife, its teeth glinting before Brokk. Stepping forward, she unbound his hands and, in one motion, grabbed his wrist and slicing the blade across his palm. Warmth spread throughout his arm, and blood pooled, dripping loudly on the floor.

Uninterested in him, the group sped over to the grouping of stones once more, flicking his blood onto them. A gentle hiss sounded, accompanied by their whispers, their foreign language taking over the silence.

He took it all in, frozen in place. For what felt like an eternity, he watched, then they finally slowed as the emerald blaze returned, crackling happily. The flame died as quickly as it came, sending them into darkness once more.

His breath hitched. He couldn't see a thing.

Breath lightly tickled the side of his face, his skin instantly crawling in reaction. They had surrounded him once more.

"We forgot to mention one tiny...little...detail."

He flinched back, bellowing, "Face me!"

He was met with silence. Suddenly, one candle was lit, and he was almost nose-to-nose with their leader. They all circled around him, breathing heavily. He couldn't look away from their eyes and undiluted fear laced through him.

His stomach dropped. "Who are you?" The fear in his voice was hard to mask.

"We are the Oilean, or maybe you will understand the term, fey. We were once wish granters, tricksters. But that's in the past. We serve a higher purpose now, and we are here to set the course right. It all begins and ends with you, Brokk Foster."

The room filled with whispers.

"We came to your world out of curiosity. There were whispers of two children being born from royalty who would destroy everything we knew and loved. We watched and saw the course set from your father. He should have known that our magic would not resonate with your world. And Adair... There is a darkness in him that cannot be undone. Now, I'm sure you are thinking that we promised. We promised to help you end this rebellion if you returned the book, yes. We personally will not harm your friends." A pause, then, "But I cannot speak for your actions."

# Heir of Lies – Part Three

*What?*

A fistful of hair was ripped from his head, and he yelped; tears pooled in his eyes. The candle was extinguished, and a metallic glow pulsed from the stones.

Blood now trickled down his cheek as well, and he heaved against an empty stomach. His arms shook when he came back to a seated position. His world spun on its axis, feeling lightheaded; he had to hold on.

They had gathered around the stones once more, throwing his hair in, and the once sickish green glow turned a burning red.

*What had he done?*

They swayed around the flame, holding hands and chanting in a language foreign to his ears. Their leader tossed one more unseen item into the flame, and with a gust of energy, an inferno rose toward the ceiling. Reds, oranges and golds twisted in the light.

"It is done," she whispered.

They all lowered their hands and gently whistled a soft, low key. The fire settled into embers, and Brokk gaped.

Movement was sifting the coals to their sides, sparks exploding as they rolled onto the floor. Slowly, human hands grasped the siding of a stone and then another. A chilled breeze rolled through the room, and in smoke and ash, his full form rose.

Brokk couldn't breathe. He couldn't move.

He was staring right at *himself*.

Golden eyes to golden eyes, the likeliness was uncanny. The Oilean erupted in a fit of laughter, admiring their job. Their leader stepped forward once again, kneeling in front of him.

He hadn't realized a steady stream of tears ran down his bruised face this entire time until a skeletal hand of one of the Oilean brushed against his cheek, wiping them away.

"The one thing we forgot to mention is that you, yourself, will not be leaving here. *Ever.* Your doppelganger over there has a *much* better understanding of our needs. Anyone who gets in his way will be killed." It shrugged. "Emory and you cannot live, which will become clear in time. How do we demolish this monarch and the rebellion while still harnessing our power? Destroy the kings and queens that started it all."

Every hope he had been clinging on to was whisked away in that moment. His head hung heavy against his chest, his hate for Nyx, for the Oilean, for Roque, for his mother, for this rebellion grew into a cold numbness that overtook every thought and feeling in his body.

They whispered something to his doppelganger and, nodding his head once, one of the Oilean pressed on the wall - a door appeared, and he left.

"Make sure he is well nourished sisters; we are far from done yet."

He begged his body to pass out in order to grant him some blissful nothingness as they enclosed on him. Unfortunately, he never did have much luck. His screams were never heard, lost in the coldness beneath the ground.

### HEIR OF LIES – PART THREE

# CHAPTER THIRTY-NINE

### Emory

The pounding of her feet echoed deep within the tunnel. Her hair came undone around her as she plummeted down the dimly lit hallway. She could hear heckles and yells of the soldiers behind her.

They were catching up.

She didn't know how long she had stood on that step, paralyzed with fear. Hoping that Memphis would come back. That someone would come back. Adair's soldiers were smarter than they looked to have found her hiding place. Or they tortured Memphis until he showed them.

*She couldn't think like that.* She had to hope Memphis and the others made it out.

Her lungs brought her back to reality, screaming for her to stop.

Pushing harder, a thousand scenarios ran through her mind, but Memphis's voice kept her going.

*Find Brokk. Don't get caught.*

Her plan could wait.

It felt like a lifetime, but finally, the hard ground started sloping upward. She was almost there. Another twenty gruelling steps and a small door came into view; she could have cried from relief. Clutching her ripped dress, she raced forward. Panicking, she shoved the door with her shoulder, trying to barrel through. It wouldn't budge. Her hands felt the creases for some sort of door handle or latch—and found nothing. She was trapped.

She screamed in frustration, "No! Come on!"

She could hear the approaching grunts and complaints of the soldiers. At least she had given them a run for their money. Emory continued to slam her body against the damp wood, and slowly, cracks of light started to dapple her skin. She wasn't fast enough.

"Well, well, well. Boys, it would seem we have finally caught our prize."

She faced two soldiers; they were clad in black and looked like brothers, their brown hair buzzed short, red sashes splayed across their chest. Nothing scared her more than the dead expressions in their eyes. She *would not* let them take her.

The last month rushed up fiercely within her. She had never gotten the privilege to grow old with her parents, but she would without a doubt protect their dream. Which was this world—*her world*.

She felt the energy surge to the palms of her hands, making her fingers tingle. She balled them into fists.

"Oh-ho. Look here. Do we have another fighter? Your blond boyfriend gave us a good go."

Stepping toward her and flicking his wrist, flame twisted around his arm and hand. His friend laughed wickedly.

"Now, we are on very strict orders not to hurt you, but if it was instigated on *your* end, I'm sure our king would see reason. Besides, he is planning on…"

Charging forward with full force, keeping her body low, she slammed her elbow deep in his gut, making him buckle for a second. And a second was all she needed.

Grabbing his wrist tight, her world turned into fire and ash. Pure power flowed through her, and she acted. Shouting, the two guards stumbled back as the fire now roared from her free palm, daring them to come closer. Taken by surprise, the guard screamed against her hold and lunged down to her arm, baring his teeth.

# Heir of Lies – Part Three

*No.*

Twisting, she sent a fireball hurtling toward the door and, letting him go, hurled herself forward. She was met with a makeshift ladder about five feet tall. She lunged up and climbed. She heard them yelling and start climbing after her. She couldn't look back.

*Faster.* Her limbs felt disconnected from her body, and she screamed in frustration when she fumbled for the next rung.

The soldiers yelled too close behind her, "Get her now!"

*No. No.*

She had maybe another ten rungs to go before land connected, and she spilled onto the grass. She was almost there...

A cold hand grabbed her ankle and pulled. Hard. She was filled with horrendous electric shocks for a second before her body absorbed the power. The current washed over her, and she felt her hands leave the ladder, gravity working against her body, causing her to free fall back toward the guards.

In a split second, she stopped falling, and Emory felt swirling air tickle her back, arms, calves. She was suspended in the air, floating. Gasping,

"What the...?"

The guard's confusion matched her own. Suddenly her body lurched forward, Emory, bewildered, shot up from the tunnel. Spinning, she landed hard on the grass, and she stayed there—her limbs shaking.

An impatient male voice snapped at her, yelling, "What are you doing? Get up!" Gruff hands pulled her up and shoved her to get going, and she stumbled forward whipping around and coming face-to-face with Alby.

Hope blossomed deep in her chest as she whispered, "Alby? You're alive?"

His red hair was dishevelled, green eyes alit. The closer Emory looked, though she didn't remember Alby being that tall—or bulky for that matter. Taut muscles were exposed from underneath his t-shirt, and she flushed deeply as he caught her staring. Movement caught her eye from behind him—the guards. Looking exasperated, he started rubbing his hands together as if he were cold.

Realizing she was still standing there, he mouthed, "*Run,*" at her.

Suddenly, a funnel cloud twisted from the now black sky devouring everything as it touched the earth. The man, who she now knew wasn't Alby, stood taller, and twirling his hands, the twister roared toward the tunnel. He was controlling it. She whipped around and sprinted to the edge of the woods, her heart sounding in her ears.

Not a minute later, screams resonated behind her, and not looking back, she wove around the trees as she broke through the edge of the forest. She spotted a rotting tree trunk tucked away behind some undergrowth. *Perfect.*

She flung herself over the trunk and rolled her body neatly behind it. Shivering and teeth chattering, the shock was settling in. That was too close. Squeezing her eyes shut, Emory concentrated on her breaths, trying to calm herself. She would not panic.

A branch cracked near her left side.

Eyes flicking open, she came face-to-face with deep green eyes. Emory screeched, "Get away from me!!"

Jumping up, she rolled from her hiding spot, tears threatening to overflow from her eyes. She sprang into a run, the stranger following close at her heels.

"Hey! Wait!"

Catching up to her, he cut off her path, arms folded across his chest. She had to stay focused.

*Find Brokk. Don't get caught.*

"Aren't you at least going to say thank you?"

Sighing, she nodded her head once in his direction. "Thank you." She tried to move around him, but he caught her arm, tightly.

"Who are you?"

# Heir of Lies – Part Three

Wrenching from his grip, she looked up at him in confusion now, assuming he was joking. His face was set with a scary determination.

"Who are *you*?" She shot the question right back at him.

"Look, since you were being trailed by Adair's soldiers, you are either dangerous or important. You came out of the Academy which I thought had been destroyed. Who exactly are you?" the man reiterated.

*Take a risk.* Her gut urged her to tell the truth, while her heart wistfully leaned toward lying. She exhaled. "I'm Emory Fae, Heir to Kiero."

It was half whispered, but his face drained of color all the same. A knife she didn't know he had on him was quickly held against her throat as he shoved her against the nearest tree. The steel bit into her skin, droplets of blood trickling down her neck.

A slight breeze tousled her hair, and his eyes flicked back and forth as he took her in. Narrowing his eyes, he murmured, "So you are both dangerous and important."

She had nothing to say to that. He huffed, talking more to himself. "Today really couldn't get any worse, could it?"

Dropping the knife, he ran his hand through his hair. "I'm assuming you have mistaken me for Alby, since we're twins. But the more important question is how he could be alive when I thought him to be dead years ago? When the Academy fell..."

She cut him off, "It never fell."

He tilted his head in question.

"Over the years, a resistance has been building, hiding from Adair until we were betrayed by one of our own. Alby was part of the Academy, but Adair...he has him now." The words came out in a rush.

"So, it was true. There were always theories, but it seemed too unrealistic that some of the most influential people of our country would stand by and do nothing while thousands died."

She cringed as if he had slapped her.

"Especially you, Emory Fae. You alone could have gotten Adair's attention and made a difference. Anyone who is anyone knows about Adair's blood feud with your family. Exactly how is it that you of all people are alive?"

Before she could answer, a husky voice called out, "Azarius!'"

He snapped to attention, the knife flashing back, holding her from running. His anger was stifling.

"Hello, Lorne." Azarius tipped his head toward his friend, his eyes never leaving hers.

Emory took in the other man, his sunkissed skin and deep eyes, dressed in a worn jacket and ripped pants. His sword was sheathed at his hip; Emory watched his hands slowly move toward it.

"What news?" Lorne asked.

"It would seem Adair's men have found what they were looking for. They left very few survivors."

*Memphis.* It felt as if someone had physically winded her. She shook her head wildly and asked, "A man with blonde hair...did you see him?"

"You don't get the privilege of knowing that!" Azarius snapped at her and shot Lorne a look that stopped him from saying anything further.

Lorne slowly asked, "Should we bring her to Morgan?" He fidgeted with his hands, the notion setting him on edge.

"No. This one I will dispose of myself. You tell Morgan there was nothing to report."

"Azarius."

"NO!" He whipped around and whispered something to Lorne in agitation.

*This is it.*

She had never thought about her death much. She thought she would live a full, quiet life. But here she was, thoughts frantically running through her mind as Lorne turned his back, walking away and leaving Azarius and her alone once more. She was frozen, her heart pounding—and *wishing.*

# Heir of Lies – Part Three

Her core warmed as those golden eyes filled her mind. *Brokk Foster.* How she needed just one moment with him—to try to explain that her fear in him was misplaced. Was fabricated all thanks to Memphis. That she had been wrong not to give him a chance.

Emory closed her eyes and, above all else, wished desperately she wasn't alone.

The wind tousled the leaves. Slowly opening her eyes, she took in Azarius. The knife glinted in the sun as he flicked it between his hands.

"It would do us both good if you could scream as convincingly as you can," he said.

*What?* "Why would I?"

His arm lashed out, and the knife soared through the air, landing with a thud in the nearest tree. "Just do it."

Sucking in breath, she exhaled and screamed as loud as she could until he nodded his head.

"We have to move fast. Lorne is not one to be misled." He set off jogging, talking as he went, "Look, you seem like you have gone through a time back there, and I can relate to that. But you and your family name don't get to dictate the future of Kiero any longer,"

"I'm trying to help bring down Adair."

"And then what would happen? Your people are indebted to you again? You become queen, follow your parents' beliefs and path? History is only bound to repeat itself. A lot of things have already been set in motion, and you returning from the dead will set a lot of things in a tailspin. So, I propose you help me find and save my brother—or I *will* kill you."

*What choice did she have?*

Emory whispered to his back, "Agreed."

Her only acknowledgement was Azarius speeding up, pushing further into the depths of the forest, and Emory followed desperately at his heels.

Time had no meaning to her in this world. There was only the constant thud of her foot against the soil and her thoughts as she and Azarius pushed further into the night. They had not stopped. They had not rested. Blisters on her heel burned as her flats rubbed them with every footstep, her torn dress muddied and in tatters. She was starting to understand her body's exhaustion. Her heart pumped violently with her every move, begging her to stop.

She had gone from being a prisoner of her own world to a prisoner of her past to Adair, and now...

Looking ahead, she stared at Azarius. Why was he so against what her parents stood for when all she had heard was stories of praise?

The thought pulled at her, ugly and loud. Had her parents balanced their duties, or had citizens suffered from their decisions for the greater good? Frustrated, she sighed, her palms tingling. She just wanted to piece it together, but nothing was clear. If Azarius was right, why wouldn't Memphis entertain the idea that more people had survived, try to pour energy into only trying to bring Adair down, not into trying to build their numbers? Banded together, they had a better chance, but alone...

Unless Adair had something Memphis wants?

*If he is still alive.*

Her life was a scattered puzzle, two halves of herself conflictingly coming into one. Would she continue to honor what her parents stood for even when she learned pieces of the truth that she didn't agree with? How would she get outside citizens to trust her when everyone has been fighting her war while she was a world away?

*She was selfish.* What she had asked Memphis and Brokk to do many years ago was so selfish. Asking them to change the course of their lives for *her.*

She wasn't the savior everyone wanted to believe she was. That *she* had believed she was. She would help free Alby. Then, she would move forward with her plan and do what she should have done when she first came back.

# Heir of Lies – Part Three

It was time for a little reunion.

She looked at the crumbling ruins in front of her. Miles and miles of destruction. The Ruined City had once been Kiero's capital, Sarthaven. A place that supposedly cultivated not only the monarchy but a rich culture. Now, deserted, Emory couldn't imagine such a city existed.

"Here?" Emory asked.

Dawn stretched across the sky, and Azarius shot a steady glare her way. "We're getting close. We don't need to be sitting ducks out in the open. This way."

He disappeared under a slab of concrete propped up sideways, and she followed, delirious from exhaustion. Squeezing through and entering what looked to be part of a house, Azarius was already positioning himself in a corner, facing her directly.

He stifled a yawn and said, "It would do us good to get some rest. I will take first watch."

It was not a question.

Sighing, she settled down. "How did you know this was here?"

He scoffed. "When you live to survive, you explore any possible option of refuge. We have scouted as far as we can walk, run. Besides, if you watch closely enough, Adair is not impossible to find."

She couldn't stifle her curiosity. "Who is *we?*" Instantly she regretted blurting out the question when she saw the stony expression cross his face.

Lost in some memory, he shook his head once and silence followed.

Emory lay down after that. She didn't know how long she laid there staring up at the molding ceiling, but eventually, she fell into a fitful sleep.

*Walking through the city, looking around at its empty streets, she called out to Brokk. It was abandoned.*

*"Emory?"*

*She dared not to hope. Anything could be possible in her dreams.*

*"Why are you here? You have to leave!" Brokk urged.*

*She turned around, and there he was, stalking toward her in agitation.*

*"Brokk," she breathed.*

*He was here. She took him in like she would study a painting, etching every detail to memory and reached out hesitantly as if touching him would only prove this wasn't real - his skin was warm against her touch.*

*Nothing held her back from crying, and she flung her arms around him. "You're alive! Brokk, I tried to find you... Where did you go?"*

*He wrapped his arms protectively around her and, breaking the embrace for a moment, searched her face. "You shouldn't be here. You have to leave."*

*"There is no one here." Emory looked around.*

*He leaned down and kissed her forehead. "Adair is always watching." The whisper was cold against her flushed cheek.*

*"What do you mean?"*

"Emory!" Rough hands shook her shoulder, and she started awake.

Azarius leaned over her, and she blinked in confusion. "We really *have* to go."

Dusk was speckling the clouds outside, and she got up. *Had it already been so long?* The more time she wasted, the more people suffered. A shiver ran down her spine, and she tried to shake the feeling of unease from her dream.

Looking at Azarius's dark circles under his eyes, she asked, "Haven't you slept?"

"No." Brushing past her, he walked outside. Following him, she was instantly yanked down to a crouched position.

"Look, you have to listen to me. Do exactly as I say." His eyes burned into hers.

*He is afraid.* Glancing around, seemingly, they were still alone in the ruins of the city.

'*He is always watching*', Brokk's words echoed in her mind, and she nodded to Azarius. He held out his hand, and she took it.

# HEIR OF LIES – PART THREE

"Stay low. Move fast." He dodged out, and she was wrenched into his world.

They were lithe and lethal. Her heart was pounding, but adrenaline pushed her forward, closer to saving Alby. They continued moving in the shadows, and suddenly, Azarius stopped and squeezed her hand. She looked past him, and two soldiers dressed in black stood about two buildings away from them.

"We have to do it quietly, no abilities." Dropping her hand, he passed her his knife, pressing it in her palm. He unsheathed another from his boot and moved forward, motioning for her to sweep around the other side.

They closed in on the guards and fast. Azarius moved first, and Emory followed. He grabbed the guard by his hair, exposing the soldier's throat. Emory gulped down her scream as Azarius's knife swiped across the stranger's flesh in a crimson smile, the man dropping dead.

Azarius moved on to the next soldier faster than she could register, killing him as well. "We have to take their clothes. You can't continue in that, and it will be our cover to get in."

Kneeling and with shaking hands, she tried to unbutton the first guard's shirt. *Don't look at his face.* She didn't realize Azarius had moved beside her until he cleared his throat.

"Let me do this. It will be faster."

She looked up, and a wave of gratitude washed over her at his gesture. Stepping away from the bodies, she ducked behind a pile of rubble a few feet away. It wasn't long before she emptied her stomach; she tried to suck in deep breaths through coughing.

This was her world. This was the violence that Azarius grew up in. It was their survival that was always at stake.

*This isn't right.* Anger, white and hot, coursed through her toward Adair, toward her family. No matter what it would cost her, she *would* set things right.

Coming back, Azarius handed her the clothes. Looking awkward he faced the other way as Emory quickly changed in the baggy uniform.

"Here, I found this. Put it on." He held out a worn cap, and she quickly put in on, tucking her hair in the back.

Azarius assessed her, and looking pleased, they set off again. They weaved through the rubble, every turn Emory preparing herself for the point of no return. They walked until the streets seemed to widen, and they came to a steep plateau.

Azarius said quietly, "There it is." He gestured to the valley at the base of what seemed to be a series of grottos, streams running along its base.

She spotted three soldiers at different locations, watching out.

"This is where we blend in. Let me do the talking."

She wanted to tell Azarius, *obviously*, but she held in the retort. Emory wiped her clammy hands on her pants and tried to steady them. *This is it.*

Setting off at a brisk pace, she kept her head slightly ducked, allowing Azarius to take the lead. It wasn't long before they approached the first cave and nearest guard.

"Urgent news to report. Rebels spotted along the Western boarder. They are armed and look to be collecting numbers," Azarius said.

The guard gave Azarius a brief look then nodded his head. "Report directly to Dex. He will want to collect them with the others."

Azarius dipped his head in recognition, and they were in.

*The others?* Numbness spread through her.

At first, everything was dark, so she stayed close to Azarius to not lose her footing. An eerie glow was their only light to navigate the hanging stalactite that hung from the cavern walls. Further and further, they traveled until a gentle slope brought them to their first room. Emory gasped at the unexpected grandeur, resulting in Azarius shooting her a glare.

Spiralling in front of them, weaving in and out of caves, was a city built in the ground. Hundreds of soldiers bustled, some

# HEIR OF LIES – PART THREE

shouting commands, groups greeting each other like old friends. Azarius didn't miss a beat. They traveled in the throng, lanterns hanging off the walls, giving them better light. Even though it was night, the city seemed more alive with energy buzzing in the air.

"Azarius."

"I know. We have to find where they are keeping them," he whispered back to her flatly.

"If we find this Dex guy, then we find them."

He nodded, and they wove through the crowds. She took in this world Adair had created, had hid away in while he destroyed what he thought wasn't good enough.

"Over there."

A younger man stood, fidgeting with his hands and looking uncomfortable as the soldiers hurried by. Azarius looked him over and then barked, "You there!"

The soldier's head snapped up, and he came over to them at once. "Yes, sir?"

He couldn't be older than fifteen, and Emory's gut wrenched.

"Where is Dex, my partner and I are to report to him immediately."

His face drained of color, and he stuttered quietly, "D-d-dex is with the prisoner's, sir. We are all to report to the stadium at once." With that, he slipped away in the crowd, not looking back at them.

"We have to split up," Emory whispered. "I'm too noticeable. Someone is bound to see that something is off. If I can find them, I can set them free."

"Absolutely not. We stick together."

"Azarius, think of Alby. Together, we don't stand a chance to find him before we are either caught or killed." Emory felt the determination burning through her, her jaw set stubbornly.

Azarius whispered, "How can I trust you?"

"Give me a chance to gain your trust."

He ran his fingers through his hair, and blowing air through his mouth, he resigned. "Fine. I will give you an hour. That's *it*. We meet back here. If things go bad and you're late, I'm not waiting up for you." Turning his back, he walked away, disappearing into the mass of black bodies.

She turned the opposite direction, her heart aching as if it was a shattering window, slowly and then all at once.

# HEIR OF LIES – PART THREE

# CHAPTER FORTY

## Brokk

He wished for death. Death would be lying in a soft bed and drifting off to his final sleep. It would be easy. Above all, it would be welcomed.

He closed his eyes and ached for relief. His body was sprawled across the wooden table *they* had built in the middle of the room. His face was beyond recognizable, open gashes covering almost every inch of his skin. They never let him fully heal—only enough to be kept alive. A giggle sounded from the corner of the room, and he visibly flinched.

They whispered from the darkness, "Do you want to hear another story?"

He didn't have the will power anymore to say no. They always took his silence for a compliant yes.

"Lovely. We start off where a collection of strangers are learning about each other. One is much more powerful than the others and would abuse his power if he *knew*. So, they send out another copy of himself to bring peace to their land. Sounding familiar so far?"

He gritted his teeth, searing pain shooting across his face. He didn't respond but watched as their hollow eye sockets stared at him.

"And so, the sisters were relieved. Soon, what had been stolen from them would be returned. The wrongs in this world would disappear. Adair will no longer sit on his broken throne, and Emory Fae will die."

*What?*

He snapped to attention. Usually their "stories" were cryptic and just repeating how they were doing him a favor—that this was for the best. Not that they were just as power hungry, twisted, and ruthless. Not at all. But there was no news about how far the doppelganger had gone—until now.

*Emory.* His heart clenched at the mention of her, worry making him want to break free and destroy these Oilean.

They continued their story as he licked his cracked lips. "And so, since the sisters knew that this was going to come to an end soon—the royal line, the Faes, and you—they figured they would share some secrets."

Giggles resonated all around him, and he flexed, trying to sit up. Trying to do anything.

"You see, Brokk Foster, we have learned such interesting facts about you. Peyton, having known your mother, can compare similarities between you two. Your shapeshifter qualities upon being induced by our serums are basic. You turn into your second form, the wolf, but the rest... Well, that is where things get more interesting, very interesting indeed."

*What had they found out?*

Curiosity built; despite everything they had done to him. Test after test. No one in his life had been able to explain *why* he had more powers. Why he was so different.

They approached him slowly, in the half light, coming closer and closer to the table. The Oilean's leader held another knife, and Brokk started whispering, "No, no, no, *please* no."

He had to hold on. He had to escape. If not for Black Dawn, for *himself.*

Determination flooded into him, lighting himself with motivation he didn't know he had. He flicked his eyes open, darting around the room. *Be resourceful, Brokk. Think.*

They had cleared the room; the only things left were cracked lamps hanging on the wall.

"Ahh. Look, sisters, we have put a spark in him."

His head snapped toward them, and he sneered at their elation.

# Heir of Lies – Part Three

"You know what we must do now...not let his hope catch." She pulled a short silver dagger from a sheath attached to her hip.

*No. No. I will not survive this.*

"Now, I will warn you, this will not be pleasant."

Laughter echoed around him.

His body felt as if he was being dragged down slowly through water. He couldn't breathe. He couldn't move. The dagger bit as it slid in between his ribs, and the world spun in pain.

# CHAPTER FORTY-ONE

### Emory

She wove further and further down into the bellows of this land. Adair's kingdom was like an ant hill, twisting and interconnected. Sweat poured off her body, and she walked as fast as she dared, trying not to draw attention to herself.

By now, the hallways had emptied besides the lingering soldiers talking in excited, hushed voices. She caught clips of the conversations, and her heart dropped like a stone. Keeping her eyes ahead, she took in everything. She had passed what looked like a market, vendors of food, clothes, wine and instruments were splayed in an attractive display. Past that, a blacksmith's shop, a beautiful woman stepping out from the front door, covered in soot and sweat.

Pushing herself faster, Emory made note of the activity within Adair's kingdom. Some children ran behind, waving goodbye as their fathers and mothers disappeared. She took a sharp turn left and was met with another series of stairs. She took them two at a time.

*Azarius will make it. He won't get caught,* she repeated this like a mantra.

"Soldier! You are to report to the stadium at once. The King's orders." The voice was as sharp as knives, and she froze.

*Come closer you. I dare you.*

"Soldier!"

She heard his footsteps when he clambered down the stairs toward her.

*It was indeed my lucky day.*

Her movements were fast and sure. She twisted around, and the guard froze, taking her in. She took the opportunity to dive behind him, holding her knife to his throat. "Make a noise, and you're dead."

He was frozen against her hold, and up close, he couldn't be older than seventeen.

*They are so young.*

He gulped, and Emory, having direct contact with him, felt the surge of energy through her. *What an ability he had!*

She whispered, "Take me to the prisoners now, or die. What do you choose, soldier?"

His voice shook as he said, "Please don't kill me. I will take you to them."

She moved the blade to his lower back. "One wrong move, and you're sealing your death. Understood?"

He gave a curt nod, and they moved forward. A layer of sweat coated his skin, and they traveled down the hallway. The black stone glistened in the light casted by the hanging lanterns. Minutes passed in silence until, finally, they rounded the corner and were met by a grey door, strange markings circling it. Without hesitation, he pressed his palm to the middle of the door, and it was as if he breathed life into it when an eerie glow started to pulse from it.

"You have to do the same," he murmured.

"What does it do?"

"To enter the dungeons, everyone has to unlock the door by disabling our abilities. It is a place of no magic. It's how no one escapes."

*Adair had thought of everything.*

Gritting her teeth, she mimicked him, and the door swung toward them. It felt like half her limbs had disappeared. They stepped into a semi-dark room, and Emory had walked straight into something of nightmares.

Hundreds of cells lined the stone walls, half starved faces peering back at her. Anger, hot and consuming, rose in her, and she flipped the blade. With all her strength, she drove the pommel into the back of the guard's head. He crumpled. Stepping over his body, she frantically ran to the closest set of bars, and grabbing them, she asked the girl in front of her, "Memphis. Do you know if a man named Memphis is here?"

"What's it to you?" Stepping forward, the girl had matted hair piled on top of her head and deep brown eyes. Her voice was a scratchy drawl, and she breathed heavily through the bars, angry scars roping her cheekbones.

"Emory?" Her name was called out, and not waiting, she sprinted toward it.

She saw him before anything else. Red hair, green eyes filled with hope. *So different than his brother's.*

"How did you get in here?" Alby asked.

She crouched down and, fidgeting, answered, "It's a long story. What's about to happen here? Why are the soldiers being gathered into the stadium?"

Alby nervously licked his cracked lips. "Adair is planning to make an example of us."

She felt nauseated. "How much time?"

"The guards have already taken Memphis out."

*Shit.*

"Alby, how do they lock the cells?"

"It's all hand code access, like we had at the Academy."

Desperation gripped her, and she ran back, returning to the unconscious guard. Bending down, knife in hand, she steadied herself. She swung down, grinding through flesh and bone, blood spurting. Holding her breath, she told herself, *Just one more cut...* Her task completed, she took the hand, running back to Alby, a blood trail splattering behind her. Revolusion twisted in her gut at what she had done.

# Heir of Lies – Part Three

She pushed the thoughts down, and gasping, she asked Alby, "Where?!"

Speechless, Alby pointed to where the first bar touched the wall. Emory pressed flesh to stone, and the cell door groaned as the barrier disappeared into the wall. Alby stepped out toward her, his legs shaking.

"We need to set them all free. Alby, there isn't time to explain, but I came here with Azarius. He is waiting for you all in the stadium. You have to save them." She motioned around her, and it was as if she had sent an electric shock through him because he stared at her wide-eyed and open mouthed.

"This is our chance, Alby. *Please move.*"

*Boom. Boom. BOOM.*

Drums, deep like a heartbeat, started above them. Alby grabbed the hand from her and started going from cell to cell until around them an orchestra of stone against metal sounded. Chaos broke out and prisoners fled, but one voice behind her rang out as the cell was unlocked.

"So. You have finally come to end this." Nyx sneered at Emory; her clothes covered in dried blood. Bruises flowered all her skin, her shirt was ripped, and her pants were rolled up, revealing fresh wounds.

Emory shot back, "Now is *not* the time,"

Nyx stepped forward with a limp, her eyes flaring with malice. "*You.* It was supposed to be enough—the information of *you.* Now Memphis..." Nyx's voiced cracked.

Using her full body weight, Emory shoved Nyx against the nearest wall, breathlessly whispering, "You sealed their fates. What did you think Adair would do? You need to show me where they took Memphis, then get *out* with Alby and the others. Have a chance."

Lowering her arm, she stared at Nyx, waiting. She barely caught what she said. "Go to the end of the cave, and there should be a staircase—down there."

Emory turned and ran, passing Alby as he corralled disoriented prisoners saying, "Okay. As soon as we are out, grab hands. I can conceal you as soon as we pass the barrier that will enable our abilities again…"

Cells blurred into a mass of grey and black, and Emory focused on her breathing. *She could do this. She had to.*

It was only a matter of minutes before she reached the makeshift staircase Nyx described. Emory grabbed a small lantern off the wall and took the steps two at time. She landed on dirt; it puffed out around her from the impact. She had entered another tunnel, wooden beams supporting the sides. She was almost hyperventilating.

What if she was too late?

Lifting the lantern, its soft light touched the walls around her. About halfway down the tunnel, natural light pooled in a circle on the floor, particles of dust floating down from the movement above. Sprinting until she reached the light, she skidded to a stop.

Looking up, she saw floorboards, small gaps between each one, and past them, a guard shifting his weight impatiently. Beside him, someone with hands bound was on his knees—Memphis.

His face was bruised; deep yellows and greens speckled his skin. Fresh blood poured from his nose onto the wood, some oozing down into the tunnel. His breath was labored, and his eyes were closed. Emory could hear the crowd's excited murmur, and she concentrated. To her left, another staircase twisted up to meet a small cellar door, its latch hanging undone before her.

Her way out.

Palms clammy, she took a step forward, and that's when a silky voice rang out, making Emory freeze and silencing the crowd immediately - "Today, I have gathered you from your duties to bring you before this rebel traitor."

Jeers sounded, and Memphis was shoved to the ground, his face colliding with the floorboards.

Emory clutched her knife and waited.

# Heir of Lies – Part Three

"Many years have passed, and *we* as a kingdom have flourished. We have weeded out anyone whose beliefs remained in the past—what the Academy stood for. Power demands to be earned, not handed out to anyone. What are the words we live by?"

"*All of might*," was chanted back at him.

"Exactly. Until recently, I thought I had buried the Academy with the Faes. Though somehow, the rebel scum survived. This man, their leader, *must pay*. What is left of the rebels must learn that I, their king, is the only one who is to rule."

The drums started once more, low and soft, and Memphis was roughly grabbed by his bound hands, and directed by the guard, they left, heading into the pit.

And out of Emory's line of sight.

*Hurry, Alby.*

She jumped up on the staircase and shoved her face against the gap, craning her neck to see. She stayed there awkwardly perched and waiting for the right moment.

*Hold.* Gingerly positioning her shoulder against the cellar door, tensing her muscles, she waited to shove through it.

That's when she felt hot breath against the nape of her neck, making her hairs stand on end. She turned around and bit down hard on her lip to stop her from screaming. The beast was easily the size of a horse, thick coarse black fur covering its body. Its claws were as long as swords, digging into the dirt. Behind him, three soldiers stood with spears prodding him along. Those eyes—a deep opaque silver flickered as his long snout sniffed her. Ears like wolves flattened against his head, and a growl like thunder started in his chest.

The soldiers froze as they spotted her.

Adair's voice continued, "As a public execution, this rebel will be faced against a beast found in the mines..."

Cheers started from the onlookers; Emory felt sick.

"And let it be known that the resistance will never survive against me!"

She took her cue: slamming her weight against the door, it exploded open, and she threw herself out, a roar following at her heels. *Move, Emory.*

Blinking hard, she spotted Memphis in the middle of the sandy pit, hundreds of soldiers surrounding it. She ran, adjusting to the light change. Memphis's usually blond hair was ridden with dirt and blood. She couldn't meet his gaze.

But there was only one person she was looking for.

Across the arena, a man with pitch black hair sat on a throne made of bones. His eyes never wavered from her unexpected appearance, as Emory sprinted full tilt toward Adair. Throwing the hat off, her black hair loosened behind her, as she pumped her arms harder.

"ADAIR!" His name ripped through her throat, the thundering of the beast following behind her.

Standing, a flurry of emotion quickly crossed Adair's face.

*There is no going back now.*

"Adair, I've come to join you!" At those words, her heart erupted into flames, turning quickly to ash, and chaos broke across the stadium.

# HEIR OF LIES – PART THREE

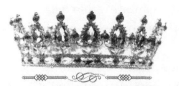

# CHAPTER FORTY-TWO

## Memphis

His hands and arms had turned numb. He heard the roar and, glancing up, was sure to see his death. Instead, he saw Emory. She was an angel inside this eternal darkness, black hair flying behind her as she ran, screaming his name.

This was torture, and it ripped fresh through him, unhinging everything. He had never thought it would be Emory that would break his resilience. Adair had tried his best, truly. But he was a stone; *he* had led Black Dawn to this fate, and the guilt layered upon him was fresh and constant.

But Emory? She was supposed to survive. To live.

He couldn't do anything more than stare as she hurtled toward him screaming, "Adair, I have come to join you!"

*What?*

Screams erupted around him, and he felt an unnatural wind pick up. Looking up, the bronze sand was funneling, forming a tornado, and growing in force with every passing second. His mind was chaos. He was surrounded by a ring of onlookers, but in the sea of black, Memphis spotted a man with fiery orange hair. *Alby?*

He was staring at Emory with visible hatred, and bringing his arms together, he clapped once, his lips moving as he did so. It was as if the world had split open. Five tornados crashed into the stadium, destroying it within seconds. Debris and bodies soared through the air as Memphis was frozen in fear. The beast that would have been his end was sucked up in the cyclone, roaring helplessly.

Emory had almost reached Adair.

All this time, she was just waiting for this moment.

"Memphis!"

His name brought him slamming back into reality as Alby materialized beside him; bruised and bloodied. "You have to come with us. My brother is waiting!"

He could feel himself shake his head, craning back to catch a glance at Emory.

"Now, Memphis! Forget about her!" Nyx appeared, eyes hard.

She unbound his restraints and shoved him upward, and as she did, Alby grabbed his hand, a refreshing coolness washing over him. This sensation had only been described to him before, but he had never experienced it.

Alby had turned them invisible.

Hushed voices encircled him, and he felt their group lurch forward. He was aware Nyx was behind him, prodding him along if he faltered. The screaming never stopped. They maneuvered out of the pit, entering a long winding staircase up to their freedom. They ran as fast as they could, which was a steady hobble.

Nyx breathed down his neck. "We have others with us. A rebel group led by someone named Morgan on the eastern border."

"Shut up, Nyx," Memphis said. He didn't have the patience to deal with her, her betrayal cutting into him just as fresh.

Alby shushed them as they climbed. "They can still hear us even if they can't see us."

Soldiers rushed past them frantically, the group catching snippets as they passed.

"No sign of them yet."

"Adair is secure."

"Fifty casualties."

# HEIR OF LIES – PART THREE

They pushed on, and soon, the stairs flattened out to join the mouth of hallway caves, and the sound of rushing water greeted them. Alby constantly searched every face, cursing under his breath. *My brother is waiting for us.*

Memphis didn't even know Alby had a brother. What else didn't he know about the people that had sacrificed everything for him? How far he had led them astray for the hope that *she* would be the key to their own freedom?

He felt as if he was being pressed into a tube, each passing second getting harder to go on, to breathe.

"*Come on, Memphis. Hold on.*" Her voice brushed up against his consciousness, and he felt her free palm gently press against his lower back.

The world spun, a cold sweat slithering down his spine. Pieces of his heart had been laid out, embedded into the wrong people.

"*Don't give her the satisfaction.*"

Brushing Nyx off, he concentrated on Alby, leading them through this maze, sweat breaking out above his brow. "Alby, do you know the way out of here?"

"We have to find Azarius. He came in here with Emory. He will wait for us and get us out."

Scanning the crowds, people dressed in black collaged together into one mass. A figure stood in the corner, jacket pulled tight around him, fiery hair a beacon in the grey of the grotto.

"There, Alby," Nyx whispered behind him.

Alby's gaze snapped to attention, taking in his brother, shock flickering across his features before he composed himself. He quickly said, "I have to be fast. Everyone stays together. Adair's men will see us. "

Alby didn't give anyone a chance to think about what this would mean. Letting go, he sprinted across the hallway, shoving soldiers out of the way, yelling, "Azarius!"

Azarius turned, taking in Alby rigidly, like he was seeing a ghost. Pushing soldiers out of the way, Alby continued to his brother. Azarius shook his head, sprinting across the room, but every soldier within the grotto had sprung into action, weapons unsheathing.

"Rebels! Restrain them!" Adair's men shouted.

Azarius grabbed the front of Alby's shirt, looking like he wanted to punch him but not before Alby grabbed his forearms, wrenching him out of the way of a soaring knife. The blade hit the stone wall where Azarius had just been standing.

Shouting desperately, every guard in the vicinity locked in on them. "Prisoners! Restrain them!"

*No*, Memphis thought, watching the chaos unfold.

Turning to run back to the group, the guards followed swiftly. In front of them, a guard locked eyes with Memphis, a grin spreading across his face as he recognized him.

"Might as well finish what Adair wanted done."

Memphis heard the knife leave the man's hand, and it cut through the air. He couldn't do anything more than look into the guard's dead eyes. He felt her throw her weight into him, shoving him out of the way. Purple hair whisked around her face - the knife landed with a thud into flesh.

Alby, in that same instant, grabbed Memphis's hand and screamed, "Everyone get in line!"

Memphis grabbed Nyx's hand, the blood pooling around her. *Where is she hit?!* The panic choked him. The hilt of the blade protruded out of her left shoulder; the steel dug in deep.

"Memphis, grab her. We have to get out of here now!" Alby yelled.

Lurching forward as if every limb was disconnected from his body, Memphis scooped up her light body, and the coolness of Alby's ability washed over them all. Her color had turned ashen; blood was spattered along her jawline. Memphis was soon covered in her fresh blood.

They moved as fast as they could around livid guards who had, in an instant, lost an entire group of fugitives.

Adair's grottos were a maze of stone walls, and they wove around and around different staircases until they came to a small waterfall and cave mouth. Azarius talked quickly and briskly to Alby.

Nyx was like a flickering candle in his arms, her pulse racing against every second that she lost more blood.

"You idiot," Memphis said to her.

A whisper of a smirk crossed her lips, and she was fixated on him for one burning moment. "Memphis...I never thought..." Her words died on her breath as she lost consciousness once again.

*She never thought it would lead to this.* But all the lives lost...what did Nyx think would happen if she went to Adair? He was ruthless. He wasn't human.

And Emory...

*No, Memphis. Let her go. Let them both go.*

Azarius barked back at them, "We move as one. If we make it to the Ruined City, we have a chance." He spoke firmly and with authority, his eyes never leaving Memphis's. Azarius had a glare of accusation burning in his gaze. Memphis's blood ran cold.

Then ducking into the waterfall, they left the buried kingdom behind and, in doing so, leaving every hope Memphis had as well.

The wind was warm against their faces when the group collapsed, and Alby allowed them to be uncovered once more. The walls of the house they were in had been smashed, concrete dust floating in the air. Alby rushed over to him and Nyx at once, inspecting her wound.

"She's lost too much blood. We have to get the blade out now and try to cauterize the wound," Alby said and bit his lip as they gently lowered her to the ground.

Azarius stood in the shadows behind them.

Memphis quickly, and with sure hands, ripped a strip off the bottom of his tattered shirt and bent down beside Nyx. Taking a deep breath, he silently wished she would stay unconscious as he gripped the weapon tight and, in one motion, ripped it from her shoulder. Warm blood spilled from her body faster than before, and he quickly tied a makeshift bandage tight, trying to stem the flow.

"She won't make it," Azarius spat.

Memphis didn't realize Azarius had moved behind him, and he straightened up to meet him.

"With the risk of infection and loss of blood, she will not survive," Azarius elaborated.

"And who are you to decide her fate?" Anger swelled in Memphis like a wave.

Narrowing his eyes, Azarius said, "Unlike you, I am a survivor. And as someone who has survived in *this world* fighting against Adair every day, I have seen wounds like this, and it does not end well."

"Azarius..." Alby said his name quietly.

Azarius looked to his brother. "No. You, I haven't even begun to start with. Stay out of this, Alby." Then Azarius drove a finger hard into Memphis's chest. "You have hid away in your *Academy* while thousands of people have died. And what was it for? The girl who just threw every hope you had away for her throne?" He snorted.

"And now, where does that leave you? Homeless, without direction, hoping that we will take your group in, while in the last years, it was *you* that left us *in the cold*."

Angry spit flew at his face, and Memphis was speechless.

"You call yourself their *leader*. You don't have the first idea about sacrifice. You have only done what's good for you, not your group, and it was all left to your selfish decisions."

Memphis's right hook was direct as his fist slammed into Azarius's jaw, cracking at the impact.

Azarius staggered back, laughing. He spat out blood and rubbed his face. "See? You can't admit to yourself that it's true. Her..." he pointed to Nyx, "...blood will be on your hands, including everyone else's." He turned away, adding, "As for you, a trial with our leader will settle it."

# HEIR OF LIES – PART THREE

Facing the group, Azarius said, "We leave at first light. We take turns being on lookout tonight and get through this together."

He stalked away, haughtily, leaving Memphis surrounded by broken people.

# Chapter Forty-Three

### Adair

The knife wedged itself deeply in the wall with a satisfying thud. The black steel was flawless, thanks to having the best smithy in Kiero. The steel was able to cut through rock and marble. Riona Welsh, time after time, had outdone herself.

Adair retrieved it quickly, pacing back and forth. The remaining light of the day spilled into his room—which was in the highest cave. An array of bookshelves and weapons scattered through it. He sent the knife flying once more, its carved hilt gleaming as it soared, and he tried to arrange his thoughts.

*How exactly had this happened?*

Over the past six years, he had managed to collect order over the entire kingdom but now...not one, but two, resistances had emerged. And Emory from her grave.

Adair grabbed the knife, twirling it between his long fingers. His next decision would dictate everything. When Emory had appeared before him, claiming she had come to join him, he was certain another hallucination had started and what ill timing it was. Yet, she was in the cells, and the rebels had infiltrated *his* halls. Not only that, but they had managed to escape with all the prisoners.

They had challenged him and succeeded.

# Heir of Lies – Part Three

Ghosts of the past had returned, and what consuming things they were...

The silver of the blade glinted as he slammed the point into the wood of his desk, his scrolls jumping from the impact. Drumming his fingers, he planned his next move. He would dance with the rebels if they wanted to dance. Finding their whereabouts wouldn't be hard if he, himself, finally took a part.

For six years, he had hidden and protected the Book of Old. It has been his teacher and the key behind building his empire. His soldiers had scoured the land, recruiting all that would join him and destroying all who wouldn't. He was their government—their *king*.

"Isn't this what you taught me? Isn't this what you *wanted?*" Shouting into the silence, his questions hung in the air. Adair gritted his teeth.

If it wasn't for Memphis and Brokk, he should have known. They had always favored her, wanting to protect her, to *love* her.

What Emory didn't realize was that she didn't have to run. He killed her parents to attain the book, and the Oilean demanded a blood price. A sacrifice for the greater good. They could have been a team—the greatest king and queen. She was his *equal*. If she wasn't a rebel spy.

Anger bubbled up inside, and he threw the knife, aiming for the back of the door. He didn't need to look to know it found its mark. Together, Emory and he could be unstoppable. But if he was wrong about her...

*"But you love her."*

The voices cooed around his mind, his cage, mocking him.

His guards had contained her as soon as the unexplainable tornadoes had started, as well as dragging him away to safety. He hadn't given her a chance to talk to him. *Should he?*

Stalking around his room, his palms tingled. There had been whispers of a rebel resistance rising because Emory Fae had returned, but he had scoffed at the rumors. It wasn't until Nyx had come to his court, showing him that the rumors were *true*.

In exchange for Emory, Nyx had foolishly believed that he would grant the rebels freedom.

He had "gifted" her with an enchanted amulet that allowed him to control her and everything that had happened that night. He had hoped she would prove him wrong. He saw Nyx kill that blue haired girl, Bryd. With her death, the Academy had appeared from its concealed state, and his soldiers destroyed it.

He was victorious—until Memphis had gotten Emory out.

Now he had nothing to worry about. She had come right to his doorstep.

As for the other rebels, their time would come.

But how far was Emory willing to go to show her allegiance to him? If she crossed him, she would pay the price with her life. The faint hint of excitement flickered through his face as the plan formed.

A curt knock brought him to the present. "Enter," he said.

Two panting guards stumbled in and bowed lowly. His captains in command of both regiments stood before him, looking very flustered.

"Captains, what news?" Sitting on the edge of his desk, interlocking his fingers, he observed them. Adair smelled the tension rolling off them in waves. He would maintain order.

"In search for the escaped rebels, we have come across another just outside the gates. He is asking for you, and sir, he is covered in fresh blood."

*Very intriguing.*

"Very well. Bring him in, but to the dungeons first. I have instructions for the current matter at hand."

The next half an hour he spent explaining what exactly was to be done in regard to Emory. Nothing was going to go amiss. Not this time.

HEIR OF LIES – PART THREE

# CHAPTER FORTY-FOUR

## Brokk

Strange tubes had been attached to his body, his blood swirling through them. Struggling for breath, Brokk fought to live.

He cracked an eye open, his left too swollen shut to move. The basement was currently empty, his only company a dimly lit candle. He had no idea how much time had passed, whether he had been here for weeks or months.

*I will not break. You are Brokk. Foster. You will not fall.* This had become his daily mantra, his lifeline.

He had undergone a series of torture, both mental and physical. Their approach, though, was completely foreign to him. Why were they collecting his blood? The tubes encompassed different parts of his body, all of them funneling to a clear basin near his feet. There were too many tubes to count, but he could hear the gentle trickle as the blood was drained.

Brokk felt lightheaded, his palms becoming clammy. *Focus.* He had to escape. Or he would die. The clarity of this sang through his body as gentle creaks of footsteps sounded, and the door creaked open. Peyton appeared, all business as usual.

"Ah, dear, things are coming along nicely here, aren't they? The Oilean will be pleased."

He rasped, "And where *are* the demons?" He didn't recognize his voice; it was a hoarse grumble.

"Ah! He does speak. And I wouldn't tell you even *if* I wanted to." She flashed a brilliant look at him, having taken on her younger form.

She continued to bustle about, humming a gentle tune. Brokk could feel the edges of his consciousness being pulled at, and he licked his lips. They were gone then, temporarily at least. He took a breath in, his mind felt clear and crisp—even if his body felt like it had been chewed through a mill.

*They had left him not drugged.* He hid his grin. Usually, they dosed him up with a serum concocted that wouldn't allow him to shapeshift, but for whatever reason... It clicked together. They needed his blood clean for their purpose.

*This would be his only chance.*

It would be a longshot. But he would try—or die doing so. It had been awhile, but it was as familiar as breathing to him. He closed his eyes, letting go. His body cracked swiftly, and with a growl that ripped through his entire body, he flung himself forward, ignoring the pain. The tubes ripped from his body—his blood flying everywhere—but he had only one target.

Peyton turned around just as he collided with her, and they were sent crashing into the brick wall. She was stunned and, with strength he didn't know he still had, slashed his claws across her chest, black blood pouring from the wounds. Her eyes went wide, and with his ears back and teeth bared, he lunged toward her jugular and ripped it apart. It was only until she stopped struggling that he stopped.

Panting heavily, he staggered back, eyes flicking toward the stones. It was pulsing an eerie green hue. Brokk could sense the energy building around the stones. A strange noise cut through the air, and the power kept building, like a bomb. *He had to get out now.*

He set out in a gallop, crashing through the door; it broke apart in a thousand shards of wood. He took the stairs almost in one leap and came into the kitchen, a thousand scents overwhelming

# Heir of Lies – Part Three

him. In that instant, the basement exploded from underneath him. Yelping, he was thrown back but, regaining his balance, hurled himself through the nearest window, shards of glass exploding around him as he was thrown into a blistering light. The sun.

Blinking hard as Brokk readjusted, he pushed himself forward and set off at a run, and each time his pads pounded the earth, it echoed *his freedom*. Trees blurred around him, and he relished the outside world in its light.

What he had gone through rippled through him, his body painfully reminding him of what they had done. He looked back over his golden fur and saw, to his delight, smoke curling toward the sky where the cottage had been. They couldn't follow him or send Peyton after him. For the time being, he was free.

His tongue licked the blood from his muzzle, and he looked to the sky. Dusk would be upon him within the hour and, with that, the night. To the west lay the Academy...but beyond that? He had always been loyal to Memphis, but he needed answers about his past. He couldn't let his friends die—if they weren't already dead.

Slowing to a trot, Brokk came upon a rushing river. He lowered down to it, the cool water rushing over his muzzle as he lapped it up. He could already feel his body healing itself with a renewed pace and sighed in satisfaction.

First, he would find out what happened to Black Dawn, which meant paying a visit to the Academy. After that... His muzzle curled into a snarl over his glistening teeth. After that, he would find his doppelganger, destroy him, and then find his answers.

He set off at a brisk lope, wishing for the night to come and swearing to himself he would turn it crimson if they had died.

# CHAPTER FORTY-FIVE

### Emory

For the first time since returning to Kiero, Emory dreamt of her mother.

Clad in a gold gown and her golden hair falling loosely, her mother was unearthly. Sitting down, Nei looked at Emory, warmth spreading through her features. They were in a long empty hallway, sunlight pouring in the bay windows surrounding them.

"Darling, how you have grown into a beautiful woman."

She felt tears prick her eyes as she reached for her mother's hand. "Where are we?"

"A safe place. They can't find us here," Nei said.

Who? A shiver ran through Emory.

"I don't have much time." Nei glanced over her shoulder as if hearing voices. "Emory, you have to stop..."

In a split second, everything dissolved, and she awoke with a gasp, sweat soaking through her shirt. She hadn't realized she had fallen asleep. The guard posted outside her cell looked smugly at her, and she made rude gestures with her hands that he chuckled at. Emory leaned against the cold stone wall, trying to make sense of her dream.

*What had that been all about?*

# HEIR OF LIES – PART THREE

For now, she tucked it away along with every other thought and sighed. "Can I speak with him *now?*" she asked.

The guard clucked his tongue at her. "No."

"Even if I say please?" she purred.

He spat on the ground, saying nothing.

"Oh, come on."

"You can shut that pretty little mouth of yours, or I will shut it for you."

Now it was her turn to look smug.

Someone else laughed a couple of cells down. Who else was in here? She had hoped all the rebels had gotten out. She licked her cracked lips; she would find out soon enough.

Her mind felt foggy, and she ran over what she would say to Adair Stratton for the millionth time...

And Emory waited.

# Chapter Forty-Six

## Memphis

Nyx hung in his arms, resembling a skeleton, while they walked, the Ruined City long behind them. Alby hadn't said a word to him since his confrontation with Azarius. Silently, they trudged on, the landscape evening out to a flowing plain before them. Tall grass swayed in the wind, mesmerizing him.

How had he gotten here? He had tried to protect Black Dawn, but set on revenge, he had, in fact, stifled their flame. Now... He looked down at Nyx. They had bound the wound the best they could, but she had lost so much blood.

He couldn't lose her and Emory both.

*Emory...* He had tried to push out any further thought of her, but tired and broken, she flooded into his thoughts. She had played him. He believed she was *his future.* He had hurt and placed doubt in his best friend; he had lied to Nyx; he had broken their rebellion. All for nothing.

Ice ran through his veins, each heartbeat painfully aware.

What had happened to Brokk? He could take care of himself, he knew, but what had he sought after? Was he dead? Alive? Blinking hard, Memphis swore he would find him. Brokk was his family, and family didn't end with blood, not when it came to Memphis.

The group moved silently and as swiftly as a shadow. The terrain had changed and then changed again, but Memphis didn't care.

Azarius stopped, stating, "We're home."

# Heir of Lies – Part Three

An excited ripple spread through the rebels. Blinking, they stood before a small thicket of trees, not yet fully grown. One had a small curved crescent moon etched into its bark, and Azarius gently grazed his hand on it.

The mark shifted, as Memphis read the words that appeared underneath it, "Pentharrow". Recognition flickered through Memphis—Pentharrow was a city east to the Academy said to have fallen years ago.

The tree was bathed in a golden light, and he stepped forward and disappeared. One by one, and without question, the group followed. Alby lingered by his side and hoarsely said, "Memph. For her."

Glancing at his friend, Alby looked as afraid as Memphis felt. Nodding, they stepped forward, and after a tingling sensation washed over him, Memphis had to stop and blink hard, trying to make sense of what he saw.

A bustling town was alive before them. Children ran through the streets, barking dogs at their heels, families laughing and talking as they wove through buildings. The smell of freshly baked bread wafted through the air, and businesses went about their day. Yells of joy spread as rebels were reunited with their loved ones.

Memphis froze.

All this time, an entire town had survived freely under Adair's eye as well as them. Azarius, arms crossed, stalked toward them. "You three are coming with me to see the healer. Now."

Alby asked, "Is this what..."

"It's exactly what it looks like, Alby." Alby cursed under his breath in awe.

Memphis looked curiously over at his friend and asked, "What's Penharrow to you?"

A small rueful emotion crossed his face, and he answered, "Home."

*Home*: the word was filled with warmth and longing. One Memphis couldn't recognize. His only home had been the Academy, which was just another memory now.

Sighing, he straightened his back and followed Azarius to a small cottage. Sage and different herbs hung from small baskets in the windows, its red brick glowing against the white shutters. Knocking once, they entered and were greeted with a squeal, "Azarius!"

A stunningly beautiful woman leaped up to throw her arms around Azarius, burrowing her face in his neck. She glanced up at them, her caramel eyes full of question. A dark green tunic and black pants fit tightly over her hazelnut skin, and she let go of Azarius, sizing them up.

"Lana, we have guests," Azarius said.

She found Nyx in Memphis's arms, and faltered. A steady stream of curses came before she ordered, "Get her on the table. Now."

She wiped some jars and scrolls aside, and Memphis gingerly laid her down.

"All three of you, out, out, OUT!!!" she spoke with her hands, shuffling them out of the door in a wave and slamming it shut behind them.

When they were outside, Azarius glanced at Memphis. "She is in the best hands possible." Then, clearing his throat, Azarius stared at him with dead eyes and said, "Now, you two. Let's pay Morgan a visit."

# HEIR OF LIES – PART THREE

# CHAPTER FORTY-SEVEN

## Adair

The fire crackled hungrily as Adair stared at it. A week had passed, and his life had returned to its routine with purpose. He glanced up at the small chest on his bookshelf that held *it*.

Tapping his foot impatiently, he turned to stare at the door. It had only been five minutes since he had given the guard the okay to bring the prisoners up. The firelight cast shadows across his face, and he settled into an emotionless mask. The instructions had been clear. Bring Emory in first and then the other prisoner.

The knock resonated through the room - through his core. The man he once was felt a nervous twinge. The voices that caged him in hissed in disapproval. He wasn't supposed to feel human emotions by this point.

Wearing a fitted black shirt, pants, and cloak with his dagger tucked away at his belt, Adair adjusting his jacket, then said, "Enter."

The door opened and Emory was shoved forward, falling on her knees before him. Her matted black hair framed her face, her cheekbones poking out. Her smell...well, rancid didn't quite cover it.

A minute passed in silence; her eyes locked with his. Then as if snapped out of a trance, she bowed her head low, saying, "Hello, Adair."

Her voice had a clarity long lost on him. Smooth as velvet and clear as crystal. He nodded. "Emory."

A pale arm extended as she helped herself up. Her clothes were in tatters, but straight backed, she searched for her words. She had his full attention. "I am here..."

He couldn't help himself when he interrupted her, "To join me, yes. That was quite an entrance you made."

Her eyes shone wickedly. "I have returned from the dead as you know."

"It would seem that way." Adair's heart stuttered painfully when he realized he had *missed her*.

He studied her, at a loss for words. There was no flicker of fear or disgust as she took him in as well, more of a curiosity blooming.

She was not broken—not yet.

"Why should I trust you? How do I not know that after so many years, you aren't here to kill me?"

Her eyes darkened. "You are my *king*. Given our history, I thought you would be interested in a deal. We both know our past does have some bearing. Besides, I have information that you will find useful." Her lips curled back in a dangerous sneer, and adrenaline coursed through him.

Rebel information. He wouldn't jump at the bait. Not yet.

"Before joining me, you will have to pass a series of trials. You must understand that I *can* and *will* sharpen you as my sword. But cross me..." he paused. "I will find out if you are trying to betray me, and I will kill you."

Raising a delicate eyebrow at him, she asked, "Aren't you interested in what I have to offer?"

Stopping in his tracks, he took her in.

"Adair, I know you want to join our families. Think about it. We are the last of our lines. Together, we would be unstoppable. I would be *your queen*."

# Heir of Lies – Part Three

The darkness within him reeled in revulsion, where as the human part of him stopped and let that sink in: *a union*.

It's what he had always wanted, always dreamed of. For a split second, hope started to course through him, but those iron doors came crashing down, trapping him once more. The voices chorused in approval as that familiar ice of nothingness filled him.

He adjusted his cuffs, saying, "I cannot trust you, and until you prove yourself to me as an equal, you will be my prisoner. As I said, I will sharpen you to be my sword." Motioning to the guard, the door opened, and another guard stepped in.

There was a flicker of something he couldn't place in Emory's eyes as the prisoner was shoved forward roughly, and he staggered into the room. He was just as dirty, his breath ragged as he stared at Adair with a predatory fixation.

He had the most golden eyes. Golden eyes that Adair would know anywhere. *Brokk Foster.*

Smirking at Emory, Adair tried to gauge her reaction.

Emory muttered something under her breath then lunged for the guard's sword behind her.

Brokk started to mutter a strange incantation, and Adair felt something stir within him. With a growl, Brokk lunged forward, hand outstretched toward his throat and far too humanly fast for Adair to react.

Emory was faster. A scream tore from her throat, and running forward, she slammed the blade deep into Brokk's gut, and it sliced him open, the life spilling from him. Emory panted heavily, staring down at him when he dropped to the floor.

Adair froze.

Her green eyes were on fire as she looked at him. "So, is that a yes?" She wiped the blade clean across her leg.

Adair buried his shock, as he took in Brokk Foster's lifeless body. In return, he raised his eyebrow at her. "We will begin tomorrow at dawn."

He watched the blood stain his carpet and turned black in the flames.

# Heir of Lies – Part Three

# Epilogue

Ash floated gently through the wind as the remnants of the house crumbled. Embers pulsed in the night, and the creatures of the forest scurried past.

Something was *off* about the forest. It was the tiniest of movements as the ground shifted, gently at first and then more frantic, coals and rubble flying. Four black figures rose up from the ground, and sickly green light pulsed off their bodies. The woods had gone silent as the first figure lowered its hood, revealing its pitiless black eyes and sickening grin.

The Oilean moved to stand in a circle, each of the sisters clutching an emerald rock. They took a deep breath in unison and whispered, "Peyton is dead."

Tucking their gems in their robes, they took in the foreign world around them. The willowy trees looked like skeletons in the night. Grinning at each other, they knew that they had succeeded: Brokk Foster had freed them from their bindings.

They had waited for years for the opportune moment, for the right person to come along. Truthfully, they were disappointed in how easily everyone had followed along.

Peyton had believed Brokk Foster was destined to die by her hand. When in truth, the Oilean hoped he would have killed Peyton faster. With Peyton dead, the Oilean opened the portal between Daer and Kiero, *finally*.

They rolled their necks, bones cracking and, in a mist of green light, started to walk, coals sparking in their wake. It was finally time to start their master's plan and burn every inch of this kingdom to the ground.

Cackling, the Oilean disappeared into the night, leaving the grass singed and smoking where they had walked.

~ *The End* ~

*To be continued...*

# ACKNOWLEDGEMENTS

I am full of gratitude as I write this, but without the following people, this series would be nothing more than a dream in my heart.

First, to my readers. Without your continuing support and enthusiasm for the world of Kiero and Emory's story, it wouldn't be out in the world, and for that I cannot express in words how eternally thankful I am—but thank you!!!

To my family and friends, for being my endless cheerleading squad and support—you are amazing!

To Jess, who read the first draft of this novel and shared my love for Kiero and its characters.

To Matt, this year has been one of the hardest, and yet this new edition came out of everything, and you are to thank for being there for me when things looked most bleak. I love you to the ends of the earth.

To Jaime, my publicist, thank you always for being an email away. I value your guidance and friendship and look forward to many more years working together!

To Emerald, this novel wouldn't be in the shape it is without you, and thank you for being my awesome editor!!!

To Rae - Thank you for your work and being my extra set of eyes for this manuscript.

To Cora Graphics, you always go above and beyond for my dreams with any cover, and Heir of Lies is no exception.

Thank you to everyone at Chapters Indigo for your continued enthusiasm for helping me schedule successful book tours.

Lastly, to Link, Lola, and Leonard, I know you can't read this, but you are the best dogs in the world.

# About the Author

© Tiny Islands Photography

Mallory McCartney currently lives in Sarnia, Ontario with her husband and their three dachshunds Link, Lola, and Leonard. When she isn't working on her next novel or reading, she can be found daydreaming about fantasy worlds and hiking. Other favorite pastimes involve reorganizing perpetually overflowing bookshelves and seeking out new coffee and dessert shops.

Follow her on Instagram @authormalmccartney.

Printed in the USA
CPSIA information can be obtained
at www.ICGtesting.com
LVHW041355130823
755092LV00001B/59